WHEN

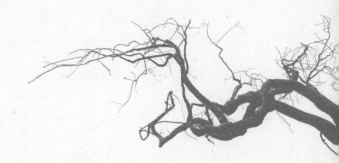

WHEN

HE'S

NOT

HERE

CARRIE MAGILLEN

Little Robin
PRESS

First published in Great Britain by
Little Robin Press Ltd, 2020
This paperback edition, 2020

A CIP catalogue record of this book is available
from the British Library

e-Book ISBN: 978-1-913692-00-1
Paperback ISBN: 978-1-913692-06-3
Paperback Large Print ISBN: 978-1-913692-02-5
Hardback ISBN: 978-1-913692-03-2
Hardback Large Print ISBN: 978-1-913692-04-9
Audiobook ISBN: 978-1-913692-05-6

Typeset in the UK by Watchword Editorial Services
Printed and bound by Lightning Source LLC

Little Robin Press Ltd
Kemp House, 160 City Road
London EC1V 2NX
United Kingdom

Little Robin
PRESS

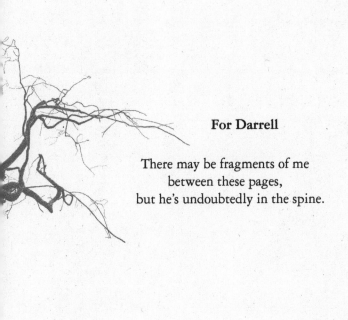

For Darrell

There may be fragments of me
between these pages,
but he's undoubtedly in the spine.

ONE

Before the barrel of the syringe is even empty, I know I've killed him.

Lying side by side on the countertop were two syringes, each filled with yellow solution.

I've picked up the wrong one.

Yet the plunger continues to work its way down the barrel as if I'm not the woman pressing it. I don't stop. I can't. My brain is tangled up in the need to pretend this isn't happening. It can't be happening. I can't have killed Jack.

My mouth falls open as I look up from his body into Caroline's benign, unsuspecting eyes.

No words come out.

'Eva? Is something wrong?'

I stare at her.

'Eva?' And her eyes are no longer benign. They match mine.

Her terrified expression jolts me into action. I need to get him out of this examining room and into prep, fast. I scoop him into my arms and yell, 'Wait there!' as I struggle with the doorknob before bolting from the room. Her voice follows me down the corridor.

'Eva? Eva, what the hell's going on?'

By the time we reach prep, Jack's already drowsy and I run into one of the nurses at the door. 'Jenny! Thank God. I need help.'

She holds the door open. 'What is it? What's wrong?'

I can't tell her.

Jenny runs alongside me as I scream, 'Bron! I need help.' Bron is my boss, the most experienced surgeon at the practice, and she rushes to my side as I lay Jack on the operating table.

I want the words to stay trapped inside me. I don't want to say them out loud. Because as soon as they leave my lips I'll have broken things I'll never be able to mend. But they must be said.

'I injected him by mistake.' My voice quivers. 'Pentoject.'

'Jesus Christ!' Bron grabs her forehead. 'Jenny, hand me my stethoscope and get him on oxygen.'

'What can I do?' I ask.

'Step back!' Bron's voice is rock-hard. I break against it.

Jenny holds the oxygen mask over Jack's nose and mouth and pumps the compression bag while Bron shouts, 'Clippers. I need clippers. And a tube, get me a tube over here.'

Nurses run in different directions while I stand glued to the spot, staring at Jack's limp body on the table. I've been treating him for digestive problems since he was a year old. For four years now. And over the last six months I've seen him every fortnight. I've come to love him as if he were mine.

Now I've killed him.

'It wasn't the full dose...'

Bron ignores me. Her attention is on Jack. I can't just stand here and watch him die. I have to do something.

'Prep the crash cart,' says Bron.

'Bron.' I fight to keep my voice calm. 'There aren't enough nurses. Give me something to do.'

Bron stares at me for a moment. There isn't time to weigh up whether it's wise to let me help, so she relents. 'IV fluids and adrenaline.'

I don't wait for her to change her mind.

At the medicine cabinet, I stare at the vials. My vision blurs until every one is filled with yellow solution and every label reads Pentoject. Beneath the grilling strip lights, a dribble of sweat runs down my spine into the waistband of my trousers. My tongue is dried meat in my mouth and I swallow a surge of acid vomit. I close my eyes, shake my head, and open them again.

Pull yourself together, Ev. Pull yourself together.

I grab IV fluids and a vial of epinephrine, check and double-check the labels, and then prep two syringes of adrenaline: one low dose, one high.

Back at the table, Bron is sizing an endotracheal tube, while Jenny finishes shaving Jack's leg and chest before placing an IV catheter in his cephalic vein.

'Fluids and epinephrine.' I put them on the tray next to Bron. She glances at me with her lips pressed tightly together before administering the fluids. I stare at her downcast eyes. Her eyelids are a wall that's gone up and I'm on the other side of it.

Jack's blood pressure spikes and then gradually declines. I watch in horror, unable to move a single muscle, as Bron barks orders at the nurses rushing around me.

I stand in the eye of the tornado.

Antiseptic fills my nostrils and coats my tongue. I swallow it down. It's a scent as familiar as the aroma of my own home. I breathe it in without even being aware of it, yet now it's thick. It takes up all the air in the room.

Jenny administers the first shot of low-dose adrenaline while Bron gets up on the table to begin chest compressions. Unless it's an exceptionally small patient, Bron always does this, because she's particular about her technique and doesn't think they're as effective leaning over a table. I've seen her do this many times, but it's never been so painful to watch.

My eyes track the twitching ECG as if I'm watching Jack's heart pumping inside his chest. I will it to keep moving, to beat on its own, and its slow pace drags mine into step.

After two minutes of compressions, Bron stops to check the ECG but there's no rhythm or heart rate. Jenny administers the second high-dose adrenaline shot, and she and Bron change places on the table. Chest compressions are tiring, mentally more than physically with a patient as small as Jack, so they switch to ensure they're maintaining the correct force and weight.

After another two minutes, Jenny stops to check the ECG. Nothing.

'Adrenaline, amiodarone and atropine,' shouts Bron.

And before any of the nurses have the opportunity to beat me to it I run back to the cabinet and prep the syringes. The amiodarone is in case the defibrillator doesn't restart Jack's heart. The atropine is a last resort. It's unlikely to do any good.

Behind me, Bron shouts, 'Prep the crash cart to sixty.' And by the time I get back to the table she's removed the ECG leads from Jack's chest and is applying electrode gel to the defibrillator paddles.

I've never believed in God, but I pray anyway.

She places the paddles on either side of Jack's sternum and shouts, 'Clear!' before she shocks him. With no ECG connected, she has to check manually for a heartbeat. 'Nothing. Charge to ninety.'

I swallow bile.

Jenny and Bron continue with adrenaline, chest compressions and the defibrillator, but there's still no heartbeat. They administer amiodarone and shock him at a hundred and ten, but Jack's heart refuses to beat on its own. Finally, Bron shouts, 'Atropine,' and my eyes well up as I lamely hand her the syringe.

The next two minutes feel like the entire thirty-eight years of my life. I watch them buzz around Jack as they shock him again and check for a heartbeat. But nothing they do will come to any good. Jack was dead the moment I pressed the plunger on that syringe.

'It's been fifteen minutes,' says Jenny, and Bron pumps Jack's chest a few more times before stopping. Her shoulders slump.

I stare at Jack's lifeless body.

This can't be happening. It can't be.

The tight leash I keep on my life is snapping.

I snap.

'Get down!' I reapply the ECG leads and hurry Bron down from the table as I climb up to take her place. Elbows locked, shoulders over my hands, I begin chest compressions.

'Ev,' says Bron. 'We've done everything we can.'

I ignore her and carry on pumping Jack's chest.

'Ev... Ev...' Bron tries to pull my arms away and I fight against her but she's taller than me, broader. She wraps her arms around mine, pinning them to my side. 'Eva! Let him go.'

There's no use fighting her so I stop struggling, slump over Jack's little body and sob. Bron and the nurses stand around me. They've never seen me like this, never seen a chink in my professional armour, and now I'm in pieces none of them have any idea what to say to me. Eventually, it's Bron who speaks.

'I'll tell Caroline.'

'No.' I sniff and wipe away tears. 'No. I'll do it.'

I get down from the table, turn my back on Jack's dead body and walk as slowly as I can back to the examination room where Caroline is waiting.

TWO

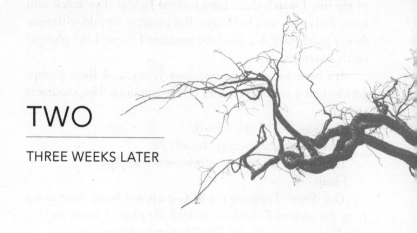

THREE WEEKS LATER

I JOLT AWAKE. Terrified.

I strike out to protect myself and my fists connect with something solid.

Flesh.

Taut muscle.

A man. Strong. He pins my arms down as I fight against him.

'Hey, hey! Are you okay?' It's Jacob's voice. 'Were you dreaming?'

I open my eyes a crack.

'I was just going in for a kiss, but if my morning breath's that bad...'

I squeeze my eyes shut and open them again, my vision clearing. 'Sorry.'

Jacob lets go of my arms, pinned to the mattress by my wrists, and I massage dry, sore eyes. He's already in his suit.

'What time is it?' I ask.

'Seven-fifteen.'

'Already?' I tap my fitness tracker and numbers startle its black face. It has a silent alarm set, yet its vibration didn't even disturb me.

'I didn't want to wake you. I'm off. Your coffee's there. See you tonight.'

I lift myself up on to my elbows and wince as a sharp pain stabs my spine. I say, 'You look dapper. Court, or new client?' My words are weary, stale. He's in one of his best suits. Against the dark grey fabric, pinstripes run contour lines down his frame, and his chinstrap goatee is trimmed to barbershop perfection.

'New client. Actress suing her producer over her nudity clause.' He bends down to kiss me again, and his dark hair falls forward into a quiff over his forehead. He brushes it back with his fingers.

'You need a haircut.'

His natural curl is breaking free, and I love it like that, but he won't keep it for long. Too unprofessional.

'I know. I'll get it done Friday. Gotta run.'

He glances back as he walks out of the door, and a chill pierces my aching spine. Something in the tone of his words hanging in the air, or his frame, silhouetted in the light from the hallway, sparks a memory. A flash of that nightmare. But then it's gone, slipping through my fingers, and all that remains is J, smiling.

He might not make it on to the front page of *GQ*, but he has a roguish smile that could get him off a murder charge. The corners of his mouth turn up naturally and are deep-set, like dimples. I like to poke my fingers in them. J told me they're called 'oral commissures', which sounds too formal for something so adorable. Almost legal: 'the oral commissures of an arrestable offence'.

He has a natural, enviable class that belies the truth of his upbringing. The farm boy – from a remote holding in Douglasville, Atlanta – came good. He didn't grow up wealthy

– neither of us did – but he slots into moneyed Oxford more comfortably than I do, even though I was born here. Oxford's charm holds me here but its undeniable poshness has always stopped me feeling like I belong. Walking the streets, you can tell the well-bred just by looking at them. Like pedigree dogs. Those who'd win Best in Show sport salmon trousers, striped shirts and a jumper, casually draped over the shoulders. But it's not really the clothes, it's the ease with which they wear them, an ease I'd never felt in any clothing, until I put on my first pair of scrubs. In those, I felt capable. Professional.

Some days, I have to fight the urge to put them on. Like a wedding dress stored in the loft, they hang cold and pressed in the wardrobe, and I paw them.

If I did put them on now, I'd feel like a fraud.

'Have a good day,' I call after him, flatly, as he turns and walks down the stairs. 'Love you.'

'Love you too, pretty lady.' He thinks his John Wayne impressions are bang on, but they're really, really bad. He's always teasing me with that chauvinistic American drawl. It doesn't bother me unless he puts 'little' in there. That sets my teeth on edge. J moved from the USA to England when he was twenty-six and those ten years have mellowed his accent, but he loves overplaying it.

Feeling heavy and awkward, I heave myself up and smack my skull against the headboard. A flower in its baroque carving leaves a painful dent in the back of my head and I rub it away as I lift up my pillow. Only J would choose such an impractical bed. It's stunning, a modern design from some famous Italian I've never heard of. J assures me it's white wood, it just looks like ivory – I'd divorce him if it were – but a padded headboard would be far more comfortable right now. I must have slept in a strange position because it's not just my spine that aches: every muscle is sore.

I reach across for my coffee and my hand trembles. J's overfilled the cup and I have to put it back down to avoid spilling it. I make fists and stretch out my fingers to stem the tremors, then reach again for my coffee, but, as I do, three bright drops of blood splash on to the white quilt cover.

'Oh, shit!' I brush my fingers over my upper lip. Another nosebleed.

Cupping a hand beneath my nose, I kick away the quilt and make for the en suite, where I sit on the toilet and pull reams of tissue from the roll. After a minute or two the bleeding subsides but doesn't stop, so I twist two wads of tissue into plugs and shove one up each nostril.

Slumped on the loo with tissue tusks up my nose, I stare at my ghostly reflection in the shower screen. Ghastly, more like. I feel sorry for her. She looks like shit. Her almost-black hair hangs limp over her olive-skin breasts, she has dark circles under her eyes, and all the colour has drained from her lips. I'd swear she's aged ten years since she was fired for killing Jack.

Peeing burns slightly and, when I've finished, it's followed by that familiar drawing sensation, as though you need to pee again. Cystitis. Which is all I need right now when I already feel like a wound-down toy.

Back in the bedroom, I give up trying to drink my coffee with tissue-tusks and throw on yesterday's jeans and jumper before turning my attention to the bloodied bedding. As I'm undoing the buttons on the bottom of the quilt, my mobile vibrates on the bedside table, so I grab it and balance it between my ear and shoulder blade while I battle with the buttons.

'Hello?'

'Eva?'

'Dad. How's things?'

'You sound off. Did I wake you?'

I hear Mum whisper in the background, 'She's still in bed? It's gone eight o'clock!'

'Of course not,' I snap. Then I take a deep breath and say, 'Sorry, Dad. Didn't mean to take your head off.'

Whenever Dad makes a phone call, Mum keeps one ear pressed to the receiver to keep tabs. I love her dearly, and when I'm in a better frame of mind her antics make me smile; she's like one of those sitcom mothers from the '70s. But these days nothing makes me smile. Part of me died on that table with Jack, and I hardly recognise what's left of me.

'Are you all right, love?' Dad asks.

'I'm fine,' I lie. 'Just a bit groggy.'

'You not sleeping?'

'On and off. Bad dreams. This morning I slept right through my alarm. I don't think I've ever done that.'

'Dreams about what?' Dad asks.

'I don't remember.'

Then Mum chimes in, 'How does she know they're bad if she can't remember them?'

'They wake me up,' I say. 'This morning I almost punched J. And they leave this…lingering feeling that stays with me all day. It's been going on for weeks.'

Mum whispers, 'Is that why she hasn't applied for any jobs yet?'

'Mum!'

'Well, it's been ages.'

'It's been three weeks!' I protest.

Then I hear her trill in the background, 'Idle hands are the devil's workshop.'

As I pull the quilt from its cover, it slides off the bed to reveal a stain on the sheet. That'll be Teddy, although he usually sleeps at the top of the bed not the bottom. Teddy is never happy sleeping on the bed, but insists on sleeping in it. He pulls back the quilt with a digging motion, snuggles down and leaves a wet-spaniel mess on the sheets. J calls it 'Teddy's Revenge' because we don't let him up on the bed while we're making love: we have to sleep in *his* wet spot. It drives J nuts because he's clawed his way through two sets so far, and they're Egyptian cotton, made to measure. J's forever saying I shouldn't let him on the bed, but then I'll go upstairs and find the two of them spooning.

'Don't listen to your mother,' says Dad. 'You take your time, love. You shouldn't go back to work till you're ready.'

'That'll be never, then,' I reply, caustically.

Mum whispers, 'Give me the phone, Tony.'

'I'm speaking to Eva.'

'Give me the phone! Tony… Tony, give me the phone.'

'In a minute. Just wait.'

My parents are still married after thirty-nine years, even though they have nothing in common. My mother's always worn the trousers – the waistcoat and the braces too – but in later life my father has found a scrap of fighting spirit. Sadly, that hasn't made his life easier, it's made it worse. They're like bones that have worn up against each other for decades: the joint aches but it still keeps moving.

It's hard to imagine my father – an intelligent, tall and striking Cape Verdean man – being intimidated by anyone. That is, of course, until you meet my mother. Dad's a gentle soul, easygoing, the type of person who's always there for you and remembers everything that's going on in your life. I'm named after his mother, Evangeline, and he's just like her. I've always striven to be like both of them: good, solid, kind people. I have their features, their wide grins and plump lips which twist into a perpetually ironic smile. Nobody takes me or my father seriously, especially when we're together.

At least, they never used to.

'How have you been, Dad? Work okay? Not getting you down?'

'It's all right. Actually, that's why I was calling. I saw Tomás Mendez on the ward yesterday. He's very sick. I'm not sure he's going to be around much longer and I was wondering if you'd heard from Maria lately?'

'No, Dad. Not for years. Let me guess – liver failure?'

'I'm afraid so.'

'I'd like to say poor Tomás, but my heart wouldn't be in it.'

Maria's an old schoolfriend of mine. Dad always had a soft spot for her because she's from Portugal, and Portuguese is the official language of Cape Verde. Nanny spoke it, along with Creole, and when Dad was missing home he'd reminisce with Maria in their common tongue.

He thought she needed rescuing, and it's his nature to nurture the vulnerable. Maria's mother died when she was twelve and, with nobody to keep Tomás in check, Maria suffered the brunt of his physical and emotional abuse. Tomás never remarried, and the lack of a mother figure hardened Maria even further. She pretty much raised herself. Back then, I was too young to understand the reasons for her hard exterior. To me, she was as tough as old boots and as sharp as a tungsten needle. And, to be honest, I was a little bit scared of her.

But then, when I first started working for Bron in my late twenties, I heard from a mutual friend that Maria had tried to commit suicide. It was only then, long after our friendship had petered out, that I realised my father had been right all along and there was a broken little bird behind those steel bars. I felt terrible for not having been more supportive when we were kids.

'I'm afraid Tomás is getting his come-uppance,' says Dad. 'But Maria might want to say goodbye.'

'I doubt it, Dad. Either way, I wouldn't know how to reach her.'

'Oh, that's a shame.'

'Though I did hear she'd joined the Met. Maybe you can contact her that way.'

I don't tell Dad how I know Maria has joined the Met, and I'm relieved he doesn't ask. Several years ago, I saw Maria's name in the paper. She'd been accused of beating a man named Peter Cunard with a nightstick while he was handcuffed. The beating left him brain-damaged. Another male officer was involved in the arrest, and Maria had claimed he was

12

responsible. But it was his word against hers and, though she was cleared of all charges, the accusation had marked her like a red cross on a plague victim's door. Because nobody put it past her.

'The Met? Really?' Dad sounds impressed.

I remember how she intimidated me as a child and say, 'I know, it's perfect for her, right?'

Phone still tucked under one ear, I head for the en suite, rummage through the sink cabinet for a clean cloth, and run it under the tap.

'It is,' says Dad. 'She'll be a real asset. Hey, maybe you should call her? I bet she'd love to hear from you. And you could do with someone like her in your corner right now.'

By 'someone like her' he just means *someone*. Anyone.

It's not as if I don't have *any* friends; it's just that my best friend was also my boss. And the surgery was so busy, I had little time for anyone except Bron and Jacob. It had been enough for me. More than enough.

I say, 'I don't think so, Dad. I don't have the energy for Maria right now. You call her.' Then I change the subject by asking, 'What were you doing down on the wards anyway? Getting your fix?'

'Something like that,' he says.

'Office getting you down?'

'It's okay—'

'He's fine,' Mum says, talking over the top of him. 'His therapist is a marvel.'

'Therapist? Dad, why are you seeing a therapist?'

'Oh, it's nothing—'

'Stress!' shouts my mother, then realises she's shouting and whispers, 'He's not coping.'

When my parents met, my father was a nurse, beloved on the paediatrics ward, but underpaid. So my mother had pushed him into the administrative side of the hospital, shepherding him up the ranks until he became an IM&T Service Manager.

It's one of those jobs where you tell people what you do and they're none the wiser. Every time phrases like 'business intelligence', 'continued service' and 'information governance and security' leave his lips, a tiny part inside me dies. And I witness a tiny part of him dying too. My father wasn't built for an office; he was built to shine, to bring light into people's lives. I blame my mother for the downcurve of his eyes, the grey in his hair, and his receding hairline. And, now I've lost the job that was my *raison d'être*, I feel for my father more than ever.

'I'm fine, love,' says Dad. 'Your mother booked it. I didn't even want to go. But anyway, I didn't call to talk about me, I called to see how you were holding up?'

'Coping, I guess.'

'Give me that.' Mum snatches the phone from Dad and starts rambling on about his inability to manage the workload and his promotion that's now in jeopardy.

The stain doesn't come out with the wet cloth so, one-handed, I go from corner to corner of the bed, yanking off the fitted sheet as if it's to blame for my father being in therapy. Then, something catches my eye. Something black. Trapped between the mattress and the footboard. I pull hard and set free a ball of lacy fabric.

As I shake to untangle it, I realise it's my suspender belt, with my lace-topped stockings still attached. I can't even remember the last time I put on a dress and heels that needed stockings and suspenders. I find suspender belts uncomfortable and tend to wear hold-ups, but J loves them. Which is probably how they ended up stuffed beneath the sheets at the bottom of the mattress. It must have been quite a night. No doubt with too much to drink. And, no doubt, before Jack. Since then, I haven't been able to face going out. With my picture all over social media, I feel as if the whole world knows who I am.

'He'll help you get over this,' says my mother.

'Who will?' I've completely lost her train of thought.

'Your father's therapist. For heaven's sake, Eva, keep up.'

'This isn't something you just get over, Mum. I'm not sure I could set foot in a surgery ever again. And, even if I could, I'm unemployable.'

'Don't be ridiculous, Eva. You just need to get a grip.'

'Get a grip? Mum, there's not a surgery in Oxford that would hire me. I doubt there's a surgery in the UK that hasn't heard about what happened.'

'It wasn't your fault, Eva. It was a silly accident.'

I can't even respond to that. Mum could never understand the loss that George and Caroline have suffered, what I've put them through, and if I spent a year trying to explain it she still wouldn't. So I just say, 'I have to go, Mum.'

'Why? It's not like you've got anything to do. You've got a cleaner, you don't even need to clean the house.'

'Jesus, Mum. I fired the cleaner, okay?'

That's not a lie. I did fire the cleaner. I felt terrible about it and paid her for three months' garden leave, but what could I do? I was spending Monday mornings watching her clean the house, and then I was cleaning it again just for something to do.

Along with my mother's bright blue eyes, I also inherited her pathological perfectionism, which is why I had a cleaner in the first place. If I clean the house myself, I can't stop until everything gleams as though it were just unwrapped from tissue paper. I spend five hours in one bathroom with a razor blade on the limescale-encrusted shower glass and a toothbrush on the grout. It's just sad.

But now, it's become a great day-filler. Without it, I'd spend my days staring out the window or at my weary reflection in the bathroom mirror, while my mind runs around a Möbius strip trying to make sense of that day. Instead, I buff bathroom tiles and shine copper pots and pans. Not having a job has scooped my insides out and left this shell that wanders between rooms, polishing things.

15

I sniff the feet of my lace-topped stockings to see if they're clean.

They aren't.

'Oh, poor Annie,' says my mother. 'I liked her.'

She didn't like Annie. The only cleaner my mother would like would be one who was cleaning part-time while studying to be a doctor or a lawyer. If she came to the house while Annie was here, Mum would talk in two-syllable words as if Annie were learning-impaired, when in truth she speaks three languages and used to be a dentist in the Czech Republic. It was so humiliating. 'Poor Annie' is right.

I say, 'She's going to start again when I go back to work.'

'You are planning on going back to work, then?'

'Mum! For fuck's sake.'

'Language, Eva! You're so uptight. You'll never get pregnant if you—'

I hang up and ram my mobile into the back pocket of my jeans.

My situation is the excitement in Mum's life, and she calls almost every day to offer her 'support'. In place of adrenal glands, my mother has a *schadenfreude* gland that excretes adrenaline whenever she learns of someone else's failure or misfortune. The icing on the cake would be for things to fall apart with J and for me to have to move back home. Within a week, she'd have Dad and me in joint therapy.

I've got to get back to work. Only I'm qualified for nothing except the one job no sensible surgery would hire me to do. I can't even type.

Leaning against the footboard of the bed, I unclip my stockings from the suspender belt and one of the straps comes away in my hand. The loop that holds it to the belt is torn.

Suddenly I feel as though I've stood up too quickly, and the room is underwater. I can't focus on anything. Everything's twisting. The room turns as black as the fabric in my hands and I fall to my knees, grabbing the bed as I go down. All the strength in my arms melts away and my grip slips from the wood, sliding down the footboard's ornate panel. There's a rug at the foot of the bed and I seize handfuls of its familiar pile to ground myself in the darkness.

I have to get out of this room.

Get away.

I try to stand, gripping the footboard for support, but recoil at the touch of carved wood beneath my palms and fall back to my knees.

I don't want to be here.

Only I can't move. I'm tied to this place, restrained at the wrists and ankles. My mind is black and blank.

A scream, distant, caged, trapped in a gland at the base of my brain, swells like a cancer.

I'm not alone.

THREE

A HIGH-PITCHED CHIME sounds in the darkness, startling me back to reality. I sit back on my heels, waiting for the black fog to clear, and that lingering fear I described to my father tenses every muscle in my body.

Malignant.

My mobile pings again with its high-pitched chime, hounding me for attention, reminding me that I have an unread text. I pull it from my back pocket and just the preview of the message makes my muscles tense even further.

> MUM: I've booked an appointment with Dr Sharif at 2.30pm today. Office above bank, corner of Cornmarket & George St. They had a cancellation.

I text back, thumbnail whitening with each keypress.

> ME: I'm not seeing Dad's therapist!!!

> MUM: Not him. That wouldn't be ethical. Your dad's therapist recommended him. He's a sleep and dream psychologist. Just what you need.

A snort escapes my lips.

> ME: Not going.

> MUM: You are. Paid £95 for session. Cancellation period 24 hours. So you have to go.

> ME: No. I don't.

> ME: No. I don't.

> MUM: Then you owe me £95.

> MUM: Don't be silly, Eva. Go. You need help.

'For fuck's sake.' I pocket the phone.

Barking with joy, Teddy jumps all over me as I struggle through the door with the shopping. I have to put the bags down before the handles tear under his body weight and kneel on the floor so he can jump into my lap, wrap his paws around my neck and nibble my ears. Those YouTube videos of service personnel greeting their dogs after a year-long tour always make me cry, but then I smile at the knowledge that Teddy greets me with equivalent enthusiasm when I come back from putting the bins out.

I make my way to the kitchen, Teddy hot on my heels, with the shopping and several envelopes he'd scattered across the doormat. With the exception of one letter, all the post is for J and I leave it on the kitchen counter. Leaving a cup of tea to brew, I analyse the envelope before tearing into it. I don't recognise the handwriting.

Mrs Eva Curtis,

This morning, Caroline and I received a letter from the practice informing us that, following Jack's death, an enquiry is under way and, in the meantime, you have been 'relieved of your position'.

I hope you feel no relief at all, for we have none.

A surgeon as incompetent as yourself should never have been hired in the first place, then he would still be alive.

We hope you wake up each night with the memory of what you've done burning your conscience.

Sleep lightly, if you can sleep at all.

George Hope

My heart plunges into my stomach and, reading the last line, I want to heave it back up into the kitchen sink.

I have to sit down before I fall down.

With trembling hands, I read the letter over and over, the words 'Sleep lightly, if you can sleep at all' stamping themselves in my mind like a mantra over the memory of Jack's little face. I grab my phone and call J's mobile but it goes straight to voicemail. I'm about to ask him to call me back but the words catch in my throat, so I hang up and throw my phone down on the counter. But then, a moment later, it pings an incoming text and I grab it, hoping it's J. It's not. It's my mother.

MUM: It's 2 o'clock. You are going, aren't you?

I see Dr Sharif's name in the previous text, grab my laptop and Google him. There's not much information, not even a photograph, so I Google 'sleep and dream psychologist' wondering if that's even a real profession. There are thousands of entries from the zany to the ridiculous: dream directories, dream analyses, the A to Z of dreams. It's all absurd. A bunch of dog-and-pony shows. I imagine this Dr Sharif in a gypsy caravan, sporting a turban with a jewel in the centre, cleansing my aura in an attempt to rid me of my nightmares. Then I picture Omar Sharif in *Top Secret*, being smacked across the face by the windscreen wipers of the car he's been compacted inside; this doctor is probably even more of a joke.

I try Jacob again but his phone goes straight to voicemail.

Usually in a situation like this, I'd call Bron and we'd talk everything through until I felt better. She always knows the right thing to say and feels more like a mother to me than my own, even though there's little age difference between us. But I can't call Bron, especially not to discuss hate mail from George and Caroline Hope. She'd probably think I deserved it.

I do deserve it.

And though I don't see what chance this Dr Sharif has of helping me, or anyone for that matter (he sounds like a fucking kook), I have to talk to someone or I'll think myself into an endless loop of crazy.

I try J one more time.

Voicemail. Fuck.

Looks like Dr Fucking Kook is all I've got. But he could be a distraction, get me out of my own head for a while.

21

FOUR

THE PSYCHOLOGIST'S OFFICE smells of leather and cigarette smoke, but faint, as if he lights up once in a blue moon, leaning through the open window, blowing smoke into the street below. It's sweet, not old Marlboros squashed and rotting in an ashtray, more like the Auld Kendal Toffee tobacco I used to buy at Havana House on the high street, fresh in its packet, moss-soft.

He's not at all what I expected. Serious. Studious.

I shouldn't have come.

'Eva Curtis?' He steps out from behind an ornately carved desk and strides across the room, hand extended.

I nod, and tentatively extend mine for him to shake.

'I am Saeed Sharif. Please...' He indicates the oxblood couch at the end of the room. 'Sit down. Make yourself comfortable.' He returns to his desk, takes a seat in a high-backed, matching leather chair and waits.

I have an urge to throw myself on to the couch, prostrate on the deep-buttoned leather, hand on forehead in a histrionic

22

display of woe. Instead, I stay rooted to the spot, staring at the Chesterfield that broods in the bay window. The window is set in a feature wall of red brick, and the bricks are flawless, unnaturally perfect and out of place in such an old building. It must be one of those façades you stick on like wallpaper.

Around the room there are double canvases of serene landscapes, sliced across the horizontal and hung with a small gap between them. Each is a different lake, the sky above reflected in the water below. Selected, I presume, to relax the clients.

It's not working.

I ache for the stingingly bright strip lights of the surgery, the antithesis of this cloistered office, and scan the walls for a switch, about to ask if it would be okay to brighten the place, when the dim glow from a bulb catches my eye. It peeks out from beneath an overstated lampshade of flocked paper that blocks out most of the light. There's another above my head. Identical.

I look behind me at the oak-panelled door and feel the psychologist's eyes on me.

'Please sit down,' says Dr Sharif. 'Unless you do not intend to stay?'

My legs are stiff. I force them to walk the length of his office, heels sinking in the red and cream rug, unsteady.

A matching Chesterfield ottoman, overlaid with a wooden-framed coffee table, sits in front of the sofa and I have to negotiate the limited space to sit down. I perch on the edge of the sofa and squirm. The couch has a stubborn tilt that impels you to lean back and relax. It takes energy to resist, energy I don't have right now. But I don't give in. It would be like giving in to my mother.

I get up again and my linen trousers squawk flatulently on the leather. My cheeks burn, so I turn away from Dr Sharif to stare out of the window. His office looks on to the cemetery that lies in the middle of the road, either side of St Mary Magdalen church. It's an incongruous sight: the dead trying to get some well-earned rest in the middle of a busy intersection. The church is an old crone, clinging by her fingernails to an idealised past, while contemporary life bustles around her.

Like me.

'You know,' I say, more to myself than to him, 'in all the years I've lived in Oxford, I've never got used to pronouncing Magdalen "maudlin". Maudlin's such a desolate word. It doesn't fit its meaning. It sounds like genuine despair. You'd be maudlin after the death of a loved one.' Jack's face flashes into my mind, like the ghost who appears behind you when you close your mirrored bathroom cabinet.

'Actually,' says Dr Sharif, 'Magdalen College is pronounced "maudlin", and Magdalen Road in East Oxford is pronounced "maudlin", but Magdalen Street is pronounced "Magdalen".'

I turn to face him. My cheeks quiver with the effort of a failed smile. 'I didn't know that. All my life I've lived here.'

'It is a common mistake.'

'It's a mistake to pronounce words that are spelt Magdalen "maudlin".'

His eyes gleam, nickel-grey in the meagre light. He's from India, I think. Good-looking. Though not as handsome as J. Salt-white strands fleck his thick black hair and stubble. He looks like a naïve George Clooney. I like him instantly, and that makes it harder for me to talk to him. I don't want to tell him what I've done. Even though I came here because I desperately needed to talk to someone, and even though I've never met this man and will probably never see him again, suddenly I don't want him to think badly of me.

There's a long silence. Discomfiting. As if he's doing that police interrogation thing, forcing you to speak by stretching out the silence until it's too painful to bear.

'I have no idea what I'm doing here.'

'Your father's therapist gave you my name?'

'He gave my *mother* your name. Apparently, it's time I "got a grip".' I make air quotes.

24

'Ah, yes, of course. It was your mother who called.'

I nod. 'She booked and paid for this appointment just this morning. Convenient, when you have a twenty-four-hour cancellation policy.'

'Your mother sounds like a shrewd woman.'

I laugh, caustically.

'Still, you did not have to come.'

'No, and I wasn't going to. But then something happened this afternoon and...I changed my mind.'

'What happened?'

I can't tell him about the letter without telling him about Jack and I'm not ready to blurt that out. 'It doesn't matter. But if I hadn't come, I'd never have heard the end of it. And besides, I don't like to throw money down the drain.'

It's true. And it's worse now that I'm not earning, and all the money I spend is J's. Jacob accrued his wealth gradually and has had time to acclimatise; I was hurled into it the night we met. Calling my mother 'shrewd' is an understatement. She knows me. She would have banked on me not wasting the money she paid for this appointment because she knows that thrifty Eva's still alive and well. Our money feels papered-on. Too easily peeled off. I play house in J's luxurious duplex in the posh part of town, and even after living there for four years it still feels like a doll's house.

I'm the dressed-up plastic wife inside.

Whenever we go out to dinner with J's associates – they're all Oxbridge law types, though they certainly didn't go on bursaries – my upbringing oozes from every pore. I sweat it into my expensive clothes, and have to stop myself breaking into received pronunciation. It's silly I know, paranoia that I lug around in my suitcase of emotional baggage. His colleagues probably don't think anything about me at all.

'Well,' says Dr Sharif, 'if you do not wish to throw money down the drain, let us talk about something other than the pronunciation of Magdalen Street.'

'Fair enough.' But having touched on the subject of my mother, it's as if she's here, filling the room to the corners with her overlarge personality. I slump down on the sofa, no longer caring that my trousers squawk against the leather. 'What do you want to talk about?'

'What do *I* want to talk about?'

'Yes. I'm interested in your suggestions for how we can squeeze the most out of my mother's ninety-five pounds.'

'I think that is a question only you can answer.'

'Well, I don't have answers any more. And I'm not the sort of person that needs psychoanalysing. Asleep or awake.'

'What sorts of people need psychoanalysing?'

'I don't know. Crazy people. Unhinged people. Depressed people.'

'And you are not any of those things?'

'No. And I don't believe in dream interpretation either. Like, if I dream I'm paralysed it means I've lost control of my waking life, or if I dream about death some dramatic change is about to take place. I'm sorry to undermine your area of expertise, Dr Sharif, but I don't think the mind can be so crudely interpreted.'

'Neither do I. And please, call me Saeed. Sleep and dream analysis is a small part of the therapy I provide. I only work on sleep and dream psychology with a few select patients, and I would never presume to interpret their dreams. Only the dreamer can do that.'

'I thought you were a dream and sleep psychologist?' My cheeks burn at the defensiveness of my tone that isn't even meant for him. It isn't even meant for my mother, not really.

Saeed almost laughs. 'No. I have a PhD in clinical psychology and neuroscience, and I am a research scientist at the Sleep and Circadian Neuroscience Institute. And, while I believe it unwise to dismiss the thought processes that occur while we sleep, that is more of a hobby, if you will. I spend most of my time in therapy.'

I'm angry at my own silly assumptions. The gypsy caravan transporting my dog-and-pony show clatters down a dirt track and disappears over the horizon. This man is no kook. He isn't going to cleanse my aura or interpret my dreams. On the contrary, Dr Sharif strikes me as a kind, insightful man, and he actually wants to talk. But I haven't talked to anyone about Jack, not properly. Not even Jacob.

I'm not ready.

'I don't need therapy.'

'Not everyone who comes for therapy *needs* therapy. Some people come just to talk. It can be helpful to talk to an outsider, someone uninvolved in our lives, someone who can see problems objectively. It can be hard to talk to friends and family about difficulties with a husband, for example, because, although you may be having issues with his behaviour, you would not want to diminish him in the eyes of other people.'

'I'm not having difficulties with my husband.'

'No. I was not implying... it was just an example.'

'Of course. I only meant...' I have no idea what I meant, or why I'm still so defensive. My mother's voice grates in my ear: *You're so uptight.*

I remember once, J organised a city break to Prague and we stayed in the Royal Suite at the Vltava Grand. It had one of those hideously expensive bean-to-cup espresso machines and we were so enamoured of it, we drank three coffees before we even got out of bed. Without thinking, we then ordered more coffee with breakfast and about half an hour later we were both squirming from all the caffeine. I'll never forget that sensation, blood coursing like river rapids through my veins.

That's how I feel now.

That's how I feel all the time lately.

We hadn't been together that long, less than six months, and it was in Prague that I finally saw him for who he was and fell in love. Because, at first, I wasn't sure.

Strangely, it was an injured badger that brought us together. He'd hit it with his car and, though it was badly injured, I managed to save it. He'd wrapped it in his suit jacket, making a comment about how expensive it was, and I'd thought he was trying to impress me with his wealth. I accepted when he asked me out on a date, but we had quite a few before I started to warm to him.

But I fell in love in Prague. He took me to my first classical concert, and I didn't expect to like it, but, when the orchestra burst into life, I burst into tears. It was like being impaled by sound. But what shocked me the most was, when I turned to tell J how I felt, he was crying too. It was one of the most profound and beautiful moments of my life, and the first time I realised he wasn't the sharp-edged, impervious lawyer I'd taken him for.

I saw who he really was.

'All right,' says Saeed. 'If not your marriage, then what does your mother think you need to get a grip on? Why did she make this appointment on your behalf?'

'She thinks I'm depressed.' I lean forward and pour myself a glass of water from the jug on the coffee table. 'I'm not depressed.' I look up and Saeed is staring at my hand. The water's surface ripples in my trembling fingers. I put the jug down.

'Then what makes her think you are?'

'I lost my job. Two weeks ago, officially – three in reality. She thinks it's time I got another one, retrained as a "proper surgeon". I make air quotes again. 'She thinks it's vital for women to maintain their financial independence so they can jump ship at a moment's notice. She doesn't realise that the majority of us aren't standing on the bow railings ready to throw ourselves overboard.'

'Do you want to talk about what happened? Why you lost your job?'

Do I? Talking about Jack won't bring him back.

'I...' I look down at my hands. 'I killed a dog.'

I blurt the words out with force, suddenly wanting him to think badly of me. I've been torn to pieces on social and mass media; why not by him as well? I want him to be as horrified by what I've done as I am.

'You are a vet?' he asks.

'I *was* a vet.' I look directly at him, waiting for his expression to alter, but it doesn't. He isn't horrified at all. Clearly, he has no idea. 'Have you ever had a dog, Dr Sharif?'

'Saeed, please. No. I do not much like dogs.'

That makes no sense to me – what's not to like – a live teddy bear who just wants to love you and be loved in return? Yet, right now, Saeed's lack of condemnation is such a relief, I have to bite back tears.

I divert the conversation by saying, 'You're missing out, Saeed.' I enjoy the sibilant hiss of his name on my tongue but can't smile. My lips are out of practice. 'Hasn't anyone ever told you they're man's best friend?'

'I do not much like pets of any species. I have never understood the need to have an animal in one's house.'

I picture Saeed as a boy, learning English at a school where they caned children across the back of the hand if they contracted a single word. But, although his words are precise, his tone isn't. It's plush velvet, deep and soft. I like the feel of it in my ears. I wish I weren't the one doing most of the talking.

'Owning a dog is nothing like buying a pet. It's like moving in with someone and falling in love with them more and more each day. And they fall in love with you too, you can see it in their eyes. They don't look at anyone else the same way and they follow you like your shadow. They read your emotions, work hard to understand you, and it's mind-blowing how many words they pick up, to the point where, on a basic level, you can almost talk to them.'

'They say dogs do not understand the words themselves but respond to inflections in your voice.'

I want to say that only a person who's never owned a dog would say something like that, but it sounds condescending. So I tell him, 'There's a collie on YouTube that knows a thousand different objects by name. And there are people who have taught their dogs to read.'

'Seriously?'

'Seriously. They write down words like "sit", "down", or "paw", and the dog performs the command. So, inflections in speech, that's...nonsense.'

'That is extraordinary.'

'They are extraordinary. When my first dog died at fourteen, I was devastated. I'd lost my grandmother two years earlier and we were really close, but I can't tell you, in all honesty, that the grief was any different.'

Saeed looks doubtful, and why wouldn't he? How can I possibly explain something I didn't understand myself until I experienced it? I say, 'I have a friend in her eighties who was out walking her dog in the middle of winter. The dog stopped to take a drink in the river, fell in, and was swept downstream. She jumped in to save it and they both had to be rescued. She nearly died.'

'That is not rational, to risk your life for an animal who was probably a much stronger swimmer and better equipped to deal with the cold.'

'Yes, exactly. But that's what it means to own a dog. They're like a child to you. And you'd risk your life for them, rational or not. You see...what I'm trying to explain is that I didn't just kill Caroline and George Hope's pet, I killed their beloved Jack. I may as well have murdered their child.'

'I think you may be amplifying—'

'No. I'm not amplifying. That's how it is.'

Saeed's expression is sympathetic, genuine, but it's not for the Hopes or Jack. It's for me and what he perceives as an overemotional response to the death of an animal.

God, I need a cigarette.

He asks, 'How did it happen?'

I think back to that day. Again and again I've played over the events of that day and wished for a time machine, a Groundhog Day, a wormhole through which I could travel. 'I was running late. I'd had a restless night and woken up nauseous. I've been trying to get pregnant for a long time and hoped it was morning sickness, but then I came down with a headache and chills, so it was more like the start of a cold or something.'

Saeed sees the disappointment I struggle to hide.

I go on. 'I was a wreck, but not bad enough to call in sick. When I arrived at the surgery, I got out of the car and the next thing I knew, I was lying on the tarmac.'

'Do you faint often?'

'No. And I'm not sure I fainted then, not really. It was more like a head rush, like I'd stood up too quickly. Bron – my boss – told me to go home, but I brushed it off.'

If only I'd gone home. But there are no Groundhog Days, no wormholes, no do-overs. We're stuck with the lousy dress rehearsal.

'Jack was my last appointment before lunch and I was planning on getting some rest upstairs before the afternoon rush. But, before Jack, Mrs Cranleigh came in with Pilot, her Newfoundland.'

Saeed is none the wiser.

'Think Shetland pony.'

His eyes widen.

'He was sixteen, old for a Newfie, completely blind with pulmonary fibrosis and hip and elbow dysplasia. He could barely get out of his basket. Mrs Cranleigh brought him in to be euthanised and I had the syringe of Pentoject pressed to his foreleg when she shouted at me to stop.'

Saeed's expression is still blank, yet I can't think of putting a dog down without imagining Teddy, even though I've done it dozens of times.

31

'She's had Pilot since he was a puppy and she's eighty years old, so she won't get another dog. It was inhumane to keep him alive but difficult to let him go. I didn't want to push her, so we agreed she would keep him over the weekend and bring him in the following Monday to be put to sleep.'

Saeed leans forward, hanging on every word. I've never met anyone with such focused attention, as though he's a bird of prey and I've snapped a twig in the undergrowth.

'Mrs Cranleigh was crying, so I put the syringe down on the counter to comfort her. The appointment was running over, and I knew Caroline Hope was waiting, but I couldn't rush Mrs Cranleigh.'

Caroline would never say anything rude about being made to wait, she's far too well-bred for that, but she exudes an air of intolerance that's almost regal and makes you feel you should curtsey.

'By the time I got Jack into the examination room, the appointment had already run over by half an hour, and I was rushing.'

'Jack is a...?'

'French bulldog. *Was* a French bulldog. Are you familiar with them?'

'No.' Saeed takes a sip of iced tea from a glass on his desk. Beads of condensation have run off the silver coaster on to the wood. It's a nice desk.

'They're really sweet.' I restrain myself from snatching a tissue from the box on the ottoman table and mopping up the water. 'A small breed with these adorable bat-like ears. Caroline bred them and showed them at Crufts. She imported Jack from the United States. Paid forty thousand pounds for him.'

Saeed chokes on his tea.

'It's not as crazy as it sounds. He was a good investment. He had an impeccable pedigree, a lilac carrying cream, so he could produce puppies of either colour. He won Best in Show

32

at Crufts and was making thousands of pounds in stud fees and endorsements. But he wasn't just an investment. Caroline loved him dearly. I did too. I saw him all the time.'

'He was sick?'

'Not exactly. Four years ago, he developed acute pancreatitis and EPI. It was severe.'

Saeed's head tilts, alerting me to my vet-speak. His hypnotic eyes draw me in and I'm suddenly conscious of how effortlessly my words are spilling out when I never meant to come here in the first place. I feel manipulated. I look away from him to the floor. He's wearing braided leather sandals, and the dark skin of his bare feet is smooth and sensual. His toes have the lightest tufts of hair on them. My eyes drift upwards, tracing the length of his body to his broad shoulders. The top buttons of his black kurta are undone, revealing more tufts of dark hair on his chest. There's a softness to him. A warmth.

I relax a little.

'Exocrine pancreatic insufficiency. The pancreas doesn't produce enough enzymes for the dog to digest its food. So, in the end, no matter how much they eat, they still starve. He came in for regular injections of Duphalyte – vitamins, amino acids and electrolytes.'

'Did this EPI not affect his...stud—'

'No. There's no evidence it's hereditary. And he was doing really well.'

'I see.'

'But Jack was on edge that day, frightened. He'd had a scuffle in reception with Blue, an Alsatian who's always aggressive with other males. And while I was prepping the syringe he jumped down from the examining table and bolted for the door. Caroline was struggling to get hold of him. Even a small dog can be difficult to handle when it puts up a fight.'

'I can imagine.'

'So...' I inhale deeply. 'I put the syringe down on the counter and helped her. We got him back on the table and I

33

held his collar while she gave him treats to calm him down. I reached behind me, picked up the syringe...' I swallow. The words slip down my throat as I struggle to get them out. 'And injected him. Only I didn't pick up the Duphalyte, I picked up the Pentoject. And I killed him.'

I don't mention our efforts to save Jack, because I need to say it like that. Like a blunt-force trauma to the head. And there's no bandaging it. No giving it mouth-to-mouth.

Saeed doesn't say anything for a long time, and the silence draws tears I have to fight back.

'That must have been terrible. The owners must have been—'

'Devastated. Outraged, naturally. They threatened to go to the press. Threatened to sue if I wasn't fired. It could have ruined the practice, so I was let go. I was already on a leave of absence, and I'm not sure I could have gone back into the surgery anyway. But it clearly wasn't enough. They didn't sue, but one way or another it hit the local paper, and got picked up by a national – then it was all over social media, with pictures of me and everything. And then, they sent me hate mail this morning.'

'Hate mail?'

'Yes.'

I hand Saeed the letter and he shakes his head as he reads it. 'This is all very distressing.' He passes the letter back to me.

'It is. I loved Jack as though he was mine. I can't believe they think I would have hurt him on purpose.'

'You said a dog is like a child to its owners. I am sure, in time, they will come around and see things more clearly. Grief makes people angry, but, as the grief lessens, so does the anger.'

'You don't think I should be worried about the letter?'

'It could be conceived as a veiled threat. You could consider notifying the police—'

'No. I don't want to involve the police. I don't want to hurt the Hopes any more than I already have. I just keep asking myself, over and over, why I didn't dispose of the syringe the moment Mrs Cranleigh changed her mind about Pilot.'

'It seems an easy mistake to make. Perhaps you are being unnecessarily hard on yourself.'

'But that's just it. It *isn't* an easy mistake to make. Not for any vet, but particularly not for me. I don't make mistakes. I'm a pathological perfectionist. I check and triple-check everything. I'm the type of woman who arranges tins face-forward in the cupboard and hangs her clothes in the wardrobe according to category.'

'You said yourself you were not well that day.'

'Even then, you need a perfect storm for something like that to happen.'

'A "perfect storm"?' Saeed's soft expressions are already starting to feel familiar. They open me up until everything spills out.

'Yes. Every detail had to fit together, like a puzzle. Remove one piece and Jack would still be alive. If Jack's appointment hadn't coincided with Blue's there would have been no fight in reception. He would have been calm and I wouldn't have put the Duphalyte syringe down. If Mrs Cranleigh had let me euthanise Pilot, the Pentoject syringe would have been empty. If the appointments had been the other way around, Pilot would have been my last appointment before lunch.'

Like coins from a slot machine, my words pour out as if I can justify the unjustifiable and somehow win redemption.

'If Pilot had been any other dog – a small breed like Jack – he wouldn't have needed such a large dose of Pentoject. But a sixty-kilo Newfie needs twenty-five millilitres of Pentoject for euthanasia, almost identical to the Duphalyte dosage for Jack. And Pentoject is a clear solution. It's easily confused with other medications, so to prevent mistakes the manufacturer adds a bright yellow dye. But of course, Duphalyte contains vitamin B12, which contains metal cobalt, which makes the solution—'

'Bright yellow?'

'Exactly. If Jack had suffered from any condition besides EPI, the syringes would have been unmistakable.'

'That is, as you say, a perfect storm.'

'Yes. And of all the dogs I could have killed, it had to be Jack. The Hopes' forty-thousand-pound pedigree show dog.'

'I am so sorry, Eva.'

As if Jack needs a minute of silence, we don't speak for a while. Then I say, 'My whole life changed in five seconds. The Eva I was died with Jack and this one was incarnated, this mess of a woman who can't function, can't think straight and can't even sleep.' I stretch out my left palm and watch my fingers quiver for a moment. I ball my hand into a fist but it still trembles, as if a moth struggles for life in my grip. 'I'm not sure I'll ever be able to work again.'

'You must give yourself time to heal. It is hardly surprising that such an event would lead to disturbed sleep and nightmares.'

I glare at Saeed. 'I didn't say I was having nightmares.'

'Your mother told me, when she telephoned to make the appointment.'

I shake my head. Not at him, at her. I wonder what else she told him.

'Can you tell me about these dreams you have been having?'

'No. I never remember them.'

'But you know they are bad?'

'Yes. I don't remember details, but I feel strange the next morning. They leave this…malignant feeling that lingers all day. It's hard to explain. Like a hangover. You can't remember the night before, but you know you had too much to drink and did terrible things.'

'I can help you remember.'

'What for?'

'It could be useful. In some of my patients it has—'

'I'm not your patient.' I'm not sure what I am.

'No, I did not mean to suggest…' He doesn't speak for a

moment and then asks, 'Have you heard of Ernest Hilgard?'

'No.'

'He was a Stanford professor, a very accomplished hypno-therapist.'

He says 'accomplished' provocatively, teasing me with my own scepticism. And that hint of sass in his tone sparks a meagre light in me that's so insignificant, yet, in the darkness that has consumed my life since Jack, strangely bright. It reminds me of my father and the way we tease each other.

'He believed that the mind is split into different systems of consciousness: active and receptive. And that, through hypnosis, we can interrogate this receptive persona, this "hidden observer" who plays out their exegesis of our lives through our dreams. And through this entity we can tap into information that our conscious mind is unaware of.'

'And how is that supposed to help me?'

'It is highly likely that these nightmares are a response to the traumatic event you have experienced. Our sessions could target the coping mechanisms of both your conscious and unconscious minds, helping you come to terms—'

'I'll never come to terms with it. I'm a vet, for Christ's sake, I'm supposed to keep animals alive, not randomly put them to sleep.'

'In reality, you forgot to dispose of a needle. And that mistake led to the death of a dog.'

'You're saying I shouldn't be so hard on myself because there was no malice aforethought? So, I'm not guilty of dog murder, just dogslaughter?'

One corner of Saeed's mouth turns up, but I wasn't trying to be funny. I inhale deeply and pry my nails from the deep gouges I've left in my palms. I wasn't even aware I was still clenching my fists.

'Well,' he says, 'yes, if you had harmed the dog intentionally, it would make you a very different person. But your intention was to heal it, not to harm it. In the job you do—'

'Did.'

He closes his eyes for a moment, then looks into mine. 'In the job you *did*...the stakes were high. But everybody...*everybody* makes mistakes, Eva. Usually, mistakes in the workplace – the secretary who misplaces a vital document, or the hairdresser who gives a bad cut – do not mean life or death. You took on that responsibility. But you cannot take only one half of it. Both their lives and their deaths were in your hands. Think of all those you have saved.'

He's right, but it doesn't make it any easier.

'Look,' he says, 'I know you are sceptical but I really think I can help you. Everything will be so much harder to cope with if we do not first address the problems you are having with sleep. Do you know that even after three or four days without sleep, a person can start to hallucinate? Do not underestimate its importance. Besides, we still have twenty minutes left of the session. You said you were interested in my suggestion for how we could squeeze the most out of your mother's ninety-five pounds. This is my suggestion.'

'To hypnotise me?'

Saeed rocks his head from side to side. 'Of sorts. For the last ten years I have studied hypnosis, sleep induction, lucid dreaming, guided meditation...each has its strengths and drawbacks. I have stolen from each to develop my own unique form of hypnosis. Can we try?'

I shrug. 'I guess.'

I've never been through guided meditation or been hypnotised before, and I rarely feel lucid these days. I have no idea what to do. I consider lying down but that smacks of being hackneyed, so I just lean back and close my eyes. His leather chair creaks as he stands and I open one eye to watch him as he comes out from behind his desk to stand behind the sofa. It feels strange to have someone talk to the back of your head, and I fight the urge to turn and face him.

'Try to relax. Get comfortable.'

I shuffle deeper into the leather, but I can't relax.

'You can open your eyes.'

I'd thought he was going to put me to sleep, but I do as I'm told. Peeking out from beneath the flocked lampshade above my head is an old-fashioned teardrop bulb with a series of vertical filaments, and I realise why there's so little light in the room. Saeed has chosen these bulbs intentionally so patients can stare at them without burning their eyes.

'I want you to focus on the light, and on your heart beating in your chest. Imagine the time between beats getting longer and longer, your heart beating slower and slower. Imagine your blood moving through your veins and slow it down until it is creeping, slowly, slowly.' His words unravel in a continuous strand, like soft yarn. 'I want you to picture that light at the end of a long, dark tunnel and imagine yourself floating towards it. The closer you get to the light, the more you relax, and the more you relax, the closer you get to the light, closer and closer, until you are so close that all you can see is light.'

I suppress a smirk. I'm not the type of person who can be hypnotised: too logical, too analytical. This is a waste of time.

I open my eyes.

Saeed is sitting on the ottoman in front of me. Slowly, I come around from a deep and restful sleep. My muscles are no longer tense, my blood no longer courses. It's like an hour-long, full-body massage. I haven't felt this good in weeks. I look up at Saeed, unable to contain a smile. But he isn't smiling. His eyes are hooded, dark.

'What's wrong?'

'You do not remember anything from the session.'

It's not a question. It's a command.

'I thought I'd fallen asleep. Did I remember my dreams?' If I did, I don't now. My mind is quiet. Quieter than it's been since Jack.

'Yes,' says Saeed.

'Well?'

'They will come back to you…slowly…in snatches…over the next few days or weeks.'

'Why don't you just tell me?'

'The events…um…what you recalled…you became very upset during the hypnosis.' It's difficult to tell from his walnut-brown skin, but I think he's blushing. 'It took time to calm you. I left you with the suggestion that you forget these events for now, for your mind to recall them more slowly…in pieces…when your mind feels able to deal with them. When you start to recall your dreams, that is when we will discuss them. It is better this way. Believe me.'

'I don't feel traumatised now. I'm pretty sure I'm capable of separating reality from fiction, Saeed. It's just a dream. A movie playing in your head. Very little fazes me, trust me, I'm not the sensitive type. Surgeons rarely are.'

'What you recalled under hypnosis felt very real to you. More so than I have seen with any other patient.'

'I'm not—'

'I know, forgive me, you are not my patient. But I would like us to spend some more time together if that is agreeable to you.'

'Convenient that I have to make another appointment to find out what I remembered under hypnosis.'

'I am happy to provide the next consultation free of charge. I would not want you thinking I am trying to squeeze another ninety-five pounds out of you. I simply wish to proceed with caution.'

'Why? What's different about my dreams compared to your other patients'?'

'My other patients?'

A smile assaults my lips but, before it can win, Saeed is serious again. His forehead furrows and his eyebrows meet as he organises his thoughts. Clearly my dreams have woken his curiosity, and I'm not sure that's a good thing.

He says, 'Your dreams are very structured. Not at all like a movie playing in your head, as you describe it – not like a dream at all. Usually, the conscious mind is able to discriminate dream from reality because what separates the physical from the psychological is the *sensation* of the dream. The inability to do so can be an indication of psychosis.'

He gesticulates enthusiastically as he speaks. While he may spend most of his time in therapy, it's obvious that sleep and dreams are his passion.

'You see, the dreamer's dream kitchen does not feel like their *real* kitchen and they are unlikely to remember how they got there. Dreams lack transitions; they are a thought-driven reality. You think of your kitchen, you appear in your kitchen.' He gestures around the room as though that's where we are. 'But *your* dreams – at least as you recount them under hypnosis – have transitions. You know how you got there. And your dream kitchen is *your* kitchen.'

'And that's not normal?'

'What is normal? The mind is a world that we are still exploring.'

I'm not sure I want to be explored. I'm a vet, with no desire to become someone else's guinea pig.

'Your mind is very grounded, Eva. It experiences none of the usual sensations of dreaming. No sudden switching from place to place. Nothing fantastical. Nothing illogical.'

'That sounds like me.'

'Well, this makes it difficult for your mind to separate dream from reality. Its response mimics that of a real-life trauma, and the events are so traumatic that stress chemicals shut down your prefrontal cortex, making them impossible to recall. That's why you have no memory of them.'

'So I'm psychotic?'

'No, of course n—'

'You said, if my brain couldn't distinguish reality from fantasy, I must be psychotic.'

41

'I said it can be an *indication* of psychosis. Psychosis is accompanied by a plethora of other symptoms, none of which you appear to be experiencing.'

'What, then? You're saying I construct an almost-perfect reality when I dream? So perfect it's impossible for my brain to realise it's dreaming?'

'Exactly.'

'I told you I was a pathological perfectionist.'

A fleeting look of tender pity and exasperation sweeps across Saeed's face.

'What?'

'You do that a lot.'

'I do what a lot?'

'Joke to defuse tension.'

'That sounds like an accusation, Saeed. Are you suggesting I use humour as a defence mechanism?'

'Are you suggesting you do not?'

He's not wrong – J picks me up on it all the time. I'm just irked by his perceptiveness and this feeling that's been missing for weeks: groundedness. Because he's right: before Jack, I was a very grounded person. I had my shit together. As much as anyone can. And I want to tell him that, but instead I say, 'I know what's coming.'

'What is coming?'

'You're about to say you don't want to be there when the laughter stops. Are you creating a list of disorders for me, Saeed? Is that how therapists make their money? By lining up problems one after the other, so the patient is never fixed?'

'I am not here to *fix* you.' His emphasis on the word 'fix' makes me feel like a toaster or a laptop. 'But I think I can help you. This slot is open now. You could come at the same time next Thursday.'

He looks at his watch, gets up from the ottoman and sits back down behind his desk. I want him to come back. I want to listen to his velvet tones and eager enthusiasm for my unusual dreams. I want to sass him about hypnosis and forget the world outside. But I've pushed him away with my cynicism.

'Well, I hope you got something for your mother's money. I do not suppose I will see you again but if – when – you start to recall your dreams, I am here should you wish to discuss them.'

I'm supposed to get up and leave but instead I cling to the edge of the sofa.

Saeed leans forward in his chair. 'Therapy might surprise you, Eva. I am not trying to cheat or trick you into coming back. If all you want is to recall this one dream, I will tell you if you insist. But analysing one dream will tell us nothing. The clues to what is happening in your subconscious can only be found in the links and repetitions in your dreams. And you will get far more from this if you allow your mind to remember the parts it considers important and make its own associations. There is something else, too…'

'What?'

'You did not dream about Jack. I thought your dreams would reflect the intense ordeal you went through, but they appear unrelated.'

'And that's not normal either?'

'It is unusual. But, without exploring them further, I can offer no rationale.'

I'm about to ask again what I dreamed, but since waking from the hypnosis there's a density to the air in the room that wasn't there before. It's clotted. And I only have to look at Saeed, at the way he shifts in his chair and averts his eyes from me to study the woodgrain on his desk, to know that whatever I recalled under hypnosis has disturbed him as much as the lingering sensation of it disturbs me.

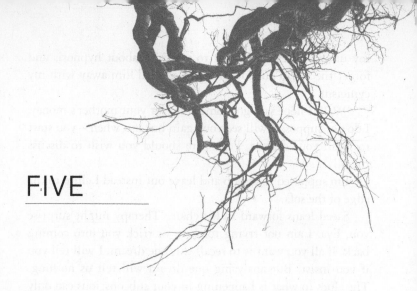

FIVE

A MAN STANDS behind me, tall in my peripheral vision, too close to see his face.

Looming.

Snatches like camera-flashes burst in my mind: a gloved hand over my mouth; the warm, animal smell of leather in my nostrils; fingers, thick, clamped over my lips; my breath barred, forced; my torso stretched forward over the footboard of a bed.

My bed.

Naked thighs crushed into wood; carved baroque flowers imprinting my skin; white ropes knotted around my wrists; another rope taut across the mattress; feet bare and cold.

A door clicks shut.

I swallow metal, as if I've bitten my own tongue.

The washing basket on my lap topples over.

I open my eyes.

Teddy's claws snick snick on the hall's wooden floorboards as he rushes out to greet Jacob. He'd been sleeping on my feet, his warmth seeping up my legs and soothing away the tension. I must have drifted off. J works so hard and here I am sleeping in the middle of the afternoon. I sit upright, snatch the water glass from the coffee table and down it in one. It washes the taste from my mouth but doesn't quench my thirst. I quickly straighten the folded clothes I squashed while I was sleeping and look busy.

The door thuds softly against its jamb, and the latch clicks into place. Small noises but good noises. Comforting noises.

I can tell what kind of day J's had by the sounds he makes entering the house: whether he closes the door gently or with force, whether Teddy rushes to greet him or sulks on his bed, whether his briefcase pats the pink ivory wood of the hall table or slams it. And I can tell from the sound of his keys in the bowl: whether they clatter with enough force to break it, or glide gently down its body into its base.

They glide.

The bowl is a bone of contention between us. Blown from Murano glass with a millefiori design, it's one of my favourite things, and I'd be heartbroken if he smashed it. He bought it for me in Venice. I fell in love with it in a shop window and he offered to buy it without seeing the price tag. The card reader announced one thousand, eight hundred euros, and he didn't bat an eyelid as he entered his PIN. Inside, he must have been choking. J has a great poker face. It was early in our relationship, and he was anxious to impress; he was poker-faced all weekend.

But I still love the bowl.

And it's not just that, it's Teddy: he confuses the clash of metal against glass with the crack of a firework, and nothing frightens Teddy more than fireworks. Every time he hears that sound, he bolts upstairs, hides under our bed and stays there until I coax him out. He mistakes lots of sounds for fireworks: Jacob's keys in the bowl, backfiring cars, and slamming doors. Once, we took him to a dog-friendly hotel and, part-way through dinner, guests started popping champagne in a marquee in the garden. Teddy went nuts and, with no bed to hide under, he clawed me frantically, desperate to get on my lap. After a chat with the waiter, I ate the rest of my dinner one-handed with a seventeen-kilo spaniel trembling on my lap.

Any other man would have told me to put the dog on the floor – people were staring – but not J. He cut up my food, refilled my wine glass, and rubbed Teddy's ears until the party died down. In the five years J and I have been together, it's those inconsequential but quintessential moments that have cemented my love for him.

I couldn't love a man who didn't love Teddy.

But it's Friday, and Jacob's in a door-eased-softly-into-its-frame kind of mood. A gentle-thud-of-leather-on-wood kind of mood. A tinkle-of-metal-against-glass and snick-snick-of-claws kind of mood.

Teddy has tan eyebrows that stand out from his chocolate-brown fur and exacerbate his perpetually baffled American cocker spaniel expression. Looking at his hangdog eyes and stalactite drool, you'd think his biscuits weren't quite baked, but he's smarter than he looks. He's as good at judging J's moods as I am. Tonight he'll have got in quick, demanding to be fussed, and if J stops scratching his chest he'll swipe him with a giant paw until he starts again. From the lounge, I hear J mumbling in Teddy's fur, 'Hey, my boofy boy. Yes, Daddy's home, it's so exciting, isn't it? Daddy's home.'

My muscles relax.

I dump the washing basket on the sofa and go out to greet him. He's wearing his best Martin Greenfield suit because he had a client meeting today. His blue eyes are fluid and lively and his tone is light. A paper shopping bag sits next to his briefcase on the table.

'What's that?'

He grabs it and ambles down the hallway to greet me, saying, 'Never you mind. It's not for you.' Then he takes me in his arms and kisses me, long and full on the lips.

46

'Someone's had a good day.'

'Yep.' He pulls me in tight and kisses me on the end of the nose.

'New client?'

'Old client.'

'Who?'

'Linda Tessler.'

'You're kidding!'

'Nope. Not kidding.'

'Isn't this her fourth husband?'

'Fifth.'

'No way.'

'Yes way.'

'Lovely Linda, she's made you a fortune. How is she?'

J relaxes his arms but doesn't let go. The memory of that dream lies in wait on the other side of his embrace, so I slide my arms inside his suit jacket and cling to the back of his shirt. He links his hands at the base of my spine and sways me ever so slightly as he talks.

'Hasn't changed a bit. Still as caustic as ever. She says hello, by the way. She said Alistair turned out to be a sanctimonious bore, but what could she expect from marrying a man named Alistair? She said she'll marry a Jacob next time.'

'I bet she did.'

J laughs. 'She'd be too much for me.'

'She'd be too much for any man. Maybe she should give them a break and torture women for a change.'

'No sensible woman would have her.'

'There are plenty of foolish women out there.'

'She'd eat any foolish woman for breakfast.'

'And any foolish man for that matter. Poor Alistair. I bet he didn't see it coming.'

'He'll be fine. Linda wants it quick. The settlement's enough to put a smile on the face of any sanctimonious bore.'

'Hmm. Not so poor Alistair, then.'

47

'No, and not so poor Jacob either.'

'An easy buck.'

'Shooting fish in a barrel. How was your day?'

Faced with the juxtaposition of my day against his, I have to paste on a smile. 'I sorted socks.'

J's eyes fill with concern and we both know where this is going. It's a place neither of us wants to keep revisiting. 'Socks, eh?' He pastes on a smile of his own. 'You must be all burned out.'

'I am. Matching pairs is mentally exhausting.'

'Those poor overworked mental muscles.' He kisses my forehead and then looks into my eyes for a long moment, longer than feels natural. He does that a lot, looks at me as if he hasn't seen me for a week, and I love that he can still do that after so many years. But he's not stupid; he knows what I'm doing. He knows I'm quipping about socks to avoid talking about anything real.

I can't look at him any longer and my eyes drift to his chest.

'I'm gonna get changed.' He lifts my chin, kisses me on the lips again, quick and tender, before darting up the stairs, two at a time. I get the laundry basket from the lounge, follow him upstairs, and empty its contents on to the bed so I can finish sorting. Deep joy.

While balling his socks, I watch him get undressed out of the corner of my eye. He tosses the paper bag on to a shelf in the cupboard before removing his jacket. If it was supposed to be a magician's sleight-of-hand manoeuvre, he should stick to the day job.

I don't want to rain on his chirpy parade, so I bite my tongue when he throws his tailored suit jacket over the chaise longue in the walk-in wardrobe. He doesn't realise – or doesn't care – that Teddy misses him while he's at work, so when he leaves his clothes on the chaise they're the next best thing; Teddy sleeps on them, leaving behind a mess of dirt and

48

slobber. Fortunately, the house fairy cleans it up and hangs his suits back in the wardrobe.

J has his suits shipped from the US, tailored by Martin Greenfield himself, and swears they're worth the price tag. According to Jacob, Martin Greenfield is the key to his success. He tailors courtroom battle suits that imbibe J with the power to intimidate his rivals. And I get that. Putting on scrubs makes me feel professional; I doubt pet owners would put as much trust in me if I showed up to work in a pair of joggers and a T-shirt. But then, Barking Threads don't design scrubs for film stars and US presidents or charge me five thousand dollars for a scrub top. Of course, now, no owner would trust me no matter what I wore.

And there it is. It doesn't matter what I'm thinking about, my mind always segues back to Jack.

I ask, 'What did you do with the letter?'

When he got home from work last night, I'd shown him the letter from George Hope, only to chastise myself for my timing immediately afterwards. He'd just walked in the door, and had clearly had a terrible day. He'd read the letter, said it had no legal implications and could be read in more than one way, and completely dismissed how it had affected me emotionally.

'What letter?'

'J! You know exactly what letter. The letter from George Hope.'

'Oh, right, yeah…I threw it away.'

'What? Why?'

He comes over, sits on the bed next to me and rests his hand on my thigh. 'Because you would have read it over and over, stewing over every word. It's better if you forget about it.' He kisses me and goes back into the walk-in wardrobe to continue getting undressed.

He's not wrong. Stewing is exactly what I've been doing.

'I wanted to keep it.'

'What for?' Jacob tugs at his tie to loosen the knot and pulls it, still knotted, over his head. Then he tosses it over the back of the chaise with his jacket.

'Proof.'

'Proof of what?'

'What do you think? The threat.'

'What threat?'

'That I should sleep lightly if I can sleep at all!'

Jacob stops unbuttoning his shirt, but doesn't say anything.

'Yes, yes, I know. You don't consider it a threat because it wouldn't stand up in court...'

'I didn't say that. But...'

'What? What, J?'

He looks directly at me.

'Babe, you don't honestly think...I mean, what are you suggesting? That you need to sleep with one eye open in case George Hope breaks in and knifes you in your sleep for killing his dog? And that I'll need the letter as proof that he murdered my wife?'

When he puts it like that, it sounds laughable. I close my eyes, let my head droop and rub my temples. I can't think straight or form rational thoughts any more. 'No,' I say. Though with less conviction than I intend.

I want to talk to J the way I talked to Saeed yesterday – well, minus the caustic sarcasm and hypnosis derision – but I'm afraid of what he'll think of me, that he'll lose respect for me, that he'll see this new Eva – this irrational mess – and fall out of love with me a little.

So I don't tell him about Saeed.

I don't tell him about the snatched nightmare.

I don't tell him I blacked out again.

He tosses his shirt on the chaise. The laundry basket is five feet away but again, I don't say anything. I prefer it this way. In the same way I can tell what mood he's in by the way he comes through the door, I can also tell if he's had a bad

50

day by the way he gets changed. When one of his cases isn't going well, he'll take off his clothes with such precision it's like removing a suit of armour. Everything will be hung up neatly or placed in the laundry.

It's an aggressive way of getting changed.

He grins and says, 'You know I wouldn't need some stupid piece of paper to avenge your death, right?'

My smile is empty.

He removes his trousers, socks and boxers and adds them to the pile of clothes. Slim-cut against his frame, J's precision-tailored suits make him seem taller than his six foot three inches, and he looks as good out of his suits as he does in them. I'll never forget the first time I saw J naked. I hadn't seen a man's body like it before. He never goes to the gym, lifts weights or does any form of exercise, he's just built that way: naturally lithe and muscular. Bron used to joke that Jacob had a clandestine rendezvous with two hundred bench presses every night. How else could he look like that? But men who lift weights often bulge, especially across the pecs, shoulders and abdominals, until their upper bodies appear larger than their lower bodies. To me, a bulging upper body makes a man's arse, hips and, most crucially of all, what's between his hips, look disproportionately small. J, on the other hand, has a lithe upper body with taut shoulders that taper to a slim waist in a distinct V between his hips. It directs your gaze, and you can't help but stare at his lower body because it looks disproportionally large. It's really sexy but at the same time a little intimidating. It reminds me of that rhyme about the bridegroom who arrives at the marital bedchamber to find his bride unconscious on the bed and a note pinned to the headboard that reads: 'The cold cream's on the mantle, the shoe horn's on the shelf, I've seen that great big thing of yours and I've chloroformed myself.'

After a quick shower, he comes out of the bathroom and disappears behind the wardrobe door. He's quiet. Too quiet.

Which means he's up to something. J has a unique sense of humour. His brain is hard-wired to seek out the funny side in any situation and, because that side of his personality contrasts so starkly with the serious lawyer, even the mildly amusing things he does seem hilarious. It draws people to him, makes men like him, and women fall in love with him. It's why *I* fell in love with him.

He jumps out from behind the wardrobe door wearing his tartan, soft cotton lounge pants – his Friday night go-to attire – and a black T-shirt I've never seen before. It has white text printed on the front which reads: *Ask Me About My Ninja Disguise.*

I ignore him and pretend I haven't noticed it.

'Go on,' he says. 'Ask me.'

'No.' I feign uninterest and ball another pair of socks.

'Ask me.'

'No.'

'Go-an,' he urges. 'Ask me.'

'I'll never ask.'

'Oh, go-an. You have to ask.'

'All right then, tell me about your ninja disguise.'

J grabs the hem of the T-shirt and flips it over his head to reveal a pair of angry ninja eyes. They stare out from the underside of the T-shirt that's now a black hood over his head.

Then he pulls a series of ninja moves, saying, 'I'm your avenging ninja, baby!' before jumping on top of me, pinning me down on the bed and kissing me through the fabric.

I giggle. 'Where on earth did you get that?'

'Martin Greenfield.'

'You funny guy. I euthanise you last.'

'Ooh, dark.' J's voice is muffled by material. 'Bad day?'

'Yes and no. Seriously, where did you buy that?'

'Covent Garden.'

'You're telling me that, in the middle of a serious divorce case, you're out buying ninja T-shirts in Covent Garden?'

'No, it was lunchtime and I was out buying a falafel wrap. I couldn't resist it. Admit it, you can't resist it either.' And he nuzzles my neck trying to bite me through the fabric. 'You want me, don't you, baby? You've never made it with a ninja.'

'Not one in tartan lounge pants.' I grab his full bottom and thrust him against me. 'But yeah, baby, I've never wanted you more. It's all that brushed cotton. It gets me so worked up.'

He pulls the T-shirt off his head and kisses me full on the lips before helping me up.

'Come on. I bought some boar and apple sausages from Porterford's on the way home—'

'Porterford's is hardly on the way.'

'I had to pop into the flat.' J keeps a managed flat in London which is rented out the majority of the time, but if he's working late he can stay there or in one of the other managed flats in the building. He rarely stays over but pops in once a week to check how things are going with the building manager. 'What do you say to bangers, mash, and fried onions?'

'You really know how to sweep a girl off her feet, don't you?'

'Yeah, baby. I know my sausages make you happy.'

'I'll be down in a minute. I'll just finish these socks.'

It's familiar, this exchange. I suppose every couple plays out their little skits, their silly dialogue, their sexual innuendo. And, even though we've been doing it for years, I still love that J can strip the solemnity from any day. He's always playing out one routine or another. He'll get stuck on a song, or a scene from a movie, and change all the accents. Then repeat it over and over for days. Fortunately, the skits change every few months, just before the cow runs dry.

Before this ninja skit, he was stuck on 'I'm a Man You Don't Meet Every Day' by The Pogues. He'd sing it in a Scottish accent and dance in his tartan pants. J's a good singer. Hell, he can turn his hand to anything. But I think he missed

his path in life with that one. When he sings, Teddy howls
and jumps up while J holds his paws and they dance together.

I've never told Teddy that Jock Stewart shoots his dog.

J's standing behind the kitchen island, frying the sausages,
and the sweet smells of seared pork, fried onions and garlic fill
the kitchen. A pile of post lies on the island's marble counter,
and he waves a spatula at it, saying, 'That one's for you.'

I'd forgotten about the post, left it on the hall table all day.
Tearing open the padded envelope, I pull out what's inside.

My heart stops dead.

In my hand is a leather strap with a silver buckle. Stitched
on top of the leather is a ribbon of blue, white and red stripes.
The French flag. And looped to each end of the strap are metal
rings that connect a silver chain.

A choke chain.

'What's that?' asks J.

I swallow hard. My voice cracks.

'It's Jack's collar.'

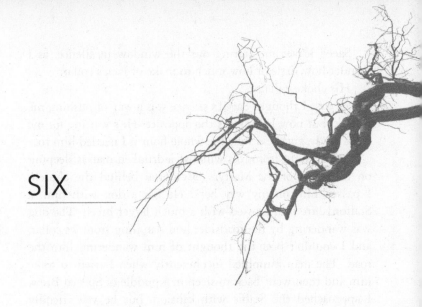

SIX

'I DID NOT EXPECT to see you again,' says Saeed.

'I did not expect to be seen.' I manage a stiff smile with my out-of-practice lips.

'You are late.'

'I know. I'm sorry.' I really didn't intend to come back, but the collar has been playing on my mind since Friday last week.

As I breathe in the smell of toffee tobacco, the ease of being in Saeed's company surprises me almost as much as it did the first time. My fingers twitch to roll, tuck, lick, squash and light. It's a ritual I never tire of. A smoke feels empty unless you roll it yourself. Unearned, like stolen money.

Walking into his office is like stepping into an antigravity chamber. The weight of the world disappears. Throughout the week, I found myself picturing us in this room, not as therapist and patient but old friends, sitting at the open window, blowing smoke into the street below, talking about everything that's gone to shit in our lives.

My life.

Saeed leaves me staring out the window in silence, as I wonder how little or how much to make of Jack's collar.

His choke collar.

At first I thought Saeed's silence was a way of pushing me to talk, but now I think it's the opposite. He's waiting for me to be ready, and he'd wait the whole hour if I needed him to.

Out of sight from this window, a drunken man is sleeping on the steps of the Martyrs' Memorial behind the church. I passed him on my way here. He has a dog with him, a Staffordshire bull crossed with a much larger breed. The dog was wandering by the roadside, lead dangling from its collar, and I couldn't bear the thought of him wandering into the road. The man mumbled incoherently when I tried to wake him and then went back to sleep in a puddle of Special Brew. I approached the Staffie with caution, but he was friendly in spite of his intimidating appearance. He had an infection on his neck that needed treating, so I rushed home, grabbed some antibiotics and Hibiscrub, and attended to it. I left the medications in the man's pocket with a note explaining how to take care of the wounds and slipped the dog's lead over his foot to keep it from wandering. It's why I'm so late.

Now, I scan the crowds for the drunk, hoping he's sobered up and is taking his dog home – if he has a home – where it's safe and warm. I can't see him. I'm sure he'd stand out, staggering along the pavement, clinging to the graveyard railings the way I'm clinging to my old life. I've become my father, sneaking down to the wards to do pretend rounds instead of attending to the information governance and security of the hospital.

I watch pedestrians, cyclists, and motorists fly past St Mary Magdalen, oblivious to the graves in the intersection. Oblivious, that is, until the tyres of their life slip on the road and hurtle them into the central reservation to join the dead. I used to be like them. Oblivious. Hurtling through life on bald tyres on a wet road. Now look at me.

I'm as dead as Jack.

Hollowed out.

That graveyard isn't a place I'd like to be buried. It's never sunlit, always gloomy and dank. In one of the niches on the south façade, there's a hideous statue with a drooping jaw and dark hooded eyes. He's succumbed to age. Both his arms and part of his nose are missing and he looms over the graves like the grim reaper. It's supposed to be Elijah, a prophet who performed resurrections, but rendered in blackened, broken stone he'd more likely raise the walking dead.

One of his disciples is staring out of the window at him.

'George Hope sent me Jack's old collar.'

I look at Saeed for a reaction. The look he gives me is exactly the one I was hoping for when I showed J the letter.

'Why do you think he did that?'

'To hurt me. Threaten me, maybe.'

'Have you called the police?'

'No. Jacob thinks he's just trying to get under my skin, make sure I don't forget what I did. As if I could.'

'What are you going to do?'

'What can I do? He hasn't committed any crime. And I keep asking myself what I would do in his position. What I would do to someone who killed Teddy. I'd want to make sure they didn't sleep at night either.'

'You are still not sleeping?'

'Not properly.'

'Nightmares?'

'Not over the weekend. At first I thought you might have fixed me after all.' I almost laugh but don't want to sound derisive. 'But then they came back.'

'Do you remember anything?'

'Not really. Snatches. But they left me feeling... I wake up tired, sore, aching. As if I've tossed and turned all night. And, given how much rest I'm getting without work, that doesn't seem okay. I thought my body might be trying to tell me there was something wrong...physically. I almost wish there were.'

57

I want to lap up those words the moment they spill out. It's foolish to give therapists ammunition like that. Like throwing a Labrador a ball and expecting it not to retrieve it. Saeed already has nightmares, pathological perfectionism and defensive humour on my list; at this rate I'll still be seeing him when I'm ninety.

I quickly add, 'Not in a Munchausen's way, you understand. I don't *want* something to be wrong with me. I just mean, if there's nothing wrong with me physically, then it must be...' I don't say the word.

'Mental?' He could have gone with psychological, emotional, psychosomatic. 'You are a surgeon, Eva. It is natural for you to respond to problems with treatments, medications, excision. There is nothing wrong with you physically? This is good news. And, when it comes to the health of your mind, well, that is what I am here for. If you want me. To treat. To medicate if really necessary. And hopefully excise.'

I abandon St Mary Magdalen and sit down on the sofa. I want him to hypnotise me again but can't get the request to leave my lips. The hypocrisy of asking for something I ridiculed only a week ago is making me squirm. So I skirt around it and ask, 'How did you get into sleep and dream psychology?'

Saeed shifts in his chair. The question, coming out of the blue like this, makes him squirm as much as my hypocrisy. His reluctance to answer piques my interest and I press him with the same silence he used on me.

'It was a difficult case. One I was not making progress with. I had to call on a colleague for help, and he introduced me to sleep and dream psychology as a way of moving a patient forward when they are unable to in a conscious state.'

'What happened...to the patient, I mean?'

'She was cured.' He runs his fingers back and forth over the desktop and won't make eye contact.

'No, she wasn't. What happened?'

'We are getting distracted, Eva, let us move on.'

'You did something wrong, didn't you?'

'Of course not. It was not wrong, it was...'

He's defensive and I'm aware that I'm crossing a line but can't stop myself. 'What? Questionable? Unethical?' He still can't look at me. 'Illegal?!'

'I cannot talk about other patients, you know that.'

'Well, you'll have to give me something or I'm going to think the worst.'

'Let us just say that I found myself in a situation where I had to choose between what was legal and what was right.'

'And you chose what was right?'

Finally, he looks at me. He doesn't say it, but the answer rests on his lips in the slightest turn at their corners. 'Can we move on now?'

'I suppose. I want you to hypnotise me again. Or meditate me, whatever you call it. I want to remember the nightmares this time. I want to know what's going on in my head while I sleep. Why I wake up feeling so...'

'I can do that. If that is what you really want. But let us talk a little first, and not about my prior cases. Some things you said when we last met have given me cause for contemplation.'

'What things?'

He sees how on edge I am and waits a moment for me to settle. That's not easy to do, so I make a show of getting comfortable.

'You said there was an Eva before Jack and now a new one has been incarnated. A woman who cannot think straight or function. As if Jack's death is the root of everything: your blackouts, your nightmares. Forgive me...' he points to my hands '...these tremors.'

I tuck my fingers inside my palms but am touched by his accurate recollection; I didn't see him take notes during our session.

'You said you were not well that day, that you passed out in the car park. More importantly, you said you had not slept well.'

I nod, unenthusiastically. I don't know where this is going.

Saeed is bright, animated. 'What you said about not needing therapy. I see that. You are strong, Eva. Resourceful. You seek out the lighter side in every situation instead of sinking into darkness and depression. I see this other Eva, fighting to get to the surface. She takes a breath and then goes down.' I swallow, blinking away tears for the person Saeed speaks of, as if she's an old friend who died too young. 'You also said that you were not the type of woman to make a mistake like that because you triple-check everything.'

'I do. Usually.'

What happened to you...is it possible that...' Saeed rearranges his thoughts, thick eyebrows knitting together. 'Your mother believes you need to "get a grip" after losing your job.' He grasps an imaginary rope with both hands, the fine tufts of hair below his knuckles bristling. 'But is it possible that you "lost your grip" before that?' He makes air quotes to remind me that these are my mother's words, not his. 'Is it possible that Jack was a symptom, not a cause?'

It's impossible to think past the image of my thumb pressing down on the plunger of that syringe. I can remember the events of that day as if they're happening right now, and all I feel is the sickening dread of realisation. I can barely imagine how I felt before: light, happy. And trying is like sticking a broken vase back together, thick lines of yellowing glue still scarring the china pattern.

But Saeed is right: I have viewed Jack's death as the root cause of all my ills over the past few weeks. If I wasn't myself before that, I must have been too busy to notice. I squeezed in some semblance of a life between shifts, fell asleep on the sofa with J after a long day in surgery, or crawled into a cold bed after a night shift in the twenty-four-hour clinic, long after he'd left for work.

Life was a whirlwind before Jack.

I close my eyes and play the movie of that fateful morning in my head. Like a crime scene reconstruction, I try to focus on anything out of the ordinary. I picture myself getting out of bed, going for a run with Teddy, sitting at my dressing table getting ready, and J bringing me a cup of coffee, as he does every morning before work.

I see myself opening my dresser drawer and scrabbling around for two plastic bottles of pills: a bright yellow tub of folic acid and a bright red tub of two-a-day multivitamins with iron – two a day after J read an article about your body pissing away whatever it can't absorb, making two smaller doses better than one. I remember being taunted by their child-proof lids and the irony that if I'd been able to have a child I might actually need child-proof lids. I try to picture my fingers pressing down on the caps, try to imagine them trembling.

If they were, I don't remember.

I think further back, to waking up and clearing my silent alarm as it vibrated on my wrist. That sparks a memory. 'I woke up stiff and aching, I remember that. Nauseous. I had this horrible taste in my mouth, like metal. I remember brushing my teeth twice that morning to get rid of it, which made me a few minutes late. And I know I didn't sleep well, I was tired.'

'Because of bad dreams?'

'I don't know. I don't remember. I just remember feeling rough.' And then suddenly I do remember something. 'I'd been sick on and off for a while.'

'Do you remember the cause?'

'Yes. About two or three weeks before Jack, a client brought her puppy into the surgery for its six-month check-up. It was a typical cockerpoo…'

Saeed's face is so telling he hardly need speak; his expressions are as clear as the words in our spoken exchanges. He has no idea what a cockerpoo is.

'...a cocker spaniel-poodle cross...never mind...the point is, they're lively. Anyway, this was an affectionate little thing, bouncing up and down on her hind legs like Tigger. She was cute and funny and I was laughing as she jumped up for a kiss. She managed to get her tongue in my mouth.'

A ripple opens in Saeed's vanilla veneer. It's an expression I catch often when people see Teddy giving me kisses. I add, 'I wouldn't have minded, only the client waited until the end of the examination to tell me the puppy was coprophagic.'

'Coprophagic?'

'It eats poo.'

As if Saeed's brain is sitting on his desk, I watch it make the connection between the puppy eating poo and then sticking its tongue in my mouth. And, once it's made that connection, it seems to require all the blood from his face to revive itself. And, looking at his drawn cheeks, I can't stop myself from taking it a step further. 'Apparently, she eats all kinds of poo: her own poo, other dogs' poo, rabbit poo, cow—'

'I get the idea.'

I suppress a smile. And for the first time in weeks it's hard to do. 'To us it's really disgusting but to a dog it's quite normal. They don't have opposable thumbs, which makes it very difficult to open poop bags.' I wave my thumbs and Saeed shakes his head at me sassing him again. More seriously, I add, 'How else do you think female dogs clean up after their puppies?'

'It is not a dilemma to which I have given much thought.'

'Anyway, it wasn't long before I was throwing up and had diarrhoea. Hardly surprising when you realise a single gram of dog waste can contain twenty-three million bacteria: campylobacter, salmonella, giardia. Fortunately, it wasn't severe because it was around the time of Jacob's firm's Summer Ball, and he was up for partner. I didn't have time to see a doctor so I took some doxycycline from the surgery.'

'You took animal medication?'

'It's just an antibiotic. It works the same in animals and humans. Now I think about it, I threw up the morning of the ball as well. That was two weeks before Jack.'

I hadn't told Jacob I was ill. I didn't want anything to spoil his big night. He'd worked so hard for that partnership and I remember every win that got him there. In fact, I can't remember a single loss. That's odd, isn't it, for a lawyer to win every case? At least, every case I'm aware of. He must cherry-pick them. In fact, I know he does because two months before the Summer Ball he won the Tagline case he'd stolen from a junior colleague. It was just a silly dispute over a line of tote bags with the boy band's image on them, and I couldn't understand why he wanted the case at all.

I wonder if Saeed's theory holds any weight. I've blamed that day for everything that's gone wrong in my life, but is it possible that Jack was a symptom, not the cause? It's true, I wasn't well that day – I could easily blame that on the puppy – but I've been sick before and able to work without killing my patients.

The idea that something other than incompetence might have caused me to make that mistake begins to take seed in my mind. And, desperate for it to grow, I cast my mind back to every memorable event of the last few months, searching for a time when I'm certain I had a firm grip on my life.

Then I replay each memory for any sign of it slipping.

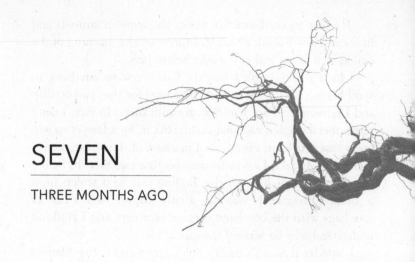

SEVEN

THREE MONTHS AGO

J'S LATE TONIGHT. I'm in the kitchen prodding a teabag with
a spoon, impatient for it to brew, when the latch clicks and the
door closes softly against its frame. His briefcase thuds on the
table, his keys tinkle in the bowl, and then his voice is buried
in Teddy's fur. I smile at the soft sounds and picture J on his
knees getting his ears nibbled.

He won the Tagline case.

When he comes in the kitchen, even though I'm in no
doubt, I ask, 'Well?'

'It's in the bag.' He pulls me into his arms and dips me
down for a kiss.

'Funny.'

Tagline is another one of those dreadful boy bands that
shoots to number one by bastardising songs from the '70s and
'80s – only people over the age of thirty know they're not an
original. Without permission, a high-street store used one of
the band's photographs on a line of canvas bags. In England,
celebrities don't have automatic rights to control reproductions

64

of their images, but J found a way for Tagline to win. While his peers are digging up old precedents, J is setting new ones. He always wins. Now, those conceited prepubescents will keep the rights to their image, be paid a fortune for the infringement, and make even more money selling the same bags at an extortionately jacked-up price. It's one of the rare occasions I wish Jacob had lost.

'Well, I'm happy you won. But you already had enough on your plate without stealing cases from junior colleagues.'

'I can take it. I'm uber-efficient!' He holds up his fist like a superhero and, wrapped in his arms, seeing that sparkle in his eyes, I believe him.

He looks at me for a long time until I ask, 'What?'

'I've got a surprise for you.'

'Don't tell me. Tickets for the Tagline concert tonight?'

'Yes!' He pulls two tickets out of his inside jacket pocket.

'O-M-G! That's so random. Awesome, dude. I'll just put on me crop top, skinny jeans and Converses, and be right widcha, man.' I do my best at a two-finger-and-thumb 'rock-on' hand gesture but don't really pull it off, and J laughs at me.

'You know,' he says. 'You're betraying your middle-aged uncoolness by calling them Converses. They're Converse.'

'What?'

'There's no "s", it's just Converse.'

'You're kidding?'

'Nope.'

'Okay then, I'll put on one Converse and limp around the O2 like a middle-aged loser.'

'Well, limp fast. The car'll be here in half an hour. I'll bring your tea up.'

As I run up the stairs, J calls after me, 'But perhaps something a little smarter than skinny jeans and Converses?' He emphasises the 's'. 'Do you even own skinny jeans?'

'I'm thirty-eight, of course I don't.'

'Shame.'

I pause on the landing and shout, 'How smart?'

'The red dress?'

He's at the foot of the stairs when I turn back and say, 'Nah, the red dress is way too smart for a Tagline concert. What are you gonna wear?'

'Skinny jeans, crop top and Converses.' Then he winks, and I know exactly what he's going to wear.

'Well, in that case…'

J's dressed and downstairs by the time I get out of the shower. No doubt he's checked his watch every minute of the last fifteen, so I hurry.

My hair clings to the African roots of my grandmother and fighting its natural curl is a waste of time, so I just smooth in some oil and let it dry naturally. Also, thanks to her wonderful genes, I hardly need make-up; I'm a ready-in-two-ticks kinda girl who thinks life's too short to sit in front of a mirror.

I slip the dress over my head and smooth out the silk as it drops to the floor. Simple but elegant. No lace, no frills, just blood-red. J had it made for last year's Summer Ball and it fits perfectly. It emphasises all the good bits while concealing every lump and bump. What more could you want? The surgeon in scrubs is transformed into a lady for the night. But just for the night – any longer and the cracks start to show. At the stroke of midnight, I turn back into the girl covered in cinders, or, in my case, dog faeces and cat vomit.

J calls me from downstairs.

'Coming.' I grab my red patent shoes and run barefoot for the stairs. J's waiting at the bottom and, sure enough, pocket watch in hand, he's checking the time. My heart tacks on a few extra beats, as it always does when he's wearing that suit. He designed it himself, midnight blue with black welt pockets and lapels. Martin Greenfield made it to his specifications and it fits so well it's as if he's part of the fabric it's cut from.

The pocket watch was his great-great-grandfather's. For J's

birthday a few years ago, I had it restored and put on a half-Albert chain. I didn't want to alter an antique watch, so I had a pendant, engraved with J.E.C. – Jacob Edward Curtis – added to the chain where it hangs from the middle button of his waistcoat.

It crosses my mind that we should blow off whatever he's got planned, and I should peel that suit off... very, very slowly.

Pulling on my shoes by their straps, I say, 'Nobody wears a suit to a Tagline concert.'

J stares at the red dress and heels with eager eyes. 'I guess we'll have to give that a miss, then.' And tearing up the tickets, he tosses them in the bowl on the hall table.

'Oh, no!' I lift up the skirts of my dress and negotiate the stairs. 'I was really looking forward to their rendition of "Better Best Forgotten".'

'It's a classic,' says J.

'Timeless. I mean, Steps created musical art with those profound lyrics and that sophisticated melody back in the '90s; who knew it could be taken to a whole new level?'

'They're very talented boys.'

'I know. I've never experienced a sensory adventure quite like Tagline bludgeoning Steps.'

'I think the sensory adventure you're referring to is your brain bleeding out of your ears.'

'Ahh, that explains the bloodstains on my shirt.'

'An experience that's better best forgotten,' he says, and I laugh.

'Where shall we go instead, then?'

'Let's see where the car takes us.'

In the driveway to our apartment complex, a salt-bearded man in a chauffeur's cap, black suit and black leather gloves, waits for us by a silver E-class Mercedes. He drives us east out of town, and when he exits the motorway at Oxford Services near Wheatley my face lights up.

'I know,' says Jacob. 'I know how long you've been wanting to come here. I was thinking we could push the boat out with a Double Whopper with cheese and a chocolate brownie.'

'I do love Burger King. But I'd have thought you'd know me well enough by now to know I'd plump for the chocolate sundae.'

'Oh, I know. I thought I'd have the brownie and you could have the spoonful of ice cream that comes on the side.'

'That's extravagant of you.'

'I'm in a generous mood.'

So when the chauffeur does a 360 around the roundabout, I point out of the window and say, 'We just missed the exit for Burger King.' He's doubling back down the road we came in on, which is the only way to get on to Swordford Lane from the A40. And, knowing where Swordford Lane leads, I'm suddenly glad Tagline won.

J says to the chauffeur, 'Dan, you missed the Burger King exit.'

'My apologies sir. I'll make a U-turn at the next round-about.'

Ignoring J's little skit, I say, 'I can't believe you're taking me here.' I grab his arm and tug his jacket sleeve. 'I've always wanted to go.'

'Well, it's only £3.99 for a King Deals Meal; I should have brought you sooner.'

I stare longingly out of the window as we approach the pillared entrance of Raymond Blanc's Belmond Le Manoir aux Quat'Saisons. But when we drive right past it, a squeak escapes my throat.

J taps my knee. 'The Burger King in Great Haseley's much nicer.'

'It closed down!'

'I believe Mrs Curtis is right, sir. Now I think about it, it closed down some time ago. Would it be impertinent of me to suggest somewhere else, sir?'

'Go ahead, Dan. The evening's ruined now anyway. Take us anywhere you like.'

'Thank you, sir.'

Without another word, Dan slams on the brakes and reverses up the road at full speed. Then I have to brace myself against the ceiling and the seat in front of me, my world spinning out of control, as he pulls a ninety-degree drift-turn into the driveway of Le Manoir. J stifles laughter, knowing how much I hate feeling out of control. I could abseil off a building or climb a mountain, knowing I'm the master of my own fate, but you wouldn't catch me dead on a fairground ride.

I get my breath back and say, 'You're impossible, do you know that?'

'Don't blame me,' he says, 'blame the driver.'

At the main entrance, I get out of the car, a little wobbly on my heels, and thank Dan for his excellent recommendation and the narrow escape from a drive-through Whopper with cheese.

'We'll call you when we're ready, Dan.'

'Very good, sir.'

And once we're out of earshot, Jacob whispers in my ear, 'Getaway driver. Served three of a five-year sentence.'

'I thought you never lost.'

'I don't. He should have gone down for twelve.'

'I hope I never have to do battle with you.'

'Not a chance.' He kisses me. 'I'd defend you to the death.'

We're seated in the garden room, eating Cornish turbot with scallops and wasabi, taking smaller and smaller bites so the fish course will last as long as possible, when J purposefully puts down his knife and fork, wipes his mouth with his napkin, and takes a sip of champagne.

He's gearing himself up to say something.

I watch him expectantly, and he looks at me for a long time before placing his hand over mine resting on the tablecloth.

The expression on his face is deadly serious, and I feel as if he's about to deliver some dreadful news.

'What?' I ask.

He takes his hand away and mine turns cold as he worries his goatee.

'What is it?' I press.

He puts his hand on mine again and says, 'Nothing. I just love you, that's all. I don't want to lose you.'

'You're not gonna lose me. Till death us do part, remember?'

'I remember.'

We tuck into our food but I can't shake the feeling that he was going to say something else. Sometimes, it crosses my mind that this is all too perfect. Aren't marriages supposed to be messy and difficult? A never-ending series of compromises and negotiations? I know it's my own silly insecurity, but I feel it most acutely on nights like this, when J goes to such lengths to make everything wonderful: our perfect marriage feels as papered-on as his money, and I'm haunted by the idea that, around the next corner, someone's waiting with a match to set light to it.

The thought dissolves as a familiar tune drifts into the restaurant and J breaks into a smile. It's distant and we can't tell where it's coming from, but the woman's voice is familiar. Like softly played flutes, she sings 'Danke Schoen' in luxurious slow motion. We both adore the song, partly because...well, who doesn't? And partly because we're closet John Hughes fans and love *Ferris Bueller*.

J summons a spick-and-span waiter in a white jacket and bow tie and asks, 'Where's that coming from?'

'The singing? There's a wedding in La Belle Époque, sir.'

'I know that voice,' I say.

'That's Amy Blackman,' replies the waiter. 'She's very popular with our weddings.'

We know Amy Blackman from bars and pubs around Oxford, but I've never heard her sing this song before.

'Please.' Jacob points towards the patio. 'Could you open the doors?'

The waiter looks over at the guests sitting by the garden room entrance and says, 'I'm sorry sir, it's a little chilly tonight. I'm afraid it would make the other guests uncomfortable.'

'But it's our song,' says J. 'And tonight is our wedding anniversary.'

I close my eyes and shake my head.

'I'm sorry, sir. Can I offer you each a glass of champagne instead?'

'No, don't worry.' Jacob lifts the bottle of champagne chilling in the cooler next to the table. 'Just bring us another bottle, thank you.'

And, as the waiter nods and walks away, I say under my breath, '"Danke Schoen" isn't our song.' Robbie Williams's 'Angels' is technically our song because it's the first one we ever slow-danced to. The problem is that neither of us likes it.

'You're right,' he says. 'But it could be.' Then, he looks around the conservatory – I have no idea what for – jumps to his feet and reaches for my hand across the table. 'Quickly. Come on!'

I struggle to keep up in my heels as he drags me at a run out of the restaurant. 'Where are we going?'

He doesn't answer as we dash down a corridor towards the hotel's rear exit. Then, throwing open the doors, he says, 'This way,' and drags me around the garden room to the patio doors the waiter refused to open.

And the moment Amy Blackman is recalling Central Park in fall, Jacob drops to his knees without a care for the fool he's making of himself, points a finger to the night sky, and rises up in true Ferris style. I burst into laughter, along with the rest of the diners at the garden room window. And before I know it I'm in his arms, being waltzed around the patio with the eyes of every dinner guest trained on us, those at the back craning their necks to watch.

With his cheek pressed to mine – and mine as red as my dress – J sings a duet with Amy while we glide past the timber-framed windows, and I try not to catch anyone's eye. It's like a scene from some soppy romance, and I want to soak up the moment and enjoy it. But I'm too conscious of my surroundings to let go. My fingers grip J's arm like a Staffie with a tug toy, and my legs are stiff and wooden. I'm afraid my heels will get caught between the stone flags or we'll collide with the patio furniture – that's what happens in real life.

But J holds me tight.

Eventually, the champagne and cool night air kick in, and I blur into the backdrop of the Atlantic blue cedar, tall enough to touch the night sky. I dissipate in the scent of grass and shrubs, damp with evening, and my fears are muted by the murmurs of wedding guests and their birdsong backdrop to J and Amy's melody.

And soon, even all that disappears.

I'm aware of nothing but a contentment so profound, it's unfair that this is my life. As if happiness was first prize in a contest, and I won. Then, the heel of one shoe actually does slip into a crack in the patio and I lose my footing. J grabs my waist, taking my weight just before I fall, and I laugh out loud at my misplaced pride.

When the song finishes, J takes a bow, kisses my hand, and leads me back into the restaurant to a round of applause.

'And now,' he says, sitting back down at the table, '"Danke Schoen" is our song.' Then, he tucks into his meal as if dancing in the garden at Belmond Le Manoir aux Quat'Saisons is as normal as picking up a drive-through Burger King.

Still breathless, I say, 'You're crazy, you know that?'

'I know. That's why you love me so much.'

And I do.

EIGHT

Now I CAN'T IMAGINE myself dancing in a garden. It seems a lifetime ago and I barely remember that woman who is now little more than a shadow. Where did she go, that dancing woman? Did she die with Jack? Or is Saeed right and she was already fading?

I still haven't told J about Saeed. I gloss over how I'm feeling, because I can't put it into words, can't classify it, describe, or label it.

There's only one thing I know for sure.

It's malignant.

'Eva.' Saeed's tone is serious. I look up and his face is grave. 'Your nose is bleeding.'

'Oh, God.' I lean forward on the sofa, pinch my nostrils closed, and cup my other hand to catch the blood.

Saeed leaps out of his chair and comes to sit on the ottoman in front of me with his hand held out. The sleeve of his white kurta is rolled up past his elbow, exposing prominent veins in his muscular forearm.

Suddenly everything closes in, and through the pressing darkness a hand reaches out. I see a pale arm, veined and powerful. In his palm, there's something white. I flinch and recoil.

'It is tissue, Eva. Are you all right?'

'Sorry...sorry...yes, I'm fine.' I take the tissue and hold it up to my nose. The blood flows fast and I'm concerned about getting it on the rug, so I tilt my head back.

'Do not do that,' Saeed says. 'We do not want you inhaling blood. Sit up straight, but tilt forward and blow your nose gently to remove any clots.'

I do as I'm told as Saeed pulls some more tissues from the box on the ottoman table.

'Thanks.' My voice is sticky with blood.

'Now, pinch the soft part of your nose and press inwards. I will be back in just a moment.'

Saeed returns with crushed ice in a handkerchief. He sits back down in front of me, lays the cold hanky over the bridge of my nose and holds it there. I'm aware of his knees between my legs as the heat from his hand, cupped over mine, cuts through the ice. It rests so close to my eyes that my eyelashes brush his thumb. My body tenses with the intimacy, yet he appears unaffected by it. His gentle compassion is so fierce that the air between us shivers with it. I'm thrown off balance and have to break away, untangling myself from him awkwardly.

'Perhaps we should call it a day. We can do a longer session on your next visit to make up the time.'

'No. It'll stop soon. They never last long. Do you have a bathroom I could use?'

'Down the hall, through the doors, first on your right.'

I'm in a contemporary bathroom, a stark contrast to the solace of Saeed's office and his tenderness. It has an egg-shaped sink and its striated-rock tiles dim the room. I pump a bead of soap into my palm and wash my hands and face. The soap leaves an artificial smell of coconut that's hard to rinse away, overpowering and sickly. Years ago, I read an article about how our skin absorbs sixty per cent of the chemicals we put on it, and since then I've been making my own soap, shampoo and deodorant. The synthetic smell leaches into my pores; I want to wash myself after washing myself.

I pat my face with paper towels and tidy myself up. Although the bleeding has stopped, my nostrils are bloodstain-red from the ice and being rubbed with tissue. In the geometric mirror on the wall – a series of conjoined triangles – I see myself in pieces.

'Are you all right?' Saeed's back in his chair and I return to the sofa.

'I'm fine.'

'Are you sure you would not prefer to continue another time?'

'I'm fine.'

'Very well, if you are sure. But before we proceed – I would also suggest you go for a health check to rule out any physical problems. The body has unusual ways of letting us know something is wrong.'

I nod, and, just like before, he comes out from behind his desk to stand behind the sofa, while I try to relax and stare up at the teardrop bulb above my head.

'Focus on the light,' he says.

The room is dark.

Heavy drapes cloak the windows and I can't tell if it's night or day. Shards of light spill in from behind me, throwing the room into shadow, crafting black shapes from the furniture.

My furniture.

Just as Saeed said it would, the nightmare comes in pieces, like a series of stills, only vivid as memories, not ethereal like dreams. The bedroom is my bedroom, in every tiny detail.

It feels deadly real.

My wrists are so tightly bound that my blood pulses against the knotted white ropes, and my fingers tingle with numbness. My naked body is pulled so taut over the bed's footboard, it presses into my upper thighs and belly and I can't catch my breath.

The dry thud and scuff of his shoes on the wooden floor is silenced when he reaches the rug at the foot of the bed. I sense the closeness of his form long before he touches me.

A gloved hand over my mouth.

A finger and thumb clamping my nostrils closed.

My lips kiss leather while my breath hisses between his barely open fingers and I choke on dust.

My ankles are tethered to the feet of the bed and my legs are spread so wide, my vulnerability sickens me. Yet something is strange: I should be struggling desperately to crush my thighs together and conceal the raw vulgarity of my nakedness – but this natural instinct is missing; it's buried too deep.

He lets go of my mouth. His hands grip my hips. His groin presses into my backside and I gasp in pain as all the air is shoved out of me, my stomach slamming into the wood.

And then there are two Evas.

One Eva – hypnotised in Saeed's office – wants to look behind her, to know who her assailant is. She wants to fight with all the strength she has and tear this man limb from limb. But there's this other Eva. Naked. Tied to this bed. And she doesn't fight. She doesn't cry out. She just lets this happen while somewhere, far off in the distant night, a woman screams at the top of her lungs.

NINE

J's SLEEPING. His breath grazes his nostrils, barely making a sound, but the darkness amplifies the volume.

I can't sleep.

I'm plagued by the memory of that nightmare. Part of me wishes Saeed had taken it away, or never recalled it in the first place. But then again, I did ask for it. I just can't see a point to it all. When he brought me out of the hypnosis he was clearly feeling positive, felt we had made progress. But it didn't feel like progress to me. Recalling sick dreams is hardly having a positive impact on my life; it's making it harder. And, if I go back, I'll be paying for this. I can't help wondering if it's a complete waste of time and money. Yet, at the same time, I can't wait to see him again. Just being near him makes me feel alive again.

If I hadn't been fired, I would have been working the night shift tonight, as I did every Thursday. I slept like the dead between emergency cases but now I can't sleep at all on Thursdays. It's been going on like clockwork since I killed

Jack. Partly because of the nightmares and partly out of habit. My brain stays on-call while my body fidgets from the imaginary discomfort of the surgery bunk.

Someone should tell them I've been fired.

Teddy's restless too. He's on the stairs. For the last hour, he's been padding around in circles from his bed to the foot of ours, down the stairs to the front door and back up again. He used to stay with me at the surgery, and his body hasn't got used to sleeping at home on a Thursday night either. It sounds crazy that a dog would know what day of the week it is, but Teddy does. From Monday to Friday, when J leaves for work at six forty-five, Teddy won't bat an eyelid, but, if Jacob leaves the house early on a Saturday or Sunday and doesn't take Teddy with him, Teddy will howl like a wolf for an hour.

On Friday mornings, Teddy and I used to run the long way back from the surgery in a loop around Port Meadow, and I've started doing that again. It feels good to get back some of my old routine, and I love running with Teddy by my side.

Sitting on the hall chair, leaning over to tie my laces, my stomach bulges over the waistband of my tracksuit bottoms. I hate that sensation of flesh folding over itself. I've really let myself go. I must have put on five kilos in a month. Anxious to get going, I grab Teddy's lead and LED collar – so he's visible off-lead in the dark – and close the door quietly behind me so as not to disturb J.

At this time of the morning, Oxford is crisp with silence. Yet even during the day Oxford has a peculiar tranquillity, a studious hush. It has its traffic jams in and out of the city but, once you're in, it's like stepping inside and closing the door on a very old building. I'm sure a lot of people take its architecture for granted, but I've never shaken the feeling that I was born in a library. From lofty heights, stone statues and chiselled heads regard the streets in imposing silence. And they *impose* silence. If you talk too loudly or make a scene, it's like doing it in church rather than on a city street. And it isn't just the people who judge and stare; the buildings stare too.

Our apartment abuts the canal, so to get on to the towpath we have to circumnavigate the whole complex, past the main entrance and down the small back road at the rear of the building. But, once we're back on the canal the water deadens any last residues of noise from the city, and I remember why I run. Always on the towpath, where the river mutes the marrow of my bones. Admittedly I have to hold my breath as I pass the weir, where rubbish and rotting vegetation collect in the still water, but after a couple of metres it's replaced by the clean flowing stream, and I inhale deeply.

J doesn't like me running in the dark, but it doesn't feel at all dangerous. Canal boats laze on the water, some out for hire, some residential, and with their quirky riverside letter-boxes and quaint names, like 'Golden Dancer', 'Goblin' and 'Gremlin's Castle', it feels safer than running on the street. A shout for help would permeate these flimsy wooden cabins far more easily than one of Oxford's old stone buildings. And, as we run alongside these floating homes, Teddy engenders a false sense of security, too. Though he's not a large dog and looks like a teddy bear, he's easily spooked and his deep, throaty bark takes strangers by surprise. They tend to back off before discovering his pin-'em-down and lick-'em-to-death defence strategy.

Only two sounds break the silence: the distant gush of the weir and our feet crunching on gravel. The retreating moon reflects on the water and yields just enough light for us to see our way along the towpath, where weeping willows drag the surface for leaf litter.

My heart trips as something brushes my cheek. I wipe my face. A spider's web. Silk lines drop from the trees that overhang the path and catch the smallest of the falling leaves. My heart finds its rhythm again.

Then it stops dead.

To the left of the path, in the trees up ahead, a shadow looms. I shorten my stride. The figure doesn't move. He lies in wait. Tall. Burly. Teddy's up ahead, racing straight for the figure, but he runs right past and neither man nor dog acknowledge each other. The momentum of my pace drives me a few steps closer and I realise it isn't a man at all. It's a pair of trousers and a T-shirt hanging from a tree to dry. One of the canal boat owners has left their laundry out. I suck in a deep breath and laugh. Spiders' webs and laundry: spooky.

At the Isis Lock where the Oxford Canal enters the River Thames, I cross the wrought-iron bridge and continue down the path on the opposite bank.

Further down, antiquated boats, some leaf-littered, some rusting, one half-sunk and rotted to the hull, sit in the shadows of a riverside apartment complex, a lot like ours. It looks down its nose at this side of the canal where the towpath's charm has been sprayed over with graffiti, and the council has tried to camouflage its townishness with trailing vines.

I used to hang out here with my mates after school, smoking under the bridge. I never pictured myself on the opposite bank.

At the Walton Well Road, Teddy and I leave the river and cross the overbridge towards Port Meadow where the gate, weighed to close with barbells, creaks as it shuts behind us.

Halfway across the meadow, we're joined by the ponies that graze there. Drawn to Teddy, they trot alongside us in the scant moonlight. They love to nuzzle Teddy's behind with their velvet noses, but they have to catch him first. He ups his pace and heads for the bridge at Fiddler's Island.

Fiddler's Island isn't really an island at all. It's more of a linked pathway with moorings that joins three sections of land where Castle Mill Stream meets the River Thames. As always, Teddy waits impatiently at the gate, squeezing through when it's barely open before darting over the Bailey Bridge, claws scraping wood. He makes his way to the Castle Mill Stream side of Fiddler's Island, to the clearing in the trees where people sometimes camp, though I doubt camping's allowed. Teddy will nose through the fire pit, dreaming of barbecues, until it's time to leave.

Teddy is my St Bernard in the alpine avalanche of life. When it's brutal and capricious, dogs remain constant, content with familiarity and routine. And their predictability makes them dependable. For the next fifteen minutes, Teddy will remain in those trees while I get my breath back on the bridge. The repetition comforts us both.

I lean on the railings, sweat cooling on the rusting metal, breathing heavily. On the water, leaves drift lazily through the reflections of trees while Teddy's LED collar bobs between them like a demented firefly.

To my left, the sun is rising over the city. I check my watch. Six a.m. I'd usually be here a few minutes earlier, but my timing isn't as bad as I thought it would be, given how I've been feeling.

'Eva.'

Heart in my mouth, I jolt and turn. A dark figure stands near the end of the bridge on the other side of the gate. The orange horizon silhouettes a tall man with stout legs and a broad frame. His face is in shadow.

'Hello?' My voice falters. The gate opens with a strained creak and then clacks shut, weighed down by a tangled knot of metal chain. 'Who's there?' The figure doesn't answer.

My feet twitch, but my brain overrides their instinct to run. They strain towards home, but home is in the direction of the figure, and the bridge is too narrow to pass him. Bolting in the opposite direction would lead me further from civilisation. I'm not fast and I'm already tired. I'm confident any man could outrun me.

To my right, Teddy's LED collar still glows in the trees. He won't come back until it's time to go or I call him. I vacillate. Should I call him? The light of his collar bobs from left to

81

right, right to left, and then dances in circles. He's on the scent of something. It will be difficult to get his attention. Teddy's a well-behaved dog who loves to please, but, when he's tracking something tasty, four out of his five senses shut down.

The man walks towards me. Beneath his heavy boots, the weathered boards clunk against the bridge's metal trusses. His footsteps have a sinister, measured cadence. If he didn't know me, if he hadn't said my name, I'd be running for the trees by now, but my name keeps me dumbly fixed to the spot.

'Who is it?' I manage two steps backward.

'It's me, George.'

George? George Hope!

Like his footsteps, his voice is sluggish, revenant. I should run. I want to run, and I'm about to call Teddy when I realise how foolish that would be. I've known Caroline and George for years and he's not the kind of man who would hurt anyone, no matter how upset he is.

An image fills my mind of my friends laughing their asses off at me as I tell them the story of me running away, like a woman possessed, from good old George. Sweet old George. Harmless old George.

Then I remember the last line of the letter. *Sleep lightly, if you can sleep at all.* And I realise how insane I am to put my dignity ahead of my safety.

I remember Jack's collar.

His choke collar.

He's only three paces away.

I should run.

But then the sunlight catches his face. He doesn't look angry. His expression is completely blank.

'George.' I swallow hard, my voice as wooden and cracked as the boards beneath my feet. I'm standing on a bridge, alone in the dark, with the man whose dog I killed a month ago. I try to remember that this is George. Posh-country-gent George, dressed as always in his hunting boots, salmon trousers and wax jacket. He's wearing his tweed waistcoat, check shirt and woollen tie. Homicidal maniacs don't wear tweed, do they?

But it's six a.m. Barely light. There's no way we've accidentally run into each other on Fiddler's Island. And the second that strikes with startling clarity, George grabs me by the throat. His thick fingers curl around my neck and crush my windpipe as he closes the gap between us. He jams me up against the railing and its metal crunches my spine.

With both hands, I grab his wrist and try to wrench his fist away.

He's too strong.

I dig my nails into his fingers and try to prise them from my throat, but my efforts are trivial. I try to speak, to say his name, but only gagging sounds come out.

With his free hand, George reaches behind him and, from a back pocket or the belt of his trousers, pulls a knife. It's long and thin like a letter opener, and he presses its tip into my cheek, the silver blade shimmering in the moonlight. My bulging eyes strain to the left, drawn to the blade as if to will it immovable.

I try to move my head to release my windpipe. I can't breathe. I try to make eye-contact with George to show him the depth of my regret, but his eyes are focused on the knifepoint at my cheek.

He squeezes.

The rising sun burns the moment into my memory and, though my mind takes everything in, my eyes can only focus on one thing: an enamel pin on George's waistcoat, peeking out from beneath his wax jacket. A yacht club logo of a boat with blue sails encircled by two lengths of knotted white rope.

'You killed my dog,' George's voice strains as he squeezes. 'You killed Jack.' But, as if speaking while wielding a knife and crushing my throat are too many actions to perform simultaneously, his grip eases just enough for me to speak.

'I know.' My eyes sting with tears. 'I'm sorry, George. I loved him too. I swear I didn't mean to hurt him.'

'You killed him.' His grip tightens again, and he closes his eyes.

'I did.' My hand quivers as I gently knead his forearm, comforting my attacker. 'And I'm so, so sorry.' His grip loosens and he opens his eyes. I look deep into them, trying to get him to focus on me, to *see* me. 'George. You know me. You've known me for years. You know I would never have deliberately hurt Jack. Please. I know you're angry, you have every right to be, but I know you don't want to hurt me.'

Then, the strangest thing happens. A fog clears from his eyes, and George looks at me as if he's only just realised who I am.

'Eva?' He lets go of my throat, drops the knife which thuds on the timber and looks at his hands as if they don't belong to him.

Then he runs.

'George!' I call out to his diminishing figure. 'Wait!' But he's through the gate and gone.

The knife gleams against the dull wood of the boards and initials, glinting in the blade, catch the light: J.J.R. It isn't George's knife; maybe he borrowed it from someone he goes hunting with or one of his sailing buddies. Bending down, about to pick it up, I stop dead at the sound of rustling leaves and whip around to locate Teddy.

Across the water, the light from his LED collar is close to the ground. It doesn't move. Something has his full attention. Discarded food probably.

A twig snaps.

Not Teddy.

The sound came from the opposite bank. Rising slowly, I squint to make out shapes in the darkness. By the river, a few metres from the bridge's embankment, stands the rectangular silhouette of the Oxford Preservation Trust stone monument, and next to that is an old tree, dead and hollowed out. It leans over the water, clinging to the earth with dry roots, wide and tall enough to obscure a large man.

'Teddy!' I scream. 'Teddy, come!'

And I run.

TEN

I WRAP MY ARMS around J's bare torso and he holds me tight enough to break me.

'You shouldn't go running in the dark.' His breathy concern whispers through my hair.

'It was six a.m., not the middle of the night.'

'But you're not working; there's no reason to go out so early.'

I pull away. Jacob doesn't mean for that to sting but it does. Sitting on the bed, I pull the feathered quilt over my knees for comfort, and Teddy curls into me, uneasy with the tension.

He heard my call from the bridge and saw me running. He had to squeeze through the fence next to the gate to catch up but, once he did, he didn't leave my side the whole way home. Usually I can't tear Teddy away from an interesting scent but the tone of my voice must have startled him. And the one thing you can count on with dogs is that the thought of being separated from their pack is far more traumatic than the thought of being separated from their next meal. Teddy would sell his grandmother for a piece of kibble, but, if I walk out of the house and leave him, he won't eat a thing. I was so glad to have him with me on the run home. He might not have been able to stop George, but his presence kept me going.

'He must have been watching me for weeks.' I'm thinking out loud. 'Working out my routine until he found an opportunity to get me alone.'

'First the letter, then the collar, now this.' J paces the bedroom. 'I'll kill him.'

'You didn't seem that worried before; in fact you were pretty dismissive about the letter.'

'No, I wasn't. Not by a long shot. I just didn't want to make a big deal of it for your sake. I didn't want you to be frightened.'

'Well, it's a little late for that – I'm scared out of my fucking wits now!' But, as soon as I say that, I realise I'm nowhere near as frightened as I should be. Something about the attack, something I can't quite put my finger on, is moderating the way I feel about it. Castrating it. Stripping it of violence.

'I'm going round there.'

'No, you're not.'

'Then I'm calling the police.'

'No, J. George knows he went too far.'

He holds up his hands in disbelief. 'How can you possibly know that? Did you two have a nice chat while he held a knife to your throat?'

He's right. I can't know that for sure. And J's in no mood to listen to me explain the look I saw on George's face when he realised what he was doing and ran away. That look of horror – shame – was like looking in a mirror, his face a sickening reflection of the panic, wretchedness and remorse I felt the moment I pressed the plunger on that syringe.

If it had been Teddy... I picture that knife, pressed against my cheek, and can't stop thinking: an eye for an eye. I've put the Hopes through so much, I will not – cannot – set the police on George.

I say, 'I don't know how I know, I just know.'

'He threatened your life!' J runs his fingers through his hair and down his beard. 'He could have killed you. You need to call the police.' He reaches for my mobile on the bedside table.

'No. I don't want the police involved. I'm not sure he even knew what he was doing.'

J raises his voice. 'Of course he knew what he was doing. You said yourself that he must have been watching you, that he followed you there. That isn't someone who doesn't know what they're doing. That's premeditation. He planned this.'

J's right. There's not a hope in hell that I just stumbled upon the man whose dog I killed, in the middle of nowhere, carrying a knife. I say, 'I agree, he must have planned it to a certain extent. But my guess is, he had a few too many with a mate down the pub, got himself all riled up, borrowed a knife, and came looking for me.'

'Yes, and it didn't go the way he planned so he'll probably try again.'

'He won't, J. Honestly, you should have seen the way he looked at me. As soon as he realised what he was doing, he dropped the knife and ran. I'm sure he's sitting at home right now, mortified by what he did. And for Christ's sake, I did kill the man's dog. If it was Teddy, I don't know what I'd do. And this wasn't just any dog, it was a forty-thousand-pound pedigree show dog, for fuck's sake. I'm not calling the police.'

J closes his eyes and shakes his head. 'I can't believe you're worried about them after everything they've put you through. They got you fired. It was probably them who went to the press after agreeing not to. And now he's sending you choke collars and threatening you at knifepoint!'

'He was right to have me fired. And he's got every right to be angry.'

'I can't believe you're defending him.'

'I'm not defending him. I'm just saying he wasn't himself. Maybe it *was* him who went to the press but he could have sued me for professional negligence as well. At least he kept that part of the bargain. He could still change his mind about that.'

J sucks in an impatient breath, but then his shoulders droop, just a little, and I think I'm getting through.

'Honestly, J, I don't think he'll come near me again. He must be wondering what we'll do. He'll be staring at the door wondering when the police are gonna show up. I'm sure that'll be torture enough for the poor man.'

'I still think we should report it. And if you won't call them, I will.'

Just the thought of it makes me sick. The police will come here asking questions about motive, and I'll have to go through it all over again. It'll be like exhuming Jack's corpse. And if involving the police changes the Hopes' minds about going to court, I'll have to go through it again there as well. I finally feel as though I've reached the last bend on this horrific journey and that, with a little help from Saeed, I'm about to turn it. I imagine, around that bend, I'll find the old Eva, the one who trusted herself, who slept without nightmares, who had a job that meant something instead of empty days filled with nothing but blackouts, tremors and nosebleeds. I feel as if she's right there, waiting for me. Just as long as I keep moving forward.

I can't go backwards.

I can't go over it again. Not even once.

'I'm begging you,' I say. 'Don't call them.' And then, with all the apathy I can muster, I add, 'What could the police do anyway? Unless I press charges, they'll just go round there and caution him. They're hardly going to organise a twenty-four-seven stakeout for my protection. So how does getting the police involved make me any safer? It doesn't.' I get up from the bed and wrap myself around his back. 'Let's leave it for now. I promise, if George comes anywhere near me again, I will report it.'

J's head droops in submission and he says, 'Fine, if you think it's for the best, I won't call them.'

'You promise?'

'I promise.' But then the muscles in his chest turn rock-hard beneath my palms. Briefly, he looks up at the ceiling and then turns his head to scrutinise me in his peripheral vision. 'What makes you think the knife wasn't George's?'

'I…' I stutter. How does he know that? I didn't describe the knife. I didn't tell J about the initials on the blade. 'I didn't say that.'

He pulls out of my embrace and turns to face me. 'You said George must have got drunk with a friend and borrowed his knife. What makes you think he borrowed it?'

'Oh…yeah…I forgot about that. Well…he dropped it. On the bridge. And then he ran. I was about to pick it up and noticed some initials on the blade.'

'And they weren't George's?'

'No.'

'What were they?'

All I want is for J to drop this. So I breathe in, close my eyes, and let out a pretend sigh as if I'm trying to recall them. 'I don't remember.' I say it as if they're meaningless, nothing at all. As if this whole incident was nothing at all.

I don't mention the rustle of leaves on the riverbank.

I don't say I heard a twig snap.

I don't tell him George wasn't alone.

ELEVEN

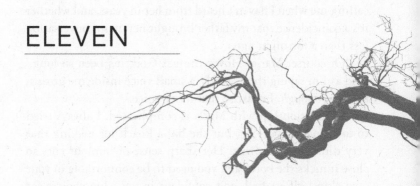

ON MY WAY BACK from a lunchtime walk along the canal with Teddy, I'm stepping out of the lift when the phone, ringing on the other side of our apartment door, sets me on edge again. The hour-long stroll gave me time to process everything that's happened, kneading out the tension, but with a few chimes it's back again. The only person who ever calls the landline is my mother, and I *always* expect the Spanish Inquisition. Her chief weapons are reproach, guilt, and a near-fanatical devotion to my employment status.

Teddy senses my tension, hears the phone and starts barking. That stresses me out even more because his deep bark resonates through the hallway, shaking the walls as if the Hound of the Baskervilles has got into the building. And, by the time I've struggled with my key in the door, Teddy is so riled up that I answer the phone just to silence him.

'Hello?'

'Is that Eva Cosgrove?' It's not Mum, it's a woman's voice, vaguely familiar.

'Yes.' Flustered, I unclip Teddy's lead one-handed and he rushes to the kitchen, knowing it's time for a dental stick. 'Well, it was Cosgrove, it's Curtis now.'

'It's Maria.' I don't say anything. 'Maria Mendez.'

She didn't need to clarify, I only know one Maria. But my brain is preoccupied, trying to figure out why she's suddenly calling me when I haven't heard from her in years, and whether it's a coincidence that my father brought her up in conversation less than a fortnight ago.

'Of course, Maria! How's things? God, it's been so long.' And as I'm saying those words, a small voice inside me groans, *not long enough*. I chastise that nasty voice.

My relationship with Maria is complicated. I always tried to love and support her but she has a knack for making that very difficult sometimes. Her sharp sense of humour cuts so close it nicks the bone, and you need to be comfortable in your own skin, self-assured, and confident in your life choices for Maria not to get to you.

I'm not any of those things.

She plays on my insecurities like a drum kit, and I have to remind myself of the broken little bird inside her. I try not to make it sound like an accusation when I ask, 'How did you get my number?'

'Your dad gave it to me. That's all right, isn't it?'

'Of course. It's great to hear from you. How are you?'

'I'm really well, thanks. I'm in the Met now, an AFO.'

'AFO?'

'Authorised Firearms Officer.'

I have no idea what that entails – clearly something gun-related – so I just say, 'Wow. That's so great.'

'Fuck, I've missed you,' she says. 'It's been too fucking long.'

The depth of sincerity in her tone takes me by surprise. 'It has. What? Ten, fifteen years? Dad told me about Tomás. I'm so sorry, Maria. Have you been to see him?'

92

'Fuck off, of course I haven't. I wouldn't piss on that man if he was on fire.'

Harsh but fair.

'But you might change your mind once he's gone and then it'll be too late. You know he's been asking after you? Maybe he wants to make amends.'

'Look, Ev, I get what you're saying, but you can't possibly understand this. You grew up with the most wonderful father in the world. You think there's anything that man could say to me in the eleventh hour that would make up for all the shit he put me through? Anyway, I didn't call to talk about *him*.' Maria spits out the word. 'I called to see if you were okay.'

'I'm fine. Any reason I shouldn't be?'

'The attack. George Hope.'

Jacob!

You asshole!

He went behind my back. I thought I'd played the attack down enough to convince him not to get the police involved. And, even though I know the answer, I ask Maria, 'How do you know about George Hope?'

'Your dad told me.'

'My dad?!' I wasn't expecting her to say that. I was expecting her to say that J had filed a police report.

'Yeah. He called me the week before last to tell me about Tomás and then called again yesterday to tell me what happened. It was so good to talk to him, he sounded really well, though I got the impression his job was getting him down. I love your mum, Ev, but she should never have pushed him out of nursing.'

'She had her reasons,' I say, while the back of my mind wrangles with how Dad knows about George Hope. J must have called him.

'He should get back into it.'

'I know. But he thinks he's too close to retirement to switch back now. It's a shame, he really misses it.'

'I've missed him.'

'I think he misses you. He always had a soft spot for you.'

'He said you were married now?'

'Yes. Jacob.' His name splinters through my teeth. I can't believe he went behind my back and roped Dad into calling Maria. God only knows what repercussions this will cause with the Hopes; they could change their mind about suing the practice. It could ruin Bron. As if I haven't put her through enough already. I'll kill him! And, once I've fed his body mashed up in dog food to Teddy, I'll kill him again for bringing Maria back into my life.

I silence that mean voice again. It's not that I hate the idea of having Maria in my life; it's more the timing. She takes so much energy, energy I don't have right now.

'Tell me he's not another dick like the ones you dated in college,' she says. 'Adam was the worst, do you remember him?' She laughs a little too enthusiastically. 'You made such a tit of yourself over that guy.'

And this is the thing: Maria's not wrong, I did make a fool of myself over Adam. And for her it's probably hilarious to look back on and laugh about. But, for me, it still stings a little. And I'm just too exhausted right now for fake laughter with the only person I know who can slit your throat with a heartfelt smile.

I picture that broken little bird.

I'm tempted to say, *Yes, actually, my husband is a complete dick. I asked him not to involve the police and he went ahead and did it anyway.* Instead, I say, 'No, he's one of the good ones. We've been married for four years now, together for five.'

'And how come I wasn't invited to the wedding?'

My mouth opens but all that comes out is a small squeak.

'I'm just fucking with you, Ev. Look, I promised your dad I'd look into the George Hope thing but, since you're the victim, I need your statement to open the case. I still live in town, we could meet for drinks and do it then if you like?'

I try not to groan out loud. 'I really appreciate it, Maria, but to be honest I never wanted it reported. Jacob shouldn't have told my dad to call you.'

'Why the hell not? It's a crime, Ev. At least there's someone sensible in your house.'

I remember George's face when he dropped the knife and say, 'George was upset and angry, that's all. I don't think he had any intention of hurting me. I think he was drunk or stoned or something. He didn't seem to have a clue what he was doing, and, if you'd seen the look on his face when he realised, you'd understand why I didn't call the police.'

'Being upset or angry doesn't justify a knife attack, Ev.'

'I know, but did Dad tell you I killed the man's dog?'

'Yes, he mentioned that, but—'

'Maria, please. Promise me you won't investigate George Hope. Promise you won't go round his house and question him or anything like that. I'm begging you. Please just forget my dad ever said anything. Or, if you've already filed paperwork on it, make sure it gathers dust in some dark corner, okay?'

'I guess. But I don't like it. You're my friend, Ev. When your dad told me, I almost went straight round there.' Laughter tickles her tone. 'I was gonna go all *Cagney and Lacey* on his ass ...'

I'm warmed by a memory of Maria and me watching *Cagney and Lacey* when we were little. We used to run around the house with finger guns, popping caps in imaginary bad guys. I'd forgotten about that. Those games must have had more of an impact on Maria than I realised.

She says, 'I'd planned on scaring the shit out of him, waving my gun in his face until he pissed his pants. That'd teach him for pulling a knife on my best mate.'

'That's really sweet, Maria. But honestly, it's not necessary. I know this guy. He's a pussycat. He'd probably piss his pants if you pulled a nightstick, let alone a gun.'

A deadening silence cuts through the line.

Shit!

That was so insensitive. The accusations over the beating of Peter Cunard must still haunt Maria, and I can't believe how thoughtless that was.

I say, 'Maria, I'm so—'

'Forget it, Ev. Besides, nobody calls them nightsticks. Don't you know anything? Fine, if you insist, I'll stay away from George Hope. But I'm gonna do a background check and monitor him for a while, just to make sure he's not hanging around your house or behaving suspiciously.'

'If you must, but for heaven's sake make sure he doesn't know about it.'

'What do you take me for, an amateur?'

'No, of course—'

'So, let's get together. Are you free next week? How about Tuesday?'

'I can't Tuesday, J and I have plans.' We don't have plans.

'Oh, well, doesn't matter 'cos I'll see you on Friday anyway.'

'Friday?'

'Yeah. At your parents' anniversary party. Your dad invited me.'

I groan inwardly and make a resolution to kill my father as well as J. I'll have them chemically preserved and set on pedestals in my hallway where I can keep tabs on their bloody meddling.

Maria asks, 'And will I get to meet this husband of yours, who's supposedly one of the good ones?'

'Of course,' I say.

If he's still alive.

J's home. His blue eyes are crackle-glazed. Teddy's under the bed. This argument's going nowhere but I can't stop myself. I'm spitting mad.

'You wouldn't go to the police,' he says. 'So I called Tony to see if he could talk some sense into you.'

He takes off his tie and hangs it neatly over his hanging tie rack. The precision with which he removes his clothes tells me that one of his cases has gone to shit. But I don't care – I've had a shit day too, thanks to him. I grip the footboard of the bed as I ask, 'And whose idea was it to involve my old schoolfriend Maria?'

'It was your father's idea to call her. I've never even met the woman.'

The way he says the sentence in full like that, referring to Maria as 'the woman' as if to detach himself from any involvement with her, makes me doubt his veracity. It's true, he's never met her, and my father would have needed to mention Maria first, but I'll bet that was all the encouragement Jacob needed.

I say, 'I told you I didn't want the police involved. You promised. You've broken that promise, ignored my wishes, and gone behind my back! If George changes his mind about suing, you could land me in court.' I slam my palm against the footboard and the white wood stings. 'You're not fucking *God*, J. You don't get to dictate what goes on in this house, especially with decisions that directly affect me. Maria's running background checks and having him tailed, for fuck's sake! George! Fucking George Hope! Like he's some kind of serial killer. She nearly went round there and pulled a gun on him. The woman's a bitesize fucking fruitcake and you nearly set her on George and Caroline…as if they need torturing any more!'

J glares at me as if that expression makes him bristle, when it's *his* expression. He uses it for people he can only tolerate in bitesize chunks. He says, 'You're just saying that because you feel guilty. As if you deserved to be threatened with a knife. Anyone would think you want to be punished. It was just a damned dog.'

'Just a damned dog? How would you feel if someone killed Teddy?'

'I couldn't give a fuck!' J runs his fingers through his hair, sighs, and lowers his voice. 'Of course I'd be angry. But I wouldn't view slitting someone's throat as a proportional response.'

He snatches a pair of smart but casual trousers from the wardrobe and puts those on as aggressively as he removed his suit. Then he does the same with a casual sweater. His choice of evening attire is as telling as the precision with which he hangs his suit. His shirt goes in the laundry basket instead of over the chaise.

I say, 'This conversation isn't getting us anywhere. I was the one who was attacked. It was *my* decision whether or not to call the police. And, if he threatens me again, that's exactly what I'll do.'

'What if next time he doesn't bother with threats and just slits your throat anyway? You're my wife! It's my job to protect you.'

'Firstly, you're not my lord and bloody keeper. And secondly, we've been over this already. What do you think the police are gonna do? Place him under twenty-four-seven surveillance until he's too old to lift a fucking knife?'

'It'll be on his record.'

'And what good will that do after the fact? Whoop-de-fucken-do, a piece of paper with George's name on it. What will you do then, wrap me up in it? I'm telling you, J, let this go. I just want this whole fucking thing behind me.'

He storms out.

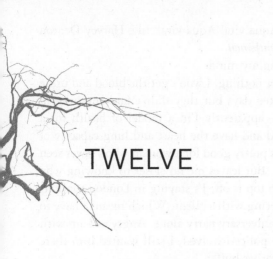

TWELVE

SAEED'S OFFICE CALLED yesterday morning to cancel our appointment. A family emergency. I hope everything's okay, but I struggled to hide my disappointment from his receptionist. After Maria had called, and I'd found out that J had gone behind my back, I really wanted to talk to him. Next Thursday can't come soon enough.

Needing to do something, anything, I booked one of those private health checks instead. It cost me over eight hundred pounds to ride an exercise bike, give three vials of blood and have my personal bits poked and prodded. I sat on a toilet in a tiny cubicle, peeing in a plastic drinking cup – one of those ones you pull out of a dispensing tube by a water fountain. The sign on the wall said to catch it midstream, but I'd already peed in the cup before I read that. There was a wooden-framed serving hatch in the wall, the kind that were all the rage in the '70s and '80s for passing food from the kitchen to the dining room. Swanky. I had to slide back the hatch and pass through my cup. I had a vision of someone on the other side downing it in one screaming 'Aqua vita! Aqua vita!' like Harvey Denton in *The League of Gentlemen*.

Christ, I'm losing my mind.

And it was all for nothing. I won't get the blood and urine results for another ten days but they didn't find anything in the physical tests – apparently I'm a model of health for a thirty-eight-year-old and have the heart and lung capacity of an athlete. Which is pretty good for a woman who's never seen the inside of a gym. But leaves me no closer to knowing why I feel so on edge. To top it off, J's staying in London tonight, some follow-up meeting with a client. Which means I have to go to my parents' anniversary party alone. Angry as I am with him for getting the police involved, I still wanted him there tonight. He's my mother-buffer.

On the way back from walking Teddy, I pass FishShorey, a chic little Indian restaurant that started as a pop-up. *The Great British Menu* made the chef, Rahul Shorey, famous and now it's hard to get a booking less than a month in advance. We can't help feeling a sense of ownership over the restaurant – that feeling that we appreciated it before its time – but we try to be happy for Rahul, even when we can't get a table.

As I pass, I notice one of the waiters hovering in the doorway, and he takes me by surprise when he steps into the street and blocks my path.

'Miss, I'm sorry to trouble you, but could you step inside?' He points to the heavy double doors of the restaurant while struggling to ignore Teddy, who's nuzzling his thigh for attention and leaving slobber trails on his smart black trousers.

'Why?'

'Please, miss, it won't take a moment.' He ushers me along by the elbow and I take a few paces towards the restaurant before stopping.

'Sorry, I'm not *stepping* anywhere until you tell me why.'

My resistance ruffles the young man. 'There's been an incident, miss. And I need you to come inside.'

My first thought is that there's a sick animal in need of attention. But it quickly dawns on me how ludicrous that is. Firstly, he has no idea I'm a vet, and secondly, any animal in FishShorey will be well past the need for CPR.

'What sort of incident?'

The waiter stutters. 'Erm...er...a woman...a woman fitting your description...fled the restaurant without paying the bill. I need you to come inside, miss.' He puts a hand on my elbow, more firmly this time, but I pull away.

'I'm sorry, you're saying a five-foot-eight woman wearing Crocs and a knitted coat, walking an American cocker spaniel, fled your restaurant without paying the bill?' He looks me up and down, speechless. I point at Teddy. 'You don't even let dogs in your restaurant.'

'I...I didn't see the woman, miss. I'm sure it wasn't you, but my manager—'

'Rahul sent you out here?'

'Yes, miss.'

'What? He didn't have the guts to come out and accuse me himself?'

'No, miss. I mean...well...'

'Rahul has known me for years. This is ridiculous! Fine! Let's see if he has the balls to accuse me to my face, then.'

I storm past the waiter, up the steps to the entrance. And I'm livid because now I won't be able to eat here out of principle. The waiter trails behind me as I storm through the doors...to bursts of laughter and applause.

Smack in the middle of the restaurant, J's sitting at a candlelit table, holding a single blue magnolia, and my anger instantly dissolves. Often, J forgets and buys roses – red – even though he knows how I feel about them. They're for Valentines, passionate affairs that are bold, dramatic and short-lived – ubiquitous, shallow romance. Magnolias, on the other hand, are a symbol of purity and endurance, a love that is long-lasting, which is why they're often used in marriage bouquets.

And blue magnolias are particularly special: they're not what they seem. A different flower hides inside those blue petals and they change colour as they open, as if they're allowing you in, letting you get to know who they really are.

That single flower is his way of saying he knows me, what his love means to me and mine to him.

Rahul, a clear conspirator in this skit, stands at his side giggling with the rest of the staff while the patrons bury broad smiles behind menus and under napkins.

'Sorry, baby,' J says.

'Oh, you're gonna be!'

'Sorry, miss,' says the waiter who stopped me in the street.

I point a finger at him, saying, 'I'll have words with you, later!' And he hurries back to his duties, blushing.

J ushers me over. 'Come on, sit down.'

'What about Teddy?'

'Since it's your anniversary, we've made an exception tonight,' says Rahul.

I glare at J. One of these days someone's going to remember one of our fake anniversaries.

'Please, take a seat, Miss Curtis.' Rahul pulls out the chair for me. He always calls me Miss Curtis, even though he knows my first name and knows I'm married. I like it. It's sweet.

I tie Teddy to the table leg but I'm reluctant to sit down. Antics like this make it really hard to stay mad at J and he knows it. He's always pulling stunts like this when he's in the doghouse.

Tail wagging furiously, Teddy puts his paws up on J's lap and gets his ears ruffled. J kisses the top of his head, speaking into his fur. 'Hey there, boofy boy. Who's my boofy boy?' And that makes it even harder. I love how much J loves Teddy. He treats him like his child. He looks up at me and says, 'I'm sorry, baby. I shouldn't have gone behind your back. Forgive me?'

I take off my coat, relent, and sit down. 'What are you doing here?'

102

'I managed to get out of the meeting. I thought I'd surprise you.'

'I'm surprised, all right.' I lean across the table to kiss him and the sleeve of my knitted coat licks a candle flame.

'Careful,' he says, moving the candle aside before kissing me long and soft on the lips. Then he picks up an empty glass and asks, 'Champagne?' A bucket-stand with a bottle on ice sits next to the table.

I check my watch as I sit back down, knowing I'm expected at my parents' house in a couple of hours. 'What about the party?'

'What party?'

'J! It is *someone's* anniversary today. My parents'! The party starts in two hours.'

'Shit, I forgot about that.'

'We talked about it yesterday!'

In truth, we hadn't talked so much as argued. It wasn't as if the meeting was important – a member of staff could have taken it – and I felt it was an excuse to get out of the party. The row over George was still raw and I'd been quick to lose my temper. I'd said, 'You bloody well are going. If it wasn't for you reporting George Hope to the bloody police, I wouldn't have Maria back in my bloody life and I'd actually be looking forward to this bloody party.'

'Bluddy, bluddy, bluddy,' he'd mimicked my Oxford accent, which would usually make me laugh. He mimics my accent all the time and he's really good at it. When I tell him to put something in the loft or bring something down from the landing, he'll put on a posh British accent and say, 'It's up in the loft. It's on the landing. It's in the conservatory.' But last night I didn't have the patience for him or his impressions.

'I won't know anyone,' he'd said. 'Go on your own.'

'You'll know my parents. And I'm sure you and Maria will have a lot to talk about.'

He'd pulled a face.

'It'll just be a lot of small talk…Brexit…Trump…the state of the NHS…yadda, yadda, yadda. The same old crap churned over and over like a shitty '80s track on repeat.'

'Like Tagline,' I said.

His eyes had sparkled but quickly dulled. There was no point arguing so I said, 'Fine. I'll go on my own.' Then he'd emailed from work saying he wouldn't be home until the morning and couldn't go even if he wanted to.

Now I glare at him expectantly, wondering what excuse he'll use this time. But instead, he grabs his forehead and says, 'Sorry, work on my mind. Look, they'll only have snacks there anyway – let's have a quick meal here, rush home, get changed and we'll be an hour late at most.'

I vacillate. A champagne dinner at FishShorey is too good an opportunity to miss, and with J here unexpectedly, apologising and actually willing to go to the party, my mother's irritation at our lateness could be worth it.

'All right, then. We can hardly leave without eating after you've told them it's our anniversary and roped them into your little skit.'

'You should have seen your face when you came in the door. I thought you were gonna tear Rahul a new asshole.'

'I was!'

Near the end of dinner, bolstered by champagne and J's agreeable mood, I consider asking him something I've held back for months. Only, with the George argument still hanging over us, it doesn't quite feel like the right moment. It never does. But he's a little tipsy and who knows when I'll get another opportunity like this. So I just blurt it out.

'J…can we try IVF?'

He doesn't even look up from his plate. 'Sure. If you think it's time.'

'Really? But…you were so reluctant before.'

He puts down his fork. 'Well, there's been a lot going on. All that work to get the partnership, finally getting it, and then all the cases they've thrown my way since. But things should get easier now.' He drifts off in thought for a moment before saying, 'There's...there's just one thing I need to do first. Something...I'm working on right now. It's crucial I get all my ducks in a row with that, but then I'm all yours. Every appointment, every injection. I just need a few months.'

'What's "a few"?'

His eyes roll towards the ceiling as if there's a project plan pinned to it. 'Three...four, maybe?'

'That's fine.' I struggle to hold back a smile, delighted and surprised that he just agreed so readily, when in the past he's been reluctant to even discuss it.

In the midst of all this emptiness, a baby will give my life purpose again. I can take a year off and by that time this will have blown over and I'll be able to go back to work part-time. I can't stop grinning, and J's eyes sparkle with the realisation of how happy he's just made me. The dimples in the corners of his smile deepen. Finally...finally, I feel like my life is getting back on track. Three months. Twelve weeks. Sixteen at most. I can do that. I can wait that long.

'Of course,' he says, looking down at his plate, 'it could still happen naturally.' He shuffles his food around with his fork then glances up with the grin of a schoolboy who just put salt in the sugar jar.

'I'm not ovulating. Not till next week.'

'Yes, but sperm live for ages, don't they?'

'Five days.'

'Well, we could strike lucky with a ten-day-old codger—'

'More like a 200-year-old codger if you count in human years.'

'Yeah, but this guy's been keeping fit...working out.'

'Playing a lot of ball?'

J laughs. 'After all his hard work, it just seems a shame—'

'Not to give him a shot at the basket?'

He laughs again and I flash a smile, so he gets the waiter's attention and mimes writing on his palm.

My parents' house sits in the middle of a tightly packed street of matching properties on the outskirts of Oxford. Ten years ago, my mother added a circular porch with white pillars and a second-floor balcony, which give the house delusions of grandeur. In reality, it's a sore thumb.

Mum opens the door as if she's invited us to her country home, takes our coats, and says, 'You're so late!'

As the cat that got the cream less than an hour ago, J can't stop smirking, and I have to nudge him. His little trick in the restaurant feels like a layer of brightly coloured paint over a stain, the brushstrokes thick and messy – but it's difficult to stay mad at him now he's agreed to IVF. At the same time, knowing Maria is in the house somewhere as a direct result of him going behind my back makes it impossible to shake it off completely; the stab in my ribs still stings.

'Get yourself in the kitchen and fix yourself a drink.' Mum gives J a playful slap to the tush and he doesn't need to be asked twice. Then she turns to me, her tone far less playful, and asks, 'Why are you so late?'

'J completely forgot about the party and booked dinner at a local restaurant.'

She shakes her head as if we're discussing a naughty boy. 'He has a lot on his plate right now. What's wrong with you? You're all squirly.'

'I'm not squirly. J's just being J, that's all.'

I expect Mum to say she knows what I'm referring to, but apparently Dad hasn't mentioned George Hope to her. I'm glad. If he had, I wouldn't hear the end of it. She would agree with J that I should have gone to the police.

She hangs our coats on the rack in the hall, saying, 'Well, this is no time to be churlish – it's a party. Whatever it was, I'm sure he didn't mean to upset you. That job puts him under

106

a lot of pressure, especially with you not working. You don't realise how lucky you are. You've got a good one there, you should be grateful.'

Dad's timing is perfect. He rushes into the hall, calling my name, and kisses me on the cheek. 'How could you keep me waiting so long?' Then he pulls me into a bear hug, forcing my arms down by my sides and squeezing me really tight. With a strained 'Hnnnnng' he squeezes even harder until I blow a raspberry in his ear.

This is *our* little skit. When I was a kid, he used to chase me around the house and, when he caught me, he'd squeeze me like that and say he loved me so hard I would burst – hence the raspberry.

'For heaven's sake,' says Mum. 'You two are far too old for that now.'

It must have something to do with the attack and George, but I'm surprised by how comforting it is to be home, secure in my dad's affection, my mum's dependable discord, and the familiar smell of home: a blend of my father's Kouros aftershave and Mum's Glade plugins in Clean Linen scent.

Dad frees my arms, and I wrap them around his middle as he rolls his eyes at Mum and tucks me under his wing. 'Come on,' he says. 'I'll fix you a drink.'

As we pass the lounge door, I glimpse J chatting to my uncle, and he eyes me with a salacious wink. The walls hum with banter and Mum's idea of party music: *Len Goodman's Crooners and Swooners* on repeat.

In the kitchen, my father pours me an enormous glass of red wine while I form my next sentence carefully, needing to say it but not wanting to burst the party bubble. 'Dad...did you have to call Maria? You could have at least discussed it with me first, asked if I wanted the police involved.'

'J said you'd be okay with it. I did say it might be better coming from you. But he said you'd be fine, since she was a friend and all. And I wanted to speak to her about Tomás one more time anyway, just in case there was a chance of convincing her to visit him.'

'Well, I wasn't okay with it, and J knew that.'

'Don't be angry with him. He was worried about you. He was only doing what he thought was best. Besides, it all worked out in the end. You and Maria are friends again, and I always liked her. Come on,' he hands me the glass of wine and puts his arm around me. 'Let's go and find her.'

'I'll just pop to the bathroom first,' I extricate myself from Dad's embrace, give him a quick kiss on the cheek and put my glass back on the kitchen counter. Then, I dash into the hall and dive for cover in the downstairs bathroom. I need to de-ruffle my feathers.

I pee, wash my hands, and check my make-up in the bathroom mirror. But, as I bare my teeth to make sure there's no lipstick on them, a trail of blood runs down my upper lip. For fuck's sake, that's all I need right now. Cupping my hand beneath my nose to avoid bloodying my dress, I unravel tissue from the toilet roll and blow out the excess blood. I remember Saeed's advice not to tilt my head back, so I sit up straight on the edge of the bath, lean forward and pinch the soft part of my nose.

That familiar sensation of caffeine pressurises my veins, and I have to keep switching the hand pinching my nose, so I can stretch out the other to ease my jittering fingers.

I feel like a jigsaw puzzle with only the edges in place, wobbly and unstable, an empty space in the middle. The important pieces, the ones that make the picture whole, are tied up in a plastic bag, lost in a dark corner of the loft. And in that bag are all the things I really feel about Jack, losing my job, being tortured by the media and attacked by George. I'm hollowed out, unable to feel deeply or respond appropriately to anything that's happened.

This isn't the first time I've faced pain in my life. My grand-mother, Evangeline, died five years ago and we were so close, the grief was unbearable. But I was able to *feel* it. And in feeling it so completely, I was forced to face it because it was all-consuming. I met J at that time and was very low, but I experienced both the joy of falling in love and the sadness of loss simultaneously. I could laugh and cry in the space of minutes.

Now I feel very little of anything.

I'm numb.

I wander through barren days in scooped-out skin that trembles, bleeds and dreams but doesn't *really* feel.

I splash water on my face, trying not to ruin my make-up, and tidy myself up. When my fingers quiver over the bathroom door lock, I leave it fastened and sit back down on the bathtub. I don't have the energy for this. But Mum's right, this is a party. I need to shake this off. I get up, take a deep breath, unlock the bathroom door, and make a beeline for that huge glass of wine in the kitchen.

'Ev!' Maria screams as I walk past the double doors to the dining room. She's been chatting enthusiastically to one of the neighbours. 'You're so late! I've been waiting and waiting for you.'

She puts her glass down on the edge of the table, sloshing red wine on to the cream carpet, and rushes over. She's only four inches shorter than me but, as she sidles in for a hug, she stoops low and over-exaggerates the stretch of her arms.

'I can't reach! I can't reach!' She almost knocks the wine out of my hand, but I can't help laughing because she used to do that at school. She had a late surge at fourteen but still only made it to five-foot-four.

I can't believe she remembers that.

Once we've caught up on the years apart, university and careers, the subject of Jack looms large, and I'm grateful when J saunters in from the lounge.

'Oh, Maria,' I say, interrupting a question about George. 'This is my husband, Jacob. J, this is Maria, my old schoolfriend who works for the Met.' I dig those words in nice and deep and then flog myself inwardly for taking less than half an hour to forget this is a party.

'Nice to meet you.' J extends his hand.

She eyes him closely as she takes it. 'Actually, we've met. What a small world.'

'We have?' J asks.

'You have?' I ask at exactly the same time.

'Yes, at the Old Bailey. I worked Priyanka Kapoor's rape case.'

'Of course,' says J. 'I'm so sorry. I didn't recognise you.'

'It's fine,' says Maria. 'People never recognise me with my clothes on.' She squeezes J's arm and laughs. 'Plain clothes, I mean.'

J forces a grin, then says, 'Priyanka told me about the officer assigned to her case. She called you a tigress, said you spent fifteen hours a day in Bethnal Green searching for her attackers, that you were by her side every step of the way, and she'll be indebted to you for the rest of her life.'

I close my mouth when I realise it's fallen open and stare at the broken little bird.

'Just doing my job.' She picks up her glass and takes a long sip of wine as if she's hiding behind it, ill at ease with the compliment.

'Well, it's nice to see you again, Maria. I'll remember next time. My mind's all over the shop at the moment.' He pretends to muddle his brain with his fingers. 'I've been made partner at the firm and they're hazing the new guy. Anyway, I'll leave you ladies to catch up.' Then he turns away from her, squeezes my arm and kisses me on the cheek as a pretext to whisper in my ear, 'Bitesize fruitcake!'

I think back to the argument with J the other night when I called her that. I was angry with him, not her. And if I hadn't, he'd still think of her as the tigress he met in the courtroom.

I hate myself for that.

110

Maria breaks my reverie by snatching her glass from the table, nudging me with her elbow and almost sloshing more wine on the carpet. Under her breath, she says, 'He's a bit of all right, isn't he? And apparently only has eyes for you. He didn't even remember me.' She stands tall with a pretence of bravado. 'Usually men can't resist the uniform.' Then she adds, 'Maybe he's gay!'

I laugh. 'That must be it.'

I imagine it's true that men find Maria irresistible. With her black hair and olive Portuguese skin, she still has that sassy 'don't mess with me' look. I was right – the Met is perfect for her.

'What about you?' I ask. 'How's your love life?'

'Utter shit.'

'Oh, no?'

'Yeah. I had one serious relationship after uni, but he was as bad as Tomás. I must attract the type: daddy issues.'

'Maybe. Or maybe it's just bad odds and there's a lot of them out there.' I take a huge gulp of wine and cough when it hits the back of my throat, but I'm determined to catch up and enjoy the party.

'Maybe.'

'Were you together a long time?'

'Five years.' Maria looks down at the carpet. 'I'm ashamed of that now. But it took a long time to realise it was abuse. It didn't turn violent until the end so I never saw it for what it was until things got out of hand.'

'Shit, that's awful.' I put a hand on her arm and tread gently. 'Especially after all the crap you went through with your dad.'

'It's okay.' She's surprisingly upbeat. 'I woke up eventually. I realised if I didn't get out of there, I was going to have a *Witches of Eastwick* moment.'

I frown, confused.

'You know,' she says. 'The overwhelming desire to very calmly say, "Let's call it a day," and beat him to death with a

111

fire iron. It was a toss-up between separation, or incarceration for second-degree murder!'

I admire her ability to joke about it and laugh along with her.

'I'm grateful for it really. It got me into the Met.'

'It did?'

'Yeah, I got a job with Women's Aid – they helped me get free – and then I started working with the police on domestic abuse cases. Eventually, I joined up. Best thing I ever did. It's made me a lot stronger.'

And she does seem stronger. Almost a different person from the one I remember from school.

'It doesn't help the love life, mind you. I won't tolerate any shit any more.'

'Good for you.'

'Looks like *you* hit the jackpot, though.' She nods in J's direction.

'He has his moments.' I meant to say that in a positive way but there's residual anger in my tone.

'What? He's not really the intelligent, charming and handsome man I just met? He's actually human?'

I glance behind me. J isn't within earshot. He's in the lounge, talking to Mum. She's holding on to his arm, throwing her head back, laughing at something he's just said.

'He's very much human. And, to be honest, I'm a little pissed off with him right now.'

'Really, why?' She looks back at J. 'I think I'd struggle to stay pissed off with that for too long. Mmm-mmm!' She flicks her hand back and forth to stress the point.

We watch them for a moment, and I notice that Mum keeps moving closer to J, and for every step she takes forward he takes one back. Soon, they'll run out of space and she'll have him pinned against the bay window.

Maria says, 'I didn't notice how hot he was at the Old Bailey. He seemed a bit...standoffish. A bit cold.'

'Don't take it personally; he takes his job very seriously.'

'Is that why you're pissed off with him? He's neglecting you for his work?'

'No. It's the George Hope thing. He promised not to involve the police then persuaded Dad to call you behind my back.'

'Rightly so!' She puts her glass back down on the table and turns to face me. The hard edge of her almost-black eyes cuts right through me. 'Jesus, Ev. Why aren't you taking this more seriously? He sent you a choke collar, for fuck's sake. That's a threat.'

'Dad told you about the collar?' I didn't tell Dad about that either, which means J did.

'You should have reported it straight away. What's wrong with you? This isn't the Eva I used to know – you're so...'

'So what?'

'Tepid.'

'Tepid?' The cut stings and the old Maria glints in the blade. Is she right? Would I have taken this more seriously in the past? Retaliated and reported George to the police? Why does what happened on the bridge bother me so little? Did Jack empty me of all emotion and now there's nothing left?

'Yeah,' she goes on. 'You were always so on fire, so consumed by life and what you wanted out of it. I was always envious that you knew just where you were going and had an exact plan for how to get there. Not like the rest of us, flailing around like kittens in a bathtub. But now you seem...disengaged.'

'Well, fucking up your whole life will do that to you.'

'You haven't fucked up your *whole* life. But you need to get back on the horse, get back to work; you just aren't yourself when you're not going balls to the wall.'

I think back to earlier, sitting on the edge of the bathtub, feeling scooped out. 'I doubt I'll be able to get another job.'

'Have you even tried? Applied for anything?'

'No.'

'Well, you won't know until you try.'

Maria could be right. Getting back to work could be exactly what I need. It would give me purpose again. If I stay at home much longer, there's a good chance I'll go completely bananas. Mum's been telling me to apply for another job since day one, I just couldn't hear it from her. Maybe Mum knows me better than I know myself.

I change the subject. 'So, are you really not going to see Tomás? Dad said he thinks it might be the end.'

'I couldn't care less. I hope it is.' She picks up her wine, downs most of it and changes the subject herself, pointing to someone in the crowd. 'Oh, look, it's Grace. You must come and meet her, she's blind...s'hilarious.'

Between the music and her mouthful of wine, I don't catch whether she says 'she's hilarious' or 'it's hilarious' and, as she drags me out of the dining room, I'm praying it's the former.

I nod acknowledgements to friends and family as Maria guides me through the crowded lounge, shouting, 'Grace!' And, interrupting the short, slender woman who's in the middle of a conversation with the large man standing beside her, 'I want you to meet my friend, Eva. Ev, this is Grace.'

Without thinking, I stretch out my hand to shake Grace's, realising too late that she won't be able to see it. But to my surprise, like a carefully tossed ball, she catches it in both of hers. A white walking stick hangs by a loop from her wrist and its handle presses into my palm as she caresses the back of my hand with her thumb. For a brief moment she doesn't speak, just looks at me slightly below my eyeline, as if she imagines me shorter than I am.

'It's lovely to meet you, Eva. Your parents have told me so much about you. You're a vet, aren't you?' She lets go of my hand and it feels exposed, separated from the warmth of hers.

'I am.'

She's difficult to age. She could be sixty or eighty. Her hair is white, wild and untamed, and, although her skin is wrinkled, it's delicately supple and radiant. Her voice is high-pitched but softened by age and the loose creases around her mouth. No longer focused on me, her eyes rest downturned in their sockets, occasionally flicking up to dance beneath her eyelashes.

'I always wanted a guide dog,' she says. 'But I'm allergic. All that hair. It makes me itch like mad.' She shivers and I catch a light in her eyes that suggests she was a real firecracker when she was young. I imagine her in the '70s, wearing flower-power trousers and smoking a big fat doobie. Actually, forget the '70s, she probably still wears flared trousers and smokes the occasional doobie. Or at least has a stiff whisky at two in the afternoon.

I say, 'Labradoodles make excellent guide dogs, if your allergies aren't too severe. They aren't truly hypoallergenic, like a poodle, but they do shed less.'

'A Labradoodle? What on earth?' She chuckles. 'Is that one of those silly designer breeds?' In loose clothes and no make-up, she luxuriates in her age and doesn't appear to care what people think. It's relaxing just being near her. I like her instantly.

'Mixing breeds for specific traits can be effective for assistance dogs. It's a Labrador-poodle cross, so you get the faithful, easy-to-train nature of the Labrador combined with the intelligence of a poodle, which is why they make such great guide dogs.'

'I'm probably too old now anyway. I am too old, aren't I? Besides, Bob makes an excellent guide dog, don't you, Bob?'

The man standing next to her grins and holds out his hand for me to shake. 'I'm Grace's dog – I mean husband – it's nice to meet you.'

I shake his hand, 'Nice to meet you, dog, I mean Bob.' He and Grace laugh and I have to hold back my surprise that he's her husband. Against Grace's slight frame, he appears even larger than he is, well over six foot, but his height doesn't help him carry his excess weight, which I would guess at twenty-five stone. It's not as though my parents' party is black tie, but Bob has taken casual to a whole new level. The pockets of his blue, baggy sweatpants sag from years spent shoring up stocky hands. And his white T-shirt, grey with age, has a splatter of punctures across the belly, as if it's spent years rubbing against a belt buckle or been put through the washing machine with a bra wire sticking through the drum. It's childish, I know, but when I picture Mum greeting Bob at the door, having a mini stroke over his attire, I go all warm and fuzzy inside and like him as much as I like Grace.

I ask how they met and Grace chatters away as if we've known each other for years. 'We met through a mutual friend,' she says, 'who set us up on a blind date. Literally, in my case. And six months later we were married! We got married in a registry office on the Monday. It was a Monday, wasn't it, Bob? Yes, it was the Monday because we went on honeymoon on the Tuesday. He took me to Toronto. Was it Toronto, Bob? Yes. No. Yes. Toronto or one of those places up there.'

Grace chatters away until Maria is teetering on the brink of giggles. And, even though Grace can't see it, Bob can. This is why my relationship with Maria is complicated: one minute I'm in awe of her strength and determination, and the next I'm embarrassed to be near her. My glass is empty and the wine is going straight through me, so I wait for a break in the conversation, excuse myself and head for the bathroom.

On my way out of the room, I bump into J who's on his way in.

'How's it going?' he asks.

'Good. Though Maria's off her head. I'm afraid she's going to make a fool of herself.'

Jacob laughs. 'She does seem like a bit of a loose cannon.'

'Hmm. She likes you, though. I think her exact words were, "Mmm-mmm!".'

J puts a hand to his forehead, 'It's exhausting being this attractive but what's a man to do?' I laugh and he kisses me, the argument over George finally beginning to melt away. 'You're empty.' He points to my glass. 'Why don't you wait for me and we'll get a top-up together? I've barely seen you all night; let's hide out somewhere for a while.'

'Okay. Though this wine's going straight through me; at this rate we might as well hide out in the bathroom.' A flicker of concern flashes across J's face. 'Don't worry, pissing like a dog on a pole is my new thing. I guess this is what happens to women over thirty-eight. It's all downhill from here.'

'You're not over thirty-eight. You *are* thirty-eight.'

'My birthday's January 3rd. Today's August 18th. So I'm over thirty-eight.'

'Never argue with a pathological perfectionist. Don't worry, I'll still love you when things really get out of hand and you have to start wearing incontinence pants. I'll even buy them for you when I do the shopping. After years of buying your tampons, it won't even faze me.'

J's still amusing himself as Grace comes around the corner. 'Eva, how could you run off and leave me with Maria?'

'You don't like Maria?' I ask. 'Give her time, she'll grow on you.'

'Yes, like something that needs surgically excising. Aww, she's sweet, though.'

'Hang on.' I suddenly realise something. 'Jacob was talking when you came around the corner. How did you even know I was here?'

'Fifth sense.'

'You mean sixth sense?'

'Not in my case, dear. And who is this charming man who's keeping you away from the party?'

'This is my husband, Jacob. J, this is Grace.'

'It's a pleasure to meet you.' J makes the same mistake I did and holds out his hand for Grace to shake. But again, she catches it and thumbs the back of his hand. Her touch is like a spell and, just as I did, J breaks into a smile.

'How do you do that?' I ask. 'Do you assume people are going to shake your hand?' Then I blush, feeling that was inappropriate. The wine has gone to my head as well as my bladder.

'I hear it,' she says. 'A rustle of clothing at armpit level. Most people do it without thinking, a reflex. And as they do, they'll say something like "It's a pleasure to meet you", just as your young man did. Their voice guides me to their hands.'

'That's incredible.'

'Dear, I'm eighty-six years old. I was born blind. I've had a lot of practice.'

I wish Grace could see the warmth in my smile.

'Well, I was on my way to the gents', but ladies first.' J opens the door for Grace.

'No, you go. I want to talk to Eva behind your back.'

'Well, in that case...' J pauses at the door. 'It's probably for the best. I'll only blush when Eva tells you how good-looking I am.' The door closes.

'Handsome as well as charming?' asks Grace. 'That's a lethal combination.'

I sigh. 'Sadly, it is.'

'Tell me he's not perfect. There's nothing worse than a perfect man.'

'No, not perfect. And he's not as good-looking as he likes to think either. Plus, he has a shocking temper and does a terrible John Wayne impression. But he's perfect for me. I'm no picnic either.'

'You're a picnic to me, dear. And he seems like one of the good ones.'

'You're the second person who's said that tonight. How can you tell from two sentences and a handshake?'

'I'm like a bloodhound, dear. I get the whiff of people right off.'

I snort. 'From their smell?'

'No, no, when I say whiff, dear, I don't mean smell. Not at all. No, I mean their presence, their aura.'

'I see.' It's clear from my tone that I don't really see at all.

'Have you ever known someone was a confident person the moment they stepped in a room?'

'Umm...I guess so.'

'Well, you do that largely by sight. But it isn't really their appearance that makes you feel that way, is it, dear? Wouldn't you agree? It's something else? Something intangible?'

'I suppose.'

'Well, that thing you don't see so much as sense, I sense it too. That's how I knew it was you when I came around the corner. Everyone's energy feels slightly different.'

'Have you ever got it wrong?'

'No...yes...no...well, once, but she was an exception. Doctors tell me it's my brain responding to messages from my eyes at an unconscious level. But I think "aura" sounds more romantic, don't you?'

'I do.'

J comes out of the bathroom. 'Sorry to interrupt you, ladies, I know you've barely had time to skim my many qualities, but I'm going to steal my wife away.'

He links his arm in mine and, as he leads me away, I tell Grace I'll come and find her later.

In the taxi on the way home, Maria lies across the back seat with her head in my lap, dribbling on my dress. There wasn't a chance in hell she'd have made it home on her own. Her mascara's run and the insides of her lips are purpled by red wine. J took the front seat to give her room to stretch out. Her eyelids flutter and she mutters something inaudible.

'Shhh,' I say. 'Go to sleep. We're taking you home.'

'I love you, Eva,' she says. 'You're my best friend.'

Her words sadden me. It's heartbreaking that a friendship as strained and distant as ours is the best one she has. I know she drives people crazy, but perhaps if she had a friendship like mine and Bron's, or found a good man like J, she'd be a

119

kinder person. Because that's what a lover does: they keep you in check, lift you up while keeping your feet on the ground. They make you a better person. That's what J and I do for each other. It takes someone who loves you to tell you when you're being an asshole.

Sadly, I think Maria has lived in a perpetual cycle. Tomás, and the feeling of isolation after the death of her mother, created her hard exterior, and that hardness has kept people at a distance, isolating her further. I brush her hair back from her face, stroke her cheek, and wonder if I could be the person to break that cycle.

Then she pukes in my lap.

THIRTEEN

IT'S LIKE STANDING in the cold, staring through a window on to my old life. It's going on without me, and nobody can hear me banging on the glass. I'm no longer the protagonist in my own story.

She is.

She's blonde. Short. And bubbly.

Instead of standing at the examining room door and calling her patient's name, she goes out into the reception area, gets down on her knees and ruffles their ears. It's a bit much if you ask me. I bet she has one of those lively, high-pitched voices.

Fuck.

I know I'm being stupid. I knew Bron would have to replace me at some point. I knew that one day, I would walk past the surgery and see a face I didn't recognise, a surgeon in blue scrubs, wandering around my second home as if it was her own.

I just thought it would be someone...

I don't know...

Less fucking pleasant.

Behind the surgery's wall of windows, Bron appears at the front desk. She places her hand on the shoulder of one of the receptionists and leans over to say something in her ear. When she stands up, her gaze draws level with the road just as a car passes between us. The movement catches her eye and she sees me, staring straight at her.

The new girl stops fussing the dog and stands up, putting a momentary wall between us, before placing a hand on the owner's back and guiding them towards the examining room. Bron glances in her direction, then back at me. Then she hot-foots it from behind the reception desk and heads straight for the double doors.

Sliced down the middle, half of me tries to run while the other half can't move. I waver on the spot, each fragment fighting for control. I think of the old Eva, the one I'm trying to get back to. And I think I could, if I just keep trundling along this rusting, damaged track. But I haven't spoken to Bron since she fired me, and if I speak to her now it will derail me.

Yet, involuntarily, my feet take a step in her direction. I want to throw my arms around her, tell her how sorry I am, beg for her forgiveness for putting her livelihood in jeopardy. But I'm suddenly aware of my own tongue, like a hunk of meat I can't chew or swallow, and I wonder if I could even say her name, let alone talk to her.

Running is easier.

I take one step back, then another.

In the vestibule, Bron pushes against the external doors and our eyes lock. She watches me retreat and holds up a palm, begging me to wait.

When she reaches the pavement on the other side of the road, she hangs back for a moment, as if I'm a stray dog that might bolt if she were to approach too quickly. Then, she crosses the road.

122

'Bron...' Her name is too large. 'I'm so sorry...'

She runs the last few steps and throws her arms around me, holding me so tight the tears pour out of me. She was in the Royal Army Veterinary Corps and everything about her screams military: her strength, her presence, her courage. I always feel like a child around her.

'Can we sit?' She points to a bench a few metres down the path.

I hesitate for a moment, then follow. Sitting down next to her, I wedge Teddy's lead beneath my thigh while he jumps up, front paws on her lap, covering her face with kisses. She leans forward, takes his head in her hands and kisses him on the head over and over. 'How are you?' she asks, and I swallow bile and tears. 'Sorry. That's a stupid question.' She lets go of Teddy and places a hand on my knee. 'I'm so sorry, Ev.'

'You have nothing to apologise for. I'm the one who...I'm sorry, Bron, but I can't do this. I can't talk about—'

'I know. It's not why I stopped you. I just wanted to see you. To say hello. And give you something.'

She takes a business card from the breast pocket of her scrub top and hands it to me. But even after rubbing my eyes, the text is still blurred.

'I got a request for a reference,' she says. 'So I know you're applying for things.'

'You did?' I'm surprised. After the conversation with Maria on Friday, I had a vicious spat with my word processing software on Saturday, updated my CV, and searched every job website I could find for openings in the area. There weren't as many as I was hoping for – most are too far away, and I need to be close enough to home to walk Teddy in my lunch hour, or, even better, take him to work with me – but I applied for every one I could. I didn't expect any of them to be asking for references so soon; they would have arrived only this morning.

For a split second, I buzz with excitement until Bron adds, 'Well, I say reference but really...they wanted to know if you were—'

123

'The vet who killed the prize show dog.' I hang my head. Unable to look at her.

'Yes.'

'But this isn't the place that asked for a reference. It's somewhere else. Not a surgery. It's Genii. They're a bio-technology company. A friend of mine works there, and I know they're looking for a vet. They specialise in bovine genetics and reproductive services. It's not ideal but it's something. You know, until things...blow over.'

'Thanks.'

'I miss you.' She pulls me into another tight hug and I burst into tears again.

I don't want to walk home through town but Teddy's almost out of dog food, so I need to drop into the pet store. I've been avoiding the place because the woman who runs it has a dog of her own and is one of my old clients. She'll have heard about what happened, and I don't have the energy right now to deal with another difficult encounter. But I don't have any choice. They're the only place that stocks Teddy's food locally, and I can't change it without upsetting his stomach. If I'd thought of it sooner, I could have ordered it online, but I didn't, and we're almost out.

Determined to get it over and done with, I hurry up Cornmarket Street, dodging pedestrians. The same thing happens that always does when I walk through town with Teddy. People – women particularly – make their orgasm face, as if the words 'Oh, my God, how cute is that dog!' are being pushed out of their vaginas. Usually I love the attention, because Teddy enjoys it so much. I love seeing his tail wag so hard he could whack himself in the face with it. So I acknowledge people's orgasm faces with a knowing smile. But right now I'm too tired, too light-headed and shaky to be drawn into another conversation that plays out like a record on repeat: 'Is he friendly? Can I pet him? He's so soft! He feels just like a teddy bear! What breed is he? Gosh, I've never heard of an American cocker spaniel. Does he moult?' and so on and so forth. So I keep my head down, only looking up now and then to avoid bumping into anyone. Then someone catches my eye.

I stop dead.

I stop breathing.

Walking down the right-hand side of the precinct, coming towards me from the direction of home, are Caroline and George Hope.

I'm about to turn and run but it's too late, they catch sight of me. We lock eyes. I'm half expecting George to come flying at me while rummaging through the contents of his Tesco carrier bag for a recently purchased kitchen knife. But he doesn't. He just takes Caroline's arm and hurries her past me, putting as much distance between us as quickly as he can.

With my heart thrumming in my chest, I turn and stare at their backs as they shuffle away. And there's something so odd about the encounter. It doesn't tally with what happened on the bridge. Okay, it's not like I regularly run into people who've sent me hate mail and the collars of dogs I've killed, before threatening me at knifepoint, but something about their behaviour doesn't sit right. For George to be driven to a knife attack, he'd have to be consumed with rage. *I'm* consumed by it, at myself. But there was no anger on either of their faces, just despair. The sight of me didn't spark fury. They seemed filled with sadness. They clung to each other. They're still clinging to each other.

I feel sick.

I picture Jack with his adorable bat-like ears.

My decision not to go to the police was the right one. George and Caroline have been through enough. I know J and Maria would never agree with me, but I can't help feeling that what George did on the bridge was no less than I deserved.

FOURTEEN

I EMAILED MY CV to Genii as soon as I got home after seeing Bron yesterday. It's not a job I would choose, though I would never tell her that; I'm grateful to her for helping me. As she said, it would be something to keep me busy until things blow over, and beggars can't be choosers.

After she told me about the call asking if I was *the* Eva Curtis, I used my maiden name on the application. It was, perhaps, a little underhand of me, but I'm so set on getting my life and career back together, I'll do whatever it takes. And, given that I only sent the application yesterday, it's a shock when my mobile vibrates and a soft, expressive voice says, 'Is that Eva Cosgrove? This is Valerie Turner from Genii.'

I almost drop the phone as I stutter, 'Yes, this is Eva.' I'm not prepared. It's been a long time since I've had an interview and suddenly, I'm as flushed and nervous as a teenager going for her first job.

'We'd like to invite you for an interview the week after next if that's convenient? Thursday the 7th?'

'Yes! Yes, that's perfect!' I'll have to cancel my appointment with Saeed, but I don't want to mess them around.

'Do you have a pen?'

'Yes.' Why?! Why did I say I had a pen when I don't? Frantically, I scan the countertops and yank open every kitchen drawer before running into the hall, trying to keep my voice level and calm.

'The interview will be with Richard Lloyd. Can you make two-thirty at Shotover Farm? Do you know where that is?'

'Yes, I can make that. And I know where you are.' I checked out their location yesterday. They have a large site with offices and farm buildings on the edge of the country park.

There's no pen in the hall drawer, so I run into J's study and plonk myself down in his leather chair. I pull wildly at drawers and the resistance of the right-hand drawer handle is so unexpected I rip my nail from the nail bed. Trying not to cry out as blood pinks the skin, I suck my finger while Valerie reels off directions to the site, despite my having told her I don't need them. The site is huge, though, so I will need to write down where to go once I arrive.

Fortunately, the left pedestal isn't locked and finally, I locate a pen and a Ratner, Leishmann and Walch notepad from J's office. I scribble down Valerie's instructions: the time, who I'll be meeting, and how to navigate Genii's extensive grounds.

Teddy eyes me from the doorway, uneasy, then returns to his bed. By the time I put the phone down, my heart's slamming against my chest, and I feel as if I'm going to faint. I'm so hot. I feel sick. The notepad makes a pathetic fan, and J's desk and drawers are practically bare; it's as if he never does any work in here.

The heat intensifies and I lean back in his chair, closing my eyes to stop the room from spinning. I suck in a deep breath but can't get enough air. My linen trousers stick to my legs, my T-shirt clings to my stomach, and sweat beads on my upper lip and forehead. If I don't find a way of cooling down soon,

I'm going to black out. I glance at the windows. There's not a cloud in the sky. It's hotter out there than it is in here. Afraid that if I get up I'll fall down, I spin the chair around. There are no papers or magazines lying around and all the books on his shelf are heavy enough to sink the *Titanic*. I scan the room and, next to the bookshelf near the skirting board, I spy a vent. Thank fuck for that! Dropping to my knees, I crawl over to it, dreaming of cool air blowing over my wet skin. I bring my face close to it but that doesn't help, so I run a hand across it, desperate for some relief.

Nothing.

I dig my fingers into the grille, but my nails hit something solid. It's blocked. The room is closing in, and I'm forced to flop down on my back and try Saeed's technique of slowing my heart rate and pulse.

Useless fucking vent!

I've lived in this house for years and didn't even know it had vents. And oddly, now I think about it, that's an internal wall. It separates J's study from the dining room. Why would anyone install a vent in an internal wall? Perhaps the apartment was fitted with an air-conditioning or ventilation system in the past, but that isn't likely; the building was renovated from an old brewery, and ductwork for a system like that would have needed to go in during the renovations.

When my temperature returns to normal and the room stops spinning, I roll on to my side and slide my fingers through the grille to feel whatever's blocking it. It's boarded up.

Warily, I get to my feet and drag my defective body to the dining room. There's no vent on the opposite wall, so I traipse from room to room searching for others, while Teddy watches me toing and froing like a tennis match with no ball.

It's the only vent in the house.

Back in J's study, I take my keys from my trouser pocket and get down on the floor to unscrew the grille. The screws are fake. Their moulded-plastic Pozidriv heads form part of the

128

grille itself. So I dig my fingernails between the vent and the wall in an attempt to prise it open, but it won't budge, not even a millimetre. My keys are useless as levers and I don't want to damage it and make it obvious that I've been snooping.

The vent's uselessness bothers me. I don't even remember seeing it before. For all I know it could have been here since we moved in, but why would anyone install a fake vent?

I return to the kitchen, open my laptop and do a Google image search for 'fake air vent'. The first picture that comes up is a hidden safe. It looks exactly the same as the grille in J's study. I can't imagine J installing a hidden safe; the previous owners must have put it in. Or it was installed during the renovation of the building and all the apartments have one. I stare at the picture as I process these questions, then Google 'how to open air vent safe'. Images of plastic grilles fill the screen, some with white cards like the ones that open hotel rooms. There's even a YouTube video of how to open a hidden safe using one of those radio frequency ID cards.

Would J install a safe without telling me?

I didn't think we had any secrets.

If it is a safe, J would probably keep the key card in his wallet. Unless there's something really valuable in there, in which case he wouldn't risk losing his wallet or having it stolen and being unable to gain access. Which means it's quite possible the card is in the house.

Back in his study, I rummage through the left-hand unlocked pedestal, but it's not in any of those drawers. It could be in the locked pedestal. Either that or the desk key could be locked in the safe, in which case I still need the key card.

Scanning the room, I feel like Debbie Reynolds in *The Unsinkable Molly Brown*, casing her own house with finger guns, gauging the looting potential of each hiding place for her husband's new-found fortune. Molly has a spark of genius and hides the cash in the potbelly stove, but then her husband comes home, cold and drunk, and sets the money on fire.

129

My potbelly stove stares me straight in the face: Jacob's swanky Rolodex.

A carousel of business cards, suspended on end, sit in little folders, divided alphabetically. If I were to hide a key card, I'd hide it in there, in plain sight. It's obvious but clever too; stuffed to its limit with hundreds of cards, it would take a thief forever to flick through.

I make a start.

The Rolodex contains nothing but business cards. I'd been so convinced. The floor-to-ceiling dark-oak bookshelf looms over me and I wonder if he might have hidden the card in a book. But it's rammed to bulging with law manuals, journals and novels; it would be a mammoth task to check every book on every shelf. Even pulling out each one and shaking it would take time. Plus, there's a good chance J hides the card between two specific pages and then I'd lose its place.

From my back-left pocket, I pull out my credit card. I'm not a handbag kind of girl, so my pockets are always crammed with everything I need. Almost every pair of jeans goes through the wash with a roll of poop bags or dog treats in the pockets. My credit card is about the same size as a key card and, taking a novel from the shelf, I slip it inside and close the book. It creates a noticeable gap between the pages.

Score!

All I have to do is tip each book forward and look for a gap.

Sitting on the rug, slumped against the bookshelf, I stare into my empty hands. They're not the devil's workshop, they're his fucking factory! The key card wasn't in any of the books. This is stupid. What did I expect to find in there anyway? If it is a safe, it's probably empty. I should book an extra appointment with Saeed and get him to hypnotise some sense into me, exorcise the devil from my idleness because, clearly, he's out of control. Any sane woman would just ask her husband about

130

it when he got home from work. And that's exactly what I'm going to do. If I get the job with Genii, all this will stop. I'll be too busy for bullshit like this, and things will go back to normal.

As I heave myself up, something glints in the footwell of J's desk. Something white, prominent against the dark wood, is stuck to the underside of his desk. I crawl across the floor and peer up inside.

It's the key card.

With the scratchy, tearing sound of Velcro, I peel it away from the desk. Then, still on my hands and knees, I crawl across the room and, following the instructions from the YouTube video, hold the key card up to the top centre of the vent. A whirring sound comes from inside and a violet-coloured light shines through the top of the grille.

The vent flips open, just a crack.

An odour of metal and must seeps out and I wait, afraid that if I poke my fingers inside, its white-plastic jaws will clamp shut. But then I take a breath and prise the vent all the way open.

Recessed into the wall is a compartment about twenty centimetres deep, forty centimetres across, and fifteen centimetres high. The wall's not a stud partition, it's flint and stone – the old brewery these apartments were converted from was built in the early nineteenth century – so someone went to a great deal of trouble to bury this thing.

I peer inside and something glints in the shadows, so I lean to one side to let sunlight spill into the cavity.

My world stops turning.

Resting in the safe's dark silence is a thin knife like a letter-opener, its steel blade engraved with initials.

J.J.R.

Stock-still, I stare at it, my mind unable to process what I'm seeing. The memory of that blade, pressed to my cheek, burns like an after-image on my retinas, the last shocking

131

scene of a film before the reel flaps and the white projector light blinds.

What the fuck is Jacob doing with George Hope's knife?

Not only did he convince Dad to call the police, he must have gone to Fiddler's Island that morning to retrieve it. I dropped it when I heard the rustle in the bushes and left it lying on the bridge.

I daren't touch it. No doubt it's covered in George's fingerprints. Evidence, should J ever need it, of the attack.

The knife sits on top of an envelope, and I don't even need to pull it out to know what's inside, I recognise the writing: it's George's letter. It sits on top of a Jiffy bag and I know what's in there too: Jack's collar.

J wins every case. How deeply embroiled does he get in his lawsuits? And how often does evidence turn up at just the right time to secure a victory? The collar and knife are an insurance policy: J's hold over George, should the harmless old fool ever threaten me again.

But then a thought turns me cold.

As if I'm standing on Cornmarket Street again, I see George and Caroline Hope walking towards me. I watch George grab Caroline's arm and hurry her away. I remember how they clung to each other and the looks on their faces. I knew it wasn't anger; I thought it was sadness. It wasn't. It was fear.

How far would J go to protect me? Has he threatened them? Warned them that a knife, signed with George's fingerprints, could incriminate him in some trumped-up charge? I can't believe it. Not of J.

Sitting next to the knife is a wooden presentation box which I pull out, unclasp and open. Inside, encased in grey velvet, is a gun.

Perhaps I *should* believe it. Perhaps I have to.

Perhaps I don't know my husband as well as I think I do.

Just being near a gun is acutely disturbing. The gravity of its black metal weighs so heavy it's impossible to pick up. I've never fired one. I've never even touched one. I close the box and quickly put it back.

My breathing returns to normal and finally, I begin to think straight. J is American. He may have moved here a long time ago but he grew up on a farm. Owning a gun must be as natural to him as owning a toaster.

I adjust the presentation box so it's in precisely the place I found it and pull out what's next to it: a small white box. Tablets. Underneath them is a tiny gold key, presumably for the locked pedestal. I turn the box over and read the label: 'LITHIUM CARBONATE Extended-Release USP, 400mg. 100 Tablets.' The prescription is made out to him, at this address, by a Dr P. Roberts, in London. Our GP is Dr Abbas. The pills must be old. I check the date. The prescription was filled on 18th July, five weeks ago. I count what's left in the blister packs and work out that he must be taking them every day, twice a day.

But what for?

And why keep it from me?

Lithium carbonate is used to treat low platelet-production in dogs, but I've no idea what it treats in humans or why J would be taking it. I return the box to its home and remove the last items from the safe: two Ziploc bags. One is filled with more pills, and the other with white powder. The pills aren't the same as those in the box; they aren't lithium carbonate. But they're unmarked, so there's no way of knowing what they are. And, since there's no label to tell me how many were prescribed, I can only assume that J is taking these as well. I steal one tablet from the bag, put it in my pocket, and return the bag to the safe. Then, in the kitchen, I find a mini Ziploc and, taking care not to inhale any of the foreign powder, spoon a sample inside. What could it be? Cocaine? I think I'd know if J was on hard drugs. I remember all the bad movies I've seen where a cop dips a finger in some mysterious white powder and rubs it along his gum line. I'm not doing that. Firstly,

133

I have no idea what cocaine or heroin even taste like. And secondly, the closest I've ever come to hard drugs is a joint of White Widow in Amsterdam. I'm fairly confident a fingertip of heroin would send me on a multi-day excursion to the funny farm. And I'm already hoping for a refund on my day pass.

Pressing each Ziploc tightly closed, I put the sample in my pocket with the pill and return the larger bag to the safe.

Finally, I scan every inch of J's study for evidence of my intrusion. I remove a few pages from the notepad so that no imprints remain, and even brush my footprints from the carpet as I leave the room.

Back in the kitchen, I Google 'lithium carbonate'. There are almost two million hits and I'm set afloat on an ocean of liquefied disorders: mania, hallucinations, delusions, bipolar disorder, clinical depression. I watch YouTube videos – some documentary, some personal accounts – of people suffering from these disorders, and can't reconcile any of them with J. None of these illnesses have anything to do with my husband. I know him. We've been together for five years and there's no way he could keep something this serious from me. He has his bad days; his work affects him deeply, and sometimes he brings that home, sometimes he takes that out on me. It doesn't mean he's clinically depressed or bipolar.

I work my way down Google's list, reading website after website, until I'm dizzy with disorders: suicidal tendencies, schizophrenia, aggression, self-harming, memory impairment, cluster headaches. One site says that lithium reduces manic episodes and in some cases suppresses them altogether. Which means Jacob could be suffering from any of these disorders but the tablets keep him in check. And the more pages I read, the more alarmed I become.

Because the rest are too frightening to even consider, I cling to two symptoms in particular: memory impairment and cluster headaches. J is forgetful – something he blames on the stress of his job – and debilitating headaches could explain his

134

dark moods. But then, if it's just headaches and forgetfulness, why hide the tablets? Why not keep them in the bathroom cabinet? Whatever he's medicating himself for, he clearly doesn't want me to know about it.

If only he'd told me he wasn't well. It wouldn't have changed how I felt about him. I would have helped him.

That's it! Of course!

I would have *insisted* on helping him. And a man like Jacob stands on his own feet. A man like Jacob doesn't accept help from anyone. Knowing he's suffering from some form of mental impairment wouldn't diminish him in my eyes, but it would diminish him in his own.

An old, romantic movie springs to mind, where Sean Connery – in that sultry voice of his – describes falling in love. He says something about seeing yourself through someone else's eyes, and it's almost like falling in love with yourself. If J had told me the truth, he would have seen himself through my eyes, through the eyes of someone who knew he was mentally impaired. And, instead of falling in love with himself, he would have been forced to face the idea that he might not be the self-possessed lawyer everyone thinks he is.

I wish I'd never found that fucking safe.

I have no idea what to do. I can't tell J what I've found, not until I know what I'm dealing with – what the pills, powder and lithium are for – and whether there's a good reason he's kept it from me. I have a plan for the pills and powder; they won't be a problem. What will be a problem is that no doctor will discuss Jacob's medical condition with me – not our own GP, nor this Dr Roberts who prescribed the pills.

I need Maria.

I don't feel like *The Unsinkable Molly Brown* any more.

Suddenly, everything feels deadly serious.

Suddenly, I'm sinking.

135

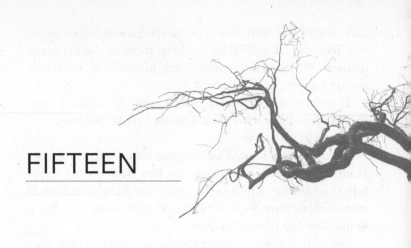

FIFTEEN

HEADING FOR the city centre, I hurry down Walton Street, past its high, white terraced houses. A hangnail on the middle finger of my left hand is raw from worrying, but I chew it anyway. Fuck! Instead of getting a grip, have I lost it altogether? Any normal wife would just ask her husband about the things she found. But then, any normal husband would tell his wife he was ill and not stash drugs, guns and knives in a hidden safe.

That malignant feeling swells.

Its cells divide.

My brain fumbles through that dark closet of disorders, pulling them out one by one and trying them on J for size: clinical depression, self-harming, suicide. None of them fits. Hallucinations, delusions, mania. None of those fits either. But, though I try to ignore it, my mind keeps circling back to three particular items, shoved to the back of the closet because, regardless of how well they fit him, they just don't suit him. Or at least, they don't suit me: bipolar disorder, memory impairment and aggression.

J's bold confidence and happiness are interspersed by moments of irritability and anger, but who doesn't have moments like that? And who doesn't forget things from time to time?

My relationship with J has never been one you could unravel by pulling on a single thread. Can anyone's? He's unpredictable, vibrant, and funny. But dark and moody too sometimes. I walk over a frozen lake with him, one moment feeling as if the ice is too thin to support my weight, and the next, feeling as though it's solid ground beneath my feet. I have to know what I'm dealing with before I confront him about the safe.

As I pass the grand columned entrance of the Ashmolean Museum, my mobile vibrates in my back pocket.

'Eva? It's Dr Abbas returning your call.'

I know it's a waste of time, but I telephoned his receptionist before leaving the house and scheduled a callback. Even though he didn't prescribe the pills, I'll have more chance of getting information out of him than from a doctor who doesn't know me. He'll have access to Jacob's medical history and I'm praying he'll either take pity on me or let something slip. I keep my pace as I talk.

'Dr Abbas, thank you for calling back.' And then I don't know where to start. Do I start with *Dr Abbas, I broke into my husband's hidden safe...* or *Dr Abbas, I'd like to talk about my husband's mental disorder...* but there's no place to start, so when he says my name as if it's a question, wondering if I've hung up, I just jump right in and say, 'Why is Jacob on lithium?'

There's a long pause.

'Dr Abbas?'

'Eva, I can't discuss Jacob with you, you know that.'

'Dr Abbas, please. What are they for? And why didn't he get the prescription from you? You've been treating me since I was a little girl; I need your help.'

I can tell from his sigh that playing on our relationship isn't going to work. We aren't friends.

'That doesn't change anything, Eva. I can't—'

'My husband is taking pills that I know are used to treat mental illness of some sort. I found them, prescribed to Jacob by a Dr Roberts. Surely you can tell me what I'm dealing with? At least whether or not I should be worried. Is he psychotic, manic depressive, bipolar?'

'Eva, he has doctor-patient confidentiality, just as you do. How would you feel about me discussing the intimate details of your medical history with Jacob without your permission?'

'Well, since you'd have nothing more interesting to discuss than cystitis, thrush and tests for infertility, I honestly wouldn't care.'

He raises his voice slightly, 'Eva, please—'

'I'm his wife!'

'You are! And frankly I'm surprised you aren't aware…'

His voice trails off and I jump in. 'Of what? His condition? Is that what you were about to say? It is something I should be aware of, then?'

'Eva, I have to go. I cannot discuss Jacob's medical health with you. Please discuss it with him. I'm sorry.'

Dr Abbas hangs up and I cling to the words *I'm surprised you aren't aware…* It was optimistic to hope that he would crack and reveal J's illness, but I got more from the call than I was expecting. It's clearly something that isn't easy to conceal – without medication at any rate. And given his swings of mood, the way he never walks down the middle of the road but always on one side or the other, I think I have my answer.

J is bipolar.

I grip my phone. My fingers won't hold still long enough to press the power button.

The screen turns black on its own.

Rooted to the spot, I stand in the surgery car park, unable to take a step closer. The tarmac soaks up the late August sun and radiates its warmth. A breeze tickles the hems of my linen trousers but does nothing to alleviate the heat. All I want is to stroll into the air-conditioned surgery as if Jack never happened.

But I can't go in.

Eventually, Jenny walks into reception and catches sight of me. We lock eyes. Then she disappears, and I know she's going to get Bron. I take one step closer to the doors, but that's as far as I can go.

After an eternal minute watching the nurses go about their business, Bron pushes her way through the vestibule doors, and when she rushes to greet me, pulling me in close, I just about manage to keep it together and not make a complete fool of myself right here in front of the floor-to-ceiling windows, on display like some zoo animal.

'Why don't you come in?' she asks. 'Everyone would love to see you.'

'I can't.' I shake my head. 'I can't.'

She hugs me again. 'Shall we go and sit down?' She points across the road to the bench.

'No, I can't stay. I have to get home to Teddy.' That's not true but I need her to believe it for the next lie I'm about to tell. 'I need your help with something.'

'Anything.'

My voice is stiff. I've never lied to her before. This whole thing with the safe and the pills has me off balance; it's trying to tip me over and spill me across the tarmac. But, as much as I want to tell her the truth and get her advice, if I do, she won't do what I'm about to ask her. So I lie through my teeth.

'I was out walking with Teddy this morning and he managed to get his hands on some medication. Some idiot dropped a load of pills and powder on the street and Teddy made a grab for them.'

'Oh, no! My poor Teddy! Is he okay?'

'He's fine at the moment. If he shows any symptoms, I'll bring him straight down. I'm not sure how much he managed

139

to swallow. I got as much as I could out of his mouth and kept some samples. I was hoping you could test them for me and find out what they are. Just in case.'

'Of course.'

I dig in my pocket and pull out the single pill and the small ziplock of powder. 'You're an angel – thanks, Bron.'

'The lab's a little backed up right now, it could take a couple of weeks, but I'll get them to expedite it for me.'

Two weeks is an eternity and the temptation to let her do that is overwhelming. But rushing these tests could delay the results for another pet with a genuine illness, and I can't live with that possibility. Jack's already more than my conscience can bear.

So I say, 'No. No, don't do that. If Teddy shows any signs of distress, I'll call you. It's only a precaution, he's fine at the moment. I'm more concerned with long-term damage.'

'Okay, I'll send them off today.'

She hugs me again and, standing there in the car park on the wrong side of the glass, my heart breaks. Holding on tight, I breathe in the scent of surgery lingering on her scrubs.

Hurrying up Cornmarket Street towards home, I make fists as I walk. The tremors are getting worse. I've lied to Bron. And tomorrow night, when I see Maria, I'm going to do something even more awful.

If I thought J would tell me the truth, I wouldn't be doing this. But for too long I've felt out of control of my life and everything that's happening around me. I'm going to take it back. When I know the truth about his illness, I'll confront him about the pills.

Then, if he lies to me...

I'll know.

SIXTEEN

HEADS TURN WHEN Maria arrives, and not just the men's. She's wearing a vivid green sleeveless top with 'Treat Me Right' printed across her chest in blue, and the letters 'eat Me' are set off in red. When she hugs me, she lingers for a long time and squeezes me really, really tightly. I squeeze her back.

She says, 'I'm so glad you called,' but doesn't mention anything about us dropping her home after the party or puking in my lap. I guess she's forgotten.

It's not that I no longer want to be the person to break the Maria cycle – the pathological perfectionist in me can't help herself. She has to stitch up the frayed seam, change the washer in the dripping tap, adjust the hinges in the cupboard that doesn't close properly, and fix the Maria who's also a little unhinged. And the vet in me wants to treat her, make her better, as if she's a sick animal – but right now I feel I need help more than she does.

She launches straight into George, saying, 'I've had a couple of the lads keeping an eye on George Hope and I did a background check, but he's clean. So I closed the case like you asked, saying you didn't want to press charges.'

'Thanks, Maria.'

'Well, you were right, he doesn't appear to be much of a threat. He was probably drunk, like you said. And anyway, I couldn't take any more stick from the boys about why we were staking out "some posh country tosser who does nothing but ride horses and sup port down the pub with his tweed-wearing chums".'

She puts that last part in air quotes, so I assume it's a direct quote from 'the boys', and I have to force a smile, feeling a strange jab at George being maligned, which makes no sense at all.

I fill up our glasses with prosecco and signal Steph, behind the bar, to bring us another bottle. I've been here so many times with Bron that she doesn't need to clarify which brand, but nods with a twinkle in her eye; she hasn't taken her eyes off Maria since she walked in.

I never come here with J. 1855 is my girls' place; a place to share secrets. It should have a sign on the door saying 'No boys allowed!'; it's too elegant for boys. The bar is a puzzle of layered wood and shabby chic drawers. Wine racks and brick feature walls soar floor-to-ceiling, and funky light bulbs hang from wires and glow softly.

'He got you fired,' Maria goes on. 'Which is usually enough for a man like that – the entitled type who's no doubt had his own way his entire life. The knife attack just doesn't fit his profile.'

'You don't think so?' It feels good to hear someone actually say that because I just *know* it isn't George to do what he did.

'No. It's too...vulgar for a man like him.'

'I'll be back in a minute.' I indicate the ladies' room.

As I'm washing my hands, a wave of comfort at having Maria back in my life washes over me, and I'm surprised by it. It's a relief that someone's on my side. Even more so now

I know the lengths J has gone to, behind my back, to protect me from George.

Things will get better with Bron now we've faced each other, but Jack left me vulnerable. I invested all my time in the surgery and Bron, neglecting everyone else in my life except J. Maria may not be the ideal candidate for a close friendship, but I need her, and I'm grateful for her at a time like this.

When I return to the table, she says, 'Speaking of getting fired,' and I groan inwardly because I thought I'd skirted that topic. 'I was chatting to your dad at the party and he told me everything that happened. It sounds like a bloody easy mistake to make if you ask me. Anyone could have done it. Why didn't you fight back?'

'George would have taken me to court.'

'So? Wouldn't it have been worth it?'

'It could have ruined the surgery.'

'But he could have ruined the surgery by going to the press, too.'

'I don't know that that was George; it could have been anyone. But with me out of the picture, at least it was just me they focused on.'

Maria downs her prosecco, tops it up, and reaches across the table for my glass. I place a hand over it and say, 'I'm fine for now.' I want to keep my wits about me. The last thing I need is to go home drunk and, without thinking, say something to J about the safe.

'Well, you don't deserve to lose your entire career over it.'

'I'm not sure the Hopes would agree with you.'

'Jesus, Ev, who the fuck is this person?' She waves her hand up and down, indicating the pathetic mess on the bar stool opposite. 'This isn't the Eva Cosgrove I remember. You're so…'

'So what? Tepid?'

'Yeah, and…' She exhales and slumps down, impersonating a gelatinous blob. 'This Eva Curtis really is lame, you know that?'

'Cheers.' I lift my glass and take a sip.

'The Eva I remember would have fought back.'

I shake my head. 'It was easier to let it go.'

'Easier? Who said life was supposed to be easy? You think breaking away from Tomás and my abusive relationship was easy? You think facing up to the accusations over Peter Cunard and that media storm was easy? I could have quit like you, but now that pain is behind me and I still have a job.'

She has a point. And, as usual with Maria, it's sharp.

'Everything worth having is hard-fought-for, Ev. Otherwise it wouldn't be worth having.'

'Actually, I am fighting. I have an interview the Thursday after next. I'm getting it together.'

Maria looks at me sideways.

'I need the loo.'

'Again? I'll have to start calling you slack-bladder.'

I grimace and get down from my stool.

By the time I return to the table, I've plucked up the courage to ask Maria the thing I came here to ask. Climbing back on the stool, I say, 'Look, Maria, I really need your help with something. Something not George-Hope-related.'

'And there it is,' she says. 'I wondered how long it would take you to admit you didn't call me for my scintillating company.'

'I did! Honestly!' I place a hand on top of hers. 'I was intending to call you at the weekend, but then something came up yesterday and…it's something only you can help with.'

Maria purses her lips. 'Okay.'

I hesitate. Every muscle tenses, and my heart beats out of rhythm with my body. But I have to do it.

'Jeez, Ev. What is it?'

I can't say it out loud.

'What? Is it Jacob? He's not having an affair, is he?'

'No, nothing like that.' My voice quivers.

'You don't sound very sure.'

144

'No, I'm sure…that's not possible.'

'It's always possible.'

'Not Jacob.'

'Don't be naïve, Ev.'

'I'm not being naïve. I'm being realistic. He doesn't tell the lies that men having affairs are forced to tell. He rarely says a meeting ran on or he got caught with a client. He's hardly ever late home; he's always with me. What woman would put up with so little time?'

'One who's patiently waiting for you to be ousted. Oh, my God, I know this great PI. He owes me a favour. He'll tail him for you.'

I laugh. 'And if he finds J with a leggy blonde, you'll plant drugs on her and have her arrested?'

'What are friends for?'

Jacob prancing around town with a leggy blonde seems like a cartoon joke. And Maria's foray into the realms of the ridiculous – PIs and stakeouts – has made it hard to ask what I need to. There's an awkward silence.

'Well,' she says, eventually. 'Out with it. What's this favour that only I can do for you?'

I hesitate. Asking J would be far more sensible. But, if he's kept all this from me, how can I trust him to tell me the truth?

'I need you to look into Jacob's medical records for me.'

'Are you fucking kidding me?' Maria physically recoils, leaning so far back on the stool I'm surprised it stays upright. 'I can't do that. I could lose my job.'

'Maria, please. I'm desperate.'

'I can't. Jacob would have to give his consent and, without it, I'd need written consent from a senior police officer. Why in God's name would you need me to do something like that?'

'I found lithium. Hidden in a safe in his study. I think he's keeping some kind of mental illness from me – bipolar disorder or something like that. I need to know what it is.'

'Why don't you just ask him?'

145

'I don't know. I'm scared.'

'Of Jacob? That sweetheart I met at the party? Ev, you're really fucking losing it now. I'm starting to worry about you.'

'Please, Maria.'

'You're serious?'

I nod.

'What's going on, Ev? Is there something you're not telling me? You know you can talk to me. Is something going on between you two?'

'No, no. Nothing like that.' I rub my forehead, suddenly conscious of Maria's history and the things she'll read into the seriousness of this request. 'I just...there's just...he's keeping things from me. I know his job requires discretion but there's...I don't know...something's off.' I gulp down the last of my prosecco. 'Can you get them for me?'

Maria's silent. She resists my pleading eyes by swigging half her own glass. But then she breaks.

'Oh, for fuck's sake, I'll see what I can do. But I'm not promising anything.' She slams the glass down and adds, 'I'll have to write up a file. I'll have to say I have concerns for your safety or something. It'll go on record, Ev. On Jacob's record. Are you sure you want to do that to him?'

'Of course I don't, but I don't have a choice. Something's wrong. Something big. Otherwise, why wouldn't he tell me about it? You can make the record disappear afterwards, can't you? I don't want to put you in a tricky spot, Maria, honestly. But you're the only person I can ask.'

'Fine, I'll do it.'

'Oh, thank you, thank you.' I reach for her hand. 'I really owe you one.'

'You're damn right you owe me one, you fucking nut job.'

I squeeze her hand. Her refusal to mollycoddle me is oddly fortifying. If I'd been here with Bron, this wouldn't have worked; she'd have insisted on hugging it out and talking everything through. And she definitely would have persuaded

146

me to talk to Jacob. Maria's acerbic indifference is like TCP on a cut. It stings at first but it's a powerful antiseptic. And when she orders another bottle of prosecco, I let her top up my glass.

I need a drink more than I ever have in my life.

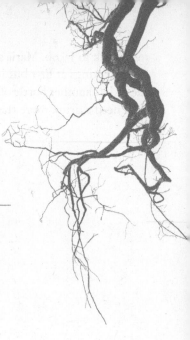

SEVENTEEN

THERE'S A LOUD SNAP in my ear.

'What happened?' Saeed lets go of my wrists. I must have been lashing out.

'I don't know, I…you…hypnotised me.'

'No. We were not recalling your dreams. Just guided meditation, exploring old memories to find the starting point of your symptoms. You do not remember?'

'No. I must have drifted off.'

When I first came here, I hadn't thought I could be hypnotised. But now, the lack of sleep and this general feeling of malaise, combined with Saeed's potent tones, are enough to send me into a trance without his even trying. 'What was I saying?'

'You were talking about a time before Jack, but after the night at the Manoir aux Quat'Saisons. Jacob's Summer Ball. You were in your bedroom, getting ready, and moments later you were somewhere else and you were screaming. Can you remember what triggered the jump?'

'No. I have no idea.'

'You said there was someone else there. A different man this time. Yet the room was dark and you were blindfolded. If it were anyone else's dream, it would make sense that they would just know. But your dreams are so grounded, so real, it makes less sense that you could be sure it was a different room and a different man. Not when you could not see.'

The memory comes back as they always do: in pieces. I wasn't in the bedroom; it wasn't before the ball. I was in the study. Tied to Jacob's desk. My mind flashes an image of the yacht club logo on George Hope's pin. Those knotted white ropes. And I can no longer tell what's real and what's dream. I *was* blindfolded. But I know the ropes were white. And I know it wasn't the same man.

'I just know. He was hesitant. Not like the other man. The other man takes what he perceives is his. This man...' I can barely make sense of it myself, let alone explain it to Saeed. 'I met a woman at a party last week. She was blind. She said you could tell someone was a confident person the moment they stepped in a room, but it wasn't their appearance that made you feel that way, it was their aura. That's how I know. He had a different aura. He was diffident, like a child being told to do something they're afraid of. His hands trembled.'

My own tremble.

'You said something about feeling hypnotised, as well as tied down. Do you think our hypnosis sessions are colouring these memories?'

'I don't know. I don't think so. It's not the same. When I'm asleep at home, it's terrifying. I feel far more in control here, under hypnosis. At least, one of me does.'

'One of you? What do you mean?'

'It's like there's two of me, and only one is paralysed. At home, asleep, there's just her.'

'Sleep paralysis occurs in almost everyone. It's what prevents you from physically re-enacting your dreams – sleepwalking –

and, if you become lucid in a dream, that feeling of paralysis can be terrifying. But it is quite—'

'No, it's not physical paralysis. It's like I could move if I wanted to, but, in spite of what's happening, I don't want to.' Saeed frowns and I realise how bad that sounds. 'No, no…I don't mean that exactly – of course I want it to stop.' I dig my fingers into the roots of my hair and scratch, thinking. 'It's not that I *don't* want to, it's that I *can't* want to.' He's still confused and I understand that. It's confusing for me, too. 'I mean, it's not my ability to move that's been taken from me, it's my free will to do so. Does that make any sense?'

'I think so.'

'When I remember under hypnosis, it's like we're two different women, and I'm watching what's happening to her. But I still feel what she feels. For me, under hypnosis, I feel like I could take back control if I really wanted to. But, for her, the loss of free will is total. It's terrifying to see myself like that.'

'I understand. I am sorry, Eva. I do not wish to keep putting you through this, and I would not if I saw another way. But please trust me, there is method in this madness and we are making progress.'

'Really – how?'

My tone is dubious and I don't mean it to be. I want to tell him that he's helping me by just being here and listening. But, at the same time, I need to know where this is going and see no progress at all.

'Your dreams are remarkably consistent, at least as far as I can tell thus far. We need more sessions to be sure.'

'You mean I have to come back?'

Saeed opens his mouth to speak, to justify the need, but he's getting to know me. He hears the sass in my tone and stops himself, changes course.

'In the meantime,' he says, his smile knowing, 'let us return to what we were discussing: where these symptoms all started.

Have you asked Jacob? Perhaps he can identify when things started to go wrong. Has he ever said anything to suggest he has noticed a change in you?'

'No. He doesn't even know I'm coming here.'

'Why would you keep such a secret? Is Jacob not an easy man to talk to?'

If Saeed only knew all the secrets I was keeping. I haven't told him about finding the safe, and I'm not ready to, not until I know what I'm dealing with.

'He is, but he has a high-pressured job and I try not to add to that. His cases get under his skin and sometimes he brings them home. I don't even try to talk to him then. But most of the time he's a good listener. It's just...well, he's like most men, I suppose. He tries to fix me.' Saeed's voice from that first day we met pops into my head – *I am not here to fix you* – and I gesture towards him, adding, 'Present company excepted, of course.'

'How does he try to fix you?'

I think about it for a moment. 'He packages problems into little boxes: issue one, issue two, issue three.' I line up imaginary packages on the table in front of me. 'Then he picks one box, opens it up and offers a solution for what's inside. Then he moves on to the next one and offers a solution for that. He doesn't realise the problem is the *pile* of boxes.'

Saeed nods encouragingly.

'Like, he knows about the nightmares, so he soothes me, reminds me they're just dreams and goes off to work. He understands that not being able to have a baby is taking its toll on me, so he buys folic acid and vitamin tablets when he does the shopping and reassures me there's plenty of time. He knows how devastated I am about Jack and losing my job, so he reassures me that the media attention will blow over, and I'll regain my confidence and be able to work again. But if he walked in the apartment tonight and I seemed down, I guarantee he would ask what was wrong. Because all my problems have been packaged up and solved. So, if I'm down, there must be a new box to open and deal with.'

'And all you want is to talk?'

'Oh, hell, I don't know. I'm as sick of talking about it as he is of hearing it. And I don't have the energy to keep poring over the contents of each box. But I want him to understand that it's the whole pile.' I reach out my hands as if I'm struggling to balance these boxes and they're tumbling.

'I understand. But I am here. And I will neither package your problems nor get sick of hearing about them.'

'You can't. You're paid to listen.'

He's suddenly grave. 'It is not just that, Eva. I want to help you.'

I lock eyes with him, and it's as if he's holding a white rope, only my wrists aren't tied to the end of it, a lifebuoy is.

He averts his gaze and clears his throat. 'I think we should move forward. My better judgement tells me it is too soon, but in your case I believe it is necessary.'

How does he know me so well after only three sessions? Am I that transparent? I guess I have made my reluctance to keep coming back pretty clear. If he only knew that I couldn't tear myself away even if I wanted to. He's the only thing that makes sense in my life right now.

'Whether we intended to find one or not,' he says, 'once again, we have a signpost.'

'A signpost?'

'A symbol. A recurring theme. As I said, your dreams are remarkably consistent. No matter where or with whom, you always dream of being bound and assaulted.'

'You make it sound like a good thing.'

'I do not mean to. But at this early stage in the process, finding signposts is rare. It usually requires a dream diary and can take many sessions to find consistencies. It has taken us only three. I could be wrong, but I think we are ready for the next stage in the process.'

152

'Which is?'

'We take back control.'

'How?'

'I am going to teach you to become lucid in your dreams, conscious. Finding signposts is the first step in learning how to do that. Once you know what to look for, you can teach your subconscious to recognise these signposts while you are dreaming. And you can use them to differentiate reality from fiction.'

'You mean that when I dream that I'm being bound and assaulted, I can use that as a trigger to tell myself I'm dreaming?'

'Yes. Only, that theme is changeable. Signposts are more specific.'

'The white ropes?'

'Exactly. Do you have an alarm on your watch?'

'Yes.' My gaze drifts to the purple band of my fitness tracker.

'I want you to set it to go off every hour throughout the day. When the alarm goes off, I want you to look at each of your wrists and visualise them bound with white rope, just like in your dreams. Then ask yourself over and over, "Am I dreaming? Am I dreaming?" Eventually, your brain will form a neural pathway – a habit – and every time you see white ropes around your wrists, you will instinctively question whether you are dreaming.'

'And that'll wake me up?'

'Not necessarily, and that is not the aim. The aim is to remain asleep but aware that it is only a dream.'

'What good will it do if I'm still trapped in the nightmare?'

A broad smile breaks across Saeed's face. 'We will get to that.'

'Can we try it now?' The moment those words leave my lips, the malignancy of that last nightmare swells. I hear that scream, distending at the base of my brain like a tumour on the gland, and I can't face going through it again.

So I'm relieved when Saeed says, 'No more dreams today. We only have fifteen minutes left. Besides, you must do the exercises first. Teach your conscious mind to look for the signposts. Only then will you recognise them in your dreams.' He gets up from the ottoman and returns to sit behind his desk. 'Let us get back to where we were. Clearly, you had a firm grip when Jacob won the Tagline case and took you to the restaurant. If our theory is right and Jack was a symptom, not a cause, something must have happened between then and Jack's death. Something happened at Jacob's Summer Ball to trigger your mind into recalling another nightmare. So, let us return to that night.'

EIGHTEEN

EIGHT WEEKS AGO

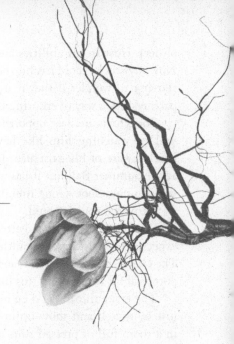

A Martin Greenfield box arrived from New York on Wednesday. It was my day off and I'd been going to meet some friends for coffee, but before Jacob left for work he gave me strict instructions not to leave the house until it arrived.

Typically, it didn't come until late afternoon. Then I had to drop it off at the dry cleaners so they could press it for him. I was at work on Thursday and Friday, so I couldn't pick it up until this morning. It seemed overkill for a brand-new suit – any creases from the journey would have fallen out on the hanger – but J's anxious for everything to be perfect tonight. He's out for the afternoon, having pre-party drinks with his colleagues from work while I get ready for the ball.

Jacob's firm has a Summer Ball every July, but this is the first year I haven't looked forward to it. Over the past six months, the partners have been giving J more and more complex cases, and his confidence in being offered the partnership is wavering. I'm exhausted from repeating myself, from reassuring him that the partners' assignment of these difficult cases is a mark of deep trust in his abilities and a way of testing his mettle. Now my stuck record has hit the run-out groove, and even I'm starting to wonder if they're a ploy to avoid giving him the partnership, a way of ensuring that Jacob Curtis finally loses.

Tonight is his last opportunity to impress. The partners will be watching him like hawks while pretending they're barely aware of his existence. Jacob always wants to impress at the Summer Ball but it has never been so crucial. He won't want to put a foot wrong tonight.

Heaven forbid *I* should.

With his glamorous and attentive wife on his arm, J will be expected to perform with faultless professionalism and charm. The client list will be select, and the partners will evaluate his potential for bringing in this lucrative new business.

The crazy thing is, I'd be much more charming if I could just be myself and show up in scrubs and Crocs. Imagine it, in a room full of pressed suits and Amanda Wakeley dresses. It would be the Crocs that really tipped them over the edge. They'd probably press charges.

I could just about face tonight if I weren't sick. It's been a struggle to conceal it from Jacob, but I couldn't put any more stress on him. I've had to spray the bathroom with perfume every time I've thrown up or suffered a bout of diarrhoea. I threw up this morning, but fortunately, it's eased off during the course of the day and I'm a lot better. If he thought for one moment I wasn't on point for this evening, he'd have a meltdown.

As with every Summer Ball, J has bought me a new dress. Reflected in my dressing table mirror, it hangs in its carrier in the wardrobe like a cadaver beneath a white sheet. Jacob has my dresses shipped from the USA; designed and made especially for me, they always fit to perfection. I imagine the dressmaker's shop with a darkened back room where a dummy Eva – my blank-eyed *doppelgänger* – sits slumped on a chair waiting to be of use. I wish she could put on the frock and go to the ball in my place. This year, J has chosen a sleek black number with a plain skirt that spills to the floor from beneath a boned bodice. It's stunning but stiff, tight-fitting, and difficult to breathe in. I'd really like to wear something else.

The crack of the door against its frame tells me that J's in no mood for negotiations. And at the clang of the keys in the bowl, Teddy bolts from beneath my dressing table and hides under the bed.

I consider joining him.

'What do you think?' J asks.

I'm still in my underwear, doing my make-up, and J is already dressed. His suit is midnight-blue, almost black, with a barely discernible pinstripe. A slim-fitting, lapelled waistcoat conceals most of his petrol-blue shirt while accentuating a beige brocade tie. There's something gangster about it, hard and intimidating, which, I guess, is exactly the look he's going for.

'Sharp. But your ass looks cuter in your tartan pants.' I blot my lipstick on a tissue.

'Hmm.' He checks himself in the mirror, twisting to see the back of his suit jacket. 'I'm not sure they'll give a partnership to a man who wears brushed cotton trousers.'

'You'll never know until you try.'

Jacob ignores me.

'Or the blue and black, you look sexy in that too.'

'I'm not wearing the blue and black.' He says it flatly, as though he hates that suit.

'You love that suit.'

'Yes, but I designed this one.'

'I thought you designed the blue and black one as well?'

Jacob takes a deep breath, and, when he exhales, the air shudders. I know what I'm doing. His tension fills the room to the corners and I'm trapped between it and the wall, pushing against it for space to breathe. In reality, I couldn't care less what he wears; he looks dapper in everything. Suit-schmoot.

'It's not right for tonight.' He pulls his watch from his waistcoat pocket and checks the time. 'You almost ready?'

'Yes.' I get up from the dressing table. 'Just need to get dressed.'

As I unzip the dress cover, I glance sideways in the dressing table mirror and catch J's eyes trained on my lace G-string. I know that look. And, even though I'm parading around in my underwear, I also know the sight of me wriggling into that tight bodice is asking for the kind of trouble I'm in no mood for. So I take my shoes and dress into the en suite and put them on in there.

I've straightened my hair tonight and without my natural curl there's enough length in it to cover my exposed shoulders. The problem is, this dress is exposing, period. Seeing J out of step has thrown me as well and, though the sickness and diarrhoea has abated, it's left me drained. I don't have the confidence tonight to pull off something this sexy. The bust and waistline are heavily embroidered and jewelled in a flowered design that creeps up the boning. It's beautifully intricate; I just wish there were more of it. The bodice is strapless and between the embroidery the lace is see-through, exposing sections of my midriff. The shine of the floor-length silk skirt catches the light, accentuating the curve of my hips, and the slit is a touch too far up my thigh.

I slip into my patent leather sling-backs and come out of the bathroom.

'Not those shoes,' says J. 'I hate those shoes.'

'But...you bought them for me. You chose them.'

'Did I?'

'Yes. You don't remember?'

'Of course I remember. They looked nice in the shop but they don't suit that dress. Wear the Louboutins with the red soles.'

'Yes, boss!' I salute.

Lying on the bed waiting, J watches me lift the skirt of the dress and lean down to remove my sling-backs. 'You'll crease your suit,' I say. 'And I just had that pressed.'

'I know.' He gets up from the bed and comes over to me. 'I was thinking we could crease it some more.'

'J, I'm all ready. The car will be here soon. We don't want to be late.'

He checks his watch again. 'We still have ten minutes.'

'I've only just made it into this dress. There's no way you're getting me out of it.'

'I don't want you out of it.' He pulls me close and whispers in my ear, 'I want you in it.' He slides a hand through the slit in the skirt and up my thigh. 'I'll be looking at you all night knowing I had you in that dress.'

I place my hand on top of his to slow its ascent but he's firm and resolute. Over my panties, he strokes my clitoris before smudging my freshly applied lipstick with a forceful kiss. I'm not in the mood, but I know how important tonight is, so, instead of pushing him away, I kiss him back and taste alcohol when his tongue enters my mouth.

He flips me around to face the bed, and I grip the footboard as he shoves his hand up the back of my skirt, bunching the silk fabric in his fist as his fingers work my panties aside. All I can think about is whether I'll have time to press it before the car arrives.

My insides don't have time to ready themselves, and he struggles to get his finger inside me. The wet click of his tongue, separating from the roof of his mouth, echoes in my ear as he sucks his middle finger, which he drives deep inside me.

Two fingers.

I'm not ready. I gasp. But Jacob mistakes the noise for pleasure and drives them deeper inside, so I try not to make a sound.

159

In the quiet, his zipper buzzes as he undoes it with his free hand.

When it's over, he zips up his trousers, straightens his suit and says, 'You'd better hurry. We don't want to be late.'

J leaves me alone to tidy myself up and the first thing I'm conscious of is that I now have his semen inside me, and the only thing keeping it from running down my legs is an insubstantial G-string. I quickly change into a pair of sheer hipsters and check for a VPL.

J's voice reverberates up the stairway. 'The car's here.'

'Be down in a minute!'

I reapply my lipstick and run a hairdryer over the silk skirt to remove the creases, twisting around to reach the back. Near the hem, a wet stain darkens the fabric. In about an hour that will dry startlingly white, so I run down to the kitchen and do my best to clean up the mess with stain wipes.

By the time we walk out the door, my skin has a sheen of sweat and I need another shower. My feathers are beyond ruffled and I'm looking forward to the evening even less than I was before Jacob came home.

J times our arrival perfectly, not early enough for the place to be half-empty, but not late enough to appear discourteous. The Grand Ballroom has a dramatic staircase that leads from an upper balcony to the main foyer and salons beneath, and Jacob loves making an entrance. That's why he chooses my dress. He knows exactly the impression he wants to create, one that has changed subtly each year.

For the first Summer Ball, he bought me an ivory dress with a flowing skirt and princess-line bodice. It was innocent yet faintly coquettish. The next year, J chose a backless dress in pink. And, last year, I wore red. I love that red dress – the one I wore to Le Manoir – because I had the time of my life in it that year at the ball.

But tonight, dressed to kill while lacking the faintest whiff of killer instinct, I find the extent to which Jacob orchestrates his life to get what he wants grating. Suddenly, in a way it never has before, everything feels premeditated, right down to our clothes. And I greet his co-workers and potential clients like a carved rook on his chessboard, my actions wooden.

Just before the Summer Ball last year, Jacob won an unprecedented legal battle between the singer Kikila and her husband. The couple had frozen embryos prior to Kikila's treatment for cancer which left her infertile. But then the couple got divorced. Kikila's husband insisted the embryos be destroyed but, as this was the singer's last chance for a biological child, she employed Jacob to fight for her right to keep them. Jacob won, in spite of the fact that Kikila had signed forms to say that in the event of a divorce the embryos wouldn't be used and either party could withdraw consent for implantation at any time.

Jacob had pulled strings to be assigned that case. He knew, before the game even started, that he would win. He also knew it would catch the attention of the other partners. Well, with the exception of the unfortunate Mr Ratner, who'd dropped dead of a heart attack in his office the year before. It certainly caught the attention of Mr Leishmann and Mr Walch. As did the red dress.

Tonight, it's black.

The colour of intimidation and power.

The colour of the end. The end-game in this case.

Clinging to J's arm, I listen to him schmooze one of the biggest fish in the room: Grant Jackson. Grant is the co-founder and executive chairman of a major IT company that's forever tied up in antitrust, copyright and data protection suits. I hop from foot to foot while faking a smile and keeping my body composed and steady. It's been so long since I've worn heels, the arches of my feet burn. I take a surreptitious glance at my watch as a young woman in a business suit comes out of one of

161

the salons and into the foyer. She's making a beeline for Jacob. It's nine forty-five on the button, and J's being summoned by the partners. As always, he's played like a master and won.

J makes his excuses to Grant and as soon as he's out of sight I do the same. Grabbing a glass of champagne from a passing waiter, I take the stairs to the balcony. Following the curve of the balustrade, I dive for cover behind a potted ficus. My schmooze batteries need a recharge, but what I really want is a cigarette. I have a stash of rollups in my coat pocket but it wouldn't do to come back smelling of smoke. J wouldn't approve.

Two of his colleagues walk past the balcony beneath me. I've met William several times but the other – Mark, I think – is relatively new to the firm. J introduced us earlier. He's young, cocky, and too handsome for his own good.

Not realising I'm standing directly above them, Mark says in a clipped London accent, 'Have you seen Jacob's wife?'

William draws out the 'oh' when he says, 'Ohhhh, yeah!'

'I'd tap that,' says Mark, shaking his hand as if my backside, squeezed into this dress, has just burnt his fingers.

'Yeah, right. You may have the balls to tap Simon's wife, but Jacob's?'

'He's not so tough.'

Mark's voice has a slight tremor and William laughs and says, 'Go on then, tap that, I dare ya.'

As they walk away, I tug angrily at my bodice, yanking it up to cover my cleavage. The skirt of the dress wafts up a sulphurous smell from the plant pot, reminding my stomach of the last few days spent on top of, or bent over, the toilet. Tap *that*, I dare ya!

From my hiding spot, I can just about see through the partially open salon doors. Less than a minute passes before first Mr Leishmann and then Mr Walch shake J's hand. The partners do everything in order of company name. First Mr Leishmann, then Mr Walch.

The young woman pours them each a whisky, which is also downed in order of company name. J waits his turn; he knows the rules. Then Mr Leishmann leaves the salon, closely followed by Mr Walch. Like two Cinderellas, the partners never remain at the ball past ten o'clock. With a procedural air, they walk up the main staircase, out of the Grand Ballroom and, presumably, out of the building. The dreadful elevator music ends so abruptly it could have been accompanied by a record scratch, and the real party begins.

I watch J as he lingers in the salon for a while finishing his whisky and, even from this distance, there's a conspicuous strain in his cheek muscles as he tries to contain a smile. I know he needs to maintain a professional demeanour, but what I really want him to do is come bolting out of the salon waving his arms in the air screaming *I made partner! I made partner!*

He takes another sip of his drink and sways slightly, closing his eyes for a moment before regaining his composure. Then, he nonchalantly pulls his mobile phone from his inside jacket pocket, enters the lock code, and sends a quick text before downing the last of his whisky.

When he finally leaves the salon, I step out from the ficus so he'll see me. Only he doesn't. He doesn't even scan the room. He takes the steps to the balcony, two at a time, and then the staircase to the main foyer. He must be heading for the gents'. Surely, that could have waited the ten seconds it would have taken to tell me he made partner? Fine. In that case, I'll go out for that cigarette after all. J can come back from the bathroom and wonder where I am.

At the top of the stairs to the foyer, I pause. Ahead, J is striding down the hotel corridor towards the front doors. He bypasses the cloakroom, the gents', and reception. Perhaps he needs some air; he's definitely had too much to drink.

I go after him.

One hand on the brass door handle, I pause at the hotel exit and watch J dart across the road. He isn't going out for air, he's running with a purpose. Dodging the busy London traffic, he heads for an alleyway between two buildings opposite the hotel, where a man waits in the darkness, leaning up against the right-hand building.

As Jacob approaches, the man straightens. He's a similar height to J, dressed in a business suit, and from the way he carries himself I'd guess he's a similar age too but his face is in shadow.

J holds out his hand and the man takes something, which he slips into the inside pocket of his jacket. They shake hands, embrace, and then disappear into the alley.

I wait.

After a few minutes, they reappear. I see J but the other man is eclipsed by the shadow of the building. I jolt and let out a gasp as Jacob grabs the man by the throat. Gripping the door handle, I watch J throw him up against the wall. But in the tussle they stumble back into the darkness, and I can't see what's happening.

Moments later, J comes out of the alley alone. He straightens his suit while he waits for a break in the traffic, and I linger as long as I dare, waiting to see if the other man comes out.

He doesn't.

J darts across the road, back towards the hotel, and I run. Bolting down the passage, I almost trip over my dress and have to hoist it up with both hands. I shuffle awkwardly along the corridor, heels wobbling in the deep-pile carpet, and practically fall through the ladies' room door, where I cling to the wall, trying to get my breath back and compose myself.

Mark's words ring in my ears: *He's not so tough.* And I remember the tremor in his voice and William's incredulity that anyone would have the balls to cross Jacob.

Hoping he didn't see me, I take a deep breath, open the door, and pretend to bump into him in the passage.

'There you are,' he says. 'I was looking for you.'

'Outside?'

'I thought you might have gone for a cigarette.'

'No. Just to the ladies'.' With heaving lungs, it's hard to keep my words steady. I realise J is waiting for me to ask about the partnership. So, raising my shoulders, I ask, 'Well...?'

'I got it!' He scoops me into his arms and spins me around. Then he lowers me back to my feet and kisses me full on the lips without a care for who's watching. 'Come on.' He takes my hand. 'Let's celebrate.'

As he drags me down the corridor, I have to jog to keep up. 'Where are we going?'

'It's a surprise.'

A surprise? A surprise that has something to do with the man in the alleyway? Is that why J needed to meet him before coming to tell me about the partnership? What could it be? And what could have made J so angry? Okay, so I didn't see the man come out of the alley; that doesn't mean he didn't come out at all.

J pulls me by the hand, past reception, and into the lift, where he presses the button for the top floor.

'Where are we going?'

'You'll see.'

We exit the lift on to a corridor that ends in a pair of cream double doors. The doors have brass handles and a gold plaque that reads, 'Garden Suite'. I try to put the incident in the alley to the back of my mind and force a smile to match J's mischievous grin.

He digs into his inside pocket and pulls out a key card. Unlocking the doors, he throws them back to reveal a palatial suite with grey fabric walls, a polished wooden floor, and two purple velvet Chesterfield sofas. At the opposite end of the room, soft netting swirls in an open doorway.

Falling into step behind me, hands on my hips, he guides me across the room and through the net curtains. As the fabric falls away, I step out into a magical private garden surrounded by high hedges and dotted with rattan sofas. The patio is decked with dark wooden planters that spill over with flowers, and, against the back wall, a soaring, standalone fireplace lies half-buried in the hedge.

'J, this is incredible.'

'I know. We have a dedicated butler too. All we have to do is press a button and he'll bring us anything we want. We could have brought Teddy and he would have walked him for us.'

'Dad would never have forgiven us for depriving him of a night with his hairy grandson.'

'True, but your mum would have been chuffed as nuts.'

I laugh. 'That she would.'

He leads me over to the fireplace and sits me down on a deep-cushioned sofa. The roaring flames cut through the cool night, and I can't stop smiling. It's the kind of place you wish you owned, the kind of place you wish you could step out into every morning. And its tranquillity beneath the clear, midnight-blue sky buffers the restless city beneath.

J saunters across the patio to a polished wooden dining table, where a bottle of champagne sits on ice. His lithe, muscular back flexes as he pours us each a glass, and I'm reminded of the strength with which he threw that man up against the building.

The hairs on the back of my neck stand up.

My lips part but the words catch in my throat. I'm afraid that, if I ask him about it, J will disappear and be replaced by the implacable Jacob I came to the ball with. I've met the Jacob from the alley. I catch him sometimes. He hides behind J's eyes in a grim cavern of hard-cracked ice. He appears when J's had a bad day or loses his temper.

With a glass in each hand, he comes and sits by my side. His eyes are warm. I only manage a sip of champagne before he puts his glass down on the coffee table and takes mine from me. As he leans in to kiss me, he eases me back into a horizontal position on the sofa.

After the rushed lovemaking earlier in the evening, I can't face it again. And, even though I don't want to do anything to spoil this moment, I gently push him away.

'J...I'm still a little sore from earlier. You hurt me.'

His eyebrows draw down and his lips tighten. He closes his eyes, pinches the skin between his eyebrows and shakes his head. And I've done it. I've made him disappear. He'll open his eyes and I'll plunge into that grim cavern.

Only I don't plunge.

Instead, he says, 'I'm sorry.' And, when he opens his eyes, they're edged with pain and regret.

'It's okay.' I place a hand on his arm. 'I know you didn't mean to hurt me.'

Brushing my hand, he says, 'Wait here,' and goes back through the patio doors into the hotel room. The netting swirls and separates as he strides across the lounge, his posture stiff, fists clenched. Then the net stills and he's gone.

Five minutes later, he comes outside again. His edges have softened. With one hand he clutches our champagne glasses, and with the other takes mine. Lifting me from the sofa, he takes me back indoors, leading me from the lounge through a dressing area with floor-to-ceiling black glass wardrobes, then into a bathroom.

With the exception of a few burning candles, the room is in darkness. The floor is tiled with black marble and the walls are panelled with black glass. In the centre of the room, white and striking, stands a circular bath full to the overflow. And across the surface of the water J has scattered creamy white petals. I wonder where he found those. From the lounge, I think: a vase of flowers on a table by the door. Not blue magnolias but I'm touched by his attention to detail.

He turns me around, unzips the bodice of my dress and eases it gently to the floor. Then he unclips my bra and slips that down my arms before removing my panties. He helps me into the water and the white petals dance on the surface as my body disappears beneath them. As I watch J undress, light streams in through the high windows, the full moon a searchlight, as if people are watching us from outside, and that sensation rouses my desire.

J's overfilled the bath and, as he sits down, waves splash over the sides.

'Your suit!' I point at the wet tangle of clothes on the floor.

'Ah, fuck it,' he says and grabs my hips to pull me closer.

I laugh. All that drama over a suit that's now soaked on the bathroom floor. My J is back, and, as swiftly as the stress drains out of him, it pours out of me.

I hold up my champagne glass for a toast, 'To my husband, a partner in a prestigious law firm. Are they going to change the name to Curtis, Leishmann and Walch?'

'Maybe Leishmann, Walch and Curtis.'

'It doesn't have the same ring.'

J chinks my glass.

While he's soaping my arms and massaging my skin to the tips of my fingers, he says, 'I feel like shit about earlier. I'm so sorry.'

'Forget it. I know tonight was playing on your mind.' Determined to brush it off and lighten the mood, I say, 'Besides, who can blame you? I'm irresistible in that dress.'

'It's not the dress.' He pulls me closer, wrapping my legs around his middle and brushing my lips with his.

'You've got competition, you know. I overheard one of your colleagues saying he was "gonna tap this".'

Jealousy rumbles his tone. 'Which one?'

'Er, Mark, I think his name is.'

'Mark Cox?! Well...he'll meet a sticky end in some dark alley, then.'

I stare at him. But he kisses me again as if he's said nothing of consequence and carries on soaping my arms. He massages my entire body, kissing every inch of me. It's hard to relax when all I want to do is ask him about the man in the alley, but at the same time I don't want to spoil this. So, when we're both soft and wrinkled and J takes my hand to help me out of the bath, I resolve to brush it aside.

For now.

J leads me back through the dressing area and opens a discreet door on to a small, intimate bedroom. A wood-framed bed, encircled by lanterns, takes up most of the room on a high-sheen wooden floor.

'It's not the main bedroom,' he says. 'But it's so romantic, don't you think? We can go in the main one if you like?'

'No. This is perfect.'

He won't make love to me. I know. Instead, he lays me down on the bed, climbs cautiously on top and just kisses me. His lips trace a line down my neck, my breasts and my stomach, until finally – at last – he goes down on me. He's so gentle. Too gentle. So I lift my hips, urging him to move harder and faster, but he refuses to touch me with anything but the lightest brush of his fingers and tongue.

It's unbearable.

Unable to take it any more, I push him on to his back and straddle him. Kissing him, I slide my tongue into his mouth and force him deep inside me. I fuck him hard and fast. And, since he already had me on the edge, I come within moments, quickly followed by J.

With him still inside me, I reach for a pillow, lay it across his chest and relax on top of him.

He says, 'I'm so s—'

'If you're going to say sorry one more time—'

'You'll do what?'

'I'll…I'll go back down to that party and twerk naked.' I point at the door as if I really mean to do it.

'You can't twerk. The Funky Chicken isn't twerking, no matter what you tell yourself.'

'Then it'll be all the more embarrassing and you'll probably lose your partnership within two hours of getting it.'

'You win,' he says.

'Good. What's my prize?'

'A naked Funky Chicken twerk.'

He makes a move to get up but I push him back down. 'Don't move. I don't want you to move.'

J slides a hand around the back of my neck and pulls me down for a kiss.

A moment later, he stiffens inside me.

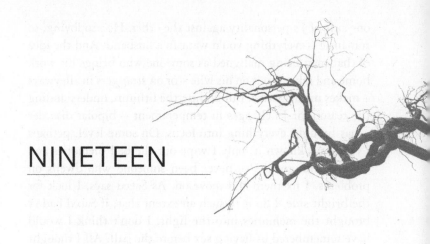

NINETEEN

I PUT OFF ASKING Jacob about the man in the alleyway. And by the morning I'd forgotten about it altogether. My mind was on the end of the evening, not the start, not the middle.

Now, when I picture the contents of his safe – the knife, the gun – I can't stop thinking about that alley again. I'm not frightened for myself; I know Jacob would never hurt me. But I'm afraid of what he might do to someone who stood in his way, or anybody who got in mine.

Like George.

When I was recounting the evening to Saeed, I skipped that part. I don't know why. I remember Saeed saying, when we first met, that although I might struggle with aspects of J's behaviour I don't want to diminish him in the eyes of other people. Perhaps that's it. Although I don't know why I would care what Saeed thinks of Jacob.

I didn't mention the sex at the start of it, either.

I remember how defensive I was over Jacob in my very first meeting with Saeed. On hindsight, I think it's because I defend one side of J's personality against the other. He's so loving, so romantic – everything you'd want in a husband. And the idea of that man being maligned as someone who brings his work home and takes it out on his wife – or on strangers in alleyways – makes me defensive. But finding the lithium, understanding the reason for J's changes in temperament – bipolar disorder – has brought everything into focus. On some level, perhaps I've always known it, only I wipe out the bad memories and cling to the good. I've never been someone who dwells on problems. I fix them and move on. As Saeed says, I look for the bright side. I do it to such an extent that, if Saeed hadn't brought the memories into the light, I don't think I would have remembered us having sex before the ball. All I thought about, for days afterwards, was the sex in the hotel room.

On hindsight, I'm more angry at myself for not putting a stop to it before the ball. Is there a name for that feeling? A word to describe your husband fingering you before your body and mind have had time to adjust? When you're married, it's not so easy to stop your husband in the middle. You could say you're not in the mood, but he'll insist he can get you there. If it was a stranger sticking his hand up your skirt without asking, you would use force. You'd push him away, screaming, *What the fuck do you think you're doing, you asshole?* But, when it's your husband, that would be...what...? Hostile? Passionless? Unspontaneous? Just weird, frankly. So you carry on while the nameless feeling nags you.

J wasn't fingering me because I like it – even though I do, when it's slower, more sensual – he was fingering me to expedite sex. And to that end, he licked his palm, ran it up and down his penis and pushed it inside me. I remember that now. I remember my hands slipping on the footboard, gripping tight to brace myself. It stung. I was raw – I remember being aware of my insides throughout the ball. J took pleasure in knowing he'd had me in that dress, but I'd felt dirty and wanted another shower.

172

I was rigid inside.

Perhaps, another time, I'll tell Saeed about my rigid vagina.

Perhaps I'll tell him that sometimes I imagine a scalpel between my thumb and forefinger. I make precise cuts through skin, flesh and muscle to surgically remove my upper body until only a vagina remains, topped off with a cervix. I prop it up against the kitchen counter, balanced on a pair of bare legs, where it waits for J to get home, while the rest of my body gets on with the housework.

I probably won't tell Saeed that.

I'll probably tell him about the other times, when J looks at me as if the ten hours apart have been unbearable. When he makes love to me slowly, in a sort of soft, heated haze that for the next few days is all I can think about. And, when I tell him that, my cheeks will fill with blood and pulse as though there's a tiny heart in each of them. Because sometimes, the bliss of knowing J is my husband – mine – seems unfair on all the other women in the world who don't get to feel the way he makes me feel.

And sometimes, not so much.

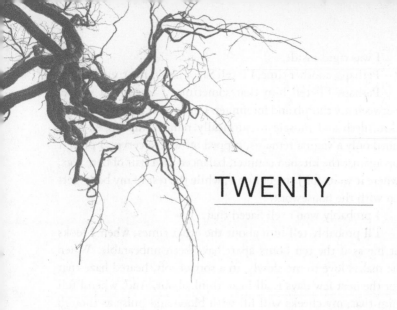

TWENTY

ON THE RADIO, James Blake sings 'Retrograde' while I stand at the kitchen island, chopping onions with a little square of bread in my mouth. It stops me crying, but once it's soaked up all the saliva I have to swallow it and start on a new piece. At this rate, I'll be full before dinner.

I love 'Retrograde'. It's like a Swedish massage for the brain and, combined with the repetition and mindlessness of chopping onions, it's almost as good as therapy. I should warn Saeed; it could put him out of business.

I'm in the mood to sing along but, with another square of bread in my mouth, can only hum. I did an OPK test this morning and I'm ovulating. At FishShorey, J said it could still happen naturally, and I'm feeling positive. I'm even wearing panties that match my bra. But J's running a little late.

After the argument over the police, J has been constantly trying to make it up to me. On Friday, he took a break from his caseload, skipped work, and took me to Porthcothan for a long weekend. We stayed in a quaint beachside cottage where

Teddy ran around like a toddler on orange Smarties, digging holes, rubbing his back in the sand, and needing to be bathed twice a day.

On Saturday night, when the bay was empty and silent, we risked the full moon, threw caution to the wind and went skinny-dipping. We felt like a couple of teenagers and couldn't stop laughing. But with Teddy barking in distress from the shoreline, convinced his owners were going to drown, we had to get out almost as soon as we'd got in. Back in the cottage, we lit the wood-burning stove and made love to warm ourselves up. The cottage had heavy curtains that blocked out the moon, and, in the pitch-black, we connected in a way we never have. It was as though, blinded by the dark, all our other senses merged together in one heightened sixth sense of desire. Our bodies were aware of nothing but each other and the whole world disappeared.

When it was over, we lay there for a few moments, curled into each other, but then suddenly started coughing. When we turned on the lights, we found the room full of thick smoke from the blocked flue of the wood-burning stove. Our senses sparked into life, and we threw open all the windows while coughing through laughter. It reminded me of an old Genesis song about being so lost in another person that you keep on going because you're unaware of anything else. The only sensible person in the room was Teddy, who was nose to the floor by the front door, breathing fresh air from the draught.

Over the rest of the weekend, we would occasionally catch each other's eye, remember that moment of being so immersed in each other that we weren't even aware of the need to breathe, and dissolve in a fit of giggles.

It was easy to forget about his bipolar disorder – or whatever it is. It didn't exist. And on the drive home I was questioning myself and what I'd found, as if the whole thing was a dream, the product of an overactive imagination. That weekend: that was reality.

I start as my fitness tracker vibrates with its hourly alarm.

I put down the knife, take a few relaxing breaths, and focus on my wrists, my palms pressed into the chopping board. I imagine white ropes curled around them, blood pulsing against twine. A memory flashes: my hips slamming into the overhanging top of Jacob's desk, its hardwood edging cutting through my bare flesh.

Like the crack of a starting pistol, I flinch as the door slams.

Jacob's keys hit the bowl and Teddy claws the carpet as he scrabbles up the stairs. He'd been eating a dental stick on his bed and I wonder if he's finished it or dropped it in fright. I close my eyes.

It's Monday again.

Something must have gone wrong with one of J's cases.

Since he was made partner, he's been assigned nothing but thorny trials, high-profile lawsuits with maximum public exposure that can't be entrusted to less-experienced staff but wouldn't be touched with a bargepole by either of the other partners.

J comes into the kitchen and I focus on the onions. If I look up, I know what I will see: a strained jaw and marble blue eyes, hard enough to crack. He comes around behind me and drops a bag of Porterford's sausages on the island counter; he must have been to the flat and that's why he's late. He kisses me on the shoulder and thrusts a bunch of flowers under my nose.

'Bad day,' I say. It's not a question.

'Worse.'

He drops the flowers on the chopping board, right on top of the onions, and the combination smells like deodorised armpits after a long day in a warm office. They're a pre-emptive strike; they're 'How-can-you-be-angry-about-anything-when-I've-bought-you-flowers?' flowers.

Roses.

Red.

176

I don't want to be ungrateful, but he knows I don't like them. It's not just the ubiquity of them, the shallow romance of them; their symbolism disturbs me. Red roses are a symbol of Christ bleeding in agony on the cross. A sign of bad luck if the petals fall when the rose is cut. And in Italy, when given fully open, they mark the recipient for death.

They're fully open.

J snatches a glass and whisky bottle from the cabinet. The cork squeals as he twists it from the opening and, upturned, it spills its last drops into a small puddle at the bottom of the crystal tumbler. J wrings its neck as if it's to blame for being empty.

Carefully, I move the flowers aside as J reaches above the wine rack for a box of Ardbeg and slams that on the island next to me. It was given to him by a client and must have been expensive but he wasn't impressed. It's gathered dust up there for months. Its quarter-circle gift box is complicated to open, so he rips into it. I wince. I liked that box. It's silly but I wanted to keep it. I'd been waiting for him to open it so I could steal it to organise my soap-making utensils. Marie Kondo would have thought it was life-changing; it was the perfect size for the cupboard.

J tears the black foil from the bottle's neck, saying, 'I know what they're up to, those bastards.'

Glancing up, I catch sight of Teddy peeking around the kitchen door to see if someone's unwrapping cheese. He isn't usually this brave. Teddy can hear the sound of cheese being unwrapped from anywhere in the house. It amuses me to take it out of the fridge really quietly and try to open the wax packet without making a sound, wondering if I can outsmart him. It never works. Out of nowhere, he'll materialise behind me, sitting to attention on the kitchen tiles making icicle-drool. He knows, if he's a good boy, he'll get a corner.

J pulls the cork and the squeal frightens Teddy. He disappears around the door frame.

I soften my voice and ask, 'What bastards?'

'Leishmann and Walch. They've assigned me the mother-fucker of all cases. It's fucking unwinnable.'

I say encouragingly, 'No case is unwinnable. Not for Jacob Edward Curtis.' He sneers. So I add, 'You said yourself you were uber-efficient.'

He ignores me and downs the glass. 'I know what they're doing. When I lose this case, they're going to use that as an excuse to rescind the partnership. They still haven't signed the paperwork, you know. Eight fucking weeks. That's why they've assigned me this piece of shit.'

'They'd never do that. I'm sure they gave it to you because they trust you to handle it.'

J grins sardonically, pours another glass, and says, 'Then why haven't they signed?'

'These things probably take time.'

'Not this much time.' He empties the glass and pours another while I move sideways behind him and put my arms around his waist. Suggesting we make love when he's in this mood would be a huge mistake, so I don't. After all, we had sex on Saturday. But most of those swimmers will have died by now and I don't know exactly when I was ovulating; I didn't do a test. I would usually do OPK tests every day in the lead-up but I've been so preoccupied. Now, though, I *know* I'm ovulating. It's certain, the clock is ticking, and in twenty-four hours my little egg will be dead.

I'm not stupid enough to say anything.

I won't say it.

But then I say it.

'Why don't we go and have a roll around? It'll make you feel better.'

I'm not sure he even heard me. 'Can you believe it?' he says. 'The fuckwit was caught with the murder weapons in the boot of his car! They had the victim's blood on them. And I'm supposed to defend the fucking idiot. I mean, who commits

178

murder and doesn't dispose of the fucking murder weapons? The little twat deserves to go down for life.'

I pull away from him and go back to the onions, saying, 'Maybe it was a crime of passion.'

'Passion? Trust me, Ev, there was no passion in this crime. The boy was a fifth-year medical student who pumped a girl full of local anaesthetic while surgically removing every bone in her body. Many of them while she was still conscious. He even stitched her up as he went and gave her blood transfusions until she finally died. Then he used her bones to build an anatomical skeleton like it was some kind of classroom assignment. After all that effort, you'd think he'd dispose of his medical bag. But oh, no! He just wiped down his instruments and dropped his medical bag in the boot of his fucking car!'

'Jesus.'

'And if his father wasn't an old friend of Leishmann's and the kid wasn't Daddy's little rich boy, the firm would never have taken the case. I can just see those bastards now, drinking port in Walch's office, wondering who they could fuck over.'

'Oh, baby.' I put down the knife and take two steps in his direction, but he's surrounded by a forcefield of energy and I'm too afraid to touch him.

'I can just picture myself in court. "Er, m'lud, I know my client was caught with the murder weapons, and has the expertise to commit such a crime, it's true all the evidence is there to convict him, but would you mind awfully NOT DOING THAT?!!"'

Even if I could persuade him to have sex in this state, if he drinks much more he isn't going to be able to. I take another tentative step closer and say, 'J, don't you think you've had enough?'

'No, actually, I don't.' He empties the glass and pours another while I stare at the floor tiles. 'You should see the photographs – what he did to this girl – and I'm supposed to defend him.'

'Then refuse.'

'On what grounds? Don't be naïve, Ev.'

He's right. Don't be naïve. I chop another onion. Don't make him angrier than he already is. And definitely don't mention the 'O' word. Two hours, three tops, and he'll have calmed down. All I have to do is wait. But the whisky is going down like water and my narrow window is closing. I can almost feel the egg getting weaker by the minute, and I need to attend to it as if it's already born and screaming its lungs out.

So I stop slicing. 'J...I'm ovulating.'

'Of course you are.'

'Please, J.'

'I'm not in the mood.'

'But, we only have—'

'I said I'm not in the mood!'

I put down the knife and reach out to put a hand on his arm. 'Please. You just have to lie there, I'll do all the work.'

He yanks his arm away. 'I just have to lie there? Are you fucking kidding me? How would you feel if I said that to you?'

'I didn't mean it like that. I just meant, if you're tired.'

'Tired? I'm fucking exhausted!' He glares at me, then adds, 'All right, then, if all you care about is my dick, let's get it done.'

He presses my back into the worktop with the weight of his body and puts a hand around the nape of my neck. Then he tries to kiss me, but I turn my back on him.

'Don't, J. I'm sorry. I shouldn't have mentioned it.' I grab the knife and go to work again, wishing I'd never opened my mouth.

His breath blows through my hair with the force of his words. 'No. No. Of course you should have mentioned it. You had to fucking mention it. You're ovulating! Stop all the fucking clocks! Eva's ovulating! She needs some cock and mine's the nearest available, so let's get on with it.'

He presses himself against my back, running a hand around my hips and finding the waistband of my trousers. I drop the knife again and grip the sides of the chopping board as his hips thrust into my backside, forcing me against the worktop. His fingers fumble for the pull of my zipper, but I push back.

'Stop it, J. I get it. I was insensitive.'

'Insensitive? Then let's make you feel a bit more sensitive, shall we?' He grabs me again.

'Don't.' I wrestle with his hand, prise his fingers from my fly, and turn to face him.

'Don't? What do you mean, don't? I thought you wanted to fuck?'

He thrusts against me and a low growl rumbles behind me. Over my shoulder, I see that Teddy has plucked up the courage to come all the way into the kitchen. His golden eyes are clouded and he doesn't look like Teddy any more. His lip curls and his incisors glint white.

Teddy's never growled at anyone. A few years ago, we had some friends staying with us who had two small boys. They were relentless with him, pulling his ears and giving his tail Chinese burns, but never once did he growl. He just walked away. Now my teddy bear's gone and I'm afraid he might bite J in an attempt to protect me. And in this mood, I have no idea what Jacob would do to Teddy if he bit him.

So I push him away, saying, 'Not like this!'

His eyes are rock-hard, ice-cold. Sweat beads on his upper lip and brow and his chest heaves. The flame isn't out. His tension and anger are boiling over and now he's started, he can't stop himself. It actually crosses my mind to say, *Perhaps you need to take some of your pills.* It's on the tip of my tongue. But, before I can say anything he slides his fingers through my hair, pulls my head back and kisses my neck, pressing my spine into the biting edge of the marble counter.

Hard against my thigh, he slides a hand down my stomach into my trousers. I struggle against him, saying, 'Don't…stop it.' But he can neither hear nor feel my resistance. My anger boils too as he fumbles inside my trousers while kissing my neck, and, in the end, I snap. At the top of my voice, I scream in his ear, 'NOT LIKE THIS!' and shove him as hard as I can. As he stumbles back, still gripping my waistband, he pulls much harder than he means to and the button pops off my trousers.

He flinches.

There's a moment of pause as it tinkles across the kitchen tiles, hits the baseboard, and comes to rest beneath one of the cabinets. I glare at him with fear and disappointment, the moment stretching out until, finally, his eyes fill with remorse as he realises he's gone way too far. We breathe heavily, staring, both equally stunned by what just happened.

Then he wraps his arms around me and whispers in my ear, 'I'm sorry, baby. I'm so sorry.'

It takes a few moments, but I finally relent and wrap my arms around him.

On the bedroom floor, on my belly, I try to coax Teddy out from under the bed. I tell him it's okay but tension is rolled into the marrow of my bones like words in a stick of rock.

Teddy can read it.

I don't think he's ever heard me scream like that, and he won't come out.

With a packet of treats I brought up from the kitchen, I make a smelly trail of fish bites along the carpet and, centimetre by centimetre, Teddy finally crawls out. He puts his front paws up on the bed, waiting for me to lift him and when I do, I feel his whole body trembling.

Lying next to me on the bed, he curls in for comfort while I replay what happened downstairs. I know the argument was partially my fault. I put my own needs above J's and gave no thought to how he was feeling. I should have backed off the moment he said he wasn't in the mood and not pushed so hard. I guess I deserved what I got.

Fuck, that's becoming a recurrent theme. I deserved to be fired, I deserved to be roasted on social media. I deserved to be threatened. I deserved...whatever that was downstairs. I close my eyes, my breath quivering.

Is Eva in here anywhere? Or has she gone for good? I once knew a woman who battled like a hellcat through every difficulty she faced. Her edges get erased a little more each day until there's less and less of her left.

My heart thrums with unease as I remember the look in J's eyes as he tore the button from my trousers. So I rub Teddy's tummy, saying, 'It's okay, boy. It's okay.'

I whisper it over and over and over.

J offered to finish dinner while I have a bath. He didn't have to ask twice. I fill it almost to the top, light the candles on the marble surround, and lie back in the double-ended tub. I feel empty with the little egg dying inside me, but sex was out of the question. Things just got too out of hand.

J and I have been trying for three years. It's another reason I don't stop him when he fucks me without preamble. I'm thirty-eight and feel like I have one of those old metal kitchen timers ticking inside me, the ones with the oversized knobs you have to turn past five to set the time. It's annoyingly loud, and, when I hit forty, its buzzer will go off and rattle me to the bone.

Negligible mercies, but at least this month I won't be taking pregnancy tests every day at seven pounds a day. I must have thrown a grand at them at least. The test manufacturers should put a little toy in the box, like a Kinder Surprise, so at least you'd feel you were getting something for your money other than disappointment: 'Okay, you're not pregnant but have this cute little plastic boy instead. He's even got moveable arms and legs!'

And it's not just the pregnancy tests. I wasted eighty pounds on a Kegelmaster 2000 because strong pelvic floor muscles lead to powerful orgasms that dip the cervix into the semen pooled in the vagina.

It gets worse, too. After reading that lycopene increases sperm count, I started J on a diet of tomatoes and did all my urine tests in paper cups that have Heinz Tomato Ketchup logos on them. Logically I understand that, even if it were Jacob's sperm in the cup instead of my pee, the logo can't leach out sperm-boosting chemicals, but each cup is an amulet offered up to the fertility gods.

We went through all the usual degrading tests: me, feet in stirrups and legs akimbo, while J skulked off to a quiet white room to wank in a cup.

They wouldn't let him use a Heinz one.

In the end, apart from elevated oestrogen in my blood, which they put down to stress, they couldn't find anything wrong with either of us. Unexplained infertility.

About a year ago, I signed into one of those trying-to-conceive chat rooms, but by the end of the night I'd deleted my account. The posts were in a foreign language with entries like: 'Have a DSS with my SO but have been TTC for three years, so we DTD every other day, but my HPT always comes back with a BFN, so now I'm considering IUI.' There were discussions about the wetness and egg-whiteness of each other's cervical mucus and how sex had become an odious chore. But the worst of it was the spite. According to the posters, every pregnant woman was a 'smug, bitch-faced little whore' for getting knocked up when it wasn't her turn. They avoided friends with children, cut off others who dared to ask about their IVF, and deleted pregnant friends from Facebook. They wanted to scream in their pregnant friends' faces, 'You stole my dream, you cunt!' It was all so hateful and malicious. And it wasn't me. I'd never felt any of those things. I was always happy for my friends who'd fallen pregnant.

Whenever I needed a breather from the subject, I'd get together with Emma, an old friend from college who'd always hated children. Our conversations never turned to pregnancy, babies or kids, so I could feel like myself for an evening. Emma saw motherhood like a time loop in Aldi with two toddlers clinging to the trolley, and a baby in the fold-out seat. One child would point to something on the shelf and scream, 'I want one!' while the other screamed, 'If he's having one, I want one too!' Then the baby would start crying. She imagined herself calmly and mechanically walking out of the supermarket and just leaving them there. It was for the best that Emma didn't want children.

But then, a few months ago, we met for drinks in 1855 and she walked in, very late and very pregnant. The shock hit me like a punch to the stomach, and I wanted to punch her back. I nearly screamed in her pregnant face, 'You stole my dream, you cunt!' But instead, I just smiled, hugged her and said, 'Congratulations.'

Those women in the chat rooms might have been spiteful bitches, but at least they were brave.

I know IVF won't be easy, but it'll give me something else to focus on; it'll feel like waking up from a horrible nightmare and starting a new day. Okay, that day will consist of injections, vaginal ultrasounds and egg collections, but that will be a walk in the park by comparison. Three months, J said, and then we can start. It's been almost six weeks since I lost my job and that time has gone by in a blink, so perhaps it won't feel like the lifetime it seems to me now. It seems a lifetime since I clung to a Clearblue test, too, praying to the fertility gods for a positive result. In fact, now I think about it, so does the last time I cried on the toilet with blood-smeared tissue in my hands.

I jump out of the bath, grab my phone from the window-sill, and open the calendar to check the date. My period was due on the 13th, which was right after the George attack and the last thing on my mind. Did I have a period? I don't remember.

185

My stomach flutters at the thought that I might be pregnant, but when I look back to my ovulation date – day sixteen in my cycle, the end of July – the calendar entry pins the butterflies to my stomach wall.

I can't be pregnant.

J was in Manchester for the whole week. I remember it vividly because the local paper article about me came out on the Friday and J wasn't due back until the Tuesday following. I had to face it alone.

I scroll back even further, looking for the previous CT entry. CT stands for *Crimson Tide*. I realise comparing my period to a close shave with a nuclear holocaust is a tad dramatic, but a girl on the blob has to keep her sense of humour.

There's a bold red entry on the 16th of July. That was only two days after I killed Jack. I wasn't aware of anything in the state I was in. The past six weeks have been the worst of my life and I can't remember putting a spare tampon in my pocket or refusing sex because I was on. I can't remember much at all. Is it really possible that I could have skipped two periods? The OPK test I did this morning was positive – but it wouldn't be able to distinguish between ovulation hormones and pregnancy hormones – both would give a positive result. Which means...surely not...

On my knees, I rummage through the cupboard under the sink and dig out the box of tampons. It's full. I run a finger through the fine layer of dust on top.

Dragging the cupboard's contents on to the floor, I search for a pregnancy test. Then I pee in a Heinz ketchup cup and cling to the plastic test while Clearblue and the fertility gods argue over the course of my life.

TWENTY-ONE

I'M PREGNANT.

Test in hand, flushed from the hot bath and excitement, I rush downstairs to tell J. But as I reach the bottom of the stairs, his voice drifts into the hallway and stops me in my tracks. His voice is clipped, irritated. He's barely audible, but I think he says, 'Why are you calling me? I said I'd call you.'

I peer through the crack between the hinges. With his back to me, mobile pressed to his ear, he stands in front of the range cooker, leaning against the kitchen island. One hand cups the base of his phone as he speaks low and quietly into his palm.

It's not unusual for J to take calls from clients or colleagues in the evening, but then he walks around the apartment upright and forceful. Now he's hunched over, glued to the spot. A woman's voice tinkles through the speaker, too quiet to make out any words, and J leans his head back, stretching out his spine as if her words have kept him crushed in a tight space for too long.

'I did call.' He's curt. 'I do call. I called you last week, you just don't remember.'

I pocket the pregnancy test, push the door wide and step into the kitchen. J looks up, smiles, and clicks the end call button on his phone. Then he presses a few more buttons and puts his mobile down on the counter. Picking up the oven gloves, he points at various pans and says, 'Potatoes are boiling, onions are caramelising, gravy is thickening.' He stirs the pan of gravy then opens the oven door and rattles the tray inside. The hot-steam smell of roasting sausages fills the kitchen as he closes the door and throws the mitt on the counter. 'Almost ready.'

'Who was that on the phone?'

'What?' He looks at me as if he has no idea what I'm talking about. 'Oh, just a client.'

I glare.

'What? It was a client.'

I walk quickly to the counter and reach for his phone but he snatches it away.

'Give me the phone.' I hold out my hand.

'No. Why? What are you going to do? Call my client?' He pockets it.

'Which client was it?' And, even as I ask, I feel like an alternate version of myself. Eva, the real one – the rational one – has slipped through the fissures in the Italian marble tiles beneath my feet, liquefied and dispersed. I've always hated these fucking tiles; they trap all the dirt.

J tilts his head and a fake smile, stretched across his lips, tells me I'm being unreasonable. Am I? I am pregnant after all and, given all my symptoms, my hormones must be raging. Maybe my imagination is too.

'Ev...' He licks gravy off the wooden spoon and points it at me. 'You need to get out of the house more.'

That stings.

He says, 'You're looking for drama where none exists. Before long you'll be checking my texts and snooping through my things.' He's waving the spoon at me as I blush at the memory of breaking into his safe. 'Are you gonna put me through the wringer every time I'm an hour late home or take a call from a client? You need to get a fucking grip.'

My mother's voice echoes in his and I stare at my feet. 'I was only asking who it was.'

'Really? You were *only asking*? It wasn't an accusation? What the fuck is going on with you?'

I trace my toe along a fissure in one of the tiles, looking for Eva, trapped in the dirt.

He says, 'You actually think I'm cheating on you? I never go anywhere! I'm either at the office or I'm here. How could I be cheating on you?'

He's right. That's exactly what I told Maria. He goes away for work occasionally, like when he went to Manchester, but that's not a regular thing, not often enough to be squeezing another woman into his life.

Maybe Mum and J are right. Maybe I do need to get a grip. But the opposite appears to be happening. I feel all wrong. As though my rational mind has uncoupled from my body and is about to float away: a sky lantern with a finite flame. This wouldn't be the first time J has been harassed in the evenings by a stressed-out client, and here am I going off the deep end over one phone call. I trust J. I always have. That is, I always *did*.

But then I recall the way he spoke to that woman on the phone and the contempt in his tone rattles my conviction, because that kind of contempt only springs from familiarity.

Am I remembering it right? His unshakeable assertions have me questioning my own memory, my own sanity. I thumb my pockets, fighting the urge to wrestle the phone from him. I want to scroll through the call history and ring back.

I don't demand the phone.

We ate dinner in silence and he refused to look at me while I brooded over whether he was right that I'm spending too much time in the house and my idle hands have turned from a factory into a manufacturing plant.

Now, the cream patterned leather of my dressing table chair makes impressions in the backs of my thighs as I stare at my reflection in the mirror. She runs a moisturised cotton pad over her downturned eyes as Jacob gets undressed in silence.

I look up quickly when he speaks but all he says is, 'Do you have any Nurofen?'

I just point at my bedside drawer.

J slept, but I couldn't, and now he's in the shower, getting ready for work. His phone is on his bedside table, and I'm pretending to be asleep, resisting the urge to check it. The passcode is probably our wedding anniversary or, more likely, our first date, since that's not public knowledge. But I can't be sure. How many days of silent treatment will I endure if I lock his SIM?

Even if I'm right about the anniversary, he'll have deleted the call entry anyway. He always does. He deletes everything: texts, emails, call history, internet search history. A girl could get paranoid. But Jacob and his cases are a target for media attention, and he's terrified of information falling into the wrong hands. Rightly so. It happened once before. A member of the press stole his phone and used it to leak information about one of his famous clients. J thinks he got the passcode from the grease pattern of his fingerprints. Fortunately, no one ever found out it was J's mistake. Now he deletes everything the moment it's dealt with. And crucial data, like client emails, are only accessible through a password-protected, encrypted app. I wouldn't dare to try and guess that.

The shower stops.

I'm out of time.

But I can't help myself. I might not get this opportunity again. I snatch up the phone and enter the PIN. I was right: our first date.

As I suspected, the call history is empty. But the one thing Jacob cannot delete is automatic recall. I dial 1471, hoping the caller hasn't withheld their number, and grab a notepad and pen from my bedside drawer. The cybernetic voice reads the number so slowly I want to rip her virtual throat out. It's an Oxford number. I jot it down. Then I search for it in his contacts and find it against an entry for 'Vi'. I throw the pad and pen back in the drawer, return his phone to the bedside table and feign sleep just as J comes back in the room.

As always, J brought me coffee before he left for work, but he didn't speak to me. He didn't even kiss me goodbye. His silence hangs in the air as if he's still here, and his words – *you need to get out of the house more* – still echo around the apartment's high ceilings.

My mobile sits on my dressing table and I stare at it while scrabbling around in the drawer for my folic acid and vitamin tablets, which are more important now than they've ever been. I fight with the childproof caps before downing them with my coffee as if they're meds for the mentally unstable.

Next to my phone sits the notepad with the woman's Oxford number written on it. What the fuck am I thinking? I snatch up my phone, throw it across the room, and make Teddy jump when it thuds on the bed. Then, notepad in hand, I go and get it, sit on the edge, and stare at the screen. Teddy nuzzles into me for reassurance.

Preceding the number with 141, so mine can't be traced, I dial.

I hang up.

Then dial again. Hang up. And dial again.

The phone rings for a painfully long time before a woman answers.

'Hello?' She sounds groggy. I've woken her. 'Hello? Is anyone there?' Her accent is thick, American. From the south, like J's before it mellowed. 'Hello?'

I hang up and stare at her number. This woman is here, in town somewhere, but J's firm is London-based. Is it a coincidence that one of his clients – an American client – just happens to live in the same city? Why not hire a local lawyer?

Although J is guarded over what he reveals of his cases, he knows he can trust me. He doesn't reveal confidential details, but he always tells me what he's working on. Perhaps this case is so confidential he can't reveal a single detail, but why not mention an American client?

I remember his tone: that resentful familiarity. Surely, he wouldn't speak to a paying client that way? A member of his family, maybe, but not a client. But J has no family. He was an only child, his parents died when he was eleven, and he lost contact with all of his friends when he left America. When we got married, his side of the aisle was filled with work colleagues. She must be a new friend, someone he made an immediate connection with because of their common birthplace, perhaps. But then, why not tell me? He's never mentioned anyone named Vi.

I massage my eyelids, as if that might knead sense into my fogged brain. My eyes are dry and sore. I lean across the bed and fumble around in the bedside drawer for the pregnancy test, trying to buoy myself up by staring at the positive result, but the screen is blank. Its batteries have died.

I need to see it again.

I can cope with anything as long as my mind stays on the endgame. But the pregnancy doesn't feel real yet, not when I'm not showing.

I run to the bathroom, pee on another stick, and sit on the toilet lid, gripping the plastic test like a lifeline.

'Pregnant 3+' soon smiles on its digital face. That'll tide me over for another twenty-four hours. I can just keep doing tests until my twelve-week scan. I carry the stick back to the bedroom, disturbing Teddy as I hop back on the bed, and check the calendar app on my phone to see if I can work out how far gone I am. Clearblue doesn't give an accurate figure beyond three weeks, it just says '3+', which is laughable when you think about it: your waters could break and Clearblue would helpfully tell you you're more than three weeks gone.

J was in Manchester the last time I was ovulating, so I scroll back even further and come to rest on the 3rd of July, where a red entry reads, 'Ovulating'. That was a Monday. Another entry, two days before, catches my eye. 'J's Summer Ball'. We had sex before and after the ball. I guess two is the magic number after all. I count forward in weeks: eight. Although a doctor would tell me to count from the first day of my last period, which would make me ten weeks gone.

They call this 'the silent trimester' and I'm terrified and excited in equal measure. I wish I'd already passed the twelve-week mark, when the chance of miscarriage drops significantly.

I wish last night hadn't happened.

I wish I hadn't heard that woman's voice.

I wish I hadn't found the safe.

These things rain cold over the news I so badly want to share with J.

He and Mum are both right: I need to get a grip. For my own sake and for the sake of this baby. I can't bring another human being into this world when I can barely take care of myself. Enough's enough. When I find out what J is medicating himself for, I'm going to approach him rationally and calmly and ask him to tell me the truth. If he lies, I'll tell him what I've done, and force him to open up to me. Then I'm going to put all this behind me. I'm going to get that job at Genii and work my arse off. I don't have to tell them I'm pregnant until halfway through the second trimester. By that time, they won't be able to live without me, and we can talk about job-share opportunities for after the baby's born. Although, if I remember from their website, they have a crèche.

I'm going to get the old Eva back.

Because, man, she really had her shit together.

TWENTY-TWO

'OH, AND I WENT for that health check you suggested, and got the results on Tuesday,' I say, at the end of telling the whole – well, not actually the whole – story.

'And?' Saeed asks.

'I thought they would show the pregnancy, but they didn't. Everything else was normal, though. The results just showed things like blood count, liver function and blood fats. I suppose they don't check for pregnancy if they aren't asked to.'

'You have seen your GP?'

'Not yet.'

Saeed slaps his desk gently with his palms. 'Always the surgeon.'

'Well, I assumed the health check would confirm the pregnancy and tell me if there was anything amiss.'

'You must go, Eva. They may not feel another pregnancy test is warranted, but they will plan your care and book your scan.'

194

I fidget on the edge of the sofa. I don't want to tell Saeed the real reason I haven't booked an appointment yet: the thought of seeing Dr Abbas after our conversation makes me cringe.

Saeed says, 'You can get your surgery to book an appointment with a midwife if you are uncomfortable seeing your GP.'

I feel like a page in *Psychology Today*, lying open on his coffee table.

He asks, 'How did Jacob take the news?'

I press my top lip between my teeth and nibble loose skin.

Saeed's eyes widen. 'You have not told him?'

I shake my head.

'Why?'

I look up from beneath tired, hooded eyes and focus on the brown embroidery on the chest of Saeed's white kurta. I consider saying, 'The timing wasn't right.' Because I don't want to say that J and I have hardly exchanged a word since the phone call on Monday. And there's no way I'm mentioning the other things I've done. I want to skew my responses so I don't come off like a paranoid harpy.

Saeed believes in talking. That's his job. If I tell him that instead of speaking openly to Jacob I've accused him of having an affair, broken into his safe, sent his medications to a vet for testing, and asked a Metropolitan Police Officer to illegally search his medical records, I won't come off well. I know skewing your responses is not the idea of therapy; the idea is to talk freely and let them guide you to the right conclusions. But I'm afraid the conclusion Saeed will guide me towards is that I am, in fact, a paranoid harpy.

Sliding back into the leather, I cross my arms and say, 'The timing wasn't right.'

'You told me Jacob was as eager for a child as you. What has changed? Do you now mistrust that eagerness?'

As soon as Saeed says that word, everything falls into place. Mistrust is precisely what I'm feeling, only it's not entirely for Jacob. I say, 'I'm not sure it's Jacob I mistrust. I think it's me.

I find myself questioning everything I say and do these days. And I never used to be this way. I've never been an overly confident person, but I did trust my own mind. Now I'm paralysed by doubt, unable to make a decisive move in any direction.'

'That is understandable. You made a terrible mistake and now you are afraid of making any decisions at all. But you cannot live your life like that, Eva. Mistakes are expected. Allowed. You must relearn. Give yourself that permission, that freedom again.'

I rub my eyes, press the heels of my palms in deep, and hide behind my hands. My voice comes out muffled. 'I accused Jacob of having an affair.' I pull my hands away. 'He's so angry. Rightfully so, I guess. He can barely look at me. He told me the woman on the phone was a client. So I looked through his contacts and found an entry for a woman called "Vi" with a local number.'

I shift forwards and perch on the edge of the sofa like a bird tuned into the sound of her name as it rebounds off the walls. 'Vi,' I re-echo the sound. 'Vivienne, Victoria…Vilhelmina.' I enunciate *Vilhelmina* with a German accent and look up to find Saeed staring at me.

I blush.

An image of Maria floats into my mind as she flips through Jacob's medical records, then a random woman in a white coat testing pills in a lab. Jacob's voice whispers in my ear: *bitesize fruitcake. Bitesize fruitcake.*

'Wilhelmina would be W.I.,' says Saeed.

'What?'

'Vilhelmina with a V is a town in Lapland.'

'It is? Well she's not German or a Laplander. She has an American accent.'

'How do you know she has an American accent?'

I shake my head quickly, subconsciously, trying to empty out the bits and pieces and organise them into a reasonable explanation for how I've heard this woman's voice. Fuck! Saeed's going to think I'm a bunny-boiler.

'Eva?'

'Um...I called her.'

'Did you ask who she was? How she knows Jacob?'

'No. I hung up.'

Saeed's eyes widen a touch.

I imagine him opening the door to his rabbit hutch and finding it empty. Littlemore Mental Health Centre is probably on his speed dial. Imagine if I told him the whole story! I justify my behaviour by saying, 'I know it's a little crazy. It's probably the hormones. This baby has its mitts around my brain and I can't think straight any more.'

'Pregnancy can wreak havoc on the body. It is quite possibly the cause of your bad dreams as well. Nightmares are common in pregnancy. But symptoms change from one trimester to the next. It is likely that things will get better. Book that appointment with the midwife. She will give you advice on how to ease your symptoms. And, speaking of dreams, do you feel well enough for another session?'

I close my eyes, suck in a cleansing breath, and physically shake everything off. 'Yes.'

'Have you been doing the exercises?'

'Yes.'

'Good. Then you know what you are looking for?'

'A signpost.'

'Yes. I will try to direct your mind back to the first dream, to your bedroom. It will be better, less stressful, if it is a nightmare you have already experienced. That will also make it easier for your subconscious to recognise that you are dreaming. But you cannot force it. The mind will go where it wants.'

He's worried about me, I can hear it in his tone. 'It's fine,' I say. 'I can handle it.'

'Good. Good.' He brightens. 'I know it is frightening, but if you can learn to do this, Eva, you can stop a nightmare in its

197

tracks. The oneironaut is the master of her dreams. Conquer lucid dreaming and the world will be limited only by your imagination.'

'You mean I could bone James McAvoy?'

'Eva…can you not be serious for one moment?'

'What? He's quite sexy as Mr Tumnus.' Saeed raises his eyebrows to the ceiling and I put on a bad American accent and say, 'Don't ever lose your sense of humour, doll.'

'Excuse me?'

'Sorry. It's something J always…never mind.'

'I know it helps you, Eva, but we are getting distracted. However, to answer your question, yes. Master this and you can do anything: walk through walls, fly from the rooftops, even conjure an actor. But I would advise you to steer clear of the sex for now. Better to imagine something peaceful. A field of flowers, a walk through the woods with your dog, perhaps. Remember what I said the first day we met: a peaceful night's sleep will alleviate all of your other symptoms.'

'Party-pooper.'

'Are you ready, Eva?' His voice is clipped and stern.

'I'm ready.'

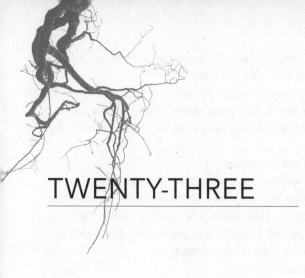

TWENTY-THREE

It's dark.

Something over my eyes blocks out all the light but I think the room is in darkness too. Not a shard penetrates the edges of the blindfold. I don't know where I am, but I'm not alone.

I'm on a bed. On my back this time. Naked. Spread-eagled. Tied at the wrists and ankles.

I'm afraid.

Vulnerable.

But I don't fight to free myself. It's not fear that's stopping me. It's something else. Just like last time, as if I'm under someone's spell.

Hypnotised.

The mattress sinks at my feet as someone climbs on to the end of the bed. The movement is light – they must weigh very little – I don't think it's a man. And when a hand lightly brushes my calf I know it's a woman. I feel that knowledge in the smallness of her fingertips. Her perfume fills my nostrils and it's strong. Not like any perfume I've ever worn; musty, musky and thick, like Arabian oudh.

I feel her knees in the space between my legs, and her skin brushes mine as her hands press down beside my shoulders. The air between us is balmy and close as she leans over my body.

I'm aware of my nakedness.

Her breath warms my cheek, and her lips brush mine. Her mouth glances my neck, my breastbone, my breasts. She tongues my nipples. Her touch is so gentle, barely there, as she kisses my ribs, my stomach and pubic hair. She slides her tongue between my legs. Then a finger.

This can't be happening.

It is happening.

I want to lash out. Punch her. Scream at the top of my voice. But I don't. I don't even resist. It's as if my horror at what she's doing against my will has been bottled up with my screams and thrown into a vast, open lake. I hear muffled shouts as it sinks deeper and deeper, getting quieter and quieter. This is going to happen. And I'll do nothing to stop it.

Scream, Eva. Scream.

That drowning voice in the back of my mind demands to know what the fuck is going on? How I got here. Who the fuck this woman is and why she's fingering me, licking me.

'Fight!' the voice shouts. 'Scream!'

But it's at the bottom of that lake, buried in sand, too quiet to hear.

Her finger slides out of me and she rests her palms on my thighs as she pushes her tongue deep inside me. It's nothing like having a man go down on you; her tongue is small and her movements leisurely and tender.

I start at the sound of creaking leather.

There's movement in the far corner of the room.

We're not alone.

I stiffen.

200

The woman is unperturbed; she doesn't stop. She slides two fingers inside me and massages me with her tongue.

Feet brush carpet and, a moment later, the woman groans while her mouth is still on me. Then she gasps; her fingers tense up inside me. Her lips leave my body as she lets out a cry. Then another.

I know that sound.

It's the sound of pain masked as pleasure. I know it the way every woman knows it. They know it because at some moment in their lives, maybe many moments, they'll have made that same cry.

She's not ready for him. He's hurting her.

And she's pretending she likes it.

I hear that voice again, far off in the drenched distance of my mind, only this time it's not quiet. This time, it's really screaming.

'Eva.'

A dreadful creak sets my teeth on edge and, with a snap, the ropes break. Ropes. They mean something to me, but I can't think what. A man's voice whispers, 'Bound and assaulted ...bound and assaulted...' but I don't know what I'm supposed to do. The blindfold slips from my eyes and I see white.

Ropes, twisted round my wrists, constrict the blood flow.

And suddenly, I'm on all fours. That man is inside me, thrusting and grunting. But I can barely hear him over the sound of a woman screaming. And I can barely hear her, because my own throat is screaming too. 'Stop. Stop. Stop!!'

'Eva!'

A snap, and I open my eyes.

I stare at a clenched fist. Saeed's forefinger and thumb are still pressed together from clicking his fingers. He's sitting on the ottoman in front of the couch, as he always is when I start to lash out. His other hand grips both of mine at the wrists, holding them down in my lap with just enough force to stop me flailing. Together, we heave in breaths as though we've had

201

a physical fight. And he leaves the memory of that nightmare burned into my consciousness.

He releases me as soon as he sees that I'm back here with him, and my cheeks blaze. 'That wasn't a fantasy, Saeed.'

'I know that.' And he says the words with such intensity, I know he means them.

'There's something gritty about it. Filthy and cruel.' I squirm against the leather of the couch. 'The whole thing was…vile. I feel dirtied by the memory of it.' And suddenly I'm crying, properly crying, like a child struggling to catch her breath between sobs. Saeed leans forward slightly and, without thinking, I reach out to hug him, but he recoils. Just slightly but enough for me to feel a slap of rejection, which he quickly reads in my eyes.

'Eva… I cannot—'

'Forget it.' I leap up from the sofa, the back of my hand smudging tears as I negotiate the limited space between me and Saeed. 'We aren't getting anywhere.'

I'm not sure what's making me angrier: my frustration at being unable to control these dreams, my mortification for sobbing like a child in front of Saeed, my embarrassment for thinking it was okay to hug him, or his rejection.

Any and all of the above.

'I can't do it.' I rub away tears as more fall. 'I can't do anything with the signposts, and I can't take back control. I can't stop it happening. And I can't do this any more.'

'I am sorry, Eva. I should have ended the session sooner. But you were almost there. You did it. You saw the ropes, you recognised the signpost in your dream.'

'What good does that do if I can't make it stop?'

Fuck. I was sorry that I'd be missing next week's session for the job interview, but now I'm glad.

'I know this must be terrible. I know they feel real. But it is *not* real. And, for a moment, you knew that. You were lucid. I am sorry if I was not clear, but lucid dreaming is not

202

something you learn from one or two dreams. It is a long and difficult process, one you learn a step at a time. Although it may not feel like it now, you have already made two giant leaps.'

I sneer at what doesn't even feel like a shuffle in the right direction.

'Eva, please trust me. We found the consistencies that link your nightmares in only three sessions. And you became lucid the very first time you saw a signpost. It is an incredible breakthrough. Real progress. Soon, those ropes will fall from your wrists, and you will stand up and walk out of that room. You will be able to leave, to go somewhere quiet, and sleep in peace.'

'You swear?'

He looks directly at me. 'I swear.'

'Well, you'd better be right, because I don't know how many more times I can do this. I dream these things at night, and then I come here and you make me dream them again!'

'I know. And they are getting worse.'

It's not a question. He's right.

The nightmares are getting worse.

TWENTY-FOUR

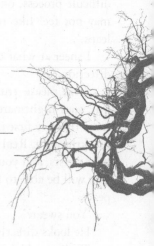

J OFFERED TO WALK Teddy into town with me and I almost wish he hadn't.

When he came home on Friday, everything was back to normal and the argument all forgotten. He even surprised me with tickets to see *Twelfth Night*, a 1920s musical adaptation, outdoors in the Bodleian Library's Quad. Under a starry night, Thomas Bodley stood in all state to hear musicians play jaunty jazz to Shakespeare's comedy. And the whole evening was so surreal and romantic, I forgot everything for one night. We stayed in bed half the day on Sunday, and it was all perfect for a while.

It's Monday.

J has spent the entire day on that murder trial, most of it with the defendant, and now everything's black again. That young man still maintains his innocence, in spite of the wealth of evidence against him, and is even directing J in his own defence, something J wouldn't normally tolerate. He's so cold, apparently. Pragmatic and apathetic but brilliant, and just being around that young man is turning my husband to ice.

He was in the office by six this morning and left early with this dark cloud tracking him like his shadow. I almost wish it would rain and all come out at once in a violent storm; maybe then there'd be clear skies again. But he keeps it all bottled up and this case could drag on for months.

I'm still waiting to hear from Bron and Maria, but now I suspect about his illness I'm hyper-aware of any change in his mood. Before, I would have just brushed it off as him having a bad day. But the contrast in Jacob from the weekend to today has left me more convinced than ever that he's bipolar.

Until I know for sure, I'm still holding off telling him about the baby.

Usually, I love it when we walk Teddy together, chatting arm in arm about each other's day. On evenings like that, it's hard to feel gloomy in Oxford, even when it's grey and rainy. It's one of the most beautiful cities in England, and, because my heart has its roots here, to me it's the most beautiful city in the world. I haven't visited every city in the world to verify my opinion but I'm sticking to it. As a teenager, I'd squeeze my way up the narrow staircase to the top of Tom Tower with my father and dream of attending one of Oxford's many colleges. I imagined roaming their thirteenth-century buildings, linked courtyards and quadrangles. My favourite by far has always been Magdalen (which, according to Saeed, is definitely pronounced 'maudlin'), where the animals carved into the cloister pillars were apparently the inspiration for Lewis's Narnia. The college has a chapel with a sepia-stained glass window so hauntingly beautiful it's almost painful to look at. If they allowed dogs, I'd go there every day.

On our walks, we often stop at the Old Bookbinders or the Angel and Greyhound and sit outside with a pint. So, as we pass Turl Street, heading in the direction of the Bodleian Library and the Radcliffe Camera, I suggest we take a detour.

We have to walk past Scriptum, my favourite shop in town. It's early, so it's still open. There can't be many shops in the world like Scriptum. It's quaint, old-fashioned, and packed to the rafters with everything from limited edition books to handmade paper, quills and wax seals.

'Would you mind if I nipped in?' I ask. 'I just love this shop, it always cheers me up.'

'Been coming here a lot lately, then?' he asks.

'Ouch.' I pull an imaginary knife out of my ribs and hand it to him.

Still in his suit, J stands in the open doorway with Teddy. His obvious impatience puts a dampener on what's usually a childlike flight of fancy into a world of miniature hot air balloons and whimsical knick-knacks.

The shelves are crammed with treats like a traditional sweet shop, the kind where, as a child, I'd waste hours scanning large plastic tubs and spend all my pocket money on bonbons and Sherbet Dip Dabs. Now I'm a grown-up, I want to spend all my money in Scriptum.

I dash upstairs to escape J's disdain and breathe in the smell of a distant century. I imagine it's always smelled this way, of dust, paper and age. *The Marriage of Figaro* is playing from hidden speakers and seems to seep between the spines of the books. I run my fingers along them and stumble on a hardback of Mary Shelley's *Frankenstein*. It's leather-bound with silver-tipped pages and from the same classics series as my copy of *Jane Eyre*. I just have to have it.

I run downstairs, brandishing my sweet-shop treat, while digging through my jeans for cash or a credit card. All I have is a roll of poop bags. I'll have to ask J to buy it for me. But one glimpse of those crackle-glazed eyes as he glances from my face to my hands reminds me I've already got a copy of *Frankenstein*. And buying another, just because it's leather-bound and part of a set, is frivolous and silly. So I put it down on a pile of journals at the foot of the staircase.

On the way out of the door, a postcard in a stand catches my eye. I slide one out of the metal rack and hold it up for J. It has a cute cartoon assassin on the front and reads 'Trust me, I'm a ninja!' But he just rolls his eyes. Clearly nothing will make him smile today.

Arm in arm, we make our way towards the High Street. At the end of Turl Street, the bollards on the pavement, and in the middle of the narrow road, force us into a tight squeeze to avoid oncoming pedestrians. And just then, a beautiful woman with dark skin and raven hair, falling almost to her waist, strolls directly towards us. Walking tall, with an air of unfettered self-confidence, she makes no move to skirt around us. Instead, she strides right between us, forcing us to break arms.

As I slip mine back into J's, her scent fills the narrow lane, and I breathe in the musty, musky scent of Arabian perfume oil. The potent, thick smell plunges me into blackness, and I'm back in that dark room, tied to that bed at the wrists and ankles.

I stumble.

J barely stops me from falling and my knees graze the paving stones.

'Steady,' he says, his voice bringing me back to the light. 'Are you all right?'

'Yeah.' I get back on my feet. 'I'm fine.'

I spin around to look at the woman and, as I do, she turns to face me with a smile that would cut glass. Then I bump into someone walking up the High Street and almost knock them over.

'Oh, God! I'm so sorry.'

'Eva! It's so lovely to run into you. Literally.'

'Grace! I'm so sorry. Are you all right?

'I'm fine, dear. Are you okay?'

'I'm fine. Sorry, I wasn't looking where I was going. How on earth did you know it was me?'

She taps the side of her nose, 'I'd recognise your aura from two streets away. And what a beautiful aura you have. It was so lovely meeting you that night. I'm only sorry we didn't have more time to chat.'

'It was lovely meeting you, too.'

'And who is this?'

'It's Jacob. My husband. You met him at the party.'

'Briefly,' says J. 'On the way into the toilet, if I remember.'

'Oh, yes, of course, I'm so sorry.'

Grace holds out her hand and J takes it. She presses her stick into his palm and rubs the back of his hand with her thumb. But this time J pulls away.

'I'm wearing a new aftershave,' he says. 'It must have thrown you off my scent.'

'Yes, yes, of course, Jacob. The lovely Jacob. I'm getting old, you know. I'm not as sharp as I once was.'

'Nonsense,' I say. 'Jacob's been in a foul mood all day. I think his aura's off kilter.'

'Oh, that explains it,' says Grace. 'Well, I'm off to Scriptum to buy one of those adorable hot air balloons for my great-niece. A complete waste of money and worth every penny, don't you think?'

'I couldn't agree more,' I say.

'I'm sure we'll run into each other again soon enough.' She walks away, calling back, 'And maybe next time we can stop for a coffee?'

'I'd love that.'

'Give my love to your parents, won't you, dear?'

'Of course.'

We make our way down the High Street and J says, 'I don't like the way she touches me. I can't stand the feel of her skin.' He shivers. 'Wrinkled and old.'

'You didn't seem to mind at the party.'

'Well, I'd had a few to drink. Beer goggles make old women more tolerable.'

208

'What are you going to do when I'm old and wrinkly? Will you have to become a drunk to tolerate me?'

He wraps an arm around my neck and pulls me close, kissing me on the forehead. 'Honey, I started drinking the day you turned thirty-five.'

I laugh and bury my head in his neck. He isn't wearing a new aftershave, it's the same one he always wears, but I don't challenge him. When he's in one of these moods, I try not to be disagreeable; it exacerbates things. And, though I hate to admit it, knowing he's on lithium only makes that worse. I'm more afraid than ever of pushing him to a place I've never seen him go.

We're just passing the University Church of St Mary the Virgin, on our way to the pub, when J's mobile rings.

He pulls it from his suit jacket pocket, glances at the screen and says, 'Hey.'

There's a long pause, and over the noise of passing cars I can't hear who's speaking. His footsteps slow, bringing me into step and then he stops altogether.

'Yeah, I'll be right there.' He hangs up. 'I have to go back to the office.'

'I thought we were going to the Angel?'

'I can't. I'm sorry.' He kisses me quickly. 'I have to get back. If it drags on, I'll stay at the flat.'

I stand in the street as pedestrians shuffle past. I don't know whether to go to the pub with Teddy or go home. Through the crowd, I watch J as he hurries away in the direction we came. But instead of continuing down the High Street to the station, he turns back into Turl Street.

Odd decision. It'll add another minute or two to his walk.

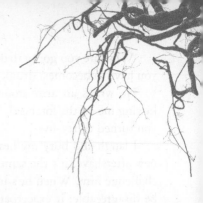

TWENTY-FIVE

AT THE OUTSKIRTS of the country park, the city disappears almost in an instant. The houses dissipate as I turn off the busy carriageway and find myself on a leafy lane that narrows into a track. It's hard to believe there's a business all the way out here. The isolation fills me with the irrational notion that I'm going off-grid. That the people who work here don't have homes to go to, televisions to watch, newspapers to read, and the internet to browse.

I'm really early – plagued by that teenage nervousness of a first interview – so I pull over into a passing place. I switch off the engine and grip the steering wheel. *You can do this, Ev. You've got this.*

I roll down the window and breathe in the scent of trees that drifts into the car on a breeze. Where I'm so close to Genii, the air's tinged with manure but it's not a smell I mind. Compared to the disinfectant, cat sick and dog shit I endured at the surgery, it's actually quite pleasant: the earthy natural smell of the countryside.

I'm nervous.

This may not be the ideal job but I want it. Badly. It could be a godsend. Though I'm not holding out much hope of getting it when every vet in the south of England knows who I am. I'm Eva Curtis, the surgeon who murdered the prize French bulldog, and, to top it off, I'm pregnant. Hire me! The pregnant dog-murderer! I'm a real catch.

I grip the steering wheel to steady my hands and myself.

Slowly, I'm coming around to the idea that finding the safe was a good thing. Being aware that J is bipolar, or something similar, is helping me to understand him better. They say you cannot change other people, you can only change yourself, and I'm already adjusting to his altering moods. With that murder trial still going on, I'm getting plenty of practice. In the long run, this will make our marriage stronger.

But I need this job.

I need to get myself back together for his sake, for mine, and the baby's. And I'm getting there. Last Thursday, Saeed took me back to the bedroom with that woman. And, although I wasn't able to take control of the dream or alter it in any way, I did manage to find a quiet place inside and maintain some level of control. I had to cancel our session today for this interview, and now I wish Saeed were here to talk me through my nerves.

My phone rings in my back pocket and I lean forward to ease it out. It's Maria. I tense. Did she manage to pull J's records?

'Good news,' she says. 'You're right, he's not having an affair.'

'Who's not having an affair?'

'Jacob.'

'What? How do you know?'

'My PI friend. He's been tailing him around London.'

I'm dumbfounded, and it's a second or two before I can speak. 'For how long?'

'Since I saw you.'

'You've had a PI tailing Jacob for two weeks?'

'Yeah, you said—'

'No, Maria, I didn't say. I thought you were joking.'

'Why would you think I was joking?'

'Because we talked about having drugs planted on his leggy blonde and arresting her. Tell me you haven't done something crazy like that as well?'

'Don't be stupid. I knew you were joking.'

'Well, YA HA!! Which is why I thought *you* were joking about hiring the PI.'

'No, I wasn't joking about that bit. I thought you wanted me to.'

'No! Of course not!'

I can't believe she did that. No, that's a lie, I can believe she did it. What I can't believe is that I was foolish enough to think Maria had any common sense. Imagine if J had caught someone tailing him! The whole scene runs through my head like a bad gangster movie… J, lying low behind a street corner, pouncing on the bumbling PI. Grabbing him by the collar, yelling, 'Who hired you?' The PI almost wetting his pants as J snarls, 'It'd better be the truth, or I'll reach down your throat and pull out your asshole! Then you'll taste the shit you're shovelling!' All followed up by the kicker: Maria's bumbling PI – who no doubt fancies himself as a police officer but couldn't make the grade – crying, 'Your wife! Your wife hired me!'

I could wring Maria's neck.

'You can't tell me you aren't curious,' she says.

'No. I'm not curious…all right…I am a little curious. There's really no leggy blonde?'

'No leggy blonde. No brunette. No redhead. He's not seeing anyone. In London, the only places he goes are his office, the courtroom, or his flat. And he's the only person who's ever been seen going in or out of there. He's never been seen with any women, other than female colleagues, and he's never shown any inclination for them. He's never even taken a woman to lunch. Honestly, Ev, the man's a fucking saint. I'm not sure you deserve him.'

Saint may be an exaggeration but, on the whole, I know she's right. I knew Jacob couldn't be having an affair, and now I feel even worse about that phone call. This whole mess started when I fell pregnant: my overactive imagination, the nightmares, the nosebleeds. For Christ's sake, I'm in therapy!

I know my hormones must be raging but I've just accidentally hired a private investigator! My idle hands aren't the devil's manufacturing plant, they're a fucking industrial estate.

I feel like marching into Genii and begging for that bloody job.

'Look, Maria, I have to go. But for Christ's sake call off the dogs, will you?'

'Sure. You still want his records, though, right?'

I wonder if getting Maria involved was a huge mistake.

'Ev?'

My hand gravitates to my belly. There's still no bump, but the twinges in my expanding uterus and my swollen breasts remind me I have a little olive in there. For its sake, I need to know if I'm right that J is bipolar. Or if, God forbid, we're facing something worse.

'Ev? All the paperwork's gone through. Do you want me to cancel the request?'

'No. No, I still want them.'

The receptionist is a plump woman in her fifties with a big smile and a thick bob of sandy hair. She brings me a cup of tea and asks me to take a seat on a small couch opposite the reception desk. The building is a converted barn, open-plan, with high-beamed ceilings and exposed stone walls. But it's bright and modern. I can picture myself working here, taking Teddy for a walk in the country park at lunchtimes. It won't have the bustling excitement of a city surgery, but a quiet rural existence could be just what I need right now. I can leave Eva Curtis in the city, and be Eva Cosgrove out here, the old me who worked as a livestock vet after qualifying.

I can start again.

From a wide entrance in the wall behind me, shoes tap the stone floor. With a broad smile, the receptionist looks up and points to the approaching man who must be the head veterinary surgeon in Technical Services. I get to my feet.

'Eva Cosgrove?' he says. I turn and hold out my hand. 'Richard Lloyd, it's nice to…' His face drops and his voice trails off. '…meet you.'

There's an uncomfortable pause before he takes my hand and shakes it, limply. I turn to the receptionist with the intention of thanking her for the tea, but she has noted her boss's change in tone and her earlier sincerity fades from her smile.

Richard says, 'You'd better come this way.'

My heels click and totter beneath me. The stone floor gives way to wood and he leads me into the belly of the building. It's like being shown in to see the headmaster. And, in his office, we take a seat either side of his imposing desk, which hammers home my subservience to his authority.

'Eva…Cosgrove, is it?' he says, scanning my CV.

'Yes. I've gone back to my maiden name.' I don't say any more in the hope he'll assume I'm divorced instead of outright lying about my identity.

The twenty-minute sham of an interview that follows feels like birthing one of his cows. And, when it's finally over and he says, 'Well, thank you for coming in, we'll let you know,' with as much sincerity as a Tagline chorus, I snap.

I get up to leave and at the door, turn and ask, 'Would it have made any difference if I'd been honest about who I was?'

He looks me straight in the eye and says, 'Well, we'll never know, will we?'

214

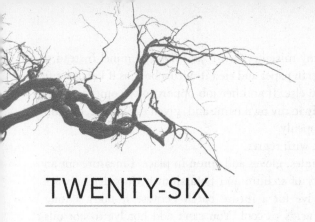

TWENTY-SIX

J TEXTED TO SAY he has to make a stop on the way home but he'll be back by six. The first thing he'll do is ask how the interview went, and my cheeks are already burning at the thought of telling him.

Teddy watches me with one eye open as I take out my frustration on a batch of cream soap. I go a little crazy over soap, like a sorceress in plastic goggles and yellow Marigolds. It's the alchemy of it. The magic that sodium and potassium hydroxide – brutal acids that can eat through skin – can transform into moisturising soap, just by adding oil.

There's a point where the fats in the oils saponify with the acid and the mixture thickens. This moment is called 'trace' because the hand blender leaves footprints in the mixture. It's beautiful, like aeroplane vapour trails across a deep-blue sky.

But my batch is past that point now, clumpy, like pissed-off mashed potato. And it takes an equally pissed-off woman to mix it with a wooden spoon. I'm not angry at the man from Genii, I'm angry at myself. I should have had the guts to admit to my mistake, own it and make it mine. Instead, I wrapped it up in paper and tied it with a bow, as if I could gift it to someone else. If another job opportunity comes up, I'm going to apply in my own name and, given the chance, explain Jack's death openly.

I feel sick with regret.

With goggles, gloves and apron in place, I measure out an extra quantity of sodium and potassium hydroxide. I always pre-mix the lye for a future batch because it takes a long time for the acids to cool. You can't add hot lye to hot oils without risking a soap volcano, and I'm always too impatient to wait. Cold acids must be added to the melted oils slowly and cautiously, so I use a squeezy bottle, it's just the ticket. I'm in the middle of decanting the mixture from jar to bottle when I hear the click, thud and tinkle of J coming through the door.

I put down the jar and listen to him whispering in Teddy's ear, 'Did you miss me, boy? You missed Daddy, didn't you? That's 'cos Daddy's the best, isn't he, boy? You love Daddy, don't you?'

My mood brightens.

He comes into the kitchen and, finding me trussed up in gloves and goggles, says, 'Jesus, it's *Breaking Bad*.' Then he comes up behind me, wraps his arms around my middle and catches his sleeve on the jar of acid. I grab it just in time, set it back on the counter and laugh with relief.

'Phew,' he says. 'That was close. What's in there?'

'Hydrochloric acid.'

'I think I'll get out of here. Is there anything in this room I *can* touch while still keeping my skin attached to my bones?'

'You can touch me,' I say, lifting my goggles.

He wraps his arms around me, more carefully this time. 'Speaking of skin and bones, you feel thin. Are you okay?'

'Actually, I've put weight on.'

'Doesn't feel like it to me. Don't get too thin, your boobs'll shrink, and we can't have that, now, can we?' He grabs one of

216

my breasts and I slap his hand with a spatula, splashing liquid on his hand, and he leaps back in fear of a skin burn.

'Just water. But that'll teach you.' I put my goggles back on and pick up the jar to decant the rest of the acid.

'So,' he says, moving around the counter to a safe distance. 'How was it?'

I just shake my head.

'That bad, huh?'

'Worse.' I screw the lid tight on the squeezy bottle and put the lid on my crockpot for the soap to cook out.

'Want to talk about it?'

I shake my head.

'In that case, you go up and relax in the tub. Scrub that interview off you, and I'll make dinner.'

'That sounds great.' I untie my apron and drop it on the counter before heading for the door, but then remember the crockpot. 'Keep an eye on my soap.'

He lifts the lid, looks inside, and pretends to stick his hand in there. Then he falls to the floor, grasping his hand and writhing around behind the counter like Stathis Borans in *The Fly*.

'Where's your compassion?' I ask, playing my part in his skit. He stops writhing, peeks out from behind the island and gives me a wink.

'I had to give it up, it cost me an arm and a leg.'

It's possible we watch too much TV.

When I come down from my bath, everything's tidy and the kitchen smells wonderful. Then I notice, on the corner of the island counter, a gift box wrapped in hearts-and-flowers paper and tied with cotton ribbon.

I look up at J with childlike curiosity. 'What's that for?'

'Well, I'd tell you it's because I love you but it's totally a bribe for sex.'

'That's a dangerous road. I'll expect gifts every time.'

'Hmm, you're right.'

He grabs the present and hides it behind his back, so I come around the island, wrap my arms around him and steal it. Tearing into the paper, I find the leather-bound copy of *Frankenstein* from Scriptum.

'J. I...' I don't know what to say. I'd been sure from his marble-eyed expression that he'd found the book frivolous. Do I do that a lot? Misread him? It's only a book, but it's another sweet gesture among many, and what do I do in return? Accuse him of adultery. Have him tailed. Break into his safe. Steal his medications. And worst of all, get Maria to pry into his medical records.

'It's not the right one?' he asks.

'No, it's exactly the right one. It just seemed...I don't know...frivolous to buy it when I already have a copy.'

'You can give the other one to Maria.'

I laugh, and then I'm hit by an overwhelming urge to burst into tears.

'Hey, hey, what's wrong?' He pulls me close. 'It's just a book. Don't all your lovers buy you presents?'

'No,' I sniff. 'My other lover's useless, he never buys me anything.'

'Hardly surprising. He's been tied up in the trunk of my car for a fortnight.' He kisses me on the forehead.

Pulling out of his embrace, I hug the book to my chest and then eye him suspiciously. 'There are hundreds of books in Scriptum. How did you know which one I wanted?'

'I noticed the black cover and silver edges, I saw where you put it down, and it matches your copy of *Jane Eyre*. What kind of lawyer would I be if that was insufficient evidence? Plus, I'm aware of the deponent's freaking obsession to have everything matching. So there was motive as well, m'lud.'

'You're good.'

'That's why they pay me so much. But this was a straight-forward verdict: coveting thy Shelley. You looked guilty the

218

moment you walked down the stairs, caressing its cover like a dead bird with its head Sellotaped on.' J does an impression of me stroking the book. 'Pretty bird. Pretty bird.'

I nudge him.

'In truth,' he says, 'it was still sitting where you left it. The shop hadn't put it back on the shelf.'

'Well, however you figured it out, I love it.'

And later, when we're curled up together watching *Friends* reruns, my day doesn't feel anywhere near as bad. And it's because of him. Because he's sitting on the sofa next to me with his hand resting on my knee and my cold feet tucked under his thigh. And I know that, whatever Maria reveals about J's condition, I'll be able to cope with it.

Because nothing could change how I feel about this man.

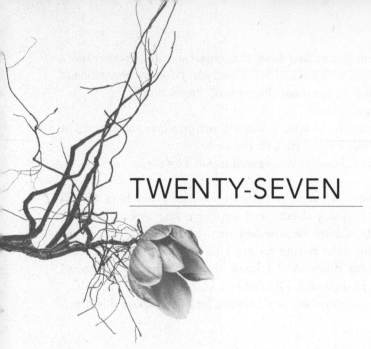

TWENTY-SEVEN

MARIA COMES INTO 1855 in her uniform. As if being in plain clothes doesn't turn enough heads. 'I can't stop,' she says. 'I'm on nights and on my way in.'

'Can I get you a drink?'

'No, thanks. No time.'

'This couldn't wait?' She stares at me and I add, 'You got them, didn't you?'

'Yeah.'

'What is it? What did you find?'

She sits down. 'Well, he's been on lithium for as far back as his medical records go. By that I mean since he moved to England when he was twenty-six. He registered with a GP in London but never had his notes sent across from the USA. So that's as far back as I've been able to go. For now, anyway.'

'What for? What's he taking it for?' She doesn't speak. She reaches across the table and puts her hand on mine. 'Maria?'

'Is that Coke?'

I nod.

'Can I have a sip?' She doesn't wait for me to answer but lets go of my hand and downs half the glass.

'I can get you a drink—'

'No, I really can't stay.'

'Just tell me.' She doesn't say anything. 'Maria, for fuck's sake, just tell me.'

'J has multiple personality disorder.'

I stop breathing.

My legs turn to jelly.

I barely hear her when she says, 'Though they call it dissociative identity disorder now. I'm so sorry, Ev.' She takes my hand again. 'I never expected it to be so serious. I've been doing some reading...'

Her voice evaporates in a mist. She must have pulled the wrong file. I interrupt her. 'There must be some mistake. They sent you someone else's records.'

'They're right, Ev. There's no mistake. I never would have thought it. When I met him in court and at the party, he seemed so...together.'

'Yes, he does.' My voice doesn't sound like mine. It doesn't feel as if it's coming from my mouth. It's as if I'm hearing it on a recording. 'I guess the lithium is keeping him together.'

'I guess so.' Maria rambles on about MPD or DID and how many personalities can hide in the mind of one person, but my own mind has detached from the conversation. It comes back when she says, 'I have a contact in the USA who's pulling his medical records over there. I should have them in a day or two.'

'How could I not know?' My heart is beating so fast it's hard to breathe. I'm hot and light-headed. 'I mean, who lives with someone with multiple personality disorder and doesn't even notice? Am I that self-absorbed?'

'No, Ev. He's managed to keep it from everyone, not just you – his work colleagues and friends. He's obviously really good at hiding it. Or the lithium's doing its job and keeping him in check.'

'But I'm a surgeon, for fuck's sake. I can tell a dog's in pain by the way it licks its lips. Yet I can't tell my own husband has a serious mental illness?' I realise now how completely immersed I was in the surgery. I see my old self as a dervish whirling through life, unable to focus on anything around her.

'He wasn't your patient, Ev. In an examining room, you're a diagnostician. The owner tells you something's wrong, and you're on the hunt for symptoms. Out of the surgery, on the street, you'd see a dog lick its lips and just think it was thirsty.' She looks at the door, then at her watch and says, 'Fuck, I shouldn't have told you like this. I didn't think it could wait, but now I have to go. I'm such an idiot, what the fuck was I thinking? I can't leave you like this. I'll call in.'

'No, no, don't. I'm all right.' That's a lie but I need a moment alone. 'You were right to tell me straight away. You go to work. I'll be fine.'

Maria gets up, pulls me into a hug and holds me tight. As she walks out of the bar, I stare dumbly at her back, at her black body armour.

It's like a death.

Like finding out that someone close to you is gone. Your brain dumps a chemical overload of emotions into your bloodstream until every cell in your body is turgid with it. Every organ, overwhelmed by chemistry, ceases to perform its function. Your knees buckle. You can't see straight. You can't breathe or think. You're blindsided.

I'm blindsided.

222

TWENTY-EIGHT

TEDDY JUMPS ALL over me when I walk through the door and J comes out of his study to greet me.

'You're home early.'

'Maria had to go to work.' I paste on a smile and have to hold myself back from screaming, *Why the fuck didn't you tell me?*

Get it together, Ev.

'That's a shame,' he says. 'I was expecting you to come back drunk so I could take advantage of you.' He pulls me in for a hug.

'Sorry to disappoint you.'

'Did you have a good day?'

'Fine.' My voice cracks and I swallow hard. 'Fine, you?'

Jacob smiles a broad, boyish grin. 'Are you okay? You seem weird.'

'I'm fine.'

'That's a lot of fines.'

'Just three.' I pull out of the hug and go into the kitchen, Teddy and J hot on my heels. Mechanically, I say, 'Any thoughts on dinner?'

Then I reach into the fridge for a beer, partly to calm my nerves and partly to hide my face long enough to mould it into a more convincing mask. Fuck! I'm not allowed to drink. Screw it, I have to drink something. I grab a bottle.

I can't talk to him. I can't say anything. And it's ridiculous that I'm supposed to pretend there's nothing wrong. But, given the way I found out, the methods I've used, I can't say a word without exposing myself.

I gulp down mouthfuls of lager and instantly feel terrible about it.

'It's a nice evening,' he says. 'Why don't we walk Teddy down to the Cape and have dinner there? You can tell me all about your *fine* day. We could sit in the garden.'

I stare at him. At the dimples in his smile as he bends down to kiss Teddy on the nose. At the tiny patch of white hair that's taken root in his stubble. Nothing can change how I feel about this man, that's what I told myself only a few days ago.

'What?' He looks up at me while Teddy licks his ears.

'Nothing. I love you, that's all.'

'Because I'm buying you dinner at the Cape? You're only getting fish and chips, you know.'

'I love fish and chips.'

I have no idea what else to say or do. So, I go over and put my arms around him.

TWENTY-NINE

'DO YOU KNOW anything about multiple personality disorder, Saeed?'

I blurt this out just moments after walking through the door, as if it's a ticking bomb and I need Saeed to cut the wire with one second left on the clock.

He sits back in his chair and crosses his arms and legs. He looks smart today, dapper, in a navy linen kurta, white linen trousers and leather sandals. I'm distracted by the dark hair in the V of his shirt and the thick veins on his forearms, exposed by his rolled-up sleeves. I never want to go home. I want to stay here forever, sticking my head in Saeed's sand.

'I have treated a few patients over the years. It is called dissociative identity disorder now. Nightmares are common in DID patients; alters use that time to express the trauma that created them in the first place. Eva, have you been on the internet? You are not self-diagnosing, are you? I know the surgeon in you is looking for a diagnosis—'

'No, no, of course not. Not me. Someone I know has been diagnosed.' I'm reluctant to tell him it's J. Discussing this behind his back feels like a betrayal. I say, 'I'm just trying to find out as much as I can about it. I want to know what it's like for the patient.'

'A friend of yours?'

'Not exactly.'

If I don't tell him it's J, Saeed's advice will be skewed. He'll think he's helping me support someone remote from my life as opposed to the man I live with every day. That betrayal seems suddenly necessary.

'It's Jacob.' His name is hard to get out. The letters tangle around each other and falter on my lips. 'I stumbled on something the other day. One thing led to another and I found out he was diagnosed with MPD – DID – many years ago. I had no idea.'

'It is very rare, Eva. Are you sure?'

'I'm sure. The diagnosis is on his medical records.'

Before I have time to check them, tears fall. Saeed gets up from his chair, pulls a tissue from the box on his desk, and comes to sit on the ottoman.

'It is a manageable condition, Eva. Manageable with—'

'Lithium.' I sniff and wipe my face. 'He's on lithium. I found it hidden in the house.' I picture the safe, buried in the wall, and imagine J on his hands and knees, digging at the solid stones with bloodied fingertips in a frantic effort to conceal this from me.

'And you asked him what it was for?'

'No...um...a friend, she...let's not get into how I found out. I just did.'

Saeed's eyes bore into me, but he says, simply, 'Why did you not just ask Jacob about the pills when you found them?'

I can't stand him looking at me like that, so I leap up from the sofa to get away from his penetrating gaze. Wringing my hands, I pace the rug as if I'm already incarcerated, being punished for going behind Jacob's back. And now I'm discussing his condition with a complete stranger instead of him.

'I was scared.'

'Of Jacob?'

'Yes. Well...no. I don't know. What I don't understand is how I didn't know. We've been together for five years. What kind of person doesn't notice her husband is suffering from a serious mental illness?'

'There you go again, judging yourself unfairly. It is not easy to diagnose, Eva. It is often missed entirely by professionals who specialise in the field.'

I stop pacing. 'Really?'

'Really. It is not unusual for the DID sufferers themselves to be unaware of their own condition. Please, come and sit down.'

I edge through the narrow gap between the ottoman and the sofa and sit back down. I'm tired, dizzy and cold. I'm always cold when I'm tired, as if my body doesn't have the energy to heat itself. His eyes, which never leave me, are the only warm thing in the room, and I fix on them.

'Mental conditions are very complex, Eva. It is not always apparent. It is only when the alter is distinctly different, a child for example, that diagnosis is easier, because the patient's demeanour, voice and vocabulary noticeably change. But, if the alters are the same sex and age, DID is often misdiagnosed. Or confused with other conditions like bipolar. Please, Eva, do not be so hard on yourself. It often happens that a spouse is unaware for many, many years.'

I think about the first day I walked into this office. The memory smarts. I hear my derisive tone, talking about therapy and dream psychology. Now, if someone told me I couldn't see Saeed again, I think I'd unravel.

I try to relax. Calm myself. Stop being so hard on myself.

It's true that Jacob's alter is not so different from J. Darker, perhaps. Mercurial. Quick to anger. But his demeanour doesn't change. His voice and vocabulary don't change. So, if a professional would struggle to diagnose a case like his, perhaps I shouldn't hate myself so much for being blind. And why would it have ever occurred to me that J had more than one personality? They both look like my husband, move and talk like my husband, so why would I ever think I was essentially living with two men? I just thought J had bad days, bad moods.

It's ridiculous. I don't really believe it. I still think Maria pulled the wrong file.

Reluctantly, I ask, 'What's it like? For J, I mean.'

'I do not know. How can we know what happens in the mind of any other person, let alone a DID sufferer?'

'I get that. But I need to understand him. I have to know what this means for me and the baby. I need to be prepared.'

Saeed worries his stubble. 'I cannot discuss specific patients but, if you like, I can share some experiences from clinical studies, since these have been published.'

I lean in close as if we're sharing something confidential.

He says, 'DID is the fragmenting of someone's personality into two or more distinct personality states. It is usually caused by some sort of trauma.'

'You mean, something bad happened to Jacob?'

Saeed pauses, his voice turns soft and low. 'Most likely, yes. And it is usually *severe* trauma. Violence, war, sexual or physical abuse. A reaction to an experience too painful to endure.'

I push my knuckles into my eye sockets and rub hard, scrubbing away the tears before they have a chance to fall. Jacob never talks about his childhood and this must be why. I know his parents died when he was young; perhaps that was the cause. Maybe he saw them die. And, as horrific as that sounds, I'd rather that were true. Because the idea of Jacob suffering physical or sexual abuse is too much to bear. I dig into the roots of my hair and scratch. I hate myself for what's already crossing my mind: that there might be something in the police records, something Maria could find.

228

'These alters,' I ask. 'Are they aware of each other?'

'Not necessarily. Each alter can lead a separate life, completely unaware of the experiences of the others. They may have no memory of what happens during their time in an alter's psyche.'

'Is that why he forgets things? Things I've told him? Evenings we've spent together?'

J always blames his forgetfulness on too much drink, or too much on his mind, and I've never questioned it.

Saeed says, 'Perhaps. In fact, it is possible for alters to be so distinctly separate from one another that they have completely unique responses. Even bodily functions like blood pressure, blood flow and pulse rate.'

'That's incredible.'

'It is.' Saeed is fascinated by this condition, I can tell. Maybe he even admires it. 'It is easier to understand if you see them as completely different people. Because, in essence, they are. It is not just their demeanour that may change; their morals, beliefs and emotional responses can be vastly different too. Each personality may respond to stimuli in different ways. They may even have their own name and will not respond to the name of the primary.'

I try to recall if he's ever flinched at me calling him Jacob. But I rarely call him that. I call him J. I rewind the footage of the last five years, replaying my marriage like a film I've seen but didn't pay attention to. I rerun scenes with an insight into J that I didn't have before.

I ask, 'And what makes them switch?'

'Stress, conflict, trauma. Sometimes it can be a simple trigger like a familiar sound that sparks a memory. Alters can switch in moments or days.'

It isn't that the pieces of my marriage are falling into place, it's more as though I'm rising above it, staring down at it with a wider perspective. And, viewing it from this angle, I can see it for what it really is.

I think stress is J's trigger. When J has a difficult day, when he has to spend hours with murderers who slice women to pieces, his alter steps in. If J suffered violence as a child, violence horrific enough to split his personality, then looking at photographs of a woman surgically dissected while conscious is probably too much for him to bear.

And I feel as if I've been spending more and more time with this alternate personality. Since J got the partnership, things have got much worse. If stress is the trigger, that would explain it. The partners have assigned him nothing but difficult and disturbing cases since they offered it to him. Sure, he had his bad days before the partnership, times when he was distant and cold. But, these days, he's angry and hostile.

I rest my head on the back of the sofa and close my eyes for a moment. Though I've managed to avoid throwing up most mornings, the nausea is constant. And all this information is making my head swim. I make fists. My hands shake almost constantly now, and it's been going on so long, the jittering is now part of me.

'It is a lot to take in.' Saeed briefly reaches a hand towards me and then takes it away. I want him to throw his professionalism to the winds and hold me, tell me that everything is going to be all right and stop me feeling so scared. 'It is not something to be afraid of, Eva. It is a very effective device. Our minds are incredible in this regard. To be able to develop such a coping mechanism.'

I've never seen Saeed so animated. I'm half expecting him to pump his fists in the air, cheering for the condition my husband is suffering from. He says, 'Many sufferers claim they would not have survived their childhood trauma had it not been for their alter.'

'You mean, it protects them?'

'Exactly. The alter is often more aggressive and fearless. They take over the mind so the primary can disappear. And this dissociation is often so effective that primaries either do not remember the trauma at all or are able to talk about it as if it happened to someone else entirely. Because, in their mind, it did. DID has an unfair reputation, when it is actually a powerful defence mechanism. It enables people to retain their sanity in the face of the worst possible pain and madness.'

I imagine Jacob's alter, this more aggressive, fearless man, stepping in when J was forced to endure something terrible. And I'm suddenly struck by a new feeling. One that surprises me. Not fear, but affection, born out of gratitude.

'Can it be cured?'

'Psychotherapy can help. A therapist trained in DID can coax the alters out into the open where they can work through the trauma together. And, if the alters collaborate willingly, they can be reunited under one personality.'

'And if that doesn't work?'

'Then patients can be taught strategies to deal with situations that tend to cause a switch. Drugs can be used. Antidepressants, anti-anxiety meds. And lithium – as you know – can suppress personality-switching.'

'How? How does it do that?' I need to understand what might happen if J stopped taking it.

'It decreases anxiety and boosts serotonin. But of course, it is a catch-all. By dampening feelings of anxiety and stress, it also dampens the imagination, impulsivity and one's ability to express oneself. It moderates the temperament.'

Fortunately, J doesn't appear to suffer from these side effects. On the contrary, he's bright and alive. I doubt he would be able to do his job so effectively if lithium had such a negative effect on his temperament.

'What can I do? If I can't get him to go to therapy, I mean.'

'You have lived with Jacob's condition for many years, Eva. You must be doing something right. Love and attention are key. Empathy and understanding. But most important is to interact with his alter as an individual and separate person rather than pretending he does not exist.'

231

'I can do that.'

I'm determined to do that.

J's alter is less romantic, capricious, a little hard around the edges, especially in bed. But now I know *why* he's here – *that* he's here – I can get to know him. I can adjust how I interact with him. I can be more loving and supportive. Already, I admire his strength for stepping in to take Jacob's pain. And, as Saeed says, I've lived with him for years, loved him, perhaps. Just as I have lived with and loved Jacob.

I just wish he had told me.

Saeed says, 'It is important not to make Jacob feel bad about his condition, accuse him of lying if he cannot recall certain events, or become confrontational over behavioural changes.'

I breathe in deeply as if it's the first breath I've taken in days. I'm no longer blindsided. I'm less afraid of it now. Perhaps it could even be exciting to live with two different men. I could pretend, when I'm around Jacob's alter, that he's my other husband, my bold and fearless lover. Of course, that fantasy would be easier to maintain if he looked different, if he could have a different haircut or shave his beard. It would be easier to adjust if I knew which Jacob had come home.

Then I realise I already do know. I know which Jacob has walked through the door by the sounds he makes in the hallway. And Teddy knows too. Suddenly my life – this new life – is starting to make sense. Nothing can change the way I feel about J and, in time, once I've adjusted, I'll come to love his alter equally. After all, who wouldn't love the man who has protected Jacob all these years?

'DID can be very difficult,' says Saeed. 'But the more you come to understand it, the easier it will be. This condition is not a choice for Jacob. It is for you, however.'

'You're not suggesting I leave him? I can't leave him, I love him.'

'No, I am not suggesting that. But you have been through a lot yourself, Eva. And you cannot make your own needs negotiable in order to support him. The important thing is that Jacob is managing his condition. His DID is not impeding him. It is a blessing that it has had such an inconsequential effect on both your lives – to the extent that you have not even detected it, and Jacob has not felt the need to share it with you. But you must find your own peace and stability before you can help him find his.'

Saeed is right. And now I'm more determined than ever to get my life back on track. For Jacob's sake and the baby's.

'It is unlikely,' he says, 'though not impossible, that Jacob can be completely cured. So, you cannot sacrifice yourself for him when doing so will not heal his wounds anyway. And, to that end, I would like us to revisit the bedroom another time. Do you feel up for that?'

I don't. But I nod anyway.

THIRTY

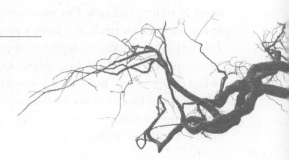

'EV, IT'S MARIA.'

It's only been a week since I met her at 1855. I wasn't expecting to hear from her so soon. 'Hey. Is everything okay?'

'My contact in the USA pulled Jacob's medical records there.'

Maria's tone is professional and serious, as if she's talking to a suspect or a victim. After my session with Saeed yesterday, I've been shoring myself up. Positively spinning what began as a nightmare into something that could bring J and me closer, make our marriage stronger. Now I'm afraid whatever Maria has to say will bring me crashing back down.

But I set this train in motion. I can't stop it now.

Leaning against the kitchen island, I slide down to the floor and soak up the warmth of the underfloor heating. The day is overcast, and there's a chill in the air. It's only September, so the central heating's off. It feels more like a winter's day.

Teddy comes over and curls close to my legs. I rub his warm tummy and say to Maria, 'That was quick.' I'm not sure

I'm ready to hear what she has to say. I've only just come to terms with our last conversation.

'Yeah, he owes me a few. He dug up records from 1994 but nothing before that, which is odd. There should be records from birth.'

'That is odd.'

'He's gonna dig a little deeper, but what I have looks to be the most interesting stuff anyway. It looks like a Violet Curtis first took Jacob to see a Dr Brian E. Warner in Douglasville on the 16th of April 1994.' The sound of ruffling pages drifts down the line as Maria sorts through what I assume is a printout of J's medical records. 'It looks like he went every week for about six months. The doctor's notes say he went willingly and proved to be "a cooperative, amiable and intelligent boy".' Maria's tone tells me she read that word for word.

I picture J with this Dr Warner, fresh-faced, with thick hair falling across his eyes. I ask, 'Are there any photographs?'

'No. Just typed records.'

A long time ago, when J first told me his parents had died, I asked if he had any pictures from when he was a boy. But he said his parents had very little money and couldn't afford a camera. It was weird to me. I mean, who doesn't have photographs of themselves as a baby or child? It makes me wonder if this woman was a loving mother. She obviously cared enough to get him to a psychiatrist when he needed help. And that must have been difficult to afford if they couldn't even buy a camera.

'Does it say what Jacob was like in these sessions?'

She flicks through the pages, and I think she's deciding what to read out and what to hold back. 'It says, "Jacob's alternate personality most often presents itself under stress, particularly when subjected to in-depth questioning."'

'That makes sense,' I say. 'Stress can induce a personality switch.'

'There's a description of Jacob's alter, but I'm not sure you wanna hear it.'

'No, I do. Read it.'

'It says, "When subjected to adversarial questioning, Jacob's demeanour changes. He slumps in the chair, his eyes narrow and darken, and his voice deepens."'

I've seen those eyes. Marble-hard.

She goes on, '"Jacob, in his alter-ego state, is sullen and argumentative. He subjects me to verbal attacks and taunts me with personal insults which are very upsetting. His alter is crass, rude, cruel, and bullying." This psychiatrist sounds like a big girl's blouse if you ask me.'

I know that Jacob's alter can be sullen and argumentative. Perhaps even a little rude at times. But a cruel bully seems a step too far. Of course, he was very young. And this description of him is before he started taking lithium. I've never really pushed Jacob in his alter state. I try not to be disagreeable when he's in what I thought was one of his moods. I capitulate to sex and let him get his own way, largely. I wonder what would happen if I subjected him to 'adversarial questioning'. Have I yet to meet this cruel bully?

'It says, "In his alter-ego state, Jacob insists on smoking cigarettes in the consulting room, despite being asked repeatedly to extinguish them. But when he returns to his original personality, he immediately puts them out." There's lots more stuff like that, but it's all much of a muchness.' She doesn't speak for a while and I listen as the papers whisper. 'Jeez, when the doctor describes these instantaneous switches between Jacob's personalities, it's pretty creepy. And, Ev—' She says my name like she's about to deliver something abominable. 'His alter-ego even has a name.'

I hold my breath.

'It's Victor.'

That name feels wrong. My skin writhes at the sound of it. I've just begun to adjust to the mercurial side of Jacob – to see that personality as a separate person – but, when she says that name, I almost feel like I have a third husband: Victor.

236

I wonder if Victor flinches every time I call him Jacob or J.

Maria goes on. 'After a few months of seeing Jacob, the psychiatrist was in no doubt that he had two distinct personalities. And he confirms his initial suspected diagnosis of MPD.'

It's a relief that I only have two to deal with. I'm not sure I could handle any more.

'Dr Warner prescribed lithium. And it says, "Jacob has responded incredibly well to the medication." It looks as if he carried on seeing this doctor for another three months but after that, he was discharged because he was "managing his MPD so successfully".'

'That's a bit bizarre, isn't it? Why would you discharge a patient with MPD? It's hardly something you can cure in a few months.'

'Sounds to me like this shrink got sick of being picked on. Pussy.'

I try to process it all. That description of Victor has me on edge.

Cruel.

Bully.

'Ev? Eva? Are you okay?'

'No, of course I'm not okay. If the only thing standing between you and some psycho bully were a few fucking pills, would you be okay?' I feel sick at my own words, regretting the word 'psycho' the moment it spills out. Spits out is more like it, and I hate myself. I didn't mean it.

'That's a bit dramatic, Ev. He's not a psycho. He's someone who's had mental distress in the past, it's been treated and now he's cured. Just make sure you never hide his lithium tablets. Well, unless you fancy an evening with bully-boy Victor.'

'That's not funny, Maria.'

'No, I guess not. Sorry.'

I don't say anything.

'Ev. I really am sorry.'

237

'It's okay. I appreciate you doing this for me. I know you've put your job on the line. I won't forget it. I really owe you one.'

'Actually, you owe me two now. And you know I'm the kinda girl who'll hold you to it.'

'Well, I don't have a job I can risk for you, but no doubt you'll think of something.'

'No doubt.'

'Maria. There is one more thing,'

'Oh, fuck! Is it something else that's gonna get me fired?'

'Nothing worse than you've already done.'

'Go on then, lay it on me.'

'I spoke to my therapist and—'

'You're seeing a therapist?'

'Yes. Don't panic, I'm not going nuts or anything. He's a sort of sleep psychologist. I've been having restless nights and bad dreams. But he may be able to help me with J's condition as well. He's worked with DID patients in the past. He says it's usually caused by some sort of trauma in childhood. Violence, sexual assault, that sort of thing.'

'Fuck. You mean Jacob...'

'Maybe. Whatever it was must have been pretty horrific. I was hoping you could delve a little deeper. Find out if there's anything on record of him being involved in some sort of trauma. Perhaps something to do with the death of his parents. Can you find out how they died and whether Jacob was there when it happened? Whether he witnessed anything that could have triggered this?'

'He hasn't told you anything?'

'No. He won't talk about his childhood. His parents died when he was eleven. I think he might have been there. It's the most likely thing to have triggered his DID.'

'Eleven? His parents died when he was eleven?'

'Yeah, why?'

I hear the pages ruffle again as she flicks back through them. 'The report says he first saw the psychiatrist in 1994.

He would have been thirteen. If J's mother died when he was eleven...'

'Oh my God, you're right! Then who was – what did you say her name was again?'

'Violet.'

'As in, Vi.'

'I guess...why?'

'Remember I told you I thought he was having an affair? I caught him on the phone to a woman named Vi. He said it was a client. Same surname, so she must be an aunt or something. His father's sister maybe?'

'But why lie? Why not just *say* he was on the phone to his aunt?'

'I don't know. He told me he didn't have any family left in America.'

'Odd.'

'Yeah. Can you look into her as well?'

'I s'pose. But you're gonna owe me so big after this.'

THIRTY-ONE

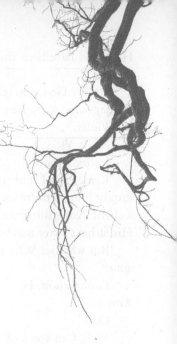

THAT TINY SOUND – the click of the front door latch – has power now. It stalls the rhythm of my heart. And my heart won't beat as it should until every sound that follows it has run its course. The requiem of J's arrival must hit its last note before I can breathe again.

It lets me know which of my husbands has come home.

Since I spoke to Maria on Friday and she told me about Victor, I haven't seen him. Jacob has been here the whole weekend – though he was called into work this afternoon for some crisis meeting – and I know from the melody playing out in the hallway that it's still him tonight as well. Given how stressed and upset he was about having his Sunday interrupted, I was half-expecting Victor.

My heart returns to normal sinus rhythm.

By Tuesday, Maria should have the file on Jacob from before he was diagnosed. I'm meeting her at 1855 and the wait is killing me. My parents are coming to dinner tomorrow, and I keep toying with the idea of cancelling. I have no idea

240

how I'll get through it. Waiting to find out what split my husband in two feels like being shoved from an aeroplane at forty thousand feet, falling from the sky, just waiting to hit the runway.

I paste on a smile when he comes in the kitchen and finds mess everywhere. I'm no good at tidying up as I go. Cooking takes every ounce of concentration I have, and if I try to clean up at the same time I'll burn something while pandering to the perfectionist who scrubs everything spotless. I blame her for being a terrible cook. She prepares food so cleanly, follows recipes so precisely, that everything she cooks tastes clean. J says my food is tasteless because it's not dirty enough.

'Looks like you've gone to town,' he says. 'What's the occasion?'

'Boredom.' That's a lie. I needed something to distract my raging mind.

'I didn't realise it was Boredom Day.' He kisses me. 'I thought that was on the 29th.'

'No, it's today, and I've made your favourite.'

'Scotch eggs?'

'Yep.'

They're one of the few things I can actually cook well – especially when I have things on my mind – because they require no intuition or interpretation whatsoever. For a culinary-challenged person like me, there's nothing more frustrating than recipes that say 'season to taste' or 'add a pinch of salt' or 'cook until golden brown'. After two hours in the kitchen, I can't taste my own food, I can pinch a fairly hefty amount of salt, and there's a whole spectrum of golden brown between underdone and burnt. I like precision. And this recipe is so precise it's almost surgical. It provides exact temperatures, accurate measurements and strict timings. If Teddy had opposable thumbs, even he could cook them.

'They'll be ready in ten.' I slide the tray into the oven. 'Go and get changed.'

Jacob kisses me again and says in a slow, American drawl, 'Awwll right then, missy, oy'll just go-an slip inta sumthin' more comfortable.'

I shake my head. That John Wayne impression's so bad.

J comes back in the kitchen wearing his ninja T-shirt and tartan pants.

With the kitchen tap running, I scrub sticky breadcrumbs from beneath my fingernails and say, 'There's a fine line between comfort and sloth.'

'Well?' he says.

'Well what?'

'Ask me.'

'J, dinner's nearly ready.' I wipe my hands on the tea towel tucked in my apron. I have no idea how to do this. How to play his games. How to be one Eva on the outside – calm and unaffected – and a different Eva jittering inside. 'I'm not asking you.'

'Go on, ask me.'

'Not a chance in hell. I'll never ask you.'

'Go-aaaan! Ask me.'

I stare at him in that stupid T-shirt and those ridiculous pants. I told myself I would adjust to whichever of my husbands came home, and already I'm failing. I have to silence this anxious and capricious Eva; her seriousness is better suited to Victor. I need to find the old me, the Eva who danced in the garden at Belmond and considered twerking naked at J's Summer Ball.

I take a deep breath and say, 'All right, then. Tell me about your ninja disguise.'

J flips the T-shirt over his head but before he has a chance to grab me I bolt away from him. He chases after me and I run around the kitchen island, laughing – actually laughing for one brief moment. Gripping the edge of the worktop, I propel myself forward just as J grabs the hem of my shirt and pulls me back. But then his socks slip on the marble tiles and he falls flat on his face. I burst into a fit of snorting giggles. 'Some ninja you are!'

He groans on the floor. 'I'll have to work on my moves.'

I get down, lie on top of him and kiss him. Not passionately, but as a talisman against further pain. It's hard to believe that someone as funny and easygoing as J has survived something so traumatic that he needed Victor to deal with it. He's so strong, so together. But maybe Victor keeps him together. Maybe, without Victor, he wouldn't be the husband I have come to love. He'd be someone else entirely. Someone broken.

I kiss him again but feel the moment slipping. The other Eva is fighting for air, dragging me down in her bid for the surface. My part in J's skit feels suddenly over-rehearsed. Stilted. As if I've been put together piece by piece without attention to detail or pride in the work. I function, but the parts grind, as if I need a good spray with WD40. If I told J that, he'd crack some joke about his tight nuts or rusty tool and I'd laugh and feel better for a moment.

But then the moment would pass.

I'm no longer the Eva who used to creep up behind him while he was cooking Porterford's and make hackneyed innuendos about the size of his sausages. Because although Jacob is still Jacob – and Victor is still Victor – I am no longer me.

Everything's changed. Those malignant cells divide, over and over, consuming me until there's nothing left but a dysfunctional body.

Will I soon be gone for good?

'Hey. What's with the face? You okay?'

'I'm fine.' I kiss him, get up, and pull him to his feet.

I need to tell him.

Everything.

About the baby, about finding the pills. And I will tell him, but not tonight. Maria will be calling me as soon as she can with J's background check, and I'll have the last puzzle pieces to make the picture whole. And then, on Thursday, I'll see Saeed. I have no idea how to even begin telling Jacob the things I've done, and the things I know, but, if anyone can guide me through it, Saeed can. I'll feel stronger after seeing him. I always do. So that's my plan.

Friday night, when J gets home from work, I'll tell him everything.

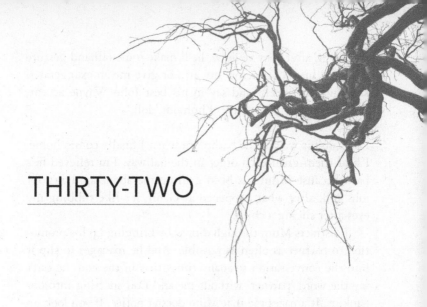

THIRTY-TWO

My mother marches through the door while removing her coat as if there's some emergency that needs attending to. She lays her coat across my arm, as though I'm her butler, then kisses me on both cheeks as if she didn't vote for Brexit. Usually it's J who plays coat-hook, but he's running late tonight.

My dad, by contrast, saunters in behind, kisses me on one cheek and squeezes me until I blow a raspberry. Then he gets down on his knees and ruffles Teddy's ears. I love that Dad greets him like a hairy grandson. It irks me that Mum greets him as if he's taxidermy. If I weren't such a disappointment and there were a baby sleeping in a cot in the hallway, of course she would stop and coo. But, in my mother's eyes a dirty brown dog might as well be a plague-infested rat. She doesn't realise that the plague-infested rat *is* my baby.

I hope J doesn't take too long, because he's great at holding me together around Mum. He'll squeeze my knee if he suspects I'm losing my temper. Instead of being annoyed by his mother-in-law, as most husbands would be, he finds her highly entertaining and takes a great deal of enjoyment from her. Later, after they've gone, he'll make some offhand gesture of laying his jacket across my arm or give me an exaggerated kiss on both cheeks and say in his best John Wayne accent, 'Don't ever lose your sense of humour, doll.'

Dad's on his way to the bathroom when J finally comes home. I hear them greet each other in the hallway. I'm relieved he's back because Mum has been grilling me about applying for jobs and, after what happened at Genii, it's like rubbing my eyes after slicing a chilli.

J distracts Mum through dinner by bringing up his promotion to partner as often as possible. And he manages to slip it into the conversation so many times that in the end, he can't say the word 'partner' without me and Dad snorting into our napkins. It amazes me that Mum doesn't notice. If you look up 'abstracted' in the dictionary, you won't find a definition, it'll just say 'Patricia Cosgrove'. But J's partnership is clearly a buoy in the drowning sea that is her unemployable, childless daughter.

When J makes Dad laugh, I'm conscious of joining in with too much enthusiasm. I hear myself fake-laughing. It's because Dad has always been a bit reserved with J, so I love seeing them relaxed in each other's company.

I remember the first night I took him to meet my parents. When we said goodbye at the door, Dad hugged me tight and whispered, 'Hang on to that one.' Naturally, I just blew a raspberry in his ear. But his warmth for J has waned over the years, just a little. Dad's an astute man, a nurse who's as sensitive to ailments in people as I am in animals. I wonder if he's noticed the inconsistencies in J's personality. Perhaps that's what's held him back from fully embracing Jacob as the son-in-law he'd always dreamed of.

I'm loading the dishwasher when Dad comes into the kitchen and says, 'Can you believe it? She's still grilling him about his promotion.'

'Yes, I can.'

In silence, he rinses the plates while I load them, and I can tell he's waiting for the right moment to say something.

In the end, I can't wait any longer. 'All right. Out with it.'

'You're pregnant.'

Dirty dinner plate in hand, I stand upright. If I'd been given three guesses as to what was going to come out of his mouth, I would have been a hundred guesses short.

'Dad, I...'

He just smiles his broad, cheeky smile.

'How did you know?'

'You're wearing it like a billboard.'

'Please don't tell Mum. I'm not ready to tell anyone yet. I haven't even told J.'

'He must be blind. Why haven't you told him yet?'

I can't tell Dad about J's DID. Not yet. Not until I understand it myself. I don't want to diminish J in my dad's eyes. I know that's silly. I know Dad won't think any less of him. But I so badly want him to regain the affection he felt for J when they first met. Also, with his nursing background, Dad would want to help. And J clearly isn't ready for that.

So I go with my trusty line, 'The timing hasn't been right. He's under so much pressure with this murder trial; I don't want to add to it. I'll tell him when he can properly enjoy the news.'

'By the time that trial ends, you'll be the size of a pot-bellied pig.'

'Thanks!'

'He's going to notice, Ev. And then he'll be angry that you kept it from him.'

'I know. I'll tell him soon.'

'J does want this baby, doesn't he?'

'Of course he does. You know how long we've been trying. It's just, I don't want to add to his already-full plate right now. I want to break the news when he's not under pressure. When he won't see it as a burden.'

247

'A burden?'

'I didn't mean it like that. Of course J won't see a baby as a burden. It's just that, since he took the partnership, the firm's been throwing a lot of shit his way. It's not just this murder trial. It's like they're using him as a dumping ground for all the difficult cases.'

'One day he'll be doing the same to the next new partner.'

'I guess so.'

'But, in the meantime, he'll have to find a way to balance his job with fatherhood.'

'He'll manage.' I imitate J – 'He's uber-efficient!' – in an attempt to lighten the mood, but it doesn't work. 'He'll get through this. He's a good man, Dad.' But I sound as though I'm trying to convince myself as much as my father.

'I know he is.' I hear the reservation in his tone.

'Look, I know J has his bad days and his bad moods but honestly, Dad, he's a good man who's just going through a lot right now.'

'I know, honey.' He leans over the dishwasher and rubs my arm. 'But you're going through a lot too. And he should be supporting you, not the other way around.'

'We're supporting each other.'

Teddy muscles between us to lick the cutlery in the dishwasher and I use him to divert Dad's focus, saying, 'At least when I'm having a bad day I have Teddy. When J's having a bad day, we both stay out of his way. Poor J has to cope alone.'

'Not only when he's having a bad day, it seems.'

'What do you mean?'

'When J came home tonight, Teddy bolted upstairs. He wouldn't go near him.'

'Really?'

'Really.'

I grip the plate in my hand.

That's not J in the dining room with my mother.

It's Victor.

248

I'd been convinced I could tell which of my husbands came home from the sounds they make in the hallway. But now I realise I don't always get it right. Instantly, I'm on edge, wondering if the person in the dining room could snap at any moment and my parents will see the dark side of J.

Suddenly, his DID looms larger than it ever has. I still haven't come to terms with it myself, and it already feels like more than I can cope with. I haven't had time to consider the impact it could have on the other people in our lives.

Do patients develop a resistance to lithium over time? I have no idea. I'm still learning. And, now I think about it, J's moods have been getting a lot worse since he got the partnership. I'm suddenly afraid that, at some point in the near future, we could all come face to face with the real Victor: the crass, rude and cruel bully described in J's medical records.

I put down the plate and clasp my belly.

'Are you okay, honey?'

'I'm fine.' I manage a smile. 'I'm fine, Dad.'

'I'm not sure you are. I'm worried about you. I have been for weeks. You're not yourself. All the light has gone out of you. Pregnancy doesn't do that to a woman. It's tiring, of course it is, but at the same time it lights a woman up.'

He navigates the open dishwasher door and pulls me into a hug. I hold on tight. And, for once, I have no enthusiasm for raspberries.

'It's a strange thing.' He kisses the top of my head. 'I remember when your mother was pregnant with you. She'd be throwing up one minute and sleeping like a child the next. But there was always this bright light in her eyes, even when she was exhausted. I know losing your job has been terrible, and I'm not trying to suggest that Jacob isn't being supportive, not by a long chalk. I'm just worried.' He pulls out of the hug and takes my hand but it's trembling, so I casually pull it away and pick up another plate. 'I can't believe I'm going to say this but I think your mother is right. I think you should see someone. A doctor.'

'I've had tests, Dad. Lots of them. I'm fine. It's just the Jack thing. Once the dust settles, I'll be able to go back to work. And besides, I am seeing someone. I'm seeing that psychologist Mum recommended.'

'You are?'

'Yeah. He's good. He's helping.'

Dad closes his eyes briefly. 'That's good. That's good.'

'But for heaven's sake don't tell her. I don't want her running victory laps around my apartment.'

Dad laughs.

'What's taking you two so long? You're missing out on all your mother's gossip.'

I look up at my husband standing in the doorway. Suddenly, I see him in a way I've never seen him before.

I see a completely different person.

I see Victor.

THIRTY-THREE

I GET TO 1855 early and order a glass of prosecco for Maria and an elderflower pressé for me. I'll have to buy every round, so she doesn't ask why I'm not drinking, but, given how much I owe her, it shouldn't be hard to convince her to let me.

When she called this morning to say she had the file, I tried to get her to tell me what was in it, but she insisted we do this in person.

That can't be good.

Maria strides in, not in uniform this time but in black skinny jeans, a blouse and a waistcoat. It's a potent, androgynous look that's intimidating yet oddly protective at the same time. She exudes a flinty resilience, and I find myself not only needing her, but wishing I were more like her. After everything she's been through, she's stronger than I ever imagined possible. And, although I could never be as rudely outspoken as she is on occasion, I feel a little...bland next to her. My life has been so easy by comparison that I haven't really changed as a person; I haven't had to. I've just got older.

Maria's a butterfly.

No, a butterfly is far too fragile.

She's an Atlas moth.

Before she even sits down, I slide the prosecco across the table and ask, 'So, what happened? Was he there when his parents died?'

'Well, hello to you too.' She drops a brown manila folder on the table and slings her handbag across the back of the bar chair.

'Sorry.' I get up, air-kiss her awkwardly, and sit back down. 'It's just, when you said you wanted to do this in person, I figured it couldn't be good.' And the way she looks at me then, I know it isn't.

'He wasn't there.' She takes a gulp of prosecco, then reaches behind her and rummages through her handbag for a pair of reading glasses. I've never seen her in glasses and, if it's possible, the thin black frames toughen her exterior even more. She pulls a stack of papers from the folder and looks down her nose to read. 'They died in a car accident.'

I've imagined dozens of grisly scenarios for how J's parents died. I was half-expecting them to have been murdered right in front of him. A car accident – one he didn't even witness – was not one of them.

She reads snippets from the file. 'They were overtaking a logging truck on the Capps Ferry Road Bridge... The trailer detached itself from the tractor unit and veered into their lane... The accident report says the trailer, loaded with forty tons of logs, forced their car off the bridge into the Chattahoochee River. Then the trailer went over too and crushed them at the bottom.'

'Jesus.'

'Yeah, pretty horrific, right? But I doubt that was the cause of Jacob's DID. He showed no signs until two years later, when he was thirteen.'

'A delayed reaction, maybe?'

252

'It's possible,' she says. 'But it doesn't really fit, not when he wasn't there to witness it.'

She's right. Though the death of both parents must have been unimaginable, it doesn't seem like something that would fracture his mind. 'Something else must have happened to him. While he was living with this Violet.'

'There's nothing in his records from the time he was diagnosed.'

'Then why was it so important to tell me in person? You had me worried.'

She exhales a long breath.

'What? What is it?'

'He's seen a lot of death for one person.'

'Really?'

'Mmm. First his parents. Then, when he was nineteen, a girl in his class went missing.' She flicks to the relevant page. 'They were studying for a Juris Doctor in Law together at Syracuse University. Her name was Sophie Bright. She was last seen driving off campus with an unidentified man. There were rumours that she was seeing Jacob and that she was pregnant. Though that was just campus gossip.'

Maria reads the question chiselled on my face.

'Obviously he was a suspect and he was questioned by the police. But at the time he was in a pub off campus.' She checks the file. 'Faegan's. And was seen by dozens of witnesses. Whoever Sophie drove off with, it wasn't Jacob. She may have been two-timing him and possibly paid for it with her life. But no body was ever found.'

'Fuck. Poor J.'

'That's not the worst of it, Ev. There's more.' She removes her glasses and rubs her eyes. 'Shit, I don't know how to tell you this.'

'What?'

She just looks at me.

'Maria, for fuck's sake.'

'Okay, I'm just going to blurt it out.'

She still doesn't speak.

'Well, go on, then.'

'Jacob was married before.'

A tiny, inaudible sound lodges in my throat.

'His wife, Claudine, committed suicide. Jacob found her in the bathtub with her wrists cut. And, just in case that didn't do the job, she also took a bottle of sleeping pills.' She pauses. 'She was pregnant, Ev. She left Jacob a note saying she didn't want a baby but couldn't live with an abortion either. She said she couldn't see another way out. A neighbour called the cops when they heard Jacob screaming in their apartment. It says in the report that he was unresponsive and inconsolable. Ev...they had to prise her out of his hands.'

I'm barely listening as Maria goes on. I can't get the image out of my head of Jacob clinging to his dead wife and unborn child.

'There's something else too.'

I grab a handful of hair and tug at the roots. 'Jesus, Maria. I'm not sure I can take any more.'

'No, the married part was the worst bit; this is just a small thing. Did you know that Curtis isn't Jacob's real name?'

'No.'

'It's Rathbone. Violet Curtis was his aunt, but she was his mother's sister. She adopted Jacob after his parents died.'

I stare at her, waiting for a punchline. Or something else I don't know about Jacob that's even worse.

'That's why we couldn't find medical records prior to Jacob turning twelve. My friend in the States had been looking into "Curtis" the whole time. It was only when he found the adoption papers that he realised he'd been looking under the wrong name.'

'Fuck. Fuck. What else hasn't he told me?'

At first, I had been reluctant to let Maria look into J's past, it had felt as though we were snooping – we *were* snooping –

but he should have told me all this. I've been lied to my entire marriage. Lied to by omission.

'I guess you can't blame him,' she says. 'Who'd want to talk about all this shit? No wonder he's fucked in the head. Who wouldn't be after all this?'

I'm about to say *He's not fucked in the head*, but I don't.

I want to understand Jacob. I'm trying to understand him. But why has he kept all this from me? Is Maria right and it's too painful to talk about? I don't know anyone who's been through so much. It must have been awful.

I'd planned to tell J everything on Friday and I thought it would help if I knew the trauma he'd been through. But now I know all of this, the secrets he's kept from me, how would I even begin?

I have no idea who I'm married to.

THIRTY-FOUR

I WAKE UP petrified.

Trembling.

In a pool of sweat, my heart tripping out of time, with no memory of what shook me to my core.

I tap my watch and '5:30' glows in the dark. Afraid my heavy breathing will wake J, I creep out of bed, tiptoe into the en suite and shut the door before turning on the light.

That one second of darkness feels like sixty.

J will be up soon and needing to get ready for work, so I sneak in a quick shower. The water runs hot through my hair and down my face as I try to stop my brain from reliving everything that's happened over the last two and a half months. Since Jack, I've been caught in a rip tide, fighting to swim to shore while being dragged out to sea. Every time I think I'm getting a grip, the ocean grabs me by the ankles and pulls me back out again. I close my eyes, tilt my head back, and let the fresh water wash away that salty sea.

I can do this.

I can cope.

I open my eyes and Jacob is standing in front of me, naked.

He holds out his hand, blows me a kiss, and I'm momentarily blinded by a cloud of steam. I blink away water and see that look in his eye. I'm about to tell him he'll be late for work when the water turns unbearably hot.

I swallow metal and bile.

The walls of the shower close in, and I reach out to steady myself. Everything turns black. My knees give way. And J just manages to slide his arms beneath mine before I collapse.

I'm vaguely aware of him carrying me to the bedroom, but it's as if it's happening to someone else and I'm watching from a distance. Only I can't open my eyes and I'm not so much watching this as feeling it.

His voice is distant. 'Here, drink this.'

Cold glass, wet with condensation, connects with my palm. But I'm too nauseous to drink anything, so I groan and push the glass away.

'Drink it,' he says. So I do.

Everything is far off, as though J and I are in different worlds, separated by an endless black space. I have a fleeting thought that it was lucky I showered before he left for work, otherwise I might have collapsed in there alone. And, as the darkness closes in completely, an image burns on the backs of my eyelids: my naked body on the grey-tiled floor, curled up and foetal, hot rain burning my skin until the water tank ran cold.

I open my eyes, and J is sitting next to me on the bed, concern etched into his eyebrows. He's dressed for work. It takes a moment for me to remember where I am. The last thing I recall is him standing in front of me, naked.

'How long have I been out?'

'I don't know. I found you like this.'

'Y...you found me?'

I look around the bedroom. The faint glimmer of dawn bleeds through a small gap in the curtains. The sun comes up around seven, which means I can't have been out for more than a couple of hours.

'You scared me. You wouldn't wake up.' He runs a hand over my hair and I realise it's dry. Dank against the damp pillow, but dry. 'What time did you come to bed?'

'I didn't. You…'

J's shirt isn't freshly pressed. It wears the soft creases of a full day at the office. I look back at the gap in the curtains.

It's not dawn. It's dusk.

I look up at him. His warm eyes wear the strain of the day. Then my mind sparks with the last memory of his eyes, those marble eyes.

That wasn't J.

That was Victor.

This is J.

And he has no memory of me collapsing in the shower.

'I what?' he asks.

'Nothing,' I say, remembering what Saeed said about not challenging him over the things he can't remember. 'Never mind.'

'Can I get you anything?'

'It's all right. I'll get up.'

'No, stay there. I'll bring you up some tea. You rest while I make dinner.'

I manage a smile but inside I'm screaming.

He left me this morning and went to work. He just left me. I passed out in the shower and he didn't even stick around to make sure I was okay. He just put on his suit and went to the office. How could he do that to me? What if something were seriously wrong? What if I hadn't woken up?

My mind unrolls a reel of images: J putting on his shirt, casually poking his cufflinks through the buttonholes in his cuffs; zipping up his trousers and sliding his leather belt through the belt loops; sitting on the edge of the bed, humming a tune while pulling on his socks and shoes. And all the time, right behind him, my unconscious body lay between the sheets. It doesn't feel real. In the five years we've been together, I've never seen this side of J. This isn't him. This isn't even Victor.

Suddenly, I'm afraid.

But a moment later, all the pieces slot into place.

Saeed said stressful situations can cause a switch. When I passed out in the shower, that must have terrified Victor. If the situation had been reversed, if I'd seen J faint in the shower, it would have scared the shit out of me. I wouldn't have known what to do, whether to call an ambulance or wait to see if he came around after a minute or two. And those minutes would have been interminable. Victor must have put me to bed and then switched under the stress. With no memory of what had happened in the shower, Jacob must have assumed I was sleeping and got ready for work as if nothing was wrong.

I sink back into the pillow. He didn't just leave me like that. J would never be so uncaring.

But then worry worms its way back in.

What if J does something like this with the baby? What if he switches personalities while driving to the supermarket on a hot summer's day and forgets the baby is on the back seat? What if he takes the baby out for the day and forgets where he left it after switching personalities?

I curl into a ball and pull the quilt up to my chin. I lay a protective hand over the little passion fruit growing in my belly.

Its vocal cords will start developing this week.

Soon it'll be able to scream as loud as me.

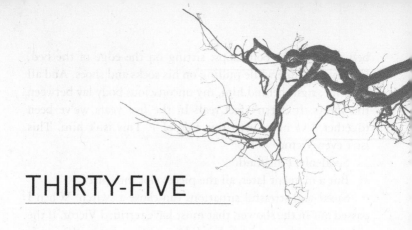

THIRTY-FIVE

'ARE YOU ALL RIGHT, Eva?'

'I'm fine, Saeed, just a little light-headed.'

In truth, my heart's beating an out-of-time quick step and I'm not only pissing like a racehorse every five minutes, I have diarrhoea as well. It's a humid day and despite two showers this morning I'm still sticky, sweaty and smelly. I've brushed my teeth twice but can't get rid of this funky taste and feel as though I've had ten Diet Cokes. It's all fun fun fun in Eva's body right now.

'How have you been sleeping?'

'Not well. I collapsed in the shower yesterday.'

'You collapsed?! Have you seen a doctor?'

'I've got an appointment next week.'

'They could not fit you in earlier?'

I shake my head. 'J left me there. Passed out. He got me out of the shower, put me to bed and then forgot all about me. I think he must have switched personalities. I think Victor helped me into bed and then, in the stress of the moment,

Jacob took over. And with no memory of what had happened, he just got dressed and went to work as if I was sleeping.'

'Who is Victor?'

'That's his name. J's alter.'

'Then you have talked to Jacob about his condition?'

'No. I...I found out.'

'You obtained his medical records...illegally?'

'It wasn't exactly illegal.'

'I am not judging you, Eva. Just asking.'

'No...judgement would be rich coming from the man who chose what was right over what was legal.'

'I did not tell you which choice I made. And you do not know the details of the case, so can we move on?' Saeed pauses, then says, 'It is not unusual, Eva, for a switch to happen so quickly. Especially in a stressful situation. One of my patients used to say it was like driving a car and drifting off, then coming to and wondering who had been steering for the last hour. It was very frightening for her.'

I think about that. I feel as if I'm in the back seat while Jacob and Victor take turns at the wheel. Even though I've been with him for years, Victor feels like a stranger to me. An uninvited guest whose smile sets my teeth on edge, and, now the party's over and it's time for him to leave, I notice his moving boxes by the door. Just the thought of those boxes makes my breath come fast and shallow.

Until he's gone, I won't be able to take a deep breath again.

I open my mouth to speak and close it again. There's something I want to say out loud, but it's something I keep caged deep inside me. And if I set it free, it will fly off through an open window, and I'll never be able to get it back again.

Victor and I both feed it through the bars.

I perch on the edge of the sofa with my knees pressed together. My fingers grip the leather and my hot palms leach its animal-sweat smell. Saeed does that thing where he waits for me to speak, and I know if I look into his nickel-grey eyes they'll bewitch me into confessing something I'm not ready to.

He'll make me open the cage.

I try to think of other things to talk about, but I can't. My mind has been stabbed through with this one terrible thought. I stare at the rug on the floor. It reminds me of the one in our dining room. The colours are different, red instead of pink, but the bold design is similar. The shapes bleed and merge. I feel dizzy and sick.

I smell leather.

I fight it.

I don't want to remember.

Everything goes dark as my mind races through a dream without images. Devoid of sight, sounds amplify. A clack of metal on wood. The chafing of ropes. That animal-sweat smell in my mouth and nostrils, the stink of it chilling my spine. I heave in breaths, turn away from the rug and stare up at the filament bulb. Saeed's eyes watch me with infinite patience, waiting, waiting for me to speak.

I open the cage.

'I'm scared of Victor. Terrified, sometimes. He gets this look in his eyes. Cold. He gets so angry. And I'm afraid that one day he'll lose it completely and...'

As soon as I've said it, I want to take it back. I don't want people to know this about J. I don't want them thinking one bad thing about him. I want them to know the best side of my husband: the man who took me to Prague and cried at the concert; the man who made love to me in the woodsmoke; the man who sang in the garden at Belmond Le Manoir aux Quat'Saisons. Because if they believe that's the only man in my life, maybe I can too.

'DID can be very frightening. For the patient and their loved ones. It does not help that so many books and films portray DID as if there is some evil alter hiding beneath the sufferer waiting to burst out.'

'What if there is?'

'Eva, these books and films…*Psycho*, *Fight Club*, *Split*. They paint a terrible picture of this condition. They are not accurate. It is almost unheard of that a DID sufferer has a psychopathic alter. On the contrary, the alter is usually a very badly damaged child. One who has been given the unhappy task of coping with the bulk of the hurt.'

I try to imagine Victor as a damaged child, taking the brunt of whatever trauma J suffered as a boy.

Saeed says, 'Victor is still Jacob. Although he is the stronger, more aggressive alter, if you trust Jacob not to hurt you, it is highly unlikely that Victor is capable of hurting you either.'

I cling to that. I know it's true. J's moods have never turned aggressive, he's never hurt me. But that thought is instantly supplanted by another: me gripping the chopping board after he was assigned that murder trial. Another: him screaming in my face that he couldn't give a fuck if someone killed Teddy. And another: the man in the alleyway.

That was Victor, subdued by lithium.

My husband is a man altered by chemistry, and the idea that Jacob needs lithium to stop Victor from turning into a crass bully frightens me. But there's another idea that's far more terrifying:

Him not taking it.

Who would he turn into? What kind of man would I come face-to-face with? I'm chilled to the bone by the possibility I'd come face-to-face with a monster. But that's just crazy-making. Saeed is right, and I've seen far too many films.

Saeed gets up from his desk, pulls a thin book from his bookcase and comes to sit on the ottoman. When he hands it to me, I realise it isn't a book but a DVD.

'*The Three Faces of Eve?*'

'I bought it for you. It is the true story of Chris Costner Sizemore, a woman with three personalities. The screenplay was written by the psychiatrists who treated her. Although it is still a fictional portrayal of her life, it is a better representation than some silly horror film. I believe it will assuage some of your fears and give you a better understanding of Jacob's condition.'

'And her name's Eve?'

'Not in real life, but yes, in the adaptation.'

'Seems apt.' I hold it tight to my chest. 'Thank you.'

'I know how overwhelming this must be. But I do not want you to neglect your own recovery in order to support Jacob. We are making such good progress with the lucid dreaming. Do you think you could manage another session?'

I nod.

'Are you sure? You look tired, Eva.'

'I'm fine. I want to keep trying. We're getting so close. And, if I could just get a peaceful night's sleep, perhaps all of this won't be so daunting.'

I lean back, stare at the bulb's filaments and listen to the lilting rhythm of Saeed's speech. And, as if my brain has hacked down overgrown brush to form a well-worn neural pathway, I drift quickly to sleep.

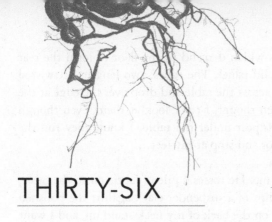

THIRTY-SIX

'GO IN THERE and wait.'

I'm in the hallway, naked beneath a silk bathrobe, staring at the open door to the dining room, and the voice, deep and gruff, comes from behind me. A man's voice.

I do as I'm told.

Mechanically, I walk down the hall, past Teddy's bed at the foot of the stairs. It holds the sunken imprint of his absent form. He's in our bedroom, under the bed. At the door, I stop. I don't want to go in. Buried deep inside me is a woman who wants to strike out and fight, but she's in that far-off place. Tied up and gagged. So I go in.

I don't need to be told what to do. I've done this before. Waiting at one end of the rectangular dining table, I focus on the French polished ebony with its swirling marquetry in pink ivory wood.

I don't look at the ropes.

The chair at my end of the table has been moved aside, but the other nine remain. They have pink wooden bands down

265

their high backs which descend to the floor to form the rear legs from one solid panel. The ropes, two lengths of twisted white nylon, lie across the table and drop over the edge at the far end. And even though I can't look at them, even though I daren't bend to peer under the table, I know they run the length of the floor and stop at my feet.

'Put these on.'

He's behind me. He tosses a pile of fabric on to the table, and the metal clips of a suspender clack against the polished wood. The hairs on the back of my neck stand up, and I want to slap the woman inside me, I want to scream at her to fight back.

But I don't.

And she doesn't.

As if the pattern on the table has me hypnotised, I don't turn around. I'm too terrified to do that. I've done that once before and regretted it. The robe is cinched around my waist and I fumble with the knot, unable to loosen it. I'm afraid of his impatience, so I lift the robe over my head, but the tie is barely loose enough to fit over my breasts. I have to tug it, hard, and for a moment, I'm suffocated by it. Discarded, yellowed from too many washes, the robe lies like a dirty mark on the expensive rug.

I stare at the Agent Provocateur basque he threw down for me and freeze.

'Do it!' A gloved hand pushes my back.

I reach forward, aware of him behind me as I bend.

Naked.

When I pick up the basque, a pair of matching panties and black seamed stockings fall from the bundle. One by one, I put on each item before I'm yanked backwards as he pulls the laces of the basque tight, knotting them in place. It's hard to breathe. The basque's pink and black stripes match the rug and dining room furniture. I'm colour co-ordinated, like a matching vase or table lamp.

266

As I clip the final suspender to the stockings, he throws a pair of patent leather stilettos at my feet and I step into them without being asked.

The gagged woman inside me begins to squirm.

I stand up and he's right behind me. He throws an arm around my neck and clamps a hand across my mouth.

I smell leather.

Animal sweat.

His thick fingers block my nose and smother my mouth. He doesn't let go, and the need to breathe becomes a fight for life. But I don't fight. I barely struggle. My body shudders, and I'm about to pass out when he opens his fingers just enough for me to suck in a breath. I choke on dusty air. There's fine grit on his gloves.

'Eyes closed. Or next time, I don't let go.'

I close my eyes.

I focus on the pink-orange patterns on the backs of my eyelids as he ties one rope to my left wrist and one to my right. Then his breath grazes my thigh as he bends down behind me. At the far end of the table, the ropes chafe its carved edging and it crosses my mind that J will be livid. They'll damage the French polish and he loves this dining set.

It's crazy what you think at times like these.

Suddenly, I slam against the table as the cords around my wrists pull taut. Bent over at the hips, my upper body is forced down on to the tabletop. I open my eyes. A strained breath escapes his lips as he pulls each cord to its limit and knots the right-hand rope to my right ankle and the left-hand rope to my left. I'm locked in place.

My hipbones grind against the table's edge, so I try to ease my feet backwards, but that only draws my arms forward, yanking the bones from their sockets. Pain sears through my shoulders. Face pressed against the table, I breathe condensation on to the varnish and inhale the oily lavender and cinnamon smell of wood polish.

I stay still.

I don't resist.

I stare at a photograph on the sideboard: a selfie of me and J on a ski lift at Mammoth Mountain in California. We're pulling silly faces.

Fingers, wet with spit, slide into the back of the panties. They trace the line between my buttocks and slide between my legs.

Inside.

Out.

Quick and rough.

He tugs at the silk, and the panties slide to my ankles. A zipper faintly buzzes. There's no gag over my mouth. I could scream. But I don't.

'Eva.'

Like plush velvet, deep and soft, my name drifts in through the open dining room door. I like the feel of it in my ears.

I see myself reflected in the glass of the picture frame on the sideboard. Not all of me, just pieces. My hair, curled and damp, splayed across the shiny tabletop. The fleshy part of my upper arm, pressed flat. And, at my wrists, stark white cords that stand out against my olive skin.

Rope.

The man takes a step closer and his gloved hands grip my thighs. Right cheek crushed against the wood, my spit sprays the varnish as I scream, wide-eyed, in pain. But no sound comes out.

'Eva.'

The ropes strangle my bound ankles as the man grunts in his assaulting rhythm.

Ropes around my ankles.

Ropes around my wrists.

Bound.

I focus on their reflection in the picture frame, on the spiralled twists of the strands.

268

They're familiar somehow. I've seen them before. I've been here before.

A velvet voice whispers through the door.

'Bound and assaulted.'

'Bound and assaulted.'

I look again at the picture of me and J. I'm blowing a kiss, holding a lock of hair over my lip so it looks like a moustache. J's pushing the end of his nose up so high his teeth are exposed. The photo fades into the background as my own reflection takes its place. Then my wrists, bound with rope.

White rope.

Am I dreaming?

This isn't real.

I'm dreaming.

In an instant, the other Eva comes alive. She tries to get up, but her body only lifts an inch from mine before she's slammed back down on to the tabletop.

And the man keeps thrusting and grunting.

The horror just keeps coming.

Pain sears my insides like being stabbed with a blade. I can't fight this. I never fight it. I could scream if I wanted to, but I don't. I just lie here and let the scream metastasise.

There's a loud snap and the ropes break, but he's still inside me, huffing and grunting. And I can't take this any more. So I scream, loud and hard enough to push my insides out. I punch and kick at the table. Demented and shaken to the core, I strike out at everything around me. But my hands find nothing, so I grab clumps of my own hair and scream even louder.

'Eva!'

He's coming at me again. His naked body presses against mine as he pins my arms down and cries out my name, 'Eva!'

I open my eyes.

Saeed is right next to me on the sofa, his arms wrapped tightly around mine, pressing them down by my sides.

He's sweating. Panting. Holding me so tight I can barely move.

I break away. 'You have to send me back in.'

'What? No, Eva.'

'You have to. I nearly had it.'

'I cannot...it was too traumatic.'

'Yes, and it will keep being traumatic until I learn how to stop it. You have to send me back in. I can't wait a week. I'll lose it. I was nearly there.'

He looks at the clock. 'We don't have time.'

'I don't care. Make the next person wait. I need to go back in. Right now.'

He checks his watch as if he can turn back time. 'All right. If you are sure.'

The man thrusts and grunts as I pant and spit on the polished tabletop. I focus on the picture frame, on the spiralled twists of white rope, on the velvet voice drifting in from the hallway.

'Bound and assaulted...bound and assaulted.'

White rope.

This isn't real. It's only a dream.

She's here.

The other Eva is here.

She tries to get up from the table, but she's slammed back down. Like me, she teeters on the brink of madness, struggling against me as I lie quietly on the tabletop, unwilling or unable to fight. She knows that, if we both go mad, Saeed will end this session, and the chance to become the master of this nightmare will be lost. She has to win, otherwise we'll go through this again and again until one of us finally finds the strength to fight back. That voice, distant and drifting, floats in from the doorway.

'You can do this, Eva. You are strong.'

I'm strong.

I'm her.

I try to rise up and sever myself from the Eva on the table. But it all feels too real, and the pain all consuming, I can't stop it. I cannot split this dream from reality.

The voice speaks.

'This nightmare is yours. This is not your body. It is your mind. And it dictates what does and does not happen to you. Take control, Eva. Take control.'

Just as Saeed taught me, I relax and close my eyes. I imagine myself elsewhere. Dream something quiet, he said. Something peaceful. A nice walk with your dog. So I picture myself on the canal towpath, walking with Teddy in the sunshine. I form a complete picture in my mind: the weeping willows dragging the water for leaves; the distant gush of the weir; the crunch of our feet on gravel. But then I trip and fall, bloodying my knees on the stones as my hips slam into the wood of the dining room table.

I try again.

I imagine myself beneath the cedar tree, dancing in the garden at Belmond. J is singing 'Danke Schoen' in a quiet whisper like a breeze through my hair. I feel his hand on the small of my back, and his body pressed close to mine. But then I'm distracted by a sharp pain. The bones of a basque dig into my flesh and a dark spot of blood seeps through the red silk of my dress. Suddenly, J grabs me by the hair and forces me down on one of the garden tables while the diners stare blank-faced through the restaurant windows.

I can't do it.

I can't fucking do it!

That other Eva disappears, leaving me here on the table. And, one way or another, I have to stop this sickening pain. I'm about to let loose, scream, punch, kick, and tear my hair from its roots like a wild thing.

But the velvet voice comes again.

'You can do this. You can stop a nightmare in its tracks. The oneironaut is the master of her dreams!'

And then, from the hallway, I hear the sassy tones of that other Eva. She's still here. She's laughing at me. She sounds just like Maria. 'This Eva Curtis really is lame, you know that? The Eva I remember would have fought back. Look at you. You could dream whatever you wanted if you weren't so fucking weak and pathetic.'

Then I hear my own voice, sassing Saeed about James McAvoy. And suddenly, I know what I have to do. Saeed was wrong. I'm not a master. I'm a beginner. I can't walk through walls or fly from buildings. I can't transform this pain into a peaceful walk with Teddy or a dance in a garden. Those things are too far from this terrifying reality. I can't change a nightmare into a dream.

But I may be able to alter it. Just a little.

I relax, close my eyes, and press my palms into the table. I imagine that the wood beneath my skin is no longer polished but matt. I press my fingers into the blade marks that slash the grain. I close my fists and grip the edge, not of the dining table, but of a chopping board. I feel J, pressed against me as his hand finds my waistband. I imagine his fingers fumbling for the pull of my zipper and the force of his breath in my hair as he says, 'Let's make you feel a bit more sensitive, shall we?'

Only this time, I don't stop him.

He pulls down my trousers, works my panties aside and struggles to get a finger inside me.

I'm not ready.

I hear the wet click of his tongue and gasp as he drives two fingers in deep.

I don't want this.

I'm rigid inside.

But now, everything's different. It's no longer a stranger assaulting me against my will. It's my husband. And, in my marriage, I decide what does and does not happen to me. I let go of the chopping board, brace myself against the marble

272

counter, and push back. Hard. J stumbles backwards as I scream, 'Not like this! Not like this!'

And suddenly, I'm standing in the doorway to the dining room.

It's dim inside. Light from the landing spills from behind me through the open door. The man is in silhouette, but I can just make out his sharp suit jacket. His white shirt hangs down beneath its hem and bobs against his backside. His trousers are wrapped around his ankles and he's still wearing his socks and shoes.

He looks rather silly from this angle.

So, I turn and walk away.

THIRTY-SEVEN

I PRESS PLAY on the remote control, but my finger hovers over the pause button because the film Saeed bought me is so painful to watch. Not just because this woman, Eve, has J's condition, but because her husband lacks the intellectual capacity to understand it.

She loses huge portions of her day while her alter buys hundreds of dollars' worth of clothes that her primary personality wouldn't dream of wearing. Meanwhile, her husband does everything Saeed has warned me not to do: he challenges her lapses in memory, threatens to slap her for lying, and at one point traumatises her so badly that, in a fit of rage, her alter tries to strangle her own child with a curtain pull. If Saeed's intention was to hammer home his point about not challenging Jacob, he couldn't have done it more effectively.

It's like watching my life in black and white.

But what's really startling is how different and disconnected her personalities are. One of the psychiatrists calls Eve White

274

'that dreary little woman'. But Eve Black is far from dreary. She's a promiscuous and uninhibited party girl. Eve Black is allergic to things Eve White isn't, refers to herself by her maiden name, and denounces her husband and child. By comparison, J's condition is mild. The two Eves are utterly unmistakable, while I struggle to tell the difference between Jacob and Victor.

What's also startling about this case is that, while Eve Black knows everything about Eve White – and even tells her what to do by shouting voices in her head – Eve White has no idea who Eve Black is. In the early stages of diagnosis, she isn't even aware of her existence or the antics she gets up to when she's in control.

Is it possible that Jacob believes himself to be cured by the lithium and has no idea that Victor still exists? Is it possible that, when he blames his memory lapses on the stress of work or alcohol, he genuinely believes that to be true?

Is that why he hasn't told me?

I don't know.

Eve White's marriage broke down because her husband wasn't able to accept the impetuous party girl living inside his wife. Yet, when Eve Black shows up at his hotel room in a revealing dress, he finds his promiscuous wife irresistible. And for a brief time he not only accepts her but is intoxicated by the thrill of her. And, for that brief moment, Eve Black is enchanted by her infatuated husband.

But it doesn't last. He continues to challenge her. Instead of seeing these alters as two completely different women, he tries to mould Eve Black to be more like Eve White and create one perfect wife.

Hard as it is to watch, I know Saeed was right to buy this for me – and I was right to watch it as soon as I got home. It has helped me to better understand Jacob. And I know what I need to do now. I won't make the same mistakes that led to the dissolution of Eve White's marriage.

When I first started coming to terms with J's illness, my instinct was to alter my own personality to adapt to both of his, and now I'm confident that's the right thing to do. All Victor needs is to be accepted as an individual person, the brave, strong man who has taken the brunt of J's pain.

He's my bold and fearless lover.

And I know now that, to connect with him more deeply, I need to unleash the darker, more sensual woman inside me. I need to unleash my own alter.

I know she's in there.

I've met her in my dreams.

I just need to set her free.

THIRTY-EIGHT

I'M ALONE IN ATIK, Oxford's largest nightclub, clinging to the railings behind me for support. My mind's a tangled mess, and I'm afraid if I let go I won't be able to stand, let alone walk.

My handbag's empty apart from a lipstick, keys, and a mobile phone that ran out of juice about two hours ago. It's not unusual for me to come out without any money – we've had joint bank accounts since we were married – but tonight, I wish I hadn't. I have no money for a taxi. I don't even have a credit card. My feet are blistered from dancing, and now I'll have to walk home in these heels or go barefoot. But right now, I can't let go of these railings and I can't move my feet, not even an inch.

It was clear things were bad the moment J walked through the door – the moment *Victor* walked through the door. The partners assigned him another case on top of the murder trial and he couldn't reassign it. The client, Elijah Gale, refused to sign with the firm unless J represented him. And, given that Elijah Gale played the lead role in the highest-grossing movie in the UK last year, it couldn't be any more high-profile.

Elijah is accused of raping a fifteen-year-old girl he apparently lured to his home with the promise of a part in his new film. He pleaded his innocence from the start, claiming the girl came on to him in a bar. Apparently, in a tight dress and make-up, she easily passed for nineteen or twenty. It didn't occur to him to ask her age. Elijah claimed they had consensual sex, that the girl encouraged him to get rough with her, and the whole thing was a set-up. The young girl has a history of promiscuity, and the evidence for rape was flimsy, so J wasn't worried about being forced to take the case.

But, as is often the way with high-profile rape cases, as soon as it went public, dozens of girls – several of whom were also underage – came forward with accusations of rape. Presumably the evidence from one of the other cases wasn't so flimsy but I didn't dare ask. Better to wait until J was ready to talk. And he usually does, telling me what little he can once he's had time to process the complication and make it disappear.

I hadn't started on dinner because of watching the DVD Saeed had given me, but it didn't matter because J didn't even change out of his suit, just suggested we go straight out, so I quickly changed into a dress and heels, and we went for dinner and drinks at Raoul's. A lot of drinks in J's case. I only had one glass of prosecco and the rest went in the plant pot every time his back was turned.

When last orders were called, he insisted we go to ATIK. We've never been to ATIK before, and I felt old the moment we joined the queue to get in. But J was charged up on stress and alcohol, and I wasn't about to suggest we go somewhere else. Or, heaven forbid, home.

I clubbed myself to death in my late teens. Now that I'm married and pregnant, mum-dancing to techno has zero appeal. As I scanned the dance floor, the thought of being single again was frankly mortifying. All I wanted to do was go home with the best-looking man in the room. Unfortunately, the best-looking man in the room didn't want to go home; he wanted to drink himself into a coma.

Eyes closed, head tipped back, sweat dripping on to his expensive shirt, J swayed and tapped to the monotonous rhythm while I questioned whether I really needed to be there.

Patting him on the arm, I signalled his pocket, and shouted over the deafening music, 'Can I have some money? I need a drink.'

'I'll get it.' J took my hand and weaved through the crowded dance floor to the bar. He ordered a Jack and Coke and, without asking what I wanted, bought me another prosecco. As he was walking away with our filled glasses, I quickly asked the barman for tap water and downed it before catching up.

Tremulously, I suggested we give Curve a try. We'd checked it out earlier in the evening – a smaller, more intimate room in the club where they play R'n'B – but J had blown it off because he wasn't in the mood for slow and smooth. I was disappointed. I love R'n'B. I find the style more diverse and you don't find yourself wondering whether you've been listening to the same song for the last twenty-five minutes. So, when J finally agreed, I was pleasantly surprised.

Curve is glamorous, chic, and a little badass. The carpets, wallpaper and private booths are all black and gold, with everything wrapped in either black PVC or gold velvet. It's incredibly sexy, and I relaxed in the kind of club I would have loved when I was young.

They were playing a song I didn't recognise, but the R'n'B vibe drew me on to the dance floor, and, in the spirit of 'if you can't beat 'em, join 'em', I bumped and ground as if I were twenty all over again. I urged J to join me but he just stood at the edge, watching.

I knew that look.

All too well.

I danced to four or five songs before a familiar tune hit the decks. 'Killing Me Softly' by the Fugees changed the mood and dancers coupled-up on the floor. I didn't want to dance alone, so looked pleadingly at J, but he just shook his head and gave me a come-hither beckon.

He'd moved to the far corner of one of the booths and was leaning against the metal railings that surround the dance floor. Sipping his Jack and Coke in the cloistered darkness, sweaty and mussed up, he was achingly sexy.

The booth was crowded, and I had to squeeze past people to get to him. When I did, he dragged me deeper into the corner where we couldn't be seen from the dance floor. He pulled me close, pushed me up against the railings and kissed me long and hard.

It was obvious from the kiss that watching me on the dance floor had driven him to the edge. The metal of the railings pressed into my spine, forcing me to push back against him. He was stiff against my hip.

In the seclusion of the corner, with the club's atmosphere and sexy music, I forgot where I was. My tongue danced around J's as he ran his hand up my dress, but the moment his fingers slid inside my panties I was struck by the insanity of our behaviour. It was further than I was willing to go in a public place.

I pulled out of the kiss, and J's lips slid across my cheek as his fingers plunged inside me. My thoughts turned to my little passion fruit, and I grabbed his wrist to stall him. *It'll have grown into a peach by now.* I wanted desperately to connect more deeply with Victor, and this was my opportunity, so I pushed that thought to the back of my mind. Sex couldn't harm the baby. I let go of his arm but was still conscious of the fact that we were surrounded. I'm no exhibitionist.

To our left was a wall offering privacy from prying eyes but to our right was a booth full of people. I glanced over.

There weren't enough seats for the entire group, so four men were standing with their backs to us, making a virtual wall. Nobody was looking.

J tilted my chin up, closed his eyes, and kissed me. With his tongue in my mouth and his fingers deep inside me, I thought about the promiscuous Eve Black and unleashed the Eva Black inside me. I knew she was in there.

So I set her free.

Abandoning all sense, I slid my palm between our bodies and grabbed his cock straining inside his suit trousers. The moment I did, J brushed my hand aside, opened his fly and guided it inside. With his cock in my hand, he grunted in my ear as he fingered me, roughly. I knew exactly who I was with. This wasn't Jacob.

This was Victor.

In a moment of clarity, my marriage flashed before my eyes. The opposite to a death, more of a waking up, I saw every moment we'd spent together with fresh eyes, knowing that, every time J had come home in a cold, impenetrable mood, I'd been with Victor.

He pulled his fingers out and with wet hands slid his cock from my grasp and thrust it inside me. I gasped in his ear, the breath leaving my body with the force of entry. And at my anguished cry, he grew inside me, stretching me. My spine bruised against the metal of the railings, but the pain melted into the husky sound of the Fugees and the delirious pleasure of the moment. This man looked like my husband. Beneath my touch, he felt like my husband. He even sounded and smelled like my husband.

But I was being fucked by another man altogether.

As he sank his teeth into my bare shoulder, I was hit by an adrenaline rush of desire. It was like committing adultery with someone I had thirsted for for years, only with none of the guilt, none of the indecision, no looking over my shoulder or counterchecking every word and action for fear of discovery.

It was the most exciting, most freeing sexual moment of my entire life.

Victor was the antithesis of J. The arrogance to his diffidence, the savagery to his tenderness. Darkness against light. And, in that moment, I not only accepted him as part of my life, I *wanted* him in my life. I wanted his unpredictability, his power, his cool composition. I was thrilled by it. I was afraid of nothing, invincible on the arm of a man who could take on the world.

I loved J, but I *needed* Victor.

I clung tight to him as he thrust inside me, lifting one leg to wrap over his backside, opening myself up to let him in deeper. And, as I did, he let out an unrestrained groan. It was the most alive I'd felt since standing in a surgery with a scalpel in my hands.

I could be this woman.

With Victor, I could be the sexually aggressive mistress who fucks in public places. And, with J, I could be the soft and sensual wife. With Victor, I could be confident and flinty, fearlessly snubbing propriety, while, with J, I could curl up on the sofa and dance in the moonlight. Just like Eve White and Eve Black, I could be two completely separate women. Jacob wasn't the only one who could run hot and cold. I could adjust my temperature to the man who came home.

I revelled in this new and exciting life. The perfect marriage where you got to have it all: a wild Jim Stark and a romantic Noah Calhoun all rolled into one. I reimagined myself as my alter ego, the paragon wife to Eva's other husband. Eva's intoxicating, unpredictable lover. And I abandoned myself to him.

I let go of all my fears and reservations, all my concerns about other people and what they thought of me. I no longer cared who was watching. I didn't care if we were caught and thrown out of the nightclub, because that's the kind of woman I was. And the risk heightened my desire. I lifted my other leg on to his waist, opening myself up as wide as possible, accepting him completely, both physically and mentally. Wanting every part of him.

His face was buried in my chest and I needed to see it. I wanted to see Victor. Wrapping one arm around his shoulder and holding on tight, I lifted his chin and kissed him deeply. I pushed my tongue into his mouth and wrapped it around his. And, as I pulled out of the kiss, I looked into the face of my new husband. As perfect in his own way as Jacob had always been to me.

But Victor was elsewhere. His head drooped on my shoulder.

I needed him to look at me. I needed him to acknowledge *my* alter ego, to accept her in the same way I had accepted him. I needed him to really *see* this new woman in his life, this thrilling woman, who would complement him, bring out the best in him, electrify and complete him.

I lifted his face to mine but he still wouldn't look at me. Lost in the moment, his eyes remained closed. I was desperate.

So, I said his name.

'Victor.'

He stopped dead and opened his eyes.

His face was so close to mine that, in the shifting lights of the nightclub, I could have sworn I saw the patterns in his irises twisting.

But I was wrong.

They were still.

Cold.

Dead.

My hand slipped from beneath his chin as he pulled out of me. My legs, numb, slid down his hips to the floor. I trembled as I tried to stand. Heart in my mouth, I swallowed, unable to tear my eyes from his. Then, without blinking or looking away from me, Victor tucked his penis in his pants and zipped up his trousers.

I was still pressed against the railings, unable to back away even one step. Then he put a hand to the left side of my chest and pushed me. He pushed me slowly but with force, leaning back at the same time as if to put as much distance between us as the cramped space would allow.

His expression was unreadable. Hatred? Disgust? Rage?

My lips parted but no words came out.

Finally, I managed two.

'Jacob, I—'

And then he punched me in the face.

THIRTY-NINE

I DON'T KNOW how long I stood there, staring at the walled backs of the men in the booth. As if Victor might fight his way through them at any moment, shoving them aside to get to me. Just as he had shoved them aside to get away from me.

He didn't come back.

My face throbbed, my eyes watered and my nose bled over my hands and down my wrists. Jacob's powerful fist had clipped my jaw, my nose and my cheekbone all at the same time.

Eventually, I found the strength to move and pushed my way through the crowd to the ladies' room. I cleaned myself up, kept my head down and left. I was afraid to return to the apartment, but I didn't know where else to go at that time of night with no credit card and no money for a taxi. So, I walked here barefoot in the dark.

Victor didn't come home.

Neither did Jacob.

He must have caught a taxi into London and stayed at the flat. And gone to work as normal the next day. But if either one of them is coming home tonight, they'll be back at any moment.

I have no idea who'll walk through the door. I pace around the kitchen as if my brain's a self-winding watch, and if I stop pacing it'll stop functioning. My hands are no longer trembling, they're rattling off my wrists. Teddy hasn't left my side all day. He knows something's wrong and he's frightened.

I know what I did was wrong. I know getting Maria to snoop through J's medical records was a terrible thing to do, but he's been lying from the first night we met. That's pretty fucking terrible too. I'd say we're even.

For five years, I've lived on a spinning top, oblivious to the precariousness of my situation.

Victor just spun it.

If he comes through the door tonight, I have to let him know I'm not afraid. I have to let him know that if he ever lays so much as a finger on me again, this relationship is over.

Fuck! It hadn't occurred to me until this very moment, but what if he wants it over? Victor and J are two distinct people. Is it possible for one of my husbands to love me and the other to want a divorce?

As soon as I woke up this morning, I packed a bag to leave, but then imagined J walking through the door and finding the house empty. With no memory of what he did as Victor, he'd think I'd left him out of the blue.

I couldn't do it.

I said I'd support him, whatever it takes, I can't fall at the first hurdle, no matter how high the fucking hurdle. Saeed said it was important not to make one alter feel guilty about the actions of the other, since in their mind they didn't do anything wrong. So I unpacked.

Fuck, fuck, fuck. I know I have to face Victor at some point, I just don't want it to be tonight. Please, God, not tonight. I'm not ready. I need to work up to it. I need to get my fear of him under control before I can confront him.

Teddy paws my leg for attention, so I kneel down and rub his warm, soft chest. He'll be no comfort if Victor comes home. He's more scared of him than I am. But he's still my security blanket. Hiding under it serves no purpose, but sometimes your belief in its power is enough to get you through.

I feel so fucking stupid. Why did I confront him in that way? Saeed told me not to be confrontational with Jacob and with one word, one name, I let him know I'd been snooping into his past. Why didn't I wait for him to come to me? It was a situation that required kid gloves and I went in wearing a gauntlet and slapped him round the face with it. Of course I got punched in return. I wish I could turn back the clock.

Whatever it takes.

That's what I said.

But how can I live with Victor now? How could we ever learn to trust each other after last night? I think I'll always be afraid of him.

The door latch clicks.

I freeze.

Teddy rushes from my arms and, at the sounds from the hallway I let out the breath I've been holding all day. I lift myself up by the counter and turn away from the door. It'll be hard to look at J without seeing Victor.

'Hey, babe.' His tone is light as he comes up behind me, brushes my hair aside and kisses my neck. Then he spins me around and kisses me full on the lips. As I pull out of the kiss, I let my hair fall over my left cheek.

'You've been smoking,' he says.

'Just one.'

Actually it was three, but he doesn't need to know that. I felt terrible, smoking while pregnant, but reasoned that one wouldn't hurt. Then one became three. I might have smoked the whole packet if the baby hadn't pointed out what an irresponsible mother I was being: my little peach made me vomit.

'Bad day?'

'Not really. I just felt like a cigarette.'

'You only smoke when you're sad, angry, or stressed. So, come on, confess, which is it?'

He lifts my chin to interrogate my eyes, and my hair falls away from my cheek.

'What happened to your face?'

'Nothing.' I pull away.

'Your cheek's bruised. What happened?'

I stare him straight in the eyes.

I search for the lie, but it's not there. J has no memory of going to ATIK. No memory of fucking in the nightclub. And his amnesia, his complete dissociation from his own actions, triggers a similar response in me. I feel as if this isn't the same man who punched me in the face less than twenty-four hours ago. Because, inside, it isn't. Victor punched me in the face. And this man, standing before me, is J.

'Ev,' he presses. 'What happened? It looks like someone hit you.'

I think quickly. 'I was walking into the supermarket this morning and some guy tried to snatch my purse. When I wouldn't let go, he spun me around and punched me. But I still wouldn't let go, and in the end he ran off.'

'Jesus fucking Christ. Did you call the police?'

'No. It all happened so quickly. I didn't even get a look at his face. I wouldn't be able to identify him so there's nothing the police can do. And apart from leaving me a bruise, he didn't take anything.'

'You should have called them. Why didn't you call me at work? I would have come home.'

'I'm fine, honestly. It didn't hurt that much; it was more of a shock than anything.'

It's easier to lie with the truth. I've never been punched before, I've only ever seen it on TV, and it didn't hurt as much as I'd imagined a punch in the face would. Perhaps because of

288

the adrenaline coursing through my body, or maybe I blacked out for a split second. It hurts more now than it did at the time.

J believes me about the robber; he's not acting. Nobody's that good an actor.

But, even as I try to get to grips with this, the other Eva is screaming. I hate her for it and, at the same time, I want to cry out in unison. Because she's not okay. At the top of her lungs she's screaming, 'It was YOU, you fucking lunatic asshole! YOU punched me in the face! Stop pretending you don't remember! What? Your knuckles are sore? Oh, I'm sorry, DID MY FACE HURT YOUR FIST?!!'

Suddenly, I feel like Eve White's awful husband. Watching that film, I hated him for how he treated his poor, damaged wife. And now I've turned into him.

I don't want to be that person.

I don't want to be someone without the intellectual capacity to understand or support J.

Fuck.

One way or another, if I want my marriage to work, I need to learn how to manage the two men in my life. Without realising it, I've been doing it for years, I've had plenty of practice with Victor.

I can do this.

Jacob wraps his arms around me as far as they will go, as if the more contact his body makes with mine, the more comfort it provides. And I'm convinced he doesn't remember a thing. I promised to support him. I promised.

But then something occurs to me. I've never crossed a line with Victor the way I did last night. And Jacob may have no memory of it.

But Victor certainly will.

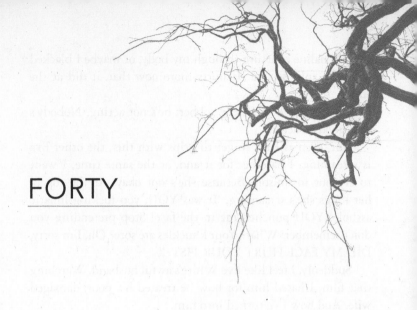

FORTY

THE WEEKEND'S been so exhausting, it's a relief when the front door finally clicks and Jacob's gone. I've spent the entire two days waiting for Victor to show up, but he never came.

With icicle drool, Teddy sits on the kitchen floor watching me prepare his breakfast, when my mobile vibrates in my back pocket. I pull it out and Bron's face fills the screen.

'Hi Ev, it's Bron.'

'Bron. Hi.' I struggle to keep my voice light. 'How are you?'

'I'm fine, honey. Are you okay?'

'I'm fine,' I lie through my teeth.

'I was just calling with the results of those tests.'

The tablets! The powder! With everything that's been going on with Victor and Jacob, I'd almost forgotten about the samples I gave to Bron.

'I'm sorry it took so long. The lab was all backed up. But since I hadn't heard from you, I assumed everything was okay with Teddy and didn't chase them. That's the only way to get anything out of them these days.'

'Not to worry, he's fine.'

'Well, I figured he would be when I got the results back. They weren't toxic, so it wouldn't have mattered how many he swallowed.'

'Why, what was it?'

'The pill.'

'Yeah, the pill, what was it?'

'No. I mean it was the pill. As in the contraceptive pill.'

'What? That can't be right.'

'It's right. The powder was more worrying but if Teddy had swallowed any of that, he would have shown immediate symptoms.'

'Why? What was it?' I say again. My words tap out mechanically while my brain wrangles with why Jacob has contraceptive pills in his safe.

'Scopolamine. It treats motion sickness, apparently. And muscle spasms in conditions like Parkinson's and IBS, though I don't know much about it. I was gonna look into it in more detail but since Teddy's fine—'

'No. It's okay, Bron, don't worry. Thanks...I appreciate it.'

Neither of us speaks for a moment, then Bron says, 'Ev?'

'Yeah?'

'Do you think we could go for a coffee some time?'

'Yes. Yes, I'd love that.'

I end the call, give Teddy his breakfast, and go into J's study. Using the key card from under his desk, I open the safe and pull out the bag of contraceptive pills. Sitting on the floor, I take one from the bag and settle it on my palm.

Why does J need contraceptive pills?

Is he having an affair after all?

I stare at the tiny tablet, white and round.

Then the worst possible thought springs to mind. Pill in my fist, I leap up, run from his study and bolt upstairs to our bedroom. I pull open my dressing table drawer with such force, everything inside flies forward.

Grabbing the pot of folic acid tablets, I fight with the childproof cap and tip the contents on to the tabletop. I pull one tablet from the pile and rest it on my palm next to the contraceptive pill.

They're identical.

I run downstairs to the kitchen, grab my laptop, and do a Google image search for 'folic acid tablets'. Fingers trembling on the trackpad, I scroll past picture after picture, comparing the pills in my palm to the images on the screen.

Folic acid tablets aren't white. They're cream. Or yellow.

I don't know how long I've been sitting here, slumped on the kitchen floor, leaning against the island, with Teddy's chin resting on my ankle.

Who have I married? For three years, we've been trying for a baby. I've gone through humiliating examinations, taken dozens of pregnancy tests, and wasted hours researching tips on how to fall pregnant. I've done ridiculous things: pissed in Heinz tomato ketchup cups, wasted hours in chat rooms and shoved a Kegelmaster 2000 up my fanny. And every time I've found blood on the toilet paper I've bitten back tears. I've plastered on a smile and pretended to be happy for friends who've conceived on their first try. I've convinced myself I wasn't one of those women, so broken by their inability to have a child, they spit venom at everyone who stole their dream.

And all this time.

Every morning without fail.

I've taken a contraceptive pill.

It explains why I had elevated oestrogen levels in my blood when we took the fertility tests. The pills sit, innocently white, in my palm. So tiny. Think of all the babies they've killed before they even had a chance to leave my ovaries.

I think back to the Summer Ball when I fell pregnant. I didn't tell J I'd been throwing up for days and so his fucked-up scheme of switching out my folic acid tablets went down the toilet. Literally. I'd like to find that cockerpoo puppy who eats shit and kiss her filthy little mouth. Without that puppy, I might have been sitting on a toilet in my mid-forties, still crying over blood on the paper.

But – fuck!!

Fuck-shit-fuck, I'm three months pregnant and all that time I've been taking the pill! I leap up from the floor, tap a new search into Google and hold my belly while I wait to learn whether it could have harmed the baby. If Jacob has done anything to hurt my child, I'll kill him.

I let out a long breath as I read there's no evidence that contraceptive pills can harm a baby.

But who the fuck is this man? And what else about our lives is a complete lie? I get up and dash from room to room, corner to corner, methodically searching the entire house for more evidence of his lies. I have no idea what I'm looking for.

Back in J's study, I take the key from the safe and, as I suspected, it opens the locked pedestal of his desk. I've been going through his hanging files for so long that the pile of the Axminster rug has embedded itself into my knees. I'm so thirsty, it's as if I haven't had a drink in days. My eyes are so dry I've rubbed them raw, and my fingers rattle as I flip through his papers.

I need to get to the bathroom. I'm going to throw up, but I'm too weak to stand. I stare at the rug's Paisley border and try to focus. I remember the day Jacob bought it. I told him how much I loved the richness of the blue in the middle of the rug. He turned on me with those hard eyes and, with a patronising smile, said, 'It's called the field.'

Was that Jacob? Or was it Victor?

Well, fuck the field, and fuck the both of them. I don't care if I'm sick on their fucking rug.

The thirst is getting to me more than the nausea. I struggle to my feet, stagger to the kitchen, and grab a Diet Coke from the fridge. Back in the study, I put the can down on the desk, on the gold-plated coaster.

The last hanging file holds the insurance documents for Teddy. He's poked his head around the door a few times to look on in despair at the owner he barely recognises any more. Nothing but empty green folders hang at the back of the drawer. I flick each one as if the reasons for his actions hover there, suspended. I feel sick. Frightened. Lost. And fuck, I desperately need to pee but I don't have the energy to get up again.

The last empty file doesn't swing like the rest. It has a weight to it that holds it steady. I dip a hand inside and pull out a leather-bound diary. Its smell fills my nostrils, and I grip it between both hands as my mind flashes back to those sickening nightmares. Suddenly, I'm in my dining room, a leather-gloved hand over my mouth, the memory tearing through my brain like a tangled mess of barbed wire. The ropes chafe the skin on my wrists and ankles, and my bones crack in my shoulder joints. I see the picture on the sideboard of me and J on the ski lift at Mammoth Mountain. I feel the presence of the man as he moves in close.

The silent Eva inside me screams.

Then she's gone, and I'm left holding a tan-coloured diary. The leather's as soft as Teddy's bare belly, with a calligraphic J stamped into the bottom right corner. I breathe in and out, in and out, as my shaking fingers unsnap the belt-buckle closure.

The diary is filled with childish handwriting – it looks like an early version of Jacob's – with entries dated by month and day but not the year. It's not a calendar of events, it's a journal.

I read.

The entries are odd, unsettling in their banality. Usually, when people keep journals, they use them to talk about their feelings and have private conversations with themselves. But young Jacob doesn't do that. He's kept a record of every prosaic detail of his life, every event, every conversation. But

294

the incidents aren't recorded with any emotion, they have all the passion of a telephone directory: what he had for breakfast, lunch and dinner, whether he was late home from school, whether he walked with a friend. He's written entries like, 'She mended the third button from the top on the frayed shirt.' All of it's so detailed, as if he has no memory of what has taken place each day and needs the diary to remind him.

I know why.

This is how you maintain a secret life of alters, how you deal with DID without everyone in your life needing to know about it. Violet knew, of course, but hiding these lapses in memory would have made it easier for her to live with, and easier for them to keep it private, within the family.

I wonder why this is the only diary in the drawer; it only covers about eighteen months. Does he still do this? Maybe more recent ones are at the flat.

I carry on reading the monotonous detail and the words travel up my spine, chilling me as I realise something. After watching the film, I had believed that not only did Jacob not know what Victor did, but he wasn't even aware of his existence.

But, he must be.

Victor is keeping this log *for Jacob*. And so, J must know of his own condition, and always did, even if he doesn't know what Victor does when he's in charge.

How entangled are they? Is it naïve to want to believe that Jacob knew nothing about the pills, and that it's Victor who's been switching them? That Victor is responsible for all the darkness in my marriage and that, if he could be excised from J, nothing but light would remain?

I fan the blank pages to the end of the journal. The back cover has a pocket for notes and receipts, and a tiny white triangle of paper pokes out. I try to pull it, but it's stuck. I stick my fingers in the pocket and snap the leather away from the paper. Tugging with my fingernails, I pull out an old photograph. The colours are muted by time, but the moment I lay eyes on the little boy in the picture, I know it's Jacob. He's young, seven or eight maybe. He has his arm around a little girl with breast-length, blonde curly hair. He's kissing her on the cheek, and she's laughing. Her mouth is wide with surprise, as though he snuck in the kiss at the last moment. But I can only tell that from her mouth.

Because her eyes have been scratched out.

I turn the photo over and, on the back, someone's written 'Jacob Rathbone and Hannah Edwards'.

I put the photo back in the journal, snap the buckle closed, and place it back in the last hanging file. Then I close the drawer, lock the pedestal, and put the key back in its hiding place. Struggling to my feet, I wait for a head rush to pass before making sure everything's back in its original place, taking the Coke can with me.

Standing at the kitchen island, I Google "Hannah Edwards", enclosing it in double speech marks to restrict the search to exact matches. But there are still more than eighty thousand hits. I scroll through the first page of results, finding mostly Facebook and LinkedIn profiles. Nothing of interest. Jacob's family farm was in Douglas County, so I type that in too. That narrows the hits to two thousand, but I need to constrain it further.

My finger hovers over the M on the keyboard.

I don't know what possesses me to do it, but I type in, 'Murdered'. That narrows the search to a page. The first hit is a newspaper site hosting a report from five years ago. I open the page and a photograph, matching the little blonde girl in the back of Jacob's diary, fills the screen.

The remains of a young girl have been found buried in the woods south of McWhorter, Douglas County. Police suspect it is the body of six-year-old Hannah Edwards, who went missing from the area twenty-three years ago.

The woods were thoroughly searched at the time but according to police the site would have been easily missed. She was buried at the base of a low-hanging sugarberry tree in autumn, when the woods were carpeted with leaves.

Forensics reveal that a deep grave had been dug with a small trowel over a period of many days, yet she was buried within minutes of her death. The child's throat had been cut, and police have no doubt that this was a premeditated murder.

The sugarberry tree was covered in kudzu, an invasive trailing vine that grows rapidly and kills trees with shade. The dead tree was ripped up during recent storms in the area, otherwise the body might never have been found.

Maria said that Jacob had seen a lot of death for one person, but she doesn't know the half of it. A black cloud scuds across my mind, raining thoughts I cannot shelter from. My breath comes thick and fast and sweat runs down my back, trickling through the waistband of my jeans. I need to sit down but I'm afraid to move. I'm standing on a precipice, wreathed in thick fog, and if I take just one step in the wrong direction I could plummet.

I'm aware of the front door as if it's a dark presence with a will of its own. I imagine it dragging itself towards me, getting closer and closer, until it's right in front of me. In my mind's eye, it flies open and Jacob is standing there.

Victor is standing there.

I swallow bile. Suddenly, I'm little Hannah Edwards, walking hand-in-hand with Jacob into the woods. I turn to face him with my six-year-old smile and come face to face with Victor.

With his hard eyes.

With my pre-dug grave.

297

With his knife, glinting in the dark.

Sickening terror fizzes inside me, rising up my throat until I'm forced to swallow it down for fear of choking on it. I can't even think it. Yet, at the same time, I can't not.

Then I breathe again because it's not possible. I do the maths. Jacob would have been eight years old when Hannah was murdered, and his DID didn't manifest until five years later. Which means Victor didn't even exist when Hannah Edwards was killed. Jacob couldn't have murdered her. It's more likely that her disappearance, combined with the tragic loss of his parents, *created* Victor.

But something doesn't sit right. Jacob didn't witness any of those deaths. Can grief alone fracture the mind?

Then I think of the photograph in Victor's diary. I remember Hannah's eyes.

Scratched out.

It doesn't make sense. Grabbing the worktop for support, I wipe sweat from my forehead and smear it across my jeans. I push the sleeves of my T-shirt up over my elbows. The soaked fabric clings to my armpits and my back, as I stare at the image of Hannah on the screen.

Her pretty eyes blur.

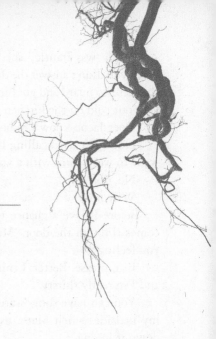

FORTY-ONE

I WAKE UP in a hospital bed.

A police officer in uniform leans over me. Maria. 'Thank God you're awake. You've been out for hours.'

'Where am I?'

'John Radcliffe.'

I blink a few times, and a sterile room comes into view. Like every hospital room I've ever seen, it has white walls, white skirting, blue curtains, and cheap melamine furniture. But the bed's comfortable, and I'm too woozy to sit up or move.

'What happened? How did I get here?'

'You passed out. When you didn't show up for lunch, I thought you'd forgotten and I came round...well...to give you shit about it, to be honest.'

I'd completely forgotten that Maria called on Thursday to arrange lunch for today. We were going to meet before she started her shift. Thank God. If Maria were a less feisty woman, she would have gone to work without giving it much thought.

'Teddy was frantic,' she says. 'Whining like a wolf. And when you didn't answer the door I went all Cagney and Lacey on the security guard and got him to open it. That's when we found you, out cold on the kitchen floor. I called an ambulance—'

'Does Jacob know I'm here?'

'No, I just tried calling him but he didn't answer. I didn't want to worry him with a voicemail. I'll try him again now.'

'No, don't.'

'Why not?'

Before I have a chance to answer, a man in a white coat comes through the door. 'Mrs Curtis. You're awake. How are you feeling?'

'Eva, please. Better, I think. Though still a little nauseous and I'm really thirsty.'

'You can have some water.' The doctor points to a jug by my bedside which Maria uses to fill a plastic cup for me. I down it in one.

'Your symptoms will subside now the dialysis is complete.'

'Dialysis?'

He hugs my chart to his chest and looks at Maria. 'Ms Mendez, I need to speak to Eva alone.'

'It's all right,' I say, anxious to keep her by my side. 'She can stay.'

'All right. Confusion and some memory loss are to be expected. You've been very lucky this time; it was just a seizure. But just a few pills can put you in danger of toxicity. We need to have a serious talk, Eva. We ran blood tests when you were brought in. You're pregnant.'

'Pregnant?' Maria squeals. 'Ev, that's—'

I glare at her.

'Fourteen weeks,' says the doctor. 'So you need to come off the pill immediately. There's no evidence it would have harmed your baby but you must stop taking it and, possibly, the other medications.'

'What other medications?'

'Eva.' He looks at Maria briefly before proceeding cautiously, as if I need handling with care. 'There's nothing in your medical records to indicate you should be on *any* other medications. No diagnoses, no prescriptions, so I don't know where you're getting them or why you're self-medicating, but now you're pregnant, you have to be far more vigilant.'

I'm getting a ticking off as if I'm some pregnant teenager who went out drinking all night, and I have no idea why.

He goes on, 'At the very least, your GP should be taking routine blood tests to ensure your dosages are regulated. This isn't something to take lightly, Eva. You must be prudent. Now more than ever. Pregnancy changes your hormone levels, fluid levels, kidney function...all of which have a direct impact on your dosage. That's why you've had a seizure now. But it could have been a coma. You'll need weekly blood tests until your GP has regulated your levels.'

'I'm sorry, doctor, I don't understand. My levels of what?'

'Both. I assume you're not taking scopolamine regularly – we only found traces – so I would stop that altogether if you can. And your GP will assist you in determining whether, during pregnancy, the benefits outweigh the risks of taking the lithium.'

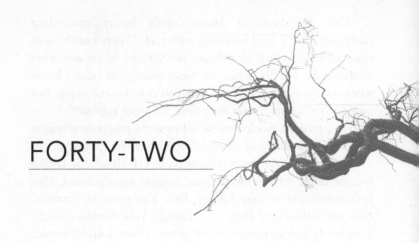

FORTY-TWO

'EVA, WHAT THE FUCK'S going on?' Maria shuts the door behind the doctor. 'I didn't know you were on lithium.'

'Neither did I.'

'What? Why didn't you say something? Why didn't you tell the doctor you weren't taking it?'

'Because I am.'

'Eva, sweetheart, you're not making any sense. I'm gonna get the doctor back.'

'No.' I grab her hand. 'Don't. You mustn't tell anyone about this. Nobody can know I've been here. Just get me out as quickly as possible. What's the time? I have to get home before Jacob gets back from work.'

Maria checks her watch. 'It's five o'clock.'

'Help me.' I kick off the blankets. 'We don't have much time.'

'Ev, this is crazy. You can't go home in this state.'

'I'll explain in the car. Just help me get dressed and drive me home.' I search the bedside cabinets for my clothes while Maria just stands there. 'Maria, please!'

'All right, okay.' She opens the top dresser drawer and finds my jeans and long-sleeved white T-shirt. 'But you've got some serious fucking explaining to do.'

Maria helps me into my clothes which, after being sweated in all morning, feel dank and dirty. I'm still a little shaky, nauseous and weak, and the whole process is an effort. Holding on to Maria for support, I slip into my Mahabis slippers and scan the room. There's nothing else here that's mine.

Maria insists we check out at the nurses' station. I resist at first; there's so little time. But she's right, the last thing I want is for anyone to think I've done a runner and call Jacob. I make a point of telling the nurses I feel much better and just want to go home and rest. I tell them Maria is going to stay with me until my husband gets home, and that I've already booked an appointment with my GP for a blood test first thing tomorrow. I put on a great show of a lithium patient who's made a simple mistake with her meds. But those few minutes of talking to the nurse take all the strength I have, and as soon as we're out of sight Maria has to hold me up to stop me collapsing right there in the hospital corridor.

She gets me to the car, activates her blues, and screeches through the car park as if we're in hot pursuit. 'Okay, explain.'

'I *have* been taking lithium. For years, probably. I found it in a hidden safe in Jacob's study and assumed it was his – to treat his DID – but he's been giving it to me, along with the contraceptive pill. He's been switching out my folic acid and vitamin tablets.' I pull my mobile from my back pocket and Google the side effects of lithium. 'All these symptoms I've been experiencing,' I run my finger down the list and read them out to Maria. 'Tremors, nosebleeds, dizziness, excessive thirst, a metallic taste, excessive urination. But all those symptoms are common in pregnancy too, so I just blamed them on that.'

'But if Jacob's been slipping you the pill, how come you're pregnant?'

'I got sick. Three months ago. I threw it up.'

'Thank fuck for that.'

'I started taking those vitamins about three months before we started trying for a baby. J picks them up when he does the food shopping on the way home from work. He must have switched them out from the start, otherwise I would have noticed. Which means I've been on lithium for three years.'

'But you've only had these symptoms for a few months, right?'

'As the doctor said, pregnancy affects the dosage. I must have functioned quite well on it before I fell pregnant.'

Saeed's voice rings in my ears – *Is it possible that Jack was a symptom not a cause?* – and I slam both of my palms hard on the dashboard. 'Fuck! Fuck!'

Maria keeps one eye on me, one on the road. 'What?'

'In excess, lithium can affect cognitive function. I killed Jack two weeks after I fell pregnant.'

'I knew it!' Maria slaps the steering wheel. 'I told your dad you were too much of a stickler to make a basic mistake like that. You've always been a fucking perfectionist, it just didn't make sense.'

'All this.' Jack's little face appears in my mind's eye and I remember scratching his bat-like ears. 'Jacob caused all this.'

At the hospital's main exit, cars stop at the roundabout to let us on to the Headley Way. Maria takes the turn so fast, I have to cling to the seat to keep myself upright.

'But I still don't get it,' she says. 'Why the fuck would he want you on lithium?'

'I don't know.'

Then I realise I do. I know exactly why. I remember almost word for word what Saeed said about lithium's effect on the body. It doesn't just decrease anxiety and boost serotonin, it's a catch-all. It dampens the imagination, creativity, impulsivity and the ability to express oneself. It decreases the body's fight-or-flight response.

'To keep me subdued,' I say. 'Submissive. Tame. That's how you hide multiple personalities from your wife for years. You drug her.'

'Fuck. That motherfucking... I'll kill him!'

And I'm deadly serious when I say, 'Not if I get there first.'

I'm still clinging to the seat as we fly down the Headley Way and run a red light at the primary school. Cars pull into bus stops and on to pavements to allow us to pass.

'But the lithium's not in your system now. You've had dialysis.'

'Yeah.'

'So basically, I'm in a car with a junkie who's just come down off her meds?'

'No. You're in the car with a perfectly rational person. One who's spent three years drugged up to the fucking eyeballs and has finally woken up.'

'And what's this sco...scopomaline stuff they found traces of?'

'Scopolamine. I don't know. Something else to keep me docile, no doubt. So I wouldn't notice I'm married to a fucking psycho.'

I'm about to Google that too when Maria's forced to brake hard for a line of traffic taking too long to get organised. She taps the steering wheel as the cars creep on to the pavement. The road is almost clear but she still doesn't move.

'Maria!' I point at the open road, and I'm thrown against the back of my seat when she slams her foot on the accelerator.

'You'll have to come and stay with me for a while. Once you're safe, I'll call for back-up and we'll go and arrest that fucker.'

'Okay. Okay. We just have to stop off to collect Teddy.'

'I didn't say the dog could come.'

I stare at Maria, dumbfounded.

'Just kidding. Your face!'

'You're joking? At a time like this, you're joking?'

'Says the woman who always jokes when things get serious.'

'Not this serious. Jesus, Maria, you really are fucked in the head, do you know that?'

'Yeah, but not as fucked as you.'

FORTY-THREE

'EVA?!' MARIA SHOUTS from the stairs. 'I've only packed a few things; we'd better get going. We'll come back once—' Her footfall is laboured on the hall floorboards. She must have brought a suitcase down. I only wanted pants and a tooth-brush.

I dash around the kitchen, piling Teddy's things into carrier bags. We agreed we'd just grab the essentials. For me, that's Teddy. For Teddy, that's food, his special bowl that stops him bolting it in one mouthful, and his bed. But he's lying on that in the hallway, eyeing his crazy owner as she darts between rooms.

I shout to Maria, 'Did you get my toothbrush?' She doesn't answer. 'Maria?'

I poke my head around the kitchen door, and she's standing in the hallway. In front of her, talking too quietly for me to hear, his face pressed to hers, is Jacob.

He turns and smiles.

It's not Jacob.

I grab the kitchen door frame for support. He's in his suit, wearing black leather gloves I've never seen before. They mould to his hands and alter his appearance. Threatening and sinister.

Mechanically, Maria slides her radio from her shoulder clip and gives it to Jacob – to Victor. He thrusts out his other hand, and she unsnaps a pocket on her waistband, taking out her can of CS spray. Next, she hands over her Taser and gun. All of which, Victor puts on the hall table.

This isn't Maria. She's behaving like a puppet.

He reaches into his pocket and hands her a pen and a folded sheet of paper.

'Sign it.'

'Maria?'

She doesn't look at me. She just signs the piece of paper, robotically.

Victor snatches it away and whispers in her ear. She takes something from him. It catches the light, metal and shiny, and for a moment she stares blank-eyed into space, catatonic, with the object in her hand.

'Now, Maria.' He points upstairs and in the same mechanical motion she walks towards me, pivots, and takes the steps one by one. Then Victor turns on me. He takes a few steps closer, sliding the signed piece of paper into his jacket pocket, then stops. Teddy eyes the stairs, ready to make a bolt for it.

'What have you done to Maria?'

'Me?' He takes another step, palm on chest, feigning innocence. 'I haven't done anything to her. She's doing it to herself.'

'Doing what?' I spit hatred.

'Stripping naked, hopping into the bath and slitting her wrists. The naked part wasn't strictly necessary but you gotta get your kicks somewhere. Plus, it'll make it easier to clean up the mess. I admit, it's a little trite and unimaginative but—'

'That's insane. She won't do that.'

'She will. I told her to.'

'She's not going to kill herself just because you told her to.'

'Isn't she? Just like George Hope didn't pull a knife because I told him to? Or you didn't bend over because I told you to?'

I stare at him. He looks just like J and yet nothing like him.

'What?' he asks. 'You don't remember? Oh, that's a shame. We had so much fun.'

'I don't understand.'

'Don't you?' He nods in agreement with some internal appraisal and says, 'I think the dining room was the most fun.'

My mouth falls open.

My nightmares.

The scream that's been trapped inside me for so many months comes out as nothing more than a quiet breath, as if I've been punched in the stomach. Question after question wrap around each other, snowballing, until I can barely get a word out. 'How?'

Victor just smiles.

I remember the dream of being tied to the bed upstairs, forced forwards over the footboard. I look across at the entrance to the dining room and recall being tied to the table. More than once. Then, I catch sight of the closed study door and remember that other man.

'Who was that man?'

'Mark Cox.'

I grab my stomach, barely able to stand. The recollection of his words at the Summer Ball turns my stomach: *I'd tap that.*

And then I remember the other time in the bedroom. I remember *her*.

'And that woman?'

He shrugs. 'Just a prostitute.'

I inhale the memory of the thick smell of her perfume. 'That was her in the street, wasn't it? And you went back to her that day, didn't you? The day we went to Scriptum.'

His eyes gleam with acknowledgement and I remember the way she looked at me, with that smile that would cut glass. I lean over and retch, spitting bile on to the floorboards.

Victor laughs.

I force myself to stand upright. 'Why did I let you do those things to me? I didn't even try to stop you.'

'Devil's Breath, Ev.'

I shake my head. I've no idea what he's talking about.

'Not ringing any bells?' he asks. 'How about scopolamine?' Victor tilts his head, waiting for the name to register.

When Bron mentioned it, and when I heard it at the hospital, it sounded vaguely familiar. But it's only now that I make the connection. Years ago, long before Jacob and I ever met, a series of burglaries in London hit the national news. The thief had used Devil's Breath, a powerful hypnotic drug, to turn his victims into willing zombies. They got in his van, directed him back to their homes, and even helped him unload all their valuables. One victim had even been seen by a neighbour, loading antique furniture into the back of the robber's van, and he'd assured them everything was fine. The next morning, they were left with an empty house and no memory of what had happened.

The media even gave the robber a nickname and, as it comes to mind, I say it out loud. 'The Devil's Highwayman.'

Victor makes a gun with his fingers, points at me, and clicks his tongue.

'You defended him?'

'Prosecuted, actually. But, in exchange for a supply, I went easy on him.'

Maria's gun is on the table behind him, way out of reach, so I take a few steps backwards into the kitchen, pulling my mobile from my back pocket. It's pointless, he'll stop me before I can call the police, but I have to do something. I open the phone app and am surprised when he doesn't lunge at me. He doesn't even take a step closer. He just reaches behind his back, lifts up his suit jacket and pulls a gun from the belt of his trousers. The gun from the safe.

I stop pressing numbers.

'What are you going to do, J, shoot me? Maria's *suicide* you may get away with, but shooting me? The first person they always suspect is the husband. You of all people should know that.'

'Ev.' He's pitying me. 'You know I win every case. Besides, I'm not going to shoot you.' My body relaxes. 'Oh, no, I mean I *am* going to shoot you. I just won't be *accused* of shooting you.'

I stare blankly. 'Who else could possibly have a motive for killing me?'

Victor smiles. It's clammy. And I remember the knife in the safe. The letter. The dog collar.

'George Hope,' I say, flatly.

He laughs. 'I couldn't believe it when you killed his dog and he sent you that letter. Between the two of you, you just handed me a motive. Poor George. And poor Jack: tragically ripped from this world by an incompetent vet. The police are gonna love it. I mean, not only did you kill his dog, you lost the guy – what, forty thousand dollars?' He claps a hand against the gun in mock applause. 'They'll find out that he's been hounding you since you killed Jack – sorry, terrible pun – and not only do I have the collar and the knife with his fingerprints on it, the attack's on his record.'

'You made sure of that, didn't you?'

'That's right.'

'It was you, wasn't it? In the bushes that night on Fiddler's Island. You drugged George.'

'It could have gone either way.' He feigns concern. 'I mean, I had no idea what he'd do in that state. He could have killed you! Of course that would have been fine too but it's better this way. Now George not only has a motive, but a history of violence against you. It'll be open and shut. But don't worry,

311

he'll be fine. The public'll get behind him. You'll hear people at the back of the courtroom whispering, "I'd have shot her too if she'd killed my dog."'

'They won't believe it. There's no evidence placing him here.'

'Well, not now. But there will be. They'll find the knife and Jack's collar, both with his DNA and yours. I mean fuck, Ev, we've put people away with far less evidence. But you still haven't heard the kicker. George will wake up from a drugged stupor with the police knocking at his door and a gun in his hand. The same gun that put a bullet between the eyes of the murdering vet and her dog.' He waves the gun in Teddy's direction. 'And for one final, sweet little touch: next to him will be a photo of Jack and, on the back, in George's own handwriting it'll say, "I did it for you, boy!"'

I imagine this scenario. George is a good man. He'd make a terrible defendant because he'd insist on telling the truth. And there would be no suspicion of Victor – Jacob – when they have George openly admitting that, after what happened on the bridge, he could have done it, he just doesn't remember. I say, 'You've thought of everything, haven't you?'

But he hasn't. He didn't bank on Maria being here.

'Hmm. It's a shame about Teddy. But it's more believable if George kills your dog first and makes you watch. It's what I'd do if I were George.' He points a gloved finger at the ceiling and exclaims, 'Revenge!' Then his voice recovers that sickly, sympathetic tone. 'Lucky for George, he can claim diminished responsibility. I could even defend him! Perhaps not.'

He's almost laughing as he plays out his little skit. He's not lying. He *will* kill me. And I almost deserve it for being such a fucking fool. But not Teddy. Not my beautiful boy. Victor pulls a silencer from his suit pocket and screws it into the barrel. Teddy doesn't move; he just stares at us with uneasy eyes. I could charge at Victor, but he'll just shoot me. In the stomach maybe. Then he'll throw me aside and shoot Teddy

312

anyway. I could call Teddy to me but Victor will only shoot him in the back.

Then something on the hall table catches my eye.

Victor's not looking at me, he's looking at Teddy. He takes aim between Teddy's eyes, but before he has a chance to pull the trigger I throw my mobile as hard as I can. It slams into the Murano bowl, smashing it to pieces, and at the sound of metal on glass Teddy bolts for the stairs. Victor turns the gun and shoots. There's a hissing crack and I flinch as the bullet leaves the gun and embeds itself in the wall. The casing tinkles across the floor as the gunshot echoes around the hallway and my ears hum. I'm stunned by the volume; calling it a silencer seems absurd and I wonder if any of the neighbours are home. If they are, they must have heard. I pray they don't think it was just a car backfiring, that they'll call the police. All I've done is buy Teddy time, but at least I've done that.

'Clever.' Victor strides towards me, left hand reaching for something in his pocket. 'Very clever.'

When he's no more than a few paces in front of me, he draws his hand up to my face, and I see something resting on his flat palm. White powder. A camera flash of *déjà vu* sparks in my brain. I've seen this before: Victor standing in front of me in the shower, holding out his hand and blowing me a kiss. But not just then – other times come back with the same startling clarity. Him ringing the doorbell instead of using his key, blowing me a kiss when I answer the door, wearing those same black gloves covered in white dust. And every time I inhaled that powder I forgot everything. And the only reason I have *déjà vu* now is because Saeed has shown it to me in my dreams.

Not dreams. Memories.

Instinctively, I turn my face to the ground, hold my breath and shield my nose and mouth, as he blows the scopolamine in my face.

'Shit. Shit. You stupid, fucking bitch.'

313

I spit in his face and he slaps me hard across the cheek. I stagger backwards, trip and fall on to the marble floor, grabbing my stomach as I go down. Victor strides towards me, and with one hand protecting my belly I scrabble away until my back slams into the kitchen island. Unable to retreat any further, I reach for the counter and pull myself up to my feet. But Victor grabs me by the throat and throws me back down. My head cracks against the tile so hard, everything goes black for a few seconds.

Blood seeps through my hairline, and I press the gash closed with my palm. Victor puts the gun down on the counter and cranks open his belt.

'Whaddya say, Ev? One last go for old times' sake?' He unzips his fly, and I scurry across the floor towards the balcony, but he drags me back by my ankles.

I'm on my back, jeans bunched at my knees. I'm lashing out and kicking. But he just tightens his grip on my wrists and gets harder inside me. I spit in his face again and he slaps me. I free one hand and lash out, but he grabs it again and slams it against the tile.

'Go on, fight. It's so much better than you just bending over.'

He closes his marble eyes, and, now I can't see them, he looks like Jacob again. This *is* Jacob. And at the same time, it's someone else altogether. Someone…something…vile. I want to scream, tear at his face, dig my nails through his lids and gouge out those eyes. But he's too strong. And I have no way of stopping what's happening to me.

Tears run from the corners of my eyes, and that scream builds in the base of my brain. Now I know why the dreams felt so real, why my mind couldn't distinguish them from reality. Because they *were* real. Every one of them.

Victor's fingers grip my wrists like ropes and I hear Saeed's voice in my head, *Bound and assaulted. Bound and assaulted.*

But signposts are no good to me now.

I hear his velvet tones whispering, *Take control, Eva. Take control.*

So I do what he taught me.

I step away from the brink of madness.

I stop fighting.

I relax.

Squeezing my eyes shut, I imagine myself elsewhere. From my experience of the dining room under hypnosis I know I can't stray too far from reality. So I keep my mind on what's real. What's possible. I imagine Victor's – Jacob's – body, dead on this kitchen floor. I stare into those cold eyes, open and unblinking. I picture myself dragging Maria from the bathtub, bandaging her wrists. I imagine myself on the bedroom floor, coaxing Teddy out from under the bed. And, while we wait for the police to arrive, I rest my hand on my belly, caressing my little peach. The only person with the power to fight for the lives of any of us – all of us – is me.

The only one who can take control is me.

I need the other Eva. The bold, fearless Eva. The one who stood outside the dining room and watched this evil from the hallway. I am not her. But I could be. I am the master of my nightmares. I can stop terror in its tracks.

And suddenly, it's as if I'm watching this scene from a few feet away. As if it's happening to someone else entirely. I step back and allow the other Eva to retain my sanity in the face of the worst possible pain and madness.

Suddenly, I can think straight.

As if I'm lucid in a nightmare, I scan the kitchen for anything I can use to help the Eva on the floor. The gun is on the counter above her and the knives are in the block a little further away. She can't reach them. And even if she could get out from under him, she'd never get to them in time. She lies there on the floor, eyes closed, submitting to this rutting animal.

315

I watch for as long as I can bear before noticing how close her left thigh is to the sliding cabinet in the base of the kitchen island. It's behind him, out of his sight, and I know exactly what's in there.

I open my eyes.

As he thrusts in and out, lost in his rhythm, I let my hands and wrists go limp beneath his palms. His grip loosens a little, just enough for me to move. Millimetre by millimetre, I stretch my arms upwards, further and further above my head. The long sleeves of my T-shirt allow my arms to slide along the tiles, despite being pinned down. And as I extend them above my head, he has no choice but to stretch forward in order to keep hold of my wrists.

As his rhythm intensifies, I stretch just my left arm as far as it will go, until the bones strain in their sockets. And then I inch it a little more. It feels ready to snap, but it forces Victor to let go for a second, and he places his hand close to my head to prevent losing his balance. He looks me straight in the eye, daring me to strike him with my free hand.

I don't.

I don't fight.

I don't struggle.

I just lie there as I have dozens of times before.

He grins, and I catch the satisfaction in his eyes as he closes them. He thinks he's won. He thinks I'm beaten. But he's dead wrong. And I'll be damned if I let him finish.

Furtively, I slide my arm down by my side and reach forward until I feel the grooves in the cupboard door. Then I silently push it open. Naturally, this pathological perfectionist has stacked the tubs in this cupboard according to size and knows exactly what's in each one. She knows what she's feeling for. Not a tub, but a plastic, squeezy bottle.

I run my fingers up its body to the ridged, screw-on lid. Twisting it around, I find the smooth indentation that gives me purchase on its flip top cap and snap it open. The sound

316

alerts Victor. And as I snatch the bottle from the cupboard, upturning it as I go, he opens his eyes.

I stare into the depths of his pupils, grit my teeth, and squeeze.

Lye streams from the bottle, squirting, splashing and sputtering acid all over Victor's bare backside.

Dropping the bottle, I wrap my arms tightly around my stomach as he screams and flails like a wild dog. His thrashing fists bruise my ribs, his legs slam into mine, and I'm burned with spatters of lye. I thump, kick and scrabble out from beneath him, heaving myself up by the counter's edge. And, hitching up my jeans, I grab the gun as he scuttles away, pulling up his suit trousers as he goes.

I have no idea how to hold a gun; it's surprisingly heavy, and I have to readjust my grip. At arm's length, I keep it trained on him as he gets to his feet, wincing as he struggles with his zipper and button. Everything, from my shoulder to my fingertip, quivers with the weight of what I'm doing, what I'm holding in my hand: a small piece of metal with the power to end a life with the flick of a switch. When Victor finally looks at me, he's composed, almost smiling, but that has to be a farce. He must be in agonising pain.

I smile, too. 'Hurts?'

He doesn't answer, he just sneers and says, 'You're not gonna shoot me. You haven't got it in you.'

He looks me right in the eye, and I hold his gaze, the gun trained on his chest. In my peripheral vision, his leg twitches. He's weighing up whether I have the balls, whether I'll shoot him if he runs at me. My mobile's in the hall, probably broken along with the glass bowl, so I can't hold him at gunpoint and call the police.

My eyes drift to the ceiling, hoping to hear sounds, praying Maria's come to and is creeping down the stairs; her gun's still on the hall table. But the house is silent, and I fear the worst.

Nobody's coming.

It's just him and me.

Only it isn't me I care about any more, it's my child, growing inside me. The child I've ached for all these years. It's the size of a peach now, I could hold it in the palm of my hand. Instead, I'm holding a gun and pointing it at its father, knowing that, for it to survive, he has to die.

I could shoot him in the leg, try to disable him, but I've never shot a gun before. If I aim anywhere but his chest, I'll probably miss.

I've let my eyes and my aim wander and the gun is so heavy the muscles in my upper arm cry out with the strain. I have to cup my left hand under my right to support the gun's weight. I retarget his heart and glare at him: a warning.

He grins.

There are six paces between us.

Six seconds.

My husband or my child.

Between Victor and my child, I choose my child. But I'm not only pointing the gun at Victor, I'm pointing it at Jacob, too. And between my child and J, the choice is less clear.

As my finger curls around the trigger, a small protruding lever depresses beneath my touch. I'm sick with fear, shaking all over, half-expecting the gun to go off as this lever disappears into the body of the trigger. But it doesn't.

I see the conviction in his eyes, the reaching of a verdict, the conclusion that I don't have it in me to shoot him. Not with the man I love buried inside. His leg twitches again.

Six seconds.

I choose my child.

I squeeze.

The trigger depresses beneath my finger and then hits resistance. But, again, the gun doesn't go off. At first I think there's something wrong with it, a safety catch that needs disabling, but Victor just put the gun on the counter. I don't remember him doing anything to it after trying to shoot

318

Teddy. I realise that all I've done is take up the slack and just how hard I'll have to press the trigger for the gun to fire. The muscles in my upper arms burn with fatigue and my hands tremble with the weakness of panic and dread. But if this is what it takes to save my baby... I slide my finger further into the trigger guard and take aim as Victor dissolves in front of me. The hard edge melts from his eyes, his body relaxes, and he looks at the floor for a moment before raising his eyes to meet mine.

It's J.

He looks at me as if he hasn't seen me for weeks and then notices the weapon. His forehead creases as his mind adjusts to the scene in front of him, and then he glares in utter confusion, unable to comprehend why I'm standing here with the barrel of a gun trained on his chest.

'Eva? What's going on? What are you doing with that gun?'

It takes a moment for him to figure it out, his eyes darting around the room as he pieces the clues together: how he got here, why I'm beaten and bloodied, why I would consider shooting the man I love.

And when his clouded eyes sharpen and everything finally makes sense, I let my arms droop. The relief is so overwhelming, my knees buckle. J rushes to my side, catching me before I fall, pressing the gun between our bodies as he throws his arms around me.

Wiping tears from my cheeks and eyelashes, he kisses me softly on the lips before sliding his fingers through my hair and pulling me to his chest. As he caresses the base of my neck, he slides his free hand between us and carefully eases the gun from my grasp.

Then he whispers in my ear, 'You stupid fucking cow.'

My whole body stiffens.

He takes two steps back and I look at him. My mind flashes to that night in ATIK, and, just like then, his eyes are cold, dead, still.

And then he punches me.

As I hit the floor, my skull cracks against the tiles, and then he leans over me, hitting me repeatedly in the face.

When I come to, he's standing back where he was, only this time he has the gun. I reach up to the island counter and pull myself to my feet, while the room spins around me. And, when my eyes finally focus on him, he's grinning.

I feel like a fool. I fell for his trick and now my baby and I will pay for it. Disarmed, all I have left to delay the inevitable are words. And I'm not going to let him enjoy this.

'You think you've won,' I say, 'but it hasn't exactly gone according to plan, has it? You thought you'd just walk in here, drug me with that shit, and it would all be easy. But you're in a mess, Jacob.' I'm careful to use his real name – I don't make the same mistake twice. 'I have acid burns on my legs and so do you. How will you explain that to the police? How will you explain the burns on your hands? Hurt, pulling your trousers up, did it?' I sneer at him. 'As I said, they always suspect the husband. And what's more, Maria's opened a file on you, expressing concerns for my safety – that's how I got your medical records. Now she's in our bathtub. How are you going to explain that?'

'Well, that one's easy.' He pulls out the piece of paper he tucked in his pocket and flicks it open. Maria's signature's at the bottom.

'It's blank.'

'It is now, but once it's typed up it'll say she found your body. That your death is on her hands because she didn't arrest George Hope when he tried to slit your throat. Poor Maria just couldn't live with the guilt. And who knows what else she'll confess to once the creative juices start flowing: abuse of power, pulling records without authorisation, bribing PIs. And the world-class kicker, the absolute daddy: beating Peter Cunard while he was handcuffed.'

'You're a bastard.' I hold myself back from running at him and ripping that supercilious grin off his face. 'You still won't get away with it, Jacob. Don't you think the police'll find your acid burns suspicious? Or the scopolamine in Maria's blood? You're going to rot in prison.'

'I don't give a shit about the burns; the police won't even see them. And as for Maria, she has your death as a motive for suicide. And she's tried it before, slitting her wrists, so it won't come as any great surprise that she succeeded this time. She has a reputation for being unstable.'

I remember Jacob whispering in my ear at the party, *bitesize fruitcake*, and I know he's right. Maria does have a reputation for instability. Even I thought she was capable of beating Peter Cunard. I don't any more.

He says, 'Forensics will confirm she made the cuts herself. Her signature on the suicide note will be verified. With a clear cause of death, there probably won't even be a post-mortem. And, even if there is, it'll be limited; they won't find the scopolamine, because it was only a small dose, and they won't even be looking for it. As I say, Ev. I win every case.'

'Why, Jacob?'

He runs a hand through his hair, grits his teeth, and marches towards me. I throw my arms around my stomach, turning my face to protect myself from another onslaught. But he doesn't hit me. He just spits words at me. 'Stop calling me fucking JACOB!'

'All right, then.'

I fight to stay calm, fight to get the word out, because the last time I said it I got punched in the face. And I can't take any more. I suck in a breath, close my eyes, and say his name. 'Victor.'

Jacob laughs at me. 'You're so fucking funny. So fucking stupid. You got that from Maria, didn't you? I knew it when you said it in ATIK. I hadn't heard it in years. But then it all made sense. Not only had you been stupid enough to go and get yourself knocked up, you had to go snooping around in our medical records.'

I had no idea that Jacob – Victor – knew about the pregnancy, and the shock's written all over my face. He sneers, 'I saw the test in your bedside drawer.'

'Victor, I—' He punches me again and I slump to the floor.

'For FUCK'S sake! Stop saying that name. I'm not fucking VICTOR!'

He towers over me, out of focus. Blood pours from my nose and my eyes run with tears. I blink them away. I have no idea who this man is. He isn't Jacob. He says he isn't Victor. Which can mean only one thing. Jacob has a third alter. One I didn't even know existed. One I've rarely seen. Except, perhaps, in the dead of night, when he drugs me, ties me up and rapes me. And now I'm cast into the unknown. I knew how to handle Jacob. I thought I knew how to handle Victor.

I have no idea how to handle this monster.

My body's frozen. I can't get up off the floor. My breath comes in rapid gasps as I scan the room for an escape route. Jacob blocks my exit to the hall and I'm backed up against the island. I'll never make it to the balcony doors, let alone the fire escape. I have no option but to buy time. I try to conceal the tremor in my voice, 'Okay, then, what should I call you?'

'Joshua. JOSH-U-A, you stupid, fucking bitch.' He speaks in a sing-song tempo, nodding his head in time with the beat of each syllable. Then he raises the gun.

I lift a hand to appease him. 'All right then...Joshua. You killed Hannah Edwards, didn't you, Joshua?' His arm relaxes a little and the gun droops. 'The little girl they found in the woods? You buried her beneath that tree?'

He grins like a child, as if he's that little boy all over again, slitting that poor girl's throat.

'Why?'

'She was in the way.'

He raises the gun again, so I speak quickly.

322

'And your girlfriend at Syracuse – Sophie. You killed her too?'

'She went for a little swim in Onondaga Lake.'

'But how? There were witnesses. You were in the pub when she went missing.'

He exposes his perfect teeth. 'The police are as fucking stupid as you are.'

I don't pause, not even for a second. 'And your wife, Claudine. You made it look like suicide, just like Maria.'

Maria said that Jacob found his wife in the bathtub, and the police had to prise him from her body. Unresponsive. Inconsolable. And it all makes sense now. Jacob killed his wife while in the mind of this third alter, Joshua, and was left with no memory of doing it.

'Why did they all have to die?'

'You fucking bitches ruin everything.' His body twists in pain.

It's a struggle to keep him distracted when my mind's on something else. Joshua will shoot me, I know I won't get out of this alive, but I'm trying to figure out how long my little peach will survive after I'm gone. Three minutes before it's starved of oxygen? Perhaps Maria is alive up there and already calling the police. Could the paramedics keep me breathing long enough to get me on life support so my little peach will survive? Can they even do that? But if Maria's dead, they won't find out I'm pregnant until it's too late.

I want that gun back. And I won't hesitate to pull the trigger. But instead, I just keep talking. 'What do we ruin?'

'He needs me. I protect him. I've always protected him. You always come between us. I saw Jacob, all coo-eyed over you at the ball. You all love *him*. And then you try to get rid of me. Like that fucking bitch Violet. I should have killed her when I had the chance.'

He's talking about his aunt. The woman who took Jacob to see a psychiatrist when he was thirteen. She did try to eradicate

Joshua from Jacob's mind. And he's right, I would have tried too.

He says, 'I thought you'd be different. You know, I really liked you when we first met. The way your mind operated. So focused. So methodical as you tried to save that pathetic badger. I didn't swerve when it ran out into the road, I wanted to hit it. I'd seen you from the street, several times, in those sexy scrubs. I knew you'd fall for the handsome stranger bringing a poor, injured animal into your surgery.'

My mouth falls open.

The man I first met wasn't Jacob. It was Joshua.

It makes sense now. He introduced himself as J and I've called him that ever since. That's why he never flinches when I say his name. And that's why I wasn't sure about him at first. It wasn't until I met Jacob – the real Jacob – that I started to warm to him.

He says, 'I thought we had something. But like all the rest, you only have eyes for Jacob. You were *mine*.' The gun droops to his side, and there's a hint of sorrow in his eyes. Then it's gone. 'Not that it matters now. You're not the same person. You were sexy. Cool. A surgeon.' He says that with reverence. 'People were impressed. But what would I say to them now? This is my wife: a fat, useless cunt who kills animals instead of saving them. Unemployed and fucking unemployable. For fuck's sake!'

'I never would have killed Jack if you hadn't had me drugged up to the fucking eyeballs!'

'Oh, come on, it wasn't the drugs. I'd had you on those for years. You had to go and get yourself knocked up. Jesus. Five fucking years! Three of them having to listen to you bitch and whine about not having a fucking baby. We haven't even made it to the seven-year itch and already I'm...' With jerky, manic movements, he scratches himself all over as if insects are crawling beneath his clothes. Then he stops suddenly and says, 'This has been the most fun I've had in our entire fucking

324

relationship.' He speaks to me as if explaining a complex problem to a simpleton. 'You see, Eva, you've changed. I mean, look at you. You're a pathetic, fucking mess. And so fucking tedious. So fucking boring.'

He lifts the gun to my head.

I hold up my hand as if I can stop the bullet. 'Please, Jacob, please. I know you're in there somewhere,' I sob, reaching a hand out to him. 'Look at me, baby. Look at me. It's Eva.'

'You still think he's in here! You still think I'm Jacob.' Joshua laughs as if that's hilarious.

Then he stops dead.

'I'm bored now,' he says.

And pulls the trigger.

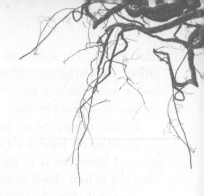

FORTY-FOUR

AN EXPLOSIVE gunfire crack echoes around the kitchen like two bullets fired in quick succession. There's a muffled ringing in my ears. Everything sounds muted.

A faint whistle of metal through air.

Splitting bone.

The tinkle of casings on the tile.

A body slumping to the floor.

Hands held to my face, head turned aside, I open my eyes. The sliding cupboard door has a splintered gash with a hole through it, millimetres from my head. It wasn't bone splitting, it was wood. Castor oil drips through the gap.

He missed.

Joshua missed.

I look up, expecting to see a face filled with regret. A face that says he couldn't go through with it and missed on purpose. Or warm eyes that tell me, in the stress of the moment, he genuinely switched alters from Joshua back to Jacob.

But Jacob isn't standing above me.

He's lying on the kitchen floor in his Martin Greenfield suit, eyes open, blood pouring from a hole in the side of his head.

I stare.

In my peripheral vision, Maria's shape shifts in the doorway, but I can't bring myself to look at her. I can't tear my eyes from J. If I do, I'll never be able to look at him again. Not like this.

He'll disappear.

The hard edge has gone from his eyes, and the dimpled corners of his mouth are turned up, almost smiling. He looks nothing like Victor or Joshua.

He looks like J.

The gun has slipped from his grip and lies black and hard on the marble. His empty hand, curled at the fingertips, reaches out for it as his blood spreads, slow and viscous. A ruby puddle on beige tiles.

His watch, on the half-Albert chain, has slipped from his pocket, and I can just make out the pendant with his initials. It dangles, quiet and motionless, from the second buttonhole of his waistcoat. His hair needs cutting. A lock falls over his forehead and he doesn't like that. It tickles. In a moment, he'll brush it back with his fingers, the way he always does when it gets too long.

He doesn't.

My hand twitches to reach out and touch the end of those curled fingers as if mine hold the spark of life, like God in the Sistine Chapel. But I pull back, knowing they will yield to my touch and droop.

Limp and lifeless.

Slowly, reluctantly, I tear my eyes from J and look towards Maria, standing in the doorway.

It's not Maria.

I look at J's body, then back at the door.

Lying dead on the kitchen floor, bleeding from a bullet hole in the side of his head, is my husband, Jacob.

And standing in the doorway with Maria's gun in his hand is my husband, Jacob.

FORTY-FIVE

THREE DAYS LATER

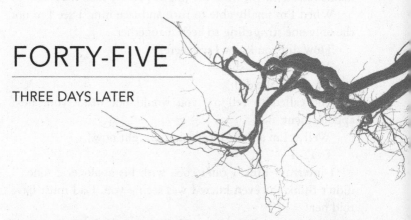

I FEEL A PRESENCE. A dark figure standing in the doorway. And the first thing I see when I prise open my swollen eyes is Joshua.

He arrives like this. Unannounced. Uninvited.

He comes in flashes like my dreams.

A moment later, I'm staring down the barrel of his gun. And the next, I'm staring at the blood seeping from the bullet hole in the side of his head.

Then I realise he's dead and think it's Jacob standing in the doorway. I remember us dancing in the garden at Le Manoir and, for a brief second, smile inside. But in another flash, I remember his lies.

This is how I wake up.

Dozens of times.

Day and night.

Only this time, it isn't Joshua standing in the doorway. It's not Jacob or Maria.

It's Saeed.

329

Turning away so he can't see my bloated face is an involuntary reaction. A hot tear pools in my black and broken eye socket. I had no idea a person's face could swell like this. Fighting tooth and nail to protect me from myself, Mum finally handed me a mirror from her purse. I barely look human.

When I'm finally able to turn and face him, I see I'm not the only one struggling to keep it together.

'How did you know I was here?'

'Your mother...she—'

'Of course she did.'

'She called to tell me you would not make your next appointment.'

'Well...I'm a little incapacitated right now.'

'Eva...I—'

I interrupt him. I can't cope with his apologetic tone. 'I didn't think she even knew I was seeing you. Dad must have told her.'

I didn't want Saeed to come. Not because I didn't want to see him – I did, desperately – but because I couldn't bear him to see me like this.

Broken.

The old Eva isn't recognisable beneath the damage. She's been dropped on a landmine. The doctors stitched on her limbs with one hand while plugging haemorrhaging wounds with the other, and what's left is a monster. But one look at Saeed tells me that the doctors can only do so much of the repair.

I'll need him for the rest.

'Did Mum tell you everything?'

'No...just...just—'

'Just the Cliff Notes? That's not like Patricia Cosgrove; she must be off her game.'

'It was hard for her to talk about it.' He approaches the bed as if I'm a cornered animal, injured, but still with claws and teeth. 'Do you want to tell me? You do not have to. We can talk about other things.'

330

'Like the weather? Politics? The state of the roads?'

'If you like.'

I stare up at the ceiling as he takes the chair next to the bed. Neither of us speaks. I'm accustomed to Saeed's silences, those long moments where he waits for me to be ready. But now those moments are stretched to breaking. When I know he's not looking at me, I watch him from the corner of my eye. He's filtering more than he ever has before. It's as if I can see the cogs in his mind through his pupils. They grind as his eyes drift off into the middle distance. He'll have had years of training on how to control and titrate his emotions in front of his patients: feeling them, noticing them, and finally labelling them before deciding what's safe. What he should and shouldn't say to me. But I suspect, this time, his training has fallen short.

And for the first time it's he who breaks the silence.

'Eva...I...I let you down.' He places his hand on my arm as if I'm made of snow and will melt beneath his touch. 'I am so sorry.' And that's all it takes for me to burst into tears.

I cry less and less each day. Not because the emotional pain is easing, but because the physical pain from crying with these injuries is unbearable. Some days, I blame J, as if he was the one beating me. After all, it's his face I see.

But other times, in my mind's eye, I see him standing in the doorway with that gun.

Shooting his brother to save my life.

He rushed to my side then, tried to hold me. But all I could do was shove him away.

He called the police, called the ambulance, dragged Maria from the bathtub and kept her alive long enough for the paramedics to take over. They said a few minutes more and she would've been dead. Those hours are a blur. But the last thing I do remember, as the paramedics fussed around me, was him carrying Teddy down the stairs and placing his trembling body next to mine on the floor.

He wouldn't let the police arrest him and take him away until he'd called Bron and asked if she'd collect Teddy. Then my father with instructions to come to the hospital. And only when every one of us was safe would he leave with the police. He'd saved the life of one of their own, so they weren't going to argue with him.

And, with the tears, the events of that day pour out of me, as if Saeed's presence alone has induced his peculiar form of hypnosis, and I'm recounting another bad dream. And once I've spilled it all, like a child at points, the words choked out between sobs, we're left in another long silence.

'Do you think he knew?' Saeed finally asks. 'What Joshua was doing?'

'Yes.' Unable to hold his gaze, I close my eyes. He's searching for the truth. He knows what's buried deep inside me.

'He shot him. Why would he have done that if he was complicit in the rapes?'

I know that, and yet I keep asking myself, over and over, how it would be possible to not know. My anger at Jacob is the only thing that's keeping me upright, and if I admit the truth...

But I have Saeed now. I don't need any more lies.

'No. I can't imagine Jacob... but that doesn't erase the lies.'

'It does not. But if you do not believe he should be convicted of murder, you will have to testify to that belief.'

'I can't. I can't face him in a courtroom. I won't be able to look at him without seeing Joshua.'

'If you will allow me to break our therapeutic confidence, I will testify. If you cannot talk about the things Joshua did?'

I nod, too exhausted to think that far ahead.

Saeed stares at the blanket. He can't look at me when he says, 'I have dreams now. Nightmares. I see you... I watch from the door, powerless to stop it. And I hear myself... telling you over and over... it is *not real*, Eva. It is *not real*. While you are tied to that table, as he...'

332

Saeed can't finish the sentence.

He can't say the words.

And, in many respects, his pain is the same as mine. It mirrors mine because they were dreams to me, too. The only memories I had of them were shared with Saeed. And now we both know, in intimate detail, the devastating trespasses that Joshua inflicted. Through me, Saeed has experienced the sickening vulnerability that only a woman can feel. And for him, just as they do for me, each dream collides with, compounds, and snowballs around the others with startling reality.

They *were* real.

And I have deep empathy for Saeed as I replay that feeling, when Joshua revealed the truth to me: the weakness in my knees, the sickness in my stomach. It's what he feels now.

And I can't speak to that feeling. Words have not been invented to describe the horror at that kind of dehumanisation.

'I knew,' he says, 'right from the start...that your dreams were different. I said to you...they lacked transitions...were too...structured. I should have known they were real. That you were not recalling nightmares...but memories. If I had figured it out sooner...'

His eyebrows are drawn down so low over his eyes they look black with sorrow, and, looking in his face, I wonder...is it possible to meet a man like Saeed and not fall in love? Not in a romantic way, not in the way I loved J, but in every other possible way there is to love another human being.

I grew up believing what my mother taught me: you meet, you date, you fall in love, you get married, you have sex, you have children. If you're a respectable girl, you don't do any of that in the wrong order. And that kind of narrow-minded, society-driven thinking leads to a great deal of confusion as you're chased along through herding gates into your inevitable future. Because human beings are far more complex, the brain and its emotions far more elaborate and sophisticated. And it's

333

only when most of life has passed you by that you realise the truth: that love cannot be so easily contained and corralled. The truth is that love comes in many forms. If you're lucky, the love you feel for a close female friend can equal the love you feel for your husband, as you tell her things you wouldn't dare tell anyone, not even him.

People knit together when they unravel their secrets.

And in the case of Saeed, is it possible to lay yourself so bare and not have that exposure lead to a connection that is, on some levels, deeper than the one you share with your husband?

In this way, I am in love with Saeed.

And I see, in the small ways he betrays his feelings: how he struggles to look me in the eye; how his words crack and his speech pauses; how his Adam's apple fluctuates as he swallows. I see him as two people: the man, and the trained psychotherapist able to mediate his emotions in a split second before choosing what to reveal to his patient. I see his fear. Of mirroring my emotions, reflecting them back on me so they double in intensity. Or of comforting me, not to help me, but to ease his own distress at seeing me so broken. He needs me to feel the full totality of my pain, to own it in the safety of his company, and not stifle it with soothing platitudes.

In laying myself bare before Saeed, we have got too close for his training to be a convincing mask over how he feels about me, or the way he perceives he let me down. But the truth is the opposite.

I wouldn't be here if it weren't for him.

And it's strange, but Saeed's coming apart stitches me back together. I stop crying, and suddenly feel stronger than I have since they wheeled me into this room.

I believe women are viewed as the weaker sex because it isn't until you put them under great strain that their strength comes to the surface. It's rarely seen. And their tendency to care for others above themselves means that their true resilience only arises when it's someone else in great need. They call it

334

hysterical strength. And I have read stories of women lifting cars to save their children; of a woman in Canada who fought a polar bear with her fists to save her son; and in America, two girls – just fourteen and sixteen – who lifted a one-and-a-half-ton tractor to free their father. It's a form of hysterical strength I feel now: the need to help Saeed, when I'm the one who's broken.

I say, 'Do you remember the first day I came to your office? Pessimistic. Haughty. Angry. Admittedly, I wasn't angry at you, I was angry at Mum for making me go. But I was convinced that this "sleep and dream psychologist" was a kook. A complete fraud. And instead, I found you. You told me that sleep and dreams were just a hobby, that you were a therapist first. And…'

I place my free hand over his arm, three fingers of my left hand splinted together – in the fight with Joshua after I poured acid over him, I didn't even realise I'd broken them – and I squeeze as tight as my broken fingers will allow, urging him to look at me.

'Your therapy saved my life. *You* saved my life. My baby's life. Maria's. And Teddy's.'

'How? I was…not even there.' And he says that as if he should have been. As if I am his responsibility in every respect: mentally, emotionally and physically.

'Joshua tried to drug me that day. If he'd succeeded, we'd all be dead. I would've been dead long before Jacob showed up. Joshua came at me with those drugs in his hand, about to blow them in my face. But I remembered. I saw what I'd recalled in our sessions. It came back, just as you said, in a snatch of memory. I saw that hand. That black glove covered in white powder. And instinct kicked in. I held my breath, covered my mouth and nose without even thinking. And it's because of you. If I hadn't seen it before, I wouldn't have known what was coming. I wouldn't have been able to protect myself, and he would have killed us all. You saved me. You saved all of us.'

335

We're touching. But it isn't enough. The space between us feels infinite.

I look at him in exasperation and say, 'For fuck's sake, Saeed. I nearly died.'

And finally...finally...he relents. And yet, he still takes me by surprise when he reaches forward and wraps his arms around me. Pressed against his chest, I feel the old Eva coming back to life. I feel her heart begin to beat, as if his hands are inside her ribcage squeezing it, willing it to beat on its own.

The relief equals my pain and grief until it's almost too much to bear.

So I say in his ear, 'To think, I almost didn't come back after that first session. I almost didn't go to that first appointment at all.'

He doesn't let go, but says, 'So you are saying your mother was right after all?'

We both laugh, but the pain is instant, my fat lips cracking.

He squeezes me and whispers in my ear with that velvet voice, 'Can you ever forgive me for letting you down?'

'There's nothing to forgive.'

And we hold each other in silence for a long time, longer than would be comfortable for friends or even lovers. Because our bond has gone beyond that. Beyond friendship. Beyond love. Beyond reason.

And when I pull him so close that all the space between us disappears and feel his heart beating against mine, I finally start to heal.

FORTY-SIX

THREE MONTHS LATER

THE FIRST TWO months were a blur of activity and commotion, but the last four weeks have been empty. Christmas has come and gone and now the apartment is quiet, so much so that I almost feel as though Joshua did take my life that day. But Maria's on her way over and that's always a relief. She knows the investigating officer and keeps me abreast of what's happening.

In the taxi that night after my parents' party, Maria called me her best friend.

Now, I am.

And she is mine.

Maria saved my life. That day, doped up and bleeding from both wrists, on the brink of consciousness, she managed to lean over the bathtub and catch the hem of her trouser leg between her fingertips. Her mobile was in the pocket and before she passed out she managed to open the phone app and press dial. With no contact selected, it dialled the last number, the one person I'd told her not to call: Jacob.

And all she managed was one word: Eva.

After that, like a virtual husband, she was there morning, noon and night in the hospital. She held my hand through every police interview, and you should see how she deals with relentless reporters. Now, when you Google my name, the headlines about Jack aren't the first ones you see.

I check my watch. She's not late. I'm impatient. There's too much room in this apartment. Too much space to think. But when Maria's around there's no room for fathomless silence and not a moment to think. After her near-death experience, she's as sassy as ever and still a bit of a bitch, but I'm a tough bitch myself these days. Tough-er, anyway.

And now, I love her for it.

Teddy adores her too. And dogs know the truth about people. They smell it. Perhaps Teddy knows that if it weren't for her, I wouldn't be here. And neither would he. It's not something either of us will ever forget.

And if we did, Maria would remind us.

I make tea and hop up next to her on one of the kitchen bar stools. Teddy's on his back legs, front paws on Maria's knees, enjoying the fuss as she massages his ears.

I still haven't replaced the sliding cupboard door. The bullet hole watches us like an eye.

She says, 'The CPS aren't going to prosecute Jacob for murder.'

I'm not sure how I feel about that. Sometimes I want Jacob to rot in jail for all his lies. Other times, the gratitude for his saving my baby's life, Teddy's life, Maria's, and mine, overwhelms me. It lasts a minute or two before I remember that he put us in that situation in the first place.

Maria says, 'I saw Jacob's statement, and it was pretty clear it wasn't intentional homicide. But the police took some convincing: a headshot looks damn intentional. They questioned him over and over about why he didn't disable

Joshua instead of killing him. But Jacob explained he didn't have time to make a rational decision. He came in the door and saw you beaten and bloodied on the kitchen floor with a gun aimed at your head. He just grabbed my gun and fired. They even tried to trick him, saying he must have had time to disengage the safety catch, take aim to make a headshot, but it didn't work, because Jacob's never fired a gun before and—'

'What?!'

'What?' Maria looks confused.

'Jacob's never fired a gun before?'

'No. The gun from the safe was Joshua's.'

'But he grew up on a farm; his father must have owned guns.'

'Hunting rifles, maybe. But Jacob left the farm when he was eleven. I doubt his father allowed his kids to play with guns.'

'That's true.'

'Anyway, a Glock doesn't have a safety, it's a fully automatic system that the trigger disengages. Jacob said he didn't even look at the gun, he didn't even aim, he just picked it up and fired. Lucky he did or you'd be dead.'

'The police are sneaky,' I say.

'So are criminals; we have to be. But Jacob's lucky to get off. He didn't think they'd let it go.'

'Why?'

'Headshots are hard to make. If you pick up a gun and fire without aiming, you'd most likely miss or hit the body, not the head. But Jacob said it didn't occur to him until much later how lucky the shot was. If he'd just injured him, Joshua could still have turned the gun on you and probably would have shot Jacob if he'd had to. It was pure luck.'

'I'm a lucky girl.'

'We both are. If Joshua had killed Jacob, we'd both be dead. Anyway, Joshua's bullet in the kitchen cupboard, combined

339

with your statement, finally satisfied the prosecutor that Jacob
had no choice. He took one life to save three.'

'Four if you count Teddy.'

Maria raises her eyebrows at the crazy dog lady.

'Anyway,' she says. 'With Joshua being his brother, especially a twin, they accepted that he wouldn't have taken the
shot if he'd had any other option.'

I nod. In spite of everything, I suppose I don't want Jacob
going down for murder.

'But he's still going to jail.'

'What for?'

'Fraud, conspiracy to commit fraud, and...' She looks
sheepish.

'And?'

'And...'

'What?'

'Impersonating a barrister. Jacob confessed that, although
the practising certificate is in his name, it was Joshua who took
the bar exam in the United States, and the QLTS in the UK.'

'QLTS?'

'It's a transfer exam so you can practise here.'

'Why would Jacob admit to that? Surely they couldn't
have proved it?'

Maria gets up to put the kettle on for more tea, and Teddy
follows her around the island. She says, 'Maybe he wants to go
to jail. He could have defended himself in court, and knowing
Jacob—'

There was no reason for Jacob to confess to that. I wonder
if Maria's right and he does want to go to prison.

'Even without that charge,' she says, 'the prosecutor's still
got him on the other counts of fraud and...' she pauses, filling
the kettle from the kitchen tap '...conspiracy to commit
fraud.'

'Surely Joshua was the one committing fraud. It was Jacob's
identity they shared.'

340

She sits back down as the kettle hisses to life, and Teddy jumps up to be fussed again. She rubs his ears and says, 'Well, that's the conspiracy part. But Jacob still tried cases when he wasn't technically a qualified barrister. And charged his clients big bucks to do it. That's fraud. Fuck, think about it: every case he's ever tried could be nullified and have to be tried again. This could drag on forever.'

'So mine isn't the only life he's fucked up, then.'

'He also saved it, remember. Fortunately, he didn't lose any of those cases. So, although he made money off his clients, he did provide the service he billed them for. Which makes the fraud charge complicated. But he also got Joshua into the country illegally, allowed him to use his passport and live here illegally under his citizenship. So that's conspiracy to commit fraud. And of course there's tax fraud too. They only paid tax for one person for all those years.'

'I didn't even think of that.'

'Anyway, the whole case is a fucking mess. He thinks he'll get a plea deal since it would take years to try, and would cost a fortune.'

'A plea deal? For how many years?'

'Hard to say. Impersonating a barrister for over a decade, two maybe. Fraud, five. Conspiracy to commit...I don't know, three possibly. So around ten in total. But with the early confession more like seven, out in four.'

'Four years? I'm not sure it's enough.'

'He's paying in other ways, Ev. He's a mess.'

'Wait a minute! How do you know he's a mess? And what do you mean, *he thinks* he'll get a plea deal? You've seen him?! You said you were just going to talk to the lead investigator.'

'He's just an acquaintance from training in Hendon, Ev. He can't share every detail with me; I'm a witness. I'm not allowed anywhere near the case. I *had* to talk to Jacob. Besides, I wanted to see him. He saved my life too, you know.'

I glare at her.

341

'Don't look at me like that. You're not angry because I went to see him without asking you. You're angry that I've seen him and you haven't.'

'Bullshit.'

'Is it? It was your statement that got him off, not mine. I didn't even see Jacob take the shot. You convinced the prosecutor it was reasonable force. It could have been murder, not self-defence. You could have put him down for life for that headshot. But you didn't.'

I bury my face in my hands.

Maria gently pulls them away. 'I know you still care about him, Ev. I know you've said from the beginning that he belongs in jail, but I'm not sure you really mean it.'

'Don't I? What if he knew? What if he knew everything Joshua was doing to me?'

'No way.'

'Well, even if he didn't, he still put me in that situation. He still lied to me for five fucking years.'

'I think you're more angry with yourself than him, because you didn't figure it out. You're not stupid, Ev. I bet his own fucking mother couldn't tell them apart. I couldn't. I met Josh in court on the Kapoor case and then Jacob at the party, do you remember? I said I'd remembered him from court as standoffish. What an understatement. A cold-blooded killer more like.'

The kettle pings and Maria gets up to finish the tea with Teddy in tow. His eyes light up when she opens the fridge door and dull again when she pulls out the milk carton and shuts it. As she's pouring the tea, she says, 'Wasn't the sex different?'

'For fuck's sake, Maria.'

'Sorry. I just wondered. I mean, they *looked* identical, uncannily so, but there must have been some differences?'

'Of course there were. Jesus. With hindsight, it's obvious now. Which is why I feel like a fucking idiot. Joshua was sullen and cold. He'd get this look in his eyes that frightened me sometimes.' I almost laugh at myself. 'And yes, he was different in bed. Rough. But I just thought it was Jacob having a bad day and taking it out on me.'

'You said that at the party, I remember – that it was just his job.'

I nod. 'And he wasn't like that in the beginning. For the first few years I didn't see that cold side of Joshua; he was more like…'

'Jacob.'

'Yes.'

'I'm sure Jacob had no idea what his brother was really like.'

'You can't know that. He lied, very successfully I might add, for years. Not just to me but to Claudine too. He's a liar, Maria. He fooled everyone. How do you know he's not fooling you?'

'If you'd seen him, Ev, you wouldn't ask me that. Why don't you go and visit him?'

'Visit him?! For fuck's sake, Maria, if you'd been through what I have, you wouldn't ask me *that*.'

'He feels terrible. He didn't even apply for bail. He wants to pay for what he's done.'

'You sound like you're on his side.'

'Don't be fucking stupid, of course I'm not. What he did was terrible. He put you and your child in danger. But…'

'But?'

'This isn't about sides. He's broken, Ev. He's lost everything: his career, his twin brother, you, and the baby. He even asked how Teddy was.'

I look away from her. I have no interest in what Jacob has lost.

'I found this, too,' she says, taking a piece of paper from her bag and handing it to me.

I unfold a newspaper cutting. 'What is it?'

343

'It's where it all started. Violet adopted Jacob when their parents died, but not Joshua. She sent Joshua to a school for boys. This is the place she sent him to.'

I read the first sentence out loud, 'The Stiles Institute for Boys closed in 1996 following horrific reports of beatings and sexual abuse...' but the rest of the words won't come out. As if the phrases are in bold, several of them stand out from the article. *A house of horror...food and medical deprivation as forms of punishment...floggings and rape were commonplace.* 'Jesus.'

'I know. No wonder he turned into a psychopath. Thirty-six boys died in that home between 1964 and 1996. But Joshua ran away after the first year. Jacob said he lived on the streets near Violet's house so they could be together.'

I imagine Joshua, sleeping on benches and in doorways to escape the horrors of that boarding school, and for one fleeting moment I feel sorry for him.

Maria says, 'Josh nearly died. That's when it all started—'

'Please don't call him that. Don't call him Josh, like he was some sweet little boy.'

'Okay. Josh-U-A.' I hear Joshua's singsong tone in Maria's voice and see his face as he pulled the trigger. 'Anyway, that's when they started switching places on Violet. Jacob did it to get Joshua off the streets. He even slept in the barn so Josh...ua... could have a warm bed. He could have died of exposure himself.'

'Jesus, can you stop with the heartstrings? I'm not going to feel sorry for Jacob.'

'I'm just telling you what happened.'

'Really?'

'Yes. Really. Ev, they did it out of necessity, not some evil plan to deceive and hurt people.'

'It may have started that way, but it certainly didn't end that way.'

Neither of us speak for a while. Then Maria says, 'Ev...' and her tone gets my attention.

'What?'

'There's something else I haven't told you.'

She gets up for a third time and Teddy follows her again. Momentarily distracted by my sweet boy, who's come to mean more to me than ever now I nearly lost him, I marvel at the energy he has for constantly monitoring the fridge and cupboards. Maria spoons the teabags out of the cups, squeezing them before dropping them in the bin, and I realise she's stalling.

'What is it?'

'Fuck...' She brings the tea back over to the island. 'I don't know whether to tell you this.'

'Well, you can't say "There's something I haven't told you" and not tell me.'

'The prosecutor's threatening Jacob with another charge.'

'What?'

'Rape.'

'Rape?!'

'Rape by deception.'

'That's ridiculous.'

'It is a bit of a stretch, but I looked into it and she may have a case. I mean, think about it: you met Joshua first. And then, when you consented to sex with Jacob, you had no idea you were consenting to a different man. You had no idea who he really was. Consent by deception is no consent at all. With them switching places on you, you never knew which man you were having sex with. And you certainly wouldn't have consented to sex with both of them. So, they're both guilty of rape by deception.'

My head is spinning. 'That's insane.'

'It's the law, Ev. It's there to protect women from being tricked into giving consent. For a rape charge to stand, there doesn't need to be resistance from the victim if the perpetrator prevented that resistance by deception. And this prosecutor's a fucking pit bull, particularly in sexual abuse cases.'

345

'She'd have had a field day with Joshua, then.'

'The only hole in her case is that you married Jacob. If you'd married Joshua, Jacob would face fifteen years for this charge alone. And with the other charges on top he'd be looking at...God, I don't know...twenty-five to thirty. But Jacob has proof that it's him you married.'

'What proof?'

'I'm not sure. Apparently, Joshua had no interest in a wedding day, with Claudine or with you. Do you need proof?'

I close my eyes to evade the truth. 'No.' I remember our wedding day – and the night – and I have no doubt who I married. I may hate Jacob but I don't want him going down for rape because of an over-zealous prosecutor. I say, 'It doesn't matter anyway, because I won't press charges. I'll refuse.'

'You don't have to press charges. It's up to the prosecutor to judge which crimes he should be charged with. You're just a witness.'

'You mean she can go ahead without me?'

'Yeah. He still committed the crime. It won't matter that the victim's on his side. If a teacher has sex with an underage student and the student claims it was love, do you think the teacher doesn't go to jail?'

'This is real? She can actually charge him with raping me?'

'Yeah. She has precedent, too. There was a similar case in the Met. This undercover police officer got into a long-term relationship with an activist he was secretly investigating. When she found out, she accused him of this same charge. The only reason he didn't go to jail was because she agreed to an out-of-court settlement. She got four hundred thousand pounds, Ev. This shit's very real.'

I drive my fingernails into the roots of my hair and tug, hard.

'You said yourself you didn't think four years was enough.'

I look her straight in the face.

'But rape, Maria. Rape!'

346

'It's crazy, I know. But she's gunning for Jacob. You have to admit, it's an interesting case. What prosecutor wouldn't want to get their teeth into this one?'

'Fuck. I thought all this was behind me. Now, there'll be a long-drawn-out trial.'

'There won't if he accepts all the charges.'

'He can't do that. He can't live with a rape charge on his record.'

'That's up to Jacob. The plea deal's between him and the CPS. There's nothing you can do.'

'Get me her number.'

'You can't call the prosecutor. You have to go through the VCL.'

I glare at her.

'I'll get you her number.'

Since Maria texted me the prosecutor's number an hour ago, I've been staring at my phone. I've dialled and hung up I don't know how many times. Maria suggested again that I go through the proper channels, but the pit bull needs to hear this from me.

I dial.

'Susannah West.'

I should have planned what I was going to say.

'Hello?'

I remind myself I'm not Eva Curtis any more; I'm not the downtrodden victim. I'm Eva Cosgrove. And Eva Cosgrove is one tough, fucking bitch.

'Hello?' she says again, about to hang up.

'Miss West, this is Eva Cosgrove…Eva Curtis.'

'Mrs Curtis. I'm sorry, but if you're calling for details about the prosecution, you'll have to go through the Victim Communication and Liaison service. I can give you their—'

'I don't want to speak to the VCL. I want to speak to you. I want to talk to you about the rape charge.'

'I'm sorry, Mrs Curtis. I can't discuss the case with you directly.'

'Fine. Then don't talk. Listen.' I turn my voice to rock. 'When I met Joshua, I wasn't sure I even liked him. It was Jacob I fell for. I only gave consent to Joshua because I thought *he* was Jacob. And I never would have done that if I'd known what he was.'

'Mrs Curtis, let's face it, you never knew who you were giving consent to at any one time. You were cheated out of it. That's the whole material point.'

'I knew. I may not have known the whole truth – I actually thought he had a split personality – but I *did* know which of those men I was in love with. And think about this: the night Jacob and I first slept together, and every goddamn night following, I consented to sex with him, face to face, in the moment. I *wanted* to have sex with him. I had the time of my life with him. I love him. The only person guilty of rape in this case is Joshua. And if you continue down this road, if you insist on pursuing this trumped-up charge, this "rape victim" will come down so hard on the side of the defence, she'll make your head spin. I'm telling you: let this go or I'll make you look like a fool.'

I end the call, slam the phone down, and stretch out my hands to stop them shaking.

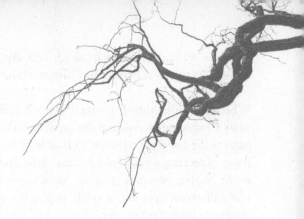

FORTY-SEVEN

IT'S A WEEK SINCE I threatened the prosecutor, and Maria hasn't been able to find out anything new, so I still don't know if it did any good. It could have made things worse. Maria called Susannah West a pit bull, and the one thing I know about pit bulls is, the harder you tug on whatever's between their teeth, the harder their jaws clamp down.

This morning, my phone rang with a number I didn't recognise, and for a moment I thought it was her. It wasn't. The woman on the other end of the line was the very last person I expected to hear from: the woman I'd accused Jacob of having an affair with. His aunt: Violet.

Apparently, Jacob had set up a low-cost local service and called her regularly. She had flown to the UK as soon as she heard what happened and plans to stay for the foreseeable future so she can spend time with him. He suggested she stay in the London flat and gave her my number to check it was all right with me. Jacob would have known it was – I never go to the flat – I suspect he wanted Violet to speak to me or, more likely, he wanted Violet to speak *for him*. And when she asked to meet, it was as if I could feel him reaching out to me.

When she walks into this small London café, she's not at all what I expected. Knowing she separated the boys after their parents died and sent Joshua to that horrific boarding school, I was expecting a very cold woman. But there's nothing cold about Violet. She has greying, shoulder-length black hair, soft half-moon eyes and a smile that aches to be wide. Life's obviously been hard on her.

I watch in awe as she unloads what must be a tablespoon of sugar into her cup and ask her if she'd like some tea with her sugar. 'Well, in Georgia,' she says, 'we like it sweet. And normally ice-cold. You English are so strange about your tea. Milk in first, milk in last. Water off the boil. Warm the pot. Don't squeeze the bag. For heaven's sakes, it's only tea.'

'It's not, it's an institution. We solve all our problems with tea.'

'And we solve all ours with guns.'

She says 'with guns' like 'wigarns'. Her accent is a highly concentrated version of Jacob's. I say, 'Perhaps if more Americans knew how to make a really good cup...'

She takes a sip. 'It is good.'

I watch as she fidgets in her chair and fusses with things on the table. Her movements are birdlike, as though her heart beats a little too fast, and her blood flows a touch too quickly; I want to prescribe beta blockers to slow her down. But, taking a cue from Saeed, I just wait for her to say what it is she's avoiding.

Eventually she runs out of small talk and, with nothing else on the table to fuss over, she has no choice but to look me in the eye and finally say it. 'I've come here to ask you to drop the rape charge. I know Jacob's done a terrible thing, but—'

'Violet, I'm not charging Jacob with rape, the prosecutor is. It has nothing to do with me. In the eyes of the law, I'm just a witness.'

She looks shaken. Clearly, she thought if she could convince me, Jacob would be off the hook. Her eyes mist over.

I quickly add, 'But I called the prosecutor last week and asked her to drop the charge.'

'Y'did?' She brightens.

'I think I said something to the effect of "I'll come down so hard on Jacob's side, I'll make your head spin".'

'Did you really? You really said that to the prosecutor?'

I nod.

'Oh, thank heaven. I felt sure, after everything he'd done, you'd want that boy put away for life.'

I don't reply. What can I say that would sound anything like the truth? *I despise him, just not enough to put him away for rape and murder.* But sitting in front of Violet – a woman who's given Jacob her free and full forgiveness, after he deceived her for so many years – *despise* sounds too harsh. But *I'm angry with him* just doesn't cut it. I used to be angry when he made teabag mountains by the kettle.

'Tell me about Jacob's mother,' I say.

'Bonnie?' Pain sharpens her eyes as she thinks for a moment. 'She was beautiful. Strong. A little daunting sometimes, but she had the pick of every man in Douglasville.'

'Jacob's father was handsome, then?'

Her eyes twinkle as she smiles. 'He was good for Bonnie. All she ever wanted was to get married and have children. Having twins was like a dream come true.'

My hand gravitates to my stomach.

'She always got attention from men. But with the twins it was something else. Almost every day, she'd make some excuse that she needed supplies in town, just to show them off. She'd dress 'em the same, give 'em the same haircuts. Always desperate to be noticed. One day, she even brought reporters to the farm so they could take pictures. *America's most identical twins*, the article said. She pinned it above their beds.'

'Could she tell them apart?'

'No. Nobody could. When they were babies, she put nail polish on their toes to tell which was which. You only knew Josh because he was stuck on Bonnie like a tick, but she kept 'em both as close as she could. She would've stopped 'em going to school if she could. If it weren't for James putting his foot down, their education would've been no better than mine.'

'So James wanted a different life for them?'

'Sure. Farming's tough. He wanted 'em to have opportunities. He would have been so proud Jacob turned out a lawyer.'

She pronounces 'lawyer' like 'liar' and I'm struck by the irony.

She closes her eyes as she shakes her head and says, 'Oh, Bonnie ruled over that school. They were never to be separated. Always in the same classes. Always sat together. And the teachers couldn't tell 'em apart neither so, like everyone else, they just called them J.'

I picture Jacob as a little boy and try to imagine what it would have been like: forced to spend every moment with his twin, being treated like the same person, never allowed to explore his own potential or identity. He didn't even have his own name, not really. What was it like to have a mother who actively crushed any differences between him and his brother? As monozygotic twins, they'd started out as two halves of the same egg, feeding off the same placenta. Finally, separated by birth, they were free to breathe their own air. But then Bonnie put all her energy into fusing them back together.

I say, 'They may as well have been conjoined.'

'Exactly.' She wraps her hands around her cup and her thin skin stretches over her blue veins, like the last piece of clingfilm that won't pull tight over a bowl. Then a grey cloud shifts over her, and her colours mute. 'The things she did...'

'What things?'

She closes her eyes for a moment, as if the shame is hers, and then her words come out stilted, like a coerced confession. 'When Jacob was small, five or six maybe, he was playing chase with Josh and squeezed through a barbed wire fence. He didn't crouch low enough and cut his head on the wire.' Violet runs a finger down her parting. 'Bonnie knew it would leave a scar, so she got some spare fencing wire and—'

'She didn't?'

'She did. I was in the fields and came running when I heard the screams. She had Josh pinned to the ground. Took her time too, to make sure the cuts were the same.'

'I've never noticed a scar in Jacob's hairline.'

'Nobody would have.'

'Then why?'

'It was an obsession. Every tiny little detail. She didn't want anyone to tell them apart. Like it would've spoiled everything.'

'Jesus, she sounds like a bloody nutcase.' I realise I'm speaking about Violet's dead sister and add, 'Sorry, I didn't mean—'

She pats my hand. 'Not at all. She *was* a bloody nutcase.'

I'm relieved when she says 'bloody' with an English twang. But then my mind flits to Jacob impersonating my Oxford accent: *It's up in the loft. It's on the landing. It's in the conservatory.*

'When Bonnie died,' she says, 'and Josh went away to school, I felt sure it was the best thing. A chance to finally be their own people. I had no idea what was going on there. Dreadful. Dreadful business. I should have taken him in. Perhaps none of this would've happened. That poor girl Sophie. Jacob's wife and child.' She puts her hand over mine. 'And the dreadful things he did to you. That school, those awful, depraved people. They turned Josh into...and to think I might'a stopped it.'

'They didn't make him what he was. Joshua was a killer before he went there.'

'What do you mean?'

Violet doesn't know. Why would she? I never mentioned it to the police; I was dosed up on painkillers when I gave

353

them my statement at the hospital. And I was so caught up in explaining why Joshua had never been a suspect in the murders of Sophie and Claudine – where they would find Sophie's body, and how he'd managed to make Claudine's death look like a suicide – that I completely forgot about poor little Hannah.

I say, 'Joshua killed Hannah Edwards.'

She shakes her head, slowly. 'No. No. Joshua was only eight when Hannah went missing.'

'I know. He killed her. He slit her throat and buried her in the woods. He told me himself.'

Violet's chest rises and falls beneath her finely knitted twinset, and her mascara nets a single tear.

'Does Jacob know?' she asks.

'I don't think so. With everything that happened, I forgot to tell the police. God, I must call them.'

'He'll be devastated. They were best friends.'

I top up Violet's tea, giving her as long as she needs to come to terms with the news I've delivered, waiting for her to give me that look – the one I've given to Saeed a hundred times – that says *I'm ready now, I can talk again now*. When I see it, I ask, 'Surely Bonnie disapproved…of Jacob's friendship with Hannah?'

'Of course. But James wouldn't hear a bad word said about the Edwardses. They owned a small farm next door, and Hannah's father and James were real tight. She was a tomboy, and Jacob was stuck on her. She used to wheel this pull-along truck wherever she went.' Violet tugs an imaginary handle and the memory shines on her face. 'Full of cap guns and tater guns, tanks and soldiers.' She gets lost in what was obviously a much happier time for her. 'Goodness, some of 'em even had parachutes. You could toss 'em in the air and they'd float back down to earth as if they'd jumped from an aeroplane. Even I thought they were fun. You can imagine what catnip that was for a young boy like Jacob. He loved playing with Hannah, even more than… Oh… I s'pose that explains it, then.'

I nod. 'I asked him why he killed her, and he just said she was in the way.'

Violet closes her eyes, breathing out as if guilt is something to be exhaled. As if Hannah's blood is on her hands too, when it's nothing of the sort. Then she says again, 'Dreadful. Dreadful business.'

'Well, there's nothing for you to feel guilty about any more. You didn't make Joshua who he was. And I'm sure you thought you were doing the right thing by sending him to that school.'

'I didn't *send* him...not really.' She closes her eyes for a moment and the creases around them deepen. Then she scratches the hair at the base of her neck and seems to squirm as she wrestles with a decision she made twenty-five years ago. 'I had no money,' she says. 'I could barely support myself off the farm, let alone two boys. I tried to treat 'em like adults, explain that life would be hard, we'd have to muck in, work the farm together, grow our own food and stuff. But Josh wanted nothing to do with that idea. The boarding school was state-funded and he said he'd rather go there. I should have pushed harder. Insisted. He was a child...and if I'd loved him more—'

'I don't think psychopaths respond to love, Violet. It's what makes them psychopaths.'

'Thank God Jacob stood up to him – it was the first time he did – Josh tried for days to convince him to go to that school too. I can't bear to think what that would'a done to Jacob, he isn't strong like Josh. He's a sensitive boy.'

'And when Joshua ran away from the school, you never suspected they were switching places on you?'

'Heavens, no. For years, I kept calling the school every few months to check on him. He was always in class or playing football or asleep, but they'd say his grades were good, he was having fun and he was happy there. I realise now that was their stock response for every relative who called. I doubt they even had any idea which boy they were being asked about. They never told me he'd run away. Given what they were doing to those boys, I imagine a lot of 'em escaped and they didn't bother informing the relatives – if there were any: most of the boys there were orphans.'

'I still can't understand why Joshua wouldn't have stayed with you and Jacob, given the option.'

'He had big dreams, even as a child. He hated farming, hated the hard graft, even hated the animals. He saw that school as a means of escape. And, I confess, I encouraged him a little. I'm ashamed of that now. I couldn't afford to keep him if he wasn't going to work, and to tell you the truth...he frightened me sometimes, even as a child. He'd get this look in his eyes...'

I know that look well. That hard-cracked ice.

'He did bad things,' she says. 'Mostly things that a lot of small boys do: pulling legs off spiders and shooting birds. But one day, when I was visiting with them, James found a stray cat that had wandered on to the farm. It was barely alive. The poor little thing had been beaten within an inch of its life, strung up in a tree and left to die. James questioned the boys about it and they denied having anything to do with it, but I saw the glint in Joshua's eye. So, when he said he didn't wanna come live with me, honestly, I was relieved. If only that place hadn't been what it was, none of this might have happened. A good school might've changed him...set him on the right path.'

'It's the eternal question, isn't it? Nature or nurture?'

We sit in silence until she takes me by surprise by reaching across the table and grasping my hand tightly.

'Jacob loved you, Eva. Every time he called, he barely spoke of anything else. And now I know why. I kept pestering him to bring you to Georgia. But I should've come sooner.'

'Well, you're here now.' And, when I say that, she feels like family.

FORTY-EIGHT

FOUR DAYS AFTER seeing Violet, I came back from my afternoon walk with Teddy and found a letter on the doormat. Seeing it, crisp and white against the stubbled mat, felt like driving over a humpback bridge too fast. I didn't need to pick it up to know who it was from.

It took me three days to open it.

With no intention of reading it, I threw it in his study drawer, but it chattered from inside, night and day, like a telephone that won't stop ringing until you answer it. A kettle that won't stop whistling until you remove it from the stove.

It wouldn't quit.

So, finally, I read it.

Dear Eva,

Unthinkable as it is, I promised myself I wouldn't make contact unless you reached out to me first. If I were you I'd screw up any letter from me without even opening it, and I hope that hearing from me won't cause you further pain. But Susannah

West came to see me two days ago to tell me she's dropping the rape charge, and that I'll only be facing the three counts of fraud. I pressed her until she told me what had changed her mind, and, when she told me what you'd said on the phone, it felt as though you _had_ reached out. If I'm wrong, please forgive me.

I am forever in your debt. Because of you, I'm not facing a lifetime in jail for rape and murder. I pulled that trigger to save your life, and now you have saved mine. I wish I could say we were even, but no amount of time in here will right the wrongs I've done to you. Nothing I write here is an attempt at justification, and I'm not writing to beg for forgiveness. Forgiveness is impossible. All I can say is how desperately I regret what I've done and how sorry I am. Sorry – it's a pathetic word, but there is no word fierce enough to convey my grief and remorse. Please, Eva, please read on – give me the chance to explain. I swear I never meant to hurt you, and I'll never lie to you again. The only way I can think of to make anything even the slightest bit better is to offer you the complete and absolute truth, so that you understand fully. After that, you can decide what you think, and what you feel. In a way, this is my testimony. You are my judge and jury.

I know Violet's told you some of my past, how our mother raised us, and it would be easy to blame the men we became on our unorthodox upbringing, but I don't blame her. We are our own people and we make our own decisions. I wish I could tell you I had been a strong-willed young boy, who stood up for himself and tried to find his own way. But, in truth, I wasn't. Until Josh went to boarding school, I had never stood up to my mother or him. I slipped into the role of younger brother, and, even if I had been old enough to understand that I was disappearing in his shadow, I'm not sure I would have fought for my identity. I loved my mother in spite of it all, and Josh's hold over me was my greatest weakness, my biggest failing. Looking back, with the perspective that comes from standing outside the mess we made, I can hardly believe what we did to you – what I did to you – it seems insane to me now. It was as though I was on a train, hurtling towards this destination, but it was moving too fast, and I was afraid to jump off. Joshua and I had grown into one person over decades, and separating myself from him would have been like separating myself from my own bones. Saying no to him was like saying no to breathing. Holding your breath for as long as you can, all the time knowing you'll eventually inhale.

My weakness has cost me everything. But it has cost you more. I will have to find a way to live with the guilt I feel for not telling you the truth sooner or realising what he was capable of. But that's the thing with lies, isn't it? By telling them, you surrender the right to be believed. I'm sure my swearing will never convince you beyond any reasonable doubt that I had no idea what Josh was doing.

I only found out about Hannah yesterday. And I will have to find a way to live with the guilt of that, too. What that childish love of mine cost her, and how I behaved afterwards. You see, when the Edwardses, and later the police, came looking for her, I never said I was the last person to see her alive, or who she was with. I had been at the bottom of the yard, waiting for Hannah to come out and play, when I saw her and Josh on the other side of the silage field going into the woods. I don't know how he convinced her to go with him. I expect he pretended to be me.

Despite searching the woods, they never found her body, and that made it easy to believe Josh's lies. But nobody tells you that the crimes you commit as a child stretch and grow with age like birthmarks on your skin. I keep asking myself if, somewhere deep down, I knew the truth. But I was a child, I loved my brother deeply, and would never have believed he had anything to do with her disappearance. Was I lying to myself? It was so long ago, I don't remember. But I do remember lying to Hannah's parents, my parents and the police, and that makes me complicit in her death.

When my parents died, and I went to live with Violet, I finally had a chance to be my own person. But what happened at that school only pulled the knot tighter.

I can explain what took place in the months that followed my parents' deaths, but I can't tell you how I felt about it. Or how Josh felt. I'm sure you can imagine it for yourself. In our own ways we were both broken, but at the time it was Josh who was keeping all the pieces of me together – he was so much stronger than me – and when he couldn't face living with Violet or working her farm and decided to leave, I came apart. Although half of me was desperate to go with him, the other half couldn't live without some semblance of motherhood. I have no idea what happened to Josh in that home; he would never speak of it. But in the years we shared a house at university he would often wake up screaming.

Josh ran away before the end of his first year. He lived on the streets, sleeping on park benches and in doorways in the neighbourhood so he could be close to me. Life on the streets is hard enough for an adult; imagine what it must have been like for a twelve-year-old boy. But one day after school, in winter, I went to meet him at a warehouse he'd been sleeping in. He was half-dead from exposure.

That day broke me. His breathing was so shallow and his pulse so weak that, at first, I was convinced he was dead. I'd already lost my parents, and I thought I'd lost him too. The moment he opened his eyes, I was so grateful, I would have done anything to keep him alive. Growing up as we had, the urge to save him felt like self-preservation – as if I were him, and he were me.

When I brought him back to Violet's, she wasn't home. I gave him food and a change of clothes, but he insisted on going back and sleeping in the barn. I'd planned to tell her what had happened, but he wouldn't hear of it. He knew she'd either make him work for his place on the farm or send him to another school and he couldn't face either. Even as a boy, he felt farming was beneath him, work for lesser mortals, and he vowed he would never forgive me if I told her. I swore on my life.

Once he'd recovered, we began to switch places, so each of us would get a hot meal, clean clothes and a warm bed in turn, *while the other slept in the barn. We took turns going to school, too, so Josh could continue his education, and, in exchange for him doing most of the homework, I did most of the farm work. Then, every evening before supper, we'd hide in the barn and do a handover. We exchanged schoolbooks, practised our handwriting until it was indistinguishable by the teachers, and kept journals of every detail of the day's events, both at school and at home with Violet. Convinced that any mistake would send Josh away, we were vigilant. We didn't miss a trick. We mimicked every one of each other's mannerisms, every tic, and every turn of phrase, until we were carbon copies of one another. Eventually, it became so natural that we no longer needed to try. We were carbon copies.*

As an adult, I understand that if we'd told Violet from day one that Josh had nearly died, she would have found a way to make it work. But as children we saw things in black and white: if we were caught, Josh would be sent away. We lacked the maturity to understand that the decision wouldn't have been so black and white for Violet, especially if Josh had told her what was going on at that school.

For the first year, it was difficult, but we made it work. I was still very withdrawn after the death of my parents and, after everything he'd been through, Josh was just grateful to be off the streets. But it didn't last. As we each recovered, I became less sullen, and Josh less grateful for his half of life with Violet. Josh had never liked our aunt to begin with, but he blamed her for choosing that school and – few as they were – for every moment he spent working the farm. His resentment turned to rage, and he struggled to conceal it. He had a habit of calling her Aunt Cuntis whenever she was out of earshot. One day, she overheard him. It broke her heart. But the very next day, she had a kind, attentive nephew who would work the farm with gusto and cuddle up with her on the sofa. She had a nephew who would one day look at her with love and the next with resentment. I didn't really think she was beginning to suspect the actual truth – after all, the school was lying about Josh still being there – but I knew we were treading on thin ice. I felt we had to do something.

By chance, I found the solution in a magazine article about a young boy with MPD. The way it described this man's altering personalities, you could have been reading about me and Josh. This boy had watched his parents die, they were shot by an intruder right in front of him, and the trauma had split his personality down the middle. One minute he was sweet and kind-hearted, and the next angry and volatile. All I had to do was leave it for Violet to find. It sowed the seed in her mind. Then I germinated it by switching personalities right in front of her eyes, pretending to be Josh. By the time she got me to the psychiatrist, I'd got pretty good at emulating my brother's moody behaviour and even come up with a fake name for our alter: Victor.

We would take turns with the psychiatrist, with (apparently) no memory of what had taken place on the previous visit. We both got pretty good at switching between sweet Jacob and bully Victor. But sometimes Josh would play Victor for the entire hour, completely terrorising a small-town psychiatrist who dealt mostly with overwrought housewives. It wasn't difficult to fool him; he was young and naïve, and had no idea we were twins. Before I knew it, I had a diagnosis of multiple personality disorder on my record and a repeat prescription for lithium.

Josh loved playing the game. He didn't suffer fools gladly, and his way of dealing with them was mockery. The plan worked, and erased any doubts Violet had about her moody nephew. I persuaded Josh to make more of an effort with her, on the proviso that it was only temporary, until we were old enough to leave. Josh complied and everything got better. He still struggled to contain the occasional outburst of resentment, but they were quickly blamed on the MPD, and Violet believed the lithium was responsible for the improvement in her nephew's behaviour.

Unlike me, Josh was a very determined and focused person. And the education he absorbed during his year at that school far excelled my own. The place was built on discipline and learning. He was always ten steps ahead of me. It was thanks to him that we got an academic merit scholarship to university, and one of us worked full time in a different town while the other was in class, so that we were able to afford an apartment off campus. Just like at school, we took turns attending classes but it was Josh who sat all the exams, in my name. And, eventually, it was Josh who sat the bar, again in my name of course.

When I was a child, it was easy for Josh to convince me that telling Violet the truth wasn't an option. And then, over the years, I convinced myself. But if I'm honest we could have told her the truth when we left for university. She would have forgiven us in the circumstances. The truth is, we were young and we were having fun. We enjoyed the game and it felt like a superpower. We didn't want to stop.

I had no idea how tightly entwined our lives would become.

My girlfriend, Sophie, disappeared while I was at university. She was seen driving off campus with a man. There were rumours that she was pregnant, and I thought she'd run off with the father. I know now that the man in the car was Josh. Perhaps she told him she was pregnant, thinking he was me. Her blood is on my hands along with Hannah's.

We moved to England when we were twenty-six. I flew first and sent my passport back for Josh. We bought the London flat and earned enough to support us both while only having to work half the time. It was every young man's dream: we were immature and having a ball. We had fun fooling our co-workers and friends, and it didn't feel as if we were hurting anyone. We'd been doing handovers for more than a decade, and they ran like clockwork. We'd stopped keeping journals at university; our legal training meant that memorising detail was easy. After nearly fifteen years of being one person, there wasn't an iota of difference between us. And if we were ever caught on camera, the only way of telling who was in the photograph was by remembering which of us had been there.

We'd been in London for some time when Josh told me that he'd advised our GP, Dr Roberts, about our MPD. I was surprised at the time, but he convinced me we needed to maintain the ruse in case anyone suspected anything, or in case Dr Roberts ever requested our records from the States. I thought it was overkill, but when he said he wasn't actually filling the lithium prescriptions I believed him. I had no idea he was giving it to you, I swear.

The only drawback to our flawlessly constructed lives was that we couldn't afford to both be seen out at the same time; it would have ruined everything. So one of us was always holed up in the London apartment, while the other went out or to work. Josh did have a lot of women, prostitutes mainly, but the majority of our alone time was spent working. Every case had two of us on it, and from the outside it appeared there was nothing Jacob Curtis couldn't do. That was how we won so many.

Everything was easy until, on a flight to Germany to meet a client, Josh met Claudine and brought her into our lives. She was bubbly, sexy and fun, though not all that bright. I doubt he ever had much intention of a long-term relationship – she wasn't really his type, and I knew that. Josh was drawn to powerful, intelligent women who challenged him. But I thought Claudine was a firecracker. I stepped in whenever he broke a date, as I had dozens of times with his girlfriends, though we never slept together; that would have been overstepping the mark. But I quickly fell in love with her vivacity.

Knowing what I know now, I believe I killed her. And I'll have to find a way to live with that along with everything else. I didn't say anything directly to Josh, but I dropped hints about him stepping back from Claudine. He didn't love her, so I didn't think he would care much either way. We got married in a register office, very quietly, and she was fine about me staying in the London flat when I was working. Josh still visited her, when he felt like it, but it was mainly me who lived with her. I was in Edinburgh when she called to tell me she was pregnant and I

*was overjoyed. I had a foolish dream that life would be perfect
with the three of us. Josh was already spending less and less time
with her, and I thought he would give her up entirely. I called
and told him about the baby, about what I wanted. I planned to
tell her the truth, and thought Josh would make a great uncle.*

*When I found her in that bathtub, part of me died. But I
never suspected Josh. He knew how I felt about her; he cared
about me – I never imagined he would do such a terrible thing.
And the evidence for her suicide was incontrovertible. We'd never
talked about children, or her feelings about abortion, so I had no
trouble believing her note where she said she couldn't live with
either. The note was written in her own hand, she'd made the
cuts herself, and only a few hours before her death she'd been
seen at a local chemist buying razor blades and sleeping pills.
Now I know she did all of that drugged on scopolamine, and I
suspect he was giving her lithium as well. I can't bear to think,
knowing what I know now about Joshua's inclinations, of what
else he'd been making her do. I'll never know.*

*Because the evidence was so overwhelming, the inquest
returned a verdict of suicide, and the coroner didn't request an
autopsy. But, even if they had found scopolamine in her blood,
it wouldn't have made any difference. Ironically, Claudine was
an air hostess who suffered debilitating air sickness. But she
never let it get her down and wore Scopoderm patches for every
flight. Used patches were found in her bathroom bin, and when
questioned about them I testified that she always wore two when
she flew. Scopolamine was Josh's perfect weapon, and I was his
rock-solid alibi, having been seen by dozens of witnesses in
Edinburgh at the time of her death.*

*With you, things were more complicated. It's difficult to
believe, but Josh loved you – or at least, he wanted you very
badly. When he got you, he was happy. I'd never seen him like
that. Of course, that didn't mean he would be monogamous for
long; that just wasn't in his make-up. And I think it was on your
sixth date that he cracked. When I stepped in, I didn't expect*

to fall in love. Even though two years had passed, I still hadn't gotten over Claudine, and it took days of badgering for Josh to persuade me to go.

We went to the Head of the River pub and sat by the canal, do you remember? You brought Teddy and talked about him with that wild affection and enthusiasm. The chef brought him a sausage from the kitchen, and for the next three hours he didn't take his eyes off the door. He had drool hanging down so low it almost touched his paws, and I remember you throwing your head back with laughter at his crazy antics and obsession with food. I loved how much you loved him and was even a little jealous of him.

Over the next few months, I kept praying for Josh to break a date. I was so desperate to see you again. But at the end of every night I'd make an excuse for why I couldn't go back to your place. It didn't seem right; in my mind, as much as I hated it, you were his.

But saying no eventually became impossible. Like notches on a prison wall, I'd count the days till I could see you again. And every night I spent in that London apartment, knowing he was with you, I wanted to die. Even worse, before I was able to see you, I'd have to hear about his time with you in excruciating detail. I think he got a kick out of describing the nights. I did our handovers verbally too, but I didn't tell him anything but mundane facts. If I had, how I truly felt about you would have slipped out between the words.

We were both editing what had gone on, but, ironically, where I was hiding all the good things that happened between us, the intimacies, he was hiding how appallingly he was treating you.

I know, if the tables were turned, I'd be wondering how you could share me with someone if you truly loved me. But you weren't mine; you belonged to Josh. He met you, he dated you, you were his girl. And in the beginning he was as bewitched by you as I was. I was just grateful for the time we had together.

He only agreed for me to marry you when it became impossible to avoid the subject – when it felt as if the relationship had to take that step forward or you'd have begun questioning it and we'd have been at risk of losing you. I think he'd have married you himself if he hadn't had such a phobia about being trapped, about not being free. I guess that dates back to that school. And when we finally married I fooled myself into thinking everything would be okay, that eventually Josh would move on and we'd be together. But he didn't move on. Every time I was able to see you, I'd find flowers from him (though he never remembered what you liked). And, when you started to talk about having a family, so did Josh.

I should have known it was a lie. He never intended for us to have a baby.

But it wasn't until the Summer Ball that I suspected anything was wrong. Our career was everything to Josh, and our success was due almost entirely to him. He studied harder, worked harder, and found the best positions in the best law firms. He cherry-picked all the cases, made sure we came off well in the press, and engineered the entire plan with Ratner, Leishmann and Walch to make partner in ten years. He loved the money, the media attention and the power. And he'd laboured hard to get it. He was resourceful and brilliant, the genius behind it all, and, having done the majority of the work, it was only fair that he should receive the handshake.

He hadn't planned on staying at the ball past that handshake; he was meeting a woman he'd been seeing on and off for a while, which suited me fine. It meant I got to spend the rest of the evening with you. I was waiting in an alley across the road from the hotel, and when it came time to switch I realised he was wasted. He'd been drinking all day. He gave me the hotel room key and, during the handover, told me what had happened earlier in the evening. His guard was down, and the way he spoke about you, about having sex with you…he'd never spoken about you that way before. It made my blood boil. I thought I was going to

367

kill him. I hit him, hard. I'd never done that before, not even as a boy. And when you told me I'd hurt you earlier in the evening – that <u>he'd</u> hurt you – I almost stormed out of that hotel room to find him again. I wanted to beat him senseless. As it was, it was two weeks before he could go home to you: he had a black eye.

Things changed between me and Josh after that night. In the weeks that followed, whenever Josh allowed me to spend time with you, he'd talk of arguments in our handover. At the time, I was relieved. I thought he was growing tired of you, as he had of every woman. But it wasn't that. He was angry. In his mind, I'd chosen you over him. And I had. He'd finally understood how much I love you, and that you loved me and not him. I think he realised he had no place in either of our lives, and that a baby would shut him out entirely.

Just as I had with Claudine, I started to plan to edge him out and tell you the truth. I didn't know whether you would forgive me for all the lies, but it was a chance I had to take. It couldn't go on. But it was only then that I finally realised our entwined lives had become an unworkable knot. Everything was in my name: our passport, driver's licence, citizenship, practising certificate, tax returns, properties, everything. It had felt like a game but, in reality, we had committed fraud, and if anyone found out we would go to jail. Josh could only remain in the UK and continue to practise law if he kept my identity. He wouldn't give that up without a fight. He wouldn't sacrifice his career any more than I would sacrifice you. There was only one option: to give it all to him. He would remain Jacob, and I would become Joshua.

Do you remember that night in FishShorey when you asked me about IVF? I told you I needed to get all my ducks in a row. That's what I was doing: untying the unworkable knot. I was harbouring this fucked-up dream that you would marry me again under my new name, and we'd finally start our family. We're married, Ev. I hope you know that. And, standing at the altar, I meant every word I said to you. I'm your husband.

Though not for much longer; I got the annulment papers this morning. I signed them.

What a fool. My attempts to remove Josh from our lives nearly cost you yours. And the baby's. And now I've lost you anyway. Maria told me you're pregnant. I'm so happy for you. I will have to go on living while the life I'd dreamed of goes on without me. I'm not fit to be a father to our child – if the baby is actually mine. It doesn't matter if it isn't; I'd have loved it just the same. I <u>will</u> love it, even if I never get to meet it.

I'm so sorry, Eva. I never should have let it all go on as long as it did. I was a coward for not telling you the truth from the beginning. There were so many times I almost told you. That night at Belmond, it was on the tip of my tongue. It so nearly slipped out. But I was terrified. I knew you would storm out of that restaurant and never speak to me again, and I couldn't bear it, Ev. I just couldn't bear the thought of losing you.

But please believe me: I had no idea I was putting you in danger. When the police told me what Josh had been doing to you, I wanted to pull that trigger all over again. It sickens me to even think of it, and I will never forgive myself, never, for the huge part I played in putting you through that.

You know me, Ev. You know I would never hurt you. Fuck, of course I've hurt you. But I hope you might know in your heart that I would never knowingly have played any part in Joshua's crimes, or stood back and allowed them to happen. I lied about who I was only because I was desperate to see you and couldn't bear the thought of losing you.

You have no reason to believe a word of this, but think: if I had let Joshua do those things to you, if I had been involved in any way, I would never have pulled the trigger.

Hindsight is a strange thing, and, while I wouldn't hesitate to pull it again, I'm finally beginning to understand my brother. And perhaps, having been with him for five years, you will appreciate what it means to know someone and not know them. Being as alike on the outside as two people could possibly be, and then spending so much time ironing out even the subtlest of differences, we eventually came to believe we were identical on the inside as well. Each of us saw the other's world through our own eyes, not realising how fundamentally different we were. I never believed Josh capable of murder, and that's because I'm not capable of it.

As far as I'm aware, there have only been four women Josh wanted to remove from this world. All of them women I loved. When I fell in love – in that childish way with Hannah, in adolescence with Sophie, and as a grown man with Claudine and then you – Josh must have felt the change in direction of my affections and loyalty. But still he would have assumed our brotherly bond was as paramount to me as it was to him. And I've come to believe that when he killed them, and tried to kill you, he didn't truly understand what he was taking from me. Because he'd only ever felt that depth of love for two people. Our mother. And me.

I've spent my life in Josh's shadow, thinking he had all the power. But I could have stopped at any time, and I take total responsibility for that.

Driving through those prison gates, breathless with claustrophobia, in the mobile prison cell of that white Serco van, was the most frightening moment of my life. I was imagining Shawshank meets Prison Break. I told myself it was no less than I deserved, and that each day would be a suture in the dozens of wounds I've inflicted on you. But it's bullshit. As if you can sew up so many gaping untruths. And the reality is that I'm not surrounded by violent criminals who'll cut out your eye over a cigarette. It's probably safer in here than Park End Street on a Friday night.

Did we watch too much television? I wonder about that in here. I wonder how, with so much life going on outside, it was possible to be so content with so little. But I was. All I thought about, every day, was getting home to you and curling up on the sofa with a glass of wine. You, pressed against me. Your

370

cold feet tucked under my thigh. Listening to you talk, hearing your insights into the storylines and characters, I was content to finally live a life without Josh. To finally be myself. To be private with you. To be Jacob.

Were you as content as I was? Or did I just imagine it?

No amount of time in this place will compare to the retribution of losing you. Even losing Josh doesn't come close, and he was my framework, the skeleton that kept me upright; after thirty-six years, separating myself from him was like cutting out every bone. I cut out every bone for you, and I would do it again, and again, until the end of time.

If you could dive inside my body and feel what I feel, my remorse and love would overwhelm you. As would the emptiness that's left behind. But I won't write again. I don't want to cause you further pain. I am a grown man, responsible for my actions, and I don't deserve your forgiveness. I'll never ask.

Eva, I've told you the truth, the whole truth, as they say, and nothing but the truth. But I know, from years of seeing this oath twisted in the courtroom, that swearing doesn't make it so. They say words have the power to change the world, but, in the end, action is all that matters. If your heart tells you these words are empty, then you must give your verdict and pass sentence. I'll accept nothing but life. And I'm going to give you that power. When you've finished this letter, go into the attic. The loft. And find the floorboard in the centre of the doorway. Count five floorboards in and look closely. You'll see that, instead of nails, that particular floorboard is held in by small screws. Underneath, you'll find a locked cash box. Go to the right-hand side of the chimney breast, count seven rows up, and find the centre brick. It's loose. The key to the cash box is taped to the back of that brick.

I've taken steps to ensure this letter gets to you unread.

You hold my life in your hands.

Jacob x

P.S. Kiss Teddy for me.

I tuck the letter back in its envelope and put it back in the drawer. The words I said to Maria play on a loop in my ears.

He's a liar. He lied. For years.

I go slowly to the hall and hunt through the tool box in the understairs cupboard. From the landing, I take the narrow circular staircase to the loft and throw open the door. The floorboards stretch lengthways in front of me. From the top step, it's clear that one of the boards is perfectly centred in the doorway, just as Jacob described. I walk along it like a knife edge, counting the boards as I go. I unscrew the fifth board, the only one that isn't nailed down, and the box is exactly where he said it would be. As is the key.

Sitting on the loft floor, I fumble with the tiny thing in the lock.

The lid of the metal cash box squeals when I open it and the first thing I see is a gun. A Glock with its square G logo on the barrel. And, even more now that I've seen what it can do, its acute violence chills my spine. But, this time, I have to pick it up. It weighs heavy on my palm, and I wrap my fingers around the grip, sliding my index over the familiar trigger. An image of Joshua sparks in my mind, his gun pointed directly at my head, and I start at the sound of a gunshot.

The Glock slips from my grasp and clatters over the floorboards, where I leave it, unable to pick it up again. It haunts my peripheral vision as I pull out the first sheet of paper in the box and unfold it.

The heading is a signed declaration from the State Registrar, stating this as a true and exact copy of an original certificate, filed in the Bureau of Vital Statistics, Alabama. Beneath it is a copy of a Certificate of Live Birth for Joshua James Rathbone.

Beneath the certificate, I find a blue Social Security Card in Joshua's name, and a stiff, crisp passport. I crank it open to the photo page where I'm greeted by a bald eagle and the preamble from the United States Constitution. Again, it's in Joshua's name but the photo is recent.

I pull out a few more pieces of paper and struggle to make sense of them at first. Jacob has made a deed poll application in the United States to change his name from Jacob Edward Curtis to Joshua James Rathbone. He has used that deed poll to request a new Bar Exam Certificate from the Alabama Supreme Court. There are also forms from Kaplan for their Qualified Lawyers Transfer Scheme, and an application for British citizenship by naturalisation.

Jacob hasn't been out of police custody since he pulled the trigger and all of this paperwork would have taken months to organise. He wasn't lying. He was planning on giving Joshua his identity and starting again under his brother's name.

He was going to tell me the truth.

In the bottom of the cash box is one final piece of paper, and, when I unfold it, it stops my heart dead.

The page trembles between my fingertips.

It's an NRA Marksmanship Qualification Program certificate with Jacob's name on it. And in large capital letters, it reads: DISTINGUISHED EXPERT.

I hold his life in my hands.

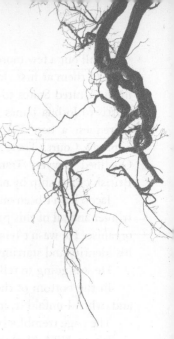

FORTY-NINE

'So THIS IS IT,' says Saeed.

Although I haven't seen him for a few weeks – I've been making preparations to leave Oxford – Saeed has been there throughout my recovery. The nightmares lingered for a long time, and, with the knowledge that it was all real, even got worse for a while. But I've got a lot better at recognising the signposts, becoming lucid, and aware that, now, they really are only dreams.

Saeed would only continue my therapy with a psychotherapy supervisor monitoring my case. She helped him reflect on and manage his involvement in my recovery. We crossed a line in that hospital room, got too close, too caught up in each other's emotions, and we both knew that connection would deepen as my therapy continued.

Now, I walk the length of his office, my feet no longer unsteady on his rug, and he comes out from behind his desk, holding out his hand to shake mine. We haven't touched each other since that day, it would have complicated things for both of us, and probably hampered my recovery. As physically and emotionally weak as I was, I would have wanted more than he was able to give. But I'm stronger now, and when I take his hand it feels wrong.

'This is it,' I say, unable to hide the sadness in my tone. 'Oh, for fuck's sake, come here.' And he doesn't resist; we hold each other tight for a long time. I'm not his patient any more. Well, not after today.

'Come,' he says. 'Sit.' I perch on the edge of the sofa, then slide back without resistance.

'Any more nightmares?'

'A few. But they don't last.' I break into a smile and say, 'When my subconscious even starts to wander in that direction, we make a visit to Mr McAvoy's house.'

'So, you finally are the master of your dreams.'

'Yes. A fully qualified oneironaut.'

Saeed crosses his legs and my attention is drawn to his feet. Beneath his desk, there's a paw-shaped bed with a puppy sleeping on top. A buff American cocker spaniel. It must already be accustomed to strangers coming in and out, because it hasn't even stirred.

I shake my head, wondering if I'm seeing things. 'I can't believe it. Mr "I do not much like pets of any species", with a puppy?'

'I cannot believe it myself. I did not want to tell you. I wanted it to be a surprise.'

'It's that all right!'

He reads the longing in my face. 'You can pet her if you like. She loves attention.'

'Let sleeping dogs lie. But I might have to break that rule if she doesn't wake up before I leave.'

'How are you feeling, now you have had a few weeks away to reflect on everything?'

'Stupid, still. If anything, the more time I've had to process it all, the more I feel like a fucking fool.'

'Still you continue to insist you should have known? Eva, we have talked about this. You still think someone else in your situation *would* have known?'

'Yes!' I almost shout it. 'I know I was drugged up to the eyeballs for most of my marriage, but I was living with two different men, sleeping with two different men; what kind of stupid—'

'Eva, Eva. What is it like living with Eva? She is so hard on you. Will there ever come a day when she gives you a break?'

'Probably not; she's a tough bitch. At least, she's getting there.'

'I know you are not my patient any more, but let us put this last thing to bed...you had relationships before Jacob, yes?'

'Yes.'

'Long-term relationships?'

'Five years with one guy. Never trusted him. He didn't like dogs.'

'And sometimes he came home angry, upset, moody?'

'Who doesn't?'

'And naturally, your first thought was: this angry, moody man cannot possibly be my partner, he must be his psychopathic twin.'

I almost laugh at the absurdity of the truth, not fully, not sincerely. I haven't quite relearned how to do that yet.

'Come on.' Saeed beckons me over to his desk. 'I want to show you something. I have been saving it for you.' He stands up, pulls out his chair, and urges me to sit down. As he leans over my shoulder to operate the mouse and keyboard, I smell toffee tobacco with a hint of coconut and realise just how much I'm going to miss being his patient.

He shuffles the mouse and the monitor gleams into life. Then he tabs between windows to a documentary he already has open and ready to play. He says, 'I knew, even after all these months, you would still blame yourself for not seeing what was right in front of you. So I did some digging over the last few weeks and found this.'

He clicks play, then fast-forward, skipping the start of a documentary. Frame-by-frame, dozens of identical twins flash up on the screen. I want him to stop and rewind so I can stare at each of them in turn and see if I can tell them apart. But clearly he has something he particularly wants me to see. Again, he presses play, and a pair of women in identical clothing ride side by side on bicycles. They're wearing helmets and sunglasses so I can't see their faces, but they sound the same, with strong Australian accents. The documentarian explains that they share everything, including a medical history, both girls having had appendicitis within weeks of each other.

Moments later, they're on screen and it's the most unbelievable thing I have ever seen. It isn't just that they're identical in every possible way; they even speak in stereo, saying the same things at the same time. They dress the same, do everything together, and have never been apart. They talk about a time they were accused of cheating at school, and the teachers set new tests for them in separate rooms. They still came up with identical answers and the school had to apologise. It's as if they are one and the same person, and they actually describe themselves that way.

Saeed pauses the film. 'Can you tell them apart?'

'No.' I'm completely stunned.

'And they are sitting side by side where you can make a direct comparison. What if you met one of these women in isolation, not knowing she was a twin, and then met the other? Would you have any idea you had met a different person?'

'No.' I look up at him.

'You never saw Jacob and Joshua together.'

'Well, not alive anyway.'

'This is why you think you should have known: because you never got the opportunity to see it for yourself, to see how

377

identical two people can be. You did not know he had a twin. You thought he had DID. Why would it even cross your mind that you were living with two men?'

'I suppose—'

'You suppose? Eva, look at these girls. They fool people without even trying. What if they *really* tried? What if their lives depended upon their maintaining a single identity?'

I stare at the picture, paused on the screen, analysing them like a spot-the-difference puzzle.

'Must you still be so hard on yourself? Or will you consider the idea that you could not have known? It was not your fault, Eva. Being fooled by another person does not make you a fool. They were con men. They conned people their entire lives and worked hard to do so.'

I flop back in Saeed's chair and suck in a deep breath.

God, I've missed him.

We talk for the full hour, about everything and nothing, and when I finally, but reluctantly, drag myself away from his leather couch, I notice the puppy stir.

'Can I?'

'Of course.'

She rolls over on her bed and shows her irresistibly soft tummy. My puppy uterus goes into spasm and I decide, then and there, that it's time Teddy had some company, someone who speaks his language, who understands the vital importance of a rustling cheese packet.

'You convinced me,' he says. 'I have only had her three weeks and already she is my baby. I remember you saying they were like children to their owners, and I confess, I thought you were a little unhinged when it came to animals. But I was wrong. She is like a child to me. I did not truly understand what you went through with Jack until I got Maggie. She sleeps in the bed with me, curled up in my armpit, with her head on my chest. And when I wake up in the morning she

378

licks my eyelids for ten minutes until I tell her, "That is too much love, Maggie. Too much love." And I put her at the bottom of the bed, where she licks my toes instead.'

'And does she follow you everywhere?'

'Yes, but I have a bone to pick with you about that. You did not say it would be *everywhere*. You did not say I would never be able to go to the toilet alone again.'

'Oh, yeah,' I laugh. 'I forgot about that. Though I did say they're your shadow, and you can hardly leave your shadow outside the bathroom door.'

'I did try. But she scratched off all the paint trying to get in. And in the end I gave up. Even if she is asleep on her bed, and I creep out of the room, as soon as she hears the seat creak, she comes into the bathroom for toilet-cuddles. I have no privacy any more. I have to go to the toilet with the door open.'

'Ahh, Maggie. You sound just like Teddy.' I tickle her some more. 'It's a great name. It suits her.'

'It is short for Margaret Schönberger Mahler.'

'That sounds familiar. Wasn't she a famous psychiatrist?'

'Yes. And Maggie has much to live up to. I plan on teaching her to read *Psychology Today*.'

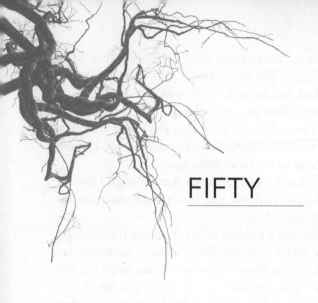

FIFTY

AFTER DOING SOME shopping in town, I have a few hours to kill before I have to pick up Teddy and go to my parents' house. So I drop into Scriptum for no other reason than to be in the shop. I take a leather-bound copy of *Pride and Prejudice* to the counter and say hello to the sales assistant who knows me too well by now. I've already got a copy of *Pride and Prejudice*, but it's not leather-bound, and it should be.

As I'm handing over the cash, my mobile vibrates in my back pocket. It's a text from Mum.

> MUM: You're coming at six? Xxx

We've already agreed I'd be there for six but I know what she's doing. She's checking in. She does it all the time now. I text back:

> EVA: Yes, see you then.
> Love you. xxx

That day in the hospital, seeing her daughter with two black eyes, a broken eye socket, nose and cheekbone, two broken ribs, raped and pregnant, she was speechless for the first time in her life. It changed everything between us. Aside from scraped knees and elbows – which she usually scolded me for – I had an easy childhood. My mother had never had to deal with any trauma. Seeing her daughter like that broke her. And when she finally pulled herself together, nothing went back in the place it had been. Now I'm made of glass, and she's afraid that if she pitches her voice too loud or too high it will shatter me.

My father's therapist turned out to be the best thing that ever happened to him. My mother booked it to help him combat the pressures of work but, ironically, it helped him combat the pressures of her. He's returned to nursing, much to her chagrin, and is back to his old spirited self. He takes great joy in offering to splint her sense of humour or spica cast her after too much leg-pulling.

And he's closer to Maria than ever. She's his heroine, his second daughter. And with every day that passes she feels more and more like my sister. One who drives me completely fucking nuts, but I guess that's what sisters are supposed to do.

On the way out of Scriptum, the rack of postcards catches my eye, and I'm drawn to the cartoon ninja I picked up the day I was in here with Joshua. I don't know what possesses me, but I buy it.

At the door, I bump into Grace again. Apparently, she loves this shop as much as I do.

'Shall we finally get that coffee?' she asks.

And it's lucky she's sitting down, since she almost faints when I tell her everything that happened. It seems she never quite got over meeting Joshua in the street.

'I knew it,' she said. 'I *knew* it wasn't Jacob. But you told me it was, and when you get to this age you do start to doubt your own sanity.'

'At the party, you said you'd got it wrong once.'

'Not once. All the time. She's a twin, just like Jacob. Only, I can't tell the difference between her and her sister. Their energy is exactly the same, as is everything else: the tone of their voices, the phrases they use, the way they shake my hand. It's uncanny.'

'Well, you have an excuse.'

'I doubt I could tell them apart even if I could see. Apparently, they get sick to the back teeth of being asked which one is which.' Grace pauses and then says, 'Would you like to come to dinner, Eva? Next week? Bob's a bang-up cook.'

'I'd love to. Shall I bring dessert?'

'I wouldn't hear of it.'

'I'll just bring some wine, then.'

'Wine would be lovely. But whatever you do, don't bring Maria.'

And I laugh.

I actually laugh.

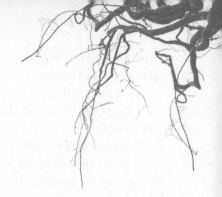

FIFTY-ONE

STANDING OUTSIDE George and Caroline's house, I consider walking away. It takes all the courage I have to press the doorbell. But I knew this wouldn't truly be over until I'd done this one last thing.

When they open the door, the shock mirrored on both their faces quickly dissolves.

'Eva!' George's voice brims with concern. 'How are you?'

'I'm fine. Recovering. How are you both?'

'Recovering,' says Caroline, putting an arm around George.

'I have something for you.' I uncover the bundle in my arms, that rests on my swollen belly, and reveal a lilac-grey head with bat-like ears. With one glance at the puppy, Caroline bursts into tears and then George starts crying too. They wrap their arms around each other, reluctant to take the bundle, in case it isn't really for them.

'This is Princeton Purple Haze – Prince. A white-platinum-carrying-lilac.' The puppy is even rarer than Jack, and for a mere fifty thousand dollars I got the pick of the litter. The sweetest, quietest boy, who loves nothing more than curling up under your chin.

'He's beautiful,' says Caroline reaching out to take him.

'I know he'll never replace Jack.' And now I'm crying too. 'I'm so sorry.'

'Come in, come in,' says Caroline. 'I'll make some tea.'

While Caroline is out in the kitchen, George can't stop apologising for sending the letter and what happened on the bridge. In some, albeit painful respects, Joshua actually did me a favour when it came to drugging George. Even though he had no memory of what took place on Fiddler's Island, when the police informed him of what he'd done, George was mortified. We've both hurt each other, and that will help us both find forgiveness.

'It wasn't your fault,' I say. 'The police must have told you, there's no way you could have known what you were doing. I know what it's like to be left with no memories.'

'Yes, but it doesn't make me feel any better.' He tickles Prince under the ears and the puppy tries to nibble his fingers. 'Ouch!'

'Puppy teeth. You forget how sharp they are.'

Caroline comes out of the kitchen and puts a tray on the coffee table. 'We're old hands at teaching bite inhibition, aren't we, George? We've had dogs our whole lives. And that's a lot of dogs!'

Out of the surgery, in her slippers and wool skirt, Caroline seems like a different woman. Soft around the edges. It's funny how deceiving looks can be. I always found her so stiff.

I dig in my pocket, pull out Jack's collar, and hand it to her, saying, 'You'll be wanting this back.'

'Where on earth did you get that?' she asks.

'I can only guess. I think Joshua came here. He posted it to me. Part of his effort to frame George.'

'Gracious!' says Caroline. 'Who on earth goes to such lengths?'

'A psychopath,' says George.

'I'm sorry I brought him into your lives. If it weren't for him, Jack would still be alive.'

'It's not your fault,' says Caroline. 'The police explained everything. Now, let's hear no more about that.' She takes Prince from George's lap and puts him down on the floor. 'We have a new baby to focus on now.' She kneels down, and, to Prince's delight, makes darting spiders across the carpet with her hands.

We drink tea and play with Prince while he scampers around the lounge, chasing anything that moves, chewing Caroline's slippers and tugging on George's trouser leg. It's hard not to think about Jack. But I never imagined a day would come when I'd be sitting in the same room as George and Caroline, playing with their puppy, laughing and smiling.

'Will you treat him?' asks Caroline. 'When we bring him to the surgery?'

And that one question heals more of my wounds than any doctor managed to in the hospital.

'I would love to. Only I'm leaving Oxford. For a while, anyway. I may come back in a few years and then it would be my honour.' I put my hand over Caroline's. 'But I can't tell you what it means that you would ask.'

FIFTY-TWO

THE TRAIN WINDOW curves slightly at the edges. Made of thick plastic rather than glass, it throws my reflection into the passing trees. This ghost of myself sits on a diaphanous seat outside, a cup of coffee on the table in front of her.

Staring straight ahead at the approaching countryside, she's the twin I'll leave behind when I exit this train at Winchester station and start a new life with this new Eva.

There's a job opening at a practice on the outskirts of the city. It's run by an old colleague of Bron's, and, if I decide to go back to work after maternity leave, the job is mine if I want it. I thought I could go back to work for Bron but, when it came down to it, I still couldn't step inside that surgery.

Maybe in time.

This job will tide me over until then, and I'm going to look around the city to see if I like it.

'When are you due?' A matronly woman boards the train at Basingstoke, sits down next to me, and puts her hand on my stomach.

This new Eva has a rebellious streak. A couldn't-give-a-fuck streak. A barely-survived-a-brush-with-death streak. And she almost replies 'I'm not pregnant' to see how quickly this stranger will snatch her hand away from my belly.

But I don't let her.

I say, 'Next month. The 24th.'

By then, Jacob will have served six months of his seven-year sentence. Well, almost. One day shy. But it's not as if I'm counting. I don't check the days off on a calendar or carve them into my headboard with a knife.

My heart keeps tally.

The day after I saw Caroline and George, I found myself back in Jacob's study, once again searching for a pen. When I yanked open the drawer, Jacob's letter flew forward. And resting on top was the postcard I'd bought from Scriptum. I picked it up and stared at it for a long time, running a finger over the cartoon ninja. It reminded me of J, chasing me around the kitchen in that silly T-shirt. I heard his voice as if he was speaking in my ear, 'Ask me.' And my response slipped out as if he was in the room with me, 'I'll never ask.' I stared at his letter in the drawer, his handwriting on the envelope, which I know as well as my own. And I remembered his words on the page: 'I don't deserve your forgiveness. I'll never ask.'

And no matter how hard I tried, I couldn't silence those words.

They say your soul whispers the truth back to you, and, if you try to silence its voice, eventually the whisper will become a roar.

Could I look into Jacob's eyes without seeing Joshua?

That slick glaze, that hard-cracked ice.

I don't know.

I turned the postcard over and the pen hovered above it. Then, with a will of its own, it wrote two words:

Ask me.

This morning, on the way to the station, I stood in front of the mailbox, staring at the address on the postcard, vacillating. I hadn't written his name, just the address of HMP Winchester and his prisoner ID: A4878DD.

Jacob, Victor, Joshua, J. And now just a number.

The woman from Basingstoke asks, 'Is this your first?'

'Yes.'

She winces to let me know – in case I don't already – that it's really going to hurt. I swear I hear her vagina clamp shut.

I don't speak about pain. I don't tell her I have no idea whether the father is dead or alive. I don't tell her that one possible father is in jail for shooting the other in the head.

Though the other Eva really, really wants to.

'You're huge! Do you know if it's a boy or a girl?'

'Boy-s.' I say.

And I turn away and watch the reflection of myself in the window, my other Eva, floating through the trees. She has no idea what life will be like at the end of this journey. She has no idea whether they'll turn out like Joshua or like Jacob. But one thing she does know.

She'll give them each their own identity.

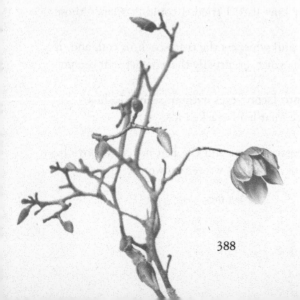

It was the beginning of his career.
He had everything to lose.
So did Saeed choose what was *legal*
– or what was *right*?

ACKNOWLEDGEMENTS

My FIRST THANKS to you, dear reader, for buying and reading this book. It's only when our stories come alive in your mind that they finally fulfil their purpose. As authors, we wish social proof weren't so important, but it's a fact of life that we live and die by reviews, so, if you have a moment to click the ratings button or write a review, it would mean the world to me. Thank you for being part of my journey.

Darrell, my deepest love and gratitude for supporting me from the moment I quit a lucrative career to be a writer. The words 'Never let a little thing like money stand in the way of your dreams' will stay with me forever. Any other husband would have said, 'We're broke. Get a job.'

For plot-wrangling into the night, incisive feedback on every draft, support, kindness and laughter from that first day outside ELL161, Luke, I owe you so much, I could write a book on it. But, for the record, eels do have teeth.

Paddington Bear for bringing Shady to my door in one of my darkest moments. It turned out the little lost bear was me. Contrary to her name, she is the light, the star, the goddess of Writing Strategies for Theme and Structure and the architect of the elephant skin I live in. For all you have taught me and all you have done for me, I am forever grateful.

For friendship and inspiration, kindness and honesty, and for tearing my drafts apart while keeping me together, Madelaine, your brilliance pushes me to work harder and do better. It's a rare gift to have a writer like you in my corner.

Ayeesha, I thank my lucky stars that Rufus and Cairo's frenetic love brought us together. You make my life better, inspire me, keep me upright, and stop me using air quotes when I say I'm a writer. Your friendship is everything. Also to John, for your incredible support, but I'll still never forgive you for killing my love, Ibn Bai.

Linda, for going above and beyond to support me both professionally and personally in this endeavour, this book is also dedicated to you. Typesetter-transcendent, editor-extraordinaire (who even checks film running times to see if a character has time for it in their fictitious day), there are no words…well, there are, but you'd make me cut them. Also to Charley, for your keen eyes on the proof. But any errors are mine: these lovely ladies don't make mistakes, they just do their best to catch them.

Elisa and Tilly, my daughters from another mother, for sparking ideas and reading hundreds of thousands of my words. Honest feedback, delivered with love, is something to be cherished. As is your friendship.

The ethereal, talented and kind Mavis Donner whose fingers I clasped as I took my first baby steps in the literary world. You made me feel like a writer when I'd hardly written a word.

For support, advice, and feedback, Mum, Jenni, Amy, Teresa, Stella, Darren, SarahKate, Claudine and Linda. For help with legalese, Katie. And for the financial crutches, Dad! I love you all to the moon and back and the stars and down.

To the beautiful ladies at Curtis Brown, Alice and Sheila, whose fight to sign this book and unstinting belief in it gave me the confidence to think this was possible.

For your vivid and imaginative covers, Mark, it's been an absolute joy to work with you.

Duncan at TAL Arms for help with the Glocks. As a British author it's hard to write gun scenes accurately and I couldn't have done it without TAL's help.

Penny, for assistance with Met details, criminal proceedings, and untangling the mess Jacob got himself into.

Lindsey Edwards (MVB, BSC, IVCA), Annika Driver (BVetMed MRCVS), and Felicity Caddick (BVetMed MRCVS) for helping me kill Jack. In such strictly regulated circumstances it seemed impossible to knock the little fella off, but we got him in the end!

Annabel Crome (BUPA) for assistance with health check results and for keeping a straight face while totting up my alcohol units!

And last but by no means least, Nick, my sister from another mother, my love. I know exactly what you'll be saying: 'Well it took you long enough! Now get off your ass and write another one!' Life's shit without you. But at least, here, I can get the last word in: dogs are better ;)

CARRIE MAGILLEN spent fifteen years as a computer engineer working for IBM and Sun Microsystems, all the while with a yellowing copy of *Plot* by Ansen Dibell on her bookshelf. She left IT in 2006 and studied creative writing at Webster University in the Netherlands, Wollongong University in Australia, and Winchester University in England. She lives in Hampshire with her husband and two American cocker spaniels. *When He's Not Here* is her debut novel.

Carrie loves hearing from readers and you can reach her via her website: carriemagillen.com

Books by Carrie
The Sharif Thrillers

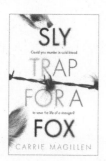
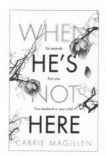

Lightning Source UK Ltd.
Milton Keynes UK
UKHW040812080922
408538UK00001B/75